C000089370

To Missy
and
Wayne

CONTENTS

BOOK I

PART 1

PART TWO

PART FOUR

O that thou wert as my brother
that sucked the breasts of my
mother!
I would lead thee and bring
thee into my mother's house,
who would instruct me:
I would cause thee to drink
of spiced wine of the juice
of my pomegranate.
For love is as strong as death.

Song of Songs
8:1, 8:2, 8:6

BOOK I

SHADOW WOMAN:
OR
ROMANCING THE DEAD

PART ONE

CHAPTER 1
WHY COME DOWN?

"Why come down?" she was asking, as she thought her last thought, the hard animal body surrounded by hundreds of calla lilies. She was reading *Decline of the West* on the 'destiny-problem',[1] in an Olympic swimsuit and shades on her West Village roof garden, a pre-war penthouse with a view of the Hudson, as she glanced at the river that seemed polluted by fate.

She looked down from above, from her solitary self, perched above Abingdon Square, the park in its midst: 60's drugged-out introverts, and the usual chaos: the continual sound of the siren, sleepless long hairs nodding out, some reading, some writing, or compulsively talking, the manic look in their eyes as they commune with the air, the darting eyes of the pushers dealing narcotics and acid, downers and speed, stuffing their pockets with money. A madman preaches the end of the world, the second coming of Jesus- the day of redemption. One dies of an over-dose, as the cops pull up. The paranoid flight, as they escape from the square. The impassive look on her face that defies time and space.

She muses a moment... "Am I in love with my analyst? ... Writes 'THE END' on her manuscript. Mused on 'the destiny problem'. She casually walks through the glass doors into a white marble hall: a giant stone lingam looms in the corner. There is a ladder in the center, above it a noose. It dangles from a big iron cross, always ready to receive her. Slowly climbing the ladder, she paused on the third rung: thinks her 'last thought'... Am I mystic or whore?"

Paused on the sixth.... "Staying for what? I will join my son in his tomb. I don't *know* what I love. It is made of the magic of projection. I am bound to 'the couch'. I am in love with my shadow... nothing neutral about her."

Paused on the ninth... "Enough magic and myth." Slips the noose round her neck. *'Love is stronger than death'.*

Nola's analyst wanders through Abingdon Square, reflexively arching her neck, as if feeling the rope. Wears a hound's tooth jacket on her Spartan frame, tailored pants, Teutonic features, early forties, an essential air; her hair like clipped wings counters her earthbound nature. She passes the newsstand on the corner, gripped by the headline in the *Utopian*: a literary paper that featured a review of Nola's' work... reading the lines as if it were part of a dream...

NOLA TROPPA HANGS HERSELF
AUTHOR OF THE MYTHIC NOVEL
DEAD AT 33

Pauses transfixed. Turns her back to the square...

Infamous for her dry mocking wit, the best-selling author inverted her poison pen and stung herself to death. She finished *Shadow Woman*, her 'novel', on the dawn of her death. She has left behind lovers and enemies, who will spin their iconic tales of her. As a cult figure, she was the heroine of the 'novel' *Lady of the Beasts*. Is it a rumor that the author was obsessed with his heroine, and hung himself on her image, in a hotel for prostitutes- or was Nola Lupa, the real author- another rumor or reality? The theme of the book, the myth of The Wolf One', the same theme as *Shadow Woman*- 'Lupa, the wolf girl'. The author, Archipova? who was hung on her cross. his body found by a prostitute: they say no man has survived her.

Nora looks over her shoulder ... "A waking dream of my death?... It's as if I were dead... It's as if it were mine"... Reads the obituary... as if she wrote it herself...

OBITUARY: GOOD FRIDAY, 1963
by NOLA LUPA

Nola Lupa, a psychic and reclusive novelist, is survived by her analyst and devoted readers. She took her own life after finishing *Shadow Woman*, her 'novel'. The theme is extracted from her life, and her Jungian analysis.

Only one session... one deadly session... Nora was thinking, gripped by her thoughts; tries changing her mind... reflects on a dream... the dream of Samara... but their shadows cross over...

Samara is hung on a hook that is thrust through her neck, hanging amidst the sheep and the goats. Her throat has been slit as a sacrifice to the mob. Her body is mum-mified; face masked by a cross.
(A complex of opposites that would need to be reconciled... but how, she had wondered... and she wondered again: how that Nola was dead, would the

3

mystery be solved)?

The Mother beside her wears a black kaftan, her two faces invisible through the transparent veil: one face mourning her death, the other bargaining for her flesh; one mumbling a prayer, the other offering a bid, as men rush to the stall and eroticize the corpse.

Nora reflects on the question: What needs to be sacrificed?... three hangings, she mused... and my son as the fourth... And her mind wanders back to Samara's last session... how Samara revealed her obsession with 'Lupa'... and surprised by her jealousy, she was trying to veil it.

"Let's face it, Nora," said Samara. I'm a sexual compulsive. Yes, I'm an Egyptian Coptic, but I practice the *ancient* religion, and worship the animal deities that were gradually humanized. I am *trying* to heal the mind/body split by *using* the sex that controls me and eroticizing 'Lupa'."

Nora tries to restrain herself, losing her analytic stance. Tries controlling her anger... but why is she angry?

"I need the wolf in her, Nora. I need it to live. It's one of my basic addictions, like my bulimia/anorexia.

Nora's anger increased at the end of the hour, when she opened the door and saw Samara in the waiting room. She was reading *Lady of the Beasts* (that she stole from my desk), and was stalking the real author, whose session followed hers. Nora took her copy back, and asked her to leave... and listened to the sound of their sex, as they taunt her in the hallway...

Pressing 'Lupa' to the wall, she jammed her knee in her cunt, sucked her breasts like a child, thrusting her finger inside her. Nora, pressed to the door, sees it all in the mind: what *she* wanted to do, when reading 'her' book- the one that she ghosted from one of her beasts.

"I want you,'Lupa', you animal. I even fuck you in my dreams. I know your body, like my own."

She strokes my marvelous ass and dares to kiss me on the lips. She seems to know what she is doing, and I give myself up to it. I put aside my preconceptions and let it happen as it may. A reckless experiment, in a mood induced by a sensation...

But why not submit to my shadow? Why not give her a taste of it- the taste of 'the wolf one' that she imagines she wants. She won't be able to handle it for more than a night, so that 'the Lupa in Nola' can taunt Nora with her repression, who will change the time of our sessions, avoiding further complications. Clearly, Nora is reading my book, and is lost in the erotic transference[5], like I am, she thought, so she could have me through her patient, and has unconsciously arranged it (obsessed with my image in my book). Well, I'll have the dread child, who wants more than my body, but such clashing worlds cannot collide, except in a dream. Even now, in my body, I can sense Nora listening. I can see the jealous anguish on her face, while she secretly listens, hating the analytic rule that binds her to her nature- the ascetic self that she suffers that lives in the dark of the mind.

"Not on the lips, please."

"I'm not a trick, Nola Lupa. I'm a whore, like yourself. I want to kiss you 'cause I can't," and 'Lupa' gave herself up to it.

When Nora opened the door, she saw Samara on her knees, licking 'Lupa' like an animal... (the way I

5

imagined I would). 'Lupa's' exquisite leg is hung over her shoulder, and she expired as Nora was slamming the door. It only made it more erotic, thought Nola... like Nora...

"That *is* the way you like it, no 'wolf girl', you animal? Only another wolf can know the way, and *I* am that wolf."

Did I unconsciously arrange it, to avoid the analytic sin?... It's nothing but transference- an illusion of the flesh, Nora was thinking, obsessed with the thought.

In the following session with Samara, Nora is compelled to reconstruct it; decides not to bring it up- to avoid her unconscious sadism. Tries to suppress it and fails, but won't let her off 'the hook'...

"The mummification process in your dream was meant to preserve you from destruction, as you submit to the mother you hate in yourself. You have replaced her with 'Lupa', your animal deity- the life force you deny, when you identify with the death instinct. And so, of course, it could backfire, and all our work would be in vain. You must stop stalking death, and remember who you are."

"But it *is* who I am. That's what you don't understand."

Was Nola aware that Samara was stalking her- her erotic obsession, when she submitted to the urge? was 'Lupa' aware of Samara's obsession, and did she find it unnerving, when she was not in disguise? Did she deny *her* obsession, to submit to the urge, and that came to a climax on the day that we met? Was she feeling possessive, as I was of her?

"What about the compulsion to give myself up?" Samara was saying, stealing her words, "to make

6

offerings of my flesh to the Devouring Mother?""

"But *you* are the offering."

"How else could it be?"

It is hard to hurt a masochist, Nora was thinking…
"Why flesh? Why not spirit?" Nora was saying.

"The world that I live in is made out of flesh... If she
is dead, I will kill myself.... Do you think she's really
dead?"

She was inducing my sadism, to respond to her
masochism. But I was still wondering about the
'syncronicity'[7] of the doubling of the hangings, and,
quelling my anger, was trying to be objective… the
dream as 'the third'… and a warning for me.

What needs to be sacrificed is my own sacrificial
attitude, and she listened with one ear and tried to block
out the other- but not entirely successful, heard more
than she wanted…

There's a confounding of submission with the spirit
of surrender; clearly, the three of us have a martyr
complex, and I am forced to watch its workings
(mixing her tenses, again, not wanting to believe it- that
Nola was dead and had finally escaped).

"I feel guilty. If I had not manipulated you into
changing my session time, she might be alive," said
Samara, intruding.

The narcissism was astounding, and I tried to look
neutral.

"I am trying, Nora. Really. Yes, I'm obsessed with
her myth, but I can't give her up. If I do I will die. It's
like I'm already dead."

"You are identified with her... and so it feels like
you're dead," I replied. It was then that I caught myself
trying to re-arrange the session times, and had almost

forgotten that Nola's time was not relevant; that I would be communing with my patient through her disem-bodied spirit. Leaving her body was a near-perfect crime that she perfected through whoring, and that my presence would interfere with.

"I will search for her in the market place," Samara was saying.

"Stalking ghosts is exhausting. Try to find her in your shadow- to not *become* what you worship, so you can make it more human." I might have been talking to myself. It was what *I* had to do.

"I will try to do what you say, but it seems quite impossible."

Impossible: a word that never existed for Nola. I could hear Nola saying, 'Never mind the time. We will continue the sessions in the lower reaches of hell, which, in any case, could be thought of as an ideal analysis'.

Nola entered the room, after her fling with Samara- and, as if it never happened, we began our first session. But the transference began when I read *Shadow Woman, (before* the first session, like a warning she sent): the book of a psychic in 'the space/time continuum- as it exists in the unconscious'[8] (and not in outer space); it compelled me to enter the fourth dimension of mind, where 'space is the Mother, time is the Son.'

Was it a symbolic death, Nora asked, to keep her on earth, to incarnate her son and her lover, who she unconsciously destroyed?

CHAPTER 2
COMMUNION

Nora sits at her desk, scanning her notes, in the timeless room reflecting an interior atmosphere: primitive statues and fetishes, tribal masks, a stone phallus, the wall-to-wall bookcase filled with psychology and myth: focused on Nola's first session, before the hanging that morning, trying to fathom the question if it was literal or symbolic...

Nola Troppa, Good Friday, '63: Her son was 'born on the day of the crucifixion of the god': still obsessed with his death, who she unconsciously murdered, and her mother's lover, his father, who incested her at twelve. Nola is dangerously dissociated, possessed by the dead. I was unable to detach, which only contributes to the problem: her idealized transference with 'the sinless Virgin' she eroticizes (the counterpart of 'The Wolf One', who is 'virgin unto herself'). The Lupa in Nola and her extreme ascetic practices involves an abstinence of the senses, (the other side of her whoring), while starving the emotional body for the freeing of the spirit; mean-while, tricking 'the father' perpetuates the split, to keep the body and spirit from 'contaminating' one another: with an unusual irony, she found a fitting analogy: 'psychic bulimia/anorexia', and explored it in reverse: 'the compulsion towards the death pole, attempting to spiritualize the body, followed by the lust for more matter, as a play on Thanatos and Eros. She is retreating to the nunnery on the lonely mountain of the mind: a world of archetypal shadows, ruled by the Mother of Death... 'one letter difference in our names', she repeated...'each the shadow of the other… only one letter difference'…

Nora closes her eyes. Covers her face with her hands. Eyes open. Continues. Always tracking the meaning…

I sensed the danger of the force that she was trying to contain, but escaping the bounds of the body, the disdain of its limits; the determined walk that was compensating for the doubt that was driving it- the wanting to turn and to run, but the will to confront her own darkness. Her eyes cut through the silence. Unmoved and immovable; but beneath an implacable surface, the raging within. The proud line of the jaw, strong classical features; a mind set in its way that would not be easy to alter. The tweed suit of disguise, hiding the sinuous body, so at odds with her nature that she wore to confuse me- brown sensible oxfords (Virginia Woolf came to mind). She entered my office, mocking her need of me, and made me feel like the patient, and that the problem was mine. Sat in the analyst's chair, looking into my soul, and, for one perverse moment, I allowed the transgression to pass. I observed her in silence, assuming an air of neutrality. Her eyes cut through the silence and dared me to know her, as I patiently waited for the next reversal of will; arching her brows, she changes her seat, fully engaged in the act of analyzing the analyst.

The ghost of a smile, while observing the trans-ference- a smile barely perceptible that derides her own bit of madness. Sees that I'm standing, now conscious of the slip, as she sits 'on the couch', but asks the analyst's question…

"Why am I here?" she is asking. "Good question," she answers. Paused and reflected, as she answered herself.

"I would avoid it, of course, but that would be absurd. I have what you call a vertical split: two different identities that attack one another. Why am I here? Because I can no longer bear it. Bear what? you are asking? my spirit imprisoned in my body. I understand that the 'psychic anorexia' is a neurotic disembodiment, and the 'psychic bulimia' the need to embody the spirit: that the symbolic 'anorexic' side is the denial of the senses, and the insatiable 'bulimic' side the man-eating prostitute, who turns men's blood into money, as I rob them of their pleasure; that my life is an experiment in the killing of desire."

"It is I who must ask- rather than asking yourself," I intruded: "Why are you here? when you seem to know more than me? Isn't that what you believe, when you make me feel that I'm unnecessary?"

"How astute. I am here because the experiment is over, and has ended in death. I have inadvertently murdered my son and my lover, in an act of revenge on the shadow of my father. I did it through my unconscious will... but I am not ready to talk about it."

"Are you ready to feel it?"

"No, not yet: only what it is to feel nothing, a feeling blacker than black- a suicidal depression filled with a poisonous self-hatred, and the rage of being human with a longing for death... But death rejects me, like a lover, and refuses to take me. If only the experiment had failed. But I have killed everything I love...Desire is dead. It is what I was working for."

"Why don't we pretend that this analysis could work? that I can grasp what you can't, and that you are merged with your shadow."

"I've been pretending all my life. I'm tired of pretending. I have written my autobiography, disguised as a novel, but I realize that these characters in my shadow play only personify collective images; archetypal patterns depersonalized, to free myself from love; and so, I'm faced with the problem of turning a cliché into a great idea. They resemble stereotypes in old movies, and I found it hard to make them real. My fear? That when I get to the end that they will finally destroy me... Destroy *what*, I keep asking, when I killed to be free?"

"Somehow, I think you'll survive, but it might destroy the analysis. I promise it will not destroy *me*. To begin with, there are two of us in the room. It will make it more interesting."

"Thank you. I needed that. You see, the second problem is clear. There is a compulsion to destroy relationship: a lack of mutuality."

"You want to be the one and the other, and so there *is* no other, is there?"

"Not until now, but it is already beginning. You are beginning to exist for me, and it's making me anxious. It must mean it's working."

"What *allows* me to exist for you?

"That I'm taken in by you- assimilated."

"Do you mean orally incorporated or understood?"

"Excellent question, and I would answer them both."

"That's what I'm afraid of. You are acting out my unconscious, and trying to steal it from me."

She laughs. "Yes, it's unfortunate that I can; it is also unfortunate that I believe if I am *not* orally incorporated, I will *not* be understood."

"How does the murder work- this murder of the self? Let's deconstruct it. Did you have a dream last night?"

"Yes. Do I want to tell it to you? No. And so, I will tell you my dream, and you will know more than I would like. It's a waking dream: part reality, part fantasy, for I am consciously observing the unconscious images...

"I enter a medieval church- there's a mural of my son in his tomb. The Magdalena is beside him, waiting for his resurrection. The nuns are imprisoned behind bars and are smiling that suffering smile, thinking that the whore is the problem, but the real problem is the Virgin, suspended in masculine space and stripped of the feminine. There is a feast before the bars, and Salome is dancing her dance, stripping the veils for the head of her saint, and then... as if starving... gorging the heart of the Lamb. The priest appears at the altar to give me Communion, to place the Eucharist in my mouth, the spiritualized body of the god, the miracle of transformation that turns the flesh into spirit, but he switches the Host for the flesh and slips his penis in my mouth. I submit and wonder why, but I go through the motions, and though I'm repelled by the act, I extract the 'spirit' from the flesh. As I perform the false sacrifice, the mural comes to life. The spirit of my son rises up... but his body remains in the tomb. It has not been transformed... and is still made of flesh... while the priest has been making the sign of the cross on my lids: 'Be closed', he is saying, reversing the words of the baptism. 'Be closed', he repeats, as if sealing the door of the tomb."

"I'm consumed by my visions, and my war with spirit and matter."

"With the holy communion with your ghosts- the dead parts of the self. They are trying to rise up to consciousness, against the will of the killer- the killer 'I' that destroys them, to believe that it's free. What do *you* think it means? Have you extracted the spirit from the dream?"

"Not entirely. It seems to be asking an impossible question: if I can reverse the false sacrifice and not escape from the earth, so I can embody my son in the tomb of my soul."

Nola was in her study, recording her impressions of Nora. There is a black Rothko, a black Stills, and a depressing black Reinhardt- three painters who suicided: a meditation on death. No place for comfort on the Arts & Crafts chairs: Wiener Werkstatte period, covered with a geometric pattern. The Tantric drawings behind them reveal a sacred geometry that seem to reconcile the inner opposites, despite the resistance of the dweller. The walls are lined with abstract formulas, reflecting universal principles, ancient temples and tombs, primal masks of the Death Mother: the masks dominate the atmosphere: an atropaic defense: to *not* become what she fears, and be annihilated by the urge. The books that she wrote in the wall-to-wall bookcase on the myth of the *Self*[14] as it continued through time; and though the form was the same, the shape kept changing its face.

She writes her impressions of Nora: tries replacing the masks, for they dominate the atmosphere... and the psyche that inhabits them...

I understood she was the instrument to understand my early influences, as she challenged my will and my magical defenses: the contradictory feelings at war with my intellect, the double nature I was born with, so at odds with the world. As I tried to escape her, she nailed every thought. I'm like a beast in the net and there *is* no way out.

Nola's 'novel' was published the day of her 'death' and created a scandal, like she knew that it would. The novel continued after the end and she remembered the future and what she wrote came to be, and it was mixed with the past in inscrutable ways. The Huntress had guided her pen on the page, and changed the *mask* of the feminine that was ripped from its face.

CHAPTER 3
SHADOW MOTHER

Looking back, it begins with the Mother of God, but then it always begins there for she lives in the core of our darkness. The only difference is that I was born inside her- the only Mother I knew, 'cause my own was kept secret from me. My tale begins on the day I was tempted to leave her, though she was weaving my fate, and the way love would end... But how can you leave what you're made of, and the cross of your destiny?

I was twelve in 1941 when I began my life in the world, on the day that he came for me and took me down from the mountain. On that day when he freed me, as in all the days of my youth, I was crouched in her shadow in the church of her name. I was sure that my purpose in life was to gaze at her mystery, while I mused on its meaning and conversed with her soul. She was black as the night in her death-like shroud, her Son nailed to her shadow, her body the cross. I was as wild in my wolfness as the beasts of the field, my feet stained with her pollen and the dust of the earth, while hers were stained with the blood of her sacrificed Son, filling the chalice below them with an unnatural light.

The nuns called me 'Lupa', 'Lupa, the wolf girl', the wild wolfish spirit that was tracking their thoughts, as I worshipped the Mother of Shadow, who is my Lady of the Beasts. I gazed at her face, like a mask of death, and talked to her image in an intimate tone, in an odd fusion I invented of the ancient tongues I combined- high Latin, low French, rough Italian, and wild Spanish- and communed with my darkness, as I searched for her Son. Her secret in Latin was carved in her back: *For What In The End Is The Son Without A Shadow*?[17] but it was like I had known it before I was born.

I am silent a moment, looking up at her image, as I try piercing her mystery, and revealing my own...

"The nuns say I'm a witch, born under a dark evil star. Is it true what they say, that I was born of a whore? Why am I different, Mother? I don't want to be different. I want to be good and belong to God. Tell me the mystery of what I am."

I wait for an answer, and I question myself: "What was I before?... Was I a whore, like my mother? Am I being punished for something I did long ago?... Did I laugh at Christ on the cross? Why can't I remember? And if *I* can't remember, how can the nuns? Tell me, Divine One, what do they know of your beast? Is my soul in my eyes, or do they know something else? That I can see in the dark, through the walls of their cells, and watch them touching and licking each other's flesh? Last night, I watched Sister Gabrielle. She likes to do it alone. She was looking into a round piece of glass, moaning and flicking her tongue like a snake. But something else, Mother, she was whispering my name: 'Lupa', she whispered, 'Lupa, the wolf girl'. When she was finished, she prayed to Our Lord for forgiveness, scourging herself, till she was covered with blood.

"It's so lonely here, Mother, shut away in God's prison. Talk to him. Talk to your crucified Son. I would ask him myself, but he won't listen to me. Tell him to send down one of his saints, and to set the child of darkness free. Tell him that I believe in his goodness, but that 'the devil wants to be redeemed'."* The bell

17

rings for Matins and the nuns enter for prayer, and as I move from the vessel, the light gradually leaves it. Like a hunted animal I run from the church, as if my devilish nature had invaded their holiness.

I was born in the high frozen peaks of the Ariège Pyrenees, where the Gothic gloom of The Mother' overshadows the landscape- like the mother who had me- who was married to the god. Each day I climbed up and down her one hundred steps and pretended to leave her and return when I would. I can see my small lonely figure at the massive medieval door, thrashed by the wind and the clouds of black dust.

The myth of the sacrifice was carved in my bones, and swept me into the present as I leapt through the door. A man on a black horse rides up the mountain, from the coal mining Biros, the village my mother was born in, a shadow town for the lost in the depths of the lowlands- a valley as black as the stones from her pit. I was sure that her Son had answered my prayer... but he came from *Perdue,* from the darkness below.

"Free me, Mother. I am ready now. Take me down to the low places, so I can learn how to love."

Through my child eyes, he looked almost god-like, with his black mane of hair, his yellow eyes like the sun, like stones that were set in the rough of his face, cut from the grit and ground to its essence. He was thirty-three at the time, and would teach me the language of men, all that I needed to know to survive on the earth...

He climbs the one hundred steps, and kisses my hand, placing a pearl on my palm of a peculiar brilliance. "It's the most perfect thing in all the world," I said in my fusion of tongues, "besides the Black

Virgin and her wounded Son."

"But the Son *is* the pearl," he said, in a Neapolitan dialect, a sound like it came from the depths of the sea.

"And the Mother?"

"The oyster."

He makes a gesture to take him into the heart of the cloister, and I defy all her laws, so I can watch him confront her: looks up at the Son, nailed to her shadow, his deep troubled eyes held by her mystery: he knows what it's like to feel the nails in the flesh, to be suspended in shadow on the Mother of matter.

Sister Gabrielle lies prostrate at the feet of the Son, her body rigid in the sign of the cross, the nun's Latin prayer wounding the silence, repenting the sin of being nothing but human. She looks at him sternly...

"I must ask you to leave. This is a cloister for penitents. Men aren't allowed in these walls," she said in her lowly French accent. His eyes penetrate hers through her invisible veil. She lowers her gaze, unable to look...

"Forgive me, sister, but I've come a long way. You wouldn't deny me your help, would you, just because I'm a man?" looks up at the Christ in the image of man.

Her eyes follow his and she can't justify it. "Follow me, I will take you to the Reverend Mother."

It was the proof that I needed that, like her Son from above, he was disguised as a man and had god-given powers, and was not merely human, but could influence a nun.

"Thank you, sister. Tell me, *who* can I thank?"

She is gone now, at his mercy. "Sister Gabrielle, *signore*," leading him through the rear door, into the quadrangle, where the nuns hid in their cells in the colonnaded arch- where no man had entered, and where none ever should. His eyes were fixed on the fountain in the center of the square, where young Magdalena was weeping for being forced to repent. On the left is an archway that leads to the garden, where the Reverend Mother was kneeling in the white calla lilies, cutting the stems for the Virgin, in the ritual act she performs.

'Lupa' leaps barefoot into the fountain, hiding behind the statue of the young Magdalena, the water engraving her face, as he peers at her saint. (It was like her face was my own and that I wept for the past... like I was held to a vow that I made long ago.) His eyes never leave her as he moves towards the statue, as if being moved by a powerful magnet...

"Do you know that the Magdalena was called 'the bitter sea, because in her repentance, she shed so many tears that she could wash God's feet with them? He drove seven devils out of her, and the hands of angels built a secret house for her, where she reflected on God and his Mother and fasted for thirty years, until her eyes became so radiant, it was like looking into the heart of the sun'.[20] Well your eyes are like that. May I call you Magdalena?"

By now, I am overcome by the passion and am burning with curiosity. "Which saint are you?"

"I am only a man, but my name's Leonardo."

"You're the first one I've seen, but I always knew they existed."

"How could you be sure?"

"God was a man (like I believed the disguise)."

"Of course. And now that I've come back to life, what do they call you?"

"They call me--"

'Lupa' leaps from the fountain and hides behind a column, plays hide and seek with the god, as the Reverend Mother approaches him. She speaks in a low discreet tone in the same primitive accent, trying to shield me from the demon of reality- the hidden soul of my mother, that I had learned to repress. I listened hard to her secret, trying to hear what they say, my cloistered ears always busy, linking the flesh and the spirit.

I am straining my senses, as he lowers his voice: "I am looking for a woman- a woman called Snow. She lived in *Perdue*, in the mining town, down below, and she used to come here to pray."

"You mean, Neige. She was a nun here." My saint was beguiled.

"I see. You thought you knew her. Here in the church, her name is Anna-Marie. I haven't seen her in twelve years- not since 'Lupa' was born."

His yellow eyes grow cold... like nails in the flesh... killing the feelings... disguised as a man...

The Mother continues to test him with almost feminine wiles, to coax him to accept what he tries to avoid: almost a woman now, subtly seducing a man. "It was a terrible birth. Neige nearly died. She was praying for death... and the death of the child- only her will that she was able to survive, but neither God nor the devil was ready for the likes of her: tempts the god- like her mother, while kneeling before him. Her only friends are the saints... and her Mother of Shadow... like Neige, so alone. It is good you have come for her."

"Now wait a minute, Mother," but she continues to lure him...

"Your brother's child. You *are* Leonardo, aren't

21

you?"

"It's impossible, Mother- quite impossible."

"That doesn't mean much here, where we *believe* in the impossible. It doesn't mean much for 'Lupa', who lives in her dreams." He is lost in his thoughts, caught in the myth of the past: "I was trying to forget her... but she appeared in a dream... She asked me to come here, and I thought I would find her. Only it wasn't her voice... it was the voice of a child."

"Impossible, isn't it? And yet, you are here. We have the same problem. Her voice is in all our dreams. The sisters think she's possessed, but she has the gift of the God."

I run to the garden, and I know what I know.

The Reverend Mother is moving him towards me. "She never really belonged here. The world is inside her- though she knows nothing of it: what she knows is the dark side, but only God knows his shadow."

I had the clue to my past now, and begin my search for my fate. I look in my *Child's Book of Saints*, to learn what miracles he performs, and why, in your wisdom, you have chosen him for me. I turn to Saint Leonardo and read the ill-fated words, that promise freedom for prisoners, knowing my fate has been written, and learn that long before I existed you had woven the plot...

"This Leonardo sets all prisoners free, and chains of iron melt before him, like wax before fire. Leonardo comes from *Legens Ardua*, one who chooses what is difficult. Or it comes from leo, which means lion. For the lion has four properties: first, he has strength in his heart, for the curbing of evil thoughts: second, the lion has cunning in two ways: he sleeps with his eyes open, and he covers his tracks when he flees: third, the lion has special power in his voice, and recalls the lion cub to life on the third day, causing every other beast to stand still in his tracks."[22]

I am having the vision, as if seeing the end, and I swallow the pearl as I wait for my destiny. "Christ in me, make me perfect for him, like this pearl." Her eyes look upward. Closes her eyes as she prays...

I ask the 'stars in the blood',[23] the eyes of the Mother, to make me your vessel, and to bring the lion cub to life. Then I turn to Magdalena, to find the missing piece. I read...

"Magdalen means *manens rea*, remaining in guilt before her conversion. Or it means armed or unconquered, with the light of perfect knowledge in her mind, and with the excellent armour of penance, devising an immolation of herself, to atone for each of the pleasures she desired. For so totally did she abandon her body to the pleasure of the senses that she was called by no other name than a woman of evil life: the 'whore' who loved too much, but who was sainted and redeemed. She fasted for thirty years and allowed no earthly satisfaction, needed no bodily food and lived on nothing but spirit."[23a]

She crosses herself and lifts her eyes up to heaven... continues to read of her fate and how it would turn into destiny... "The Magdalena was present at the crucifixion, standing alone at the foot of the cross:"* 'the holy whore' who was waiting at the foot of the tomb, for the god to rise from the dead and make her 'hearer of the Word'.

Why else would I hear it, but to bring the lion cub to life?... the third day from Good Friday... the day he rose from the dead." I kneel in the lilies, making my vow...

"Tell him, dark goddess, tell him to take me, and I will fast for thirty-three years- three more than the Magdalen- and I swear to renounce all bodily pleasure, till the cub of the lion is raised from the dead."

Leonardo reaches his hand out, pulling me up...

"Too much prayer is not good for the soul. C'mon Magdalena, do you want to be my new partner?"

I look in his eyes as he lifts me up on his horse...

"Nothing lies...nothing lies…"

"Just wait, you will see."

And we rode down the mountain to the valley of men, where I began mining the shadow and the rough stone of the self, but in my magical thinking, how could I know what I prayed for?

CHAPTER 4
SUBMISSION?

Paris, '63, off Boulevard Clichy, as 'Lupa' poses as a street whore on Rue de Martyr, the sign revealing her complex, her face masked with cheap make-up. Her red dress clings in the rain to her animal body. Seams drip down her thighs to the high black stilettos, as she hooks a heel to the sign of 'ROOMS' by the hour, throws her head back against it, and gets engaged in the role. It was a bit of nostalgia as she remembers Leonardo, his rejection of her body and her childish bout with prostitution. Now she was doing research on a book on the Greco/Roman feminine, and the sacralizing of submission as an offering to the goddess-till the compulsion took over and she was unable to stop.

Only three months had passed when he took me down from 'The Mother', till I was bringing my saint down by working the streets. Keeping my promise to the Mother of Shadow, I practiced starving my senses, like the Magdalen at the tomb, while walking the alleyways and wearing the mask of the feminine. Thirty-three years of fasting- the year Christ was crucified, and she had freed me from dogma, only to enslave me to the flesh."

Three whores look her over, eyes full of envy and hatred. They wanted her dead, and they want her to know it. She looks back at them coolly, letting them know she can take it.

"Who's the foreign bitch?" asks whore #1.

"Never saw her before," says whore #2.

"Well, what's she doin' here?" asks whore #3.

"We'll get her on the rebound," says whore #1.

Leonardo leans in a doorway, an ironic smile on his face, as if amused by the game, pretending, like her.

Twelve, the last time I saw him, and now every night for a week, watching the ritual from a distance, as he leans in a doorway. Still trying to find me... but I wasn't about to give in, and yet, I still wasn't sure why I was escaping from love. In his mid-fifties now- twenty-one years had gone by. The rough cast of his face, but a seasoned elegance about him. The yellow stones for the eyes that doubted the god; his nature forged on the street that was at odds with his grace: a deep sadness there that he hid with his gun."

His eyes take me in. He can't look away- like the first time he saw me on the steps of 'The Mother'. I feel his eyes looking into me, while I am tapping the whore, and begin reconstructing the past, as I watch it fade like a dream.

The coarse voice of a trick rouses me from my reverie: "Hey, you with the wet dress, how much for ten minutes?"

"Three hundred francs" (in the primitive accent of 'Lupa')- the whores are a hundred. They watch her with hatred.

It was like I was born in the role. Like it was nothing but fate. Making the numbers work out, like some abstraction in physics, trying to prove the equation, as I was tossing the dice. It was the going rate in a whorehouse, but not on the street, in the twisted alleys of fate, run by the whores and the thieves.

"Three hundred francs?" (he is stunned). "Why? You special or something? The others are only a hundred."

"Then take one of the others." I give him the look, surly and hot- like the common whore I perfected. "Why don't you take him?" tossing it over my shoulder, as I throw them the meat, while I fantasize my death. How they wish they were me- the one I created… and how I wished that I hadn't… but such a wish was a dream.

"No, wait a minute. I like your mouth. I bet it sucks real good."

"Sure. It swallows too."

I regain my objectivity, and treat it like research, but I knew in the end I would edit the filth. Just an exorcism of love- at least, that's how it started.

The trick follows me to the door, as I enter the seedy hotel, Leo's eyes always on me, with his hand on his gun. I let their hatred inspire me, as I enter for a ten-minute hour, while I get in the mood for a light supper in hell.

I look through the window into the past, at the man who 'freed' me from God, to show me the shadow of men. Eyes lock for a moment... Try breaking the spell...

"Give me the money." He gives me two hundred francs. "Six or it's over," (turning the tables). He gives me six more, submissively, like one of my beasts. "Now get undressed, and wait till I'm ready to give it to you."

I try to control what others call feeling- that in my split-off shadow state seem to distract from the play: the production I'm writing, directing, designing and editing; while pretending that there *is* no unconscious, no mad god possessing me; that I'm not really trying to pass my life off as fiction. I straddle the bidet and the old images flood me...

Again, I was twelve, dressed as a boy, and carry a black bag of instruments for a safecracking job, as we walk, like we did, through a deserted war zone in Naples.

"Now I want you to concentrate on all the things that I taught you," said Leo. "Remember, it's the little things that get you. Any one of them could be fatal. It takes years of mistakes to be a good thief. But you, well, you're lucky. It's in your blood."

"Is that what the sisters call fate?" I was asking my 'saint'.

On the opposite side of the street, in the bombed-out shell of a building, two German soldiers were raping two boys… maybe nine. Leo grabs me and pulls me into the shadows. I stare fascinated and begin touching myself. He is watching me strangely and seems to see something else; stares at my young boyish body and is lost in the past. It was my first erotic moment, besides the masturbating nuns. He pulls me roughly round the corner to my debut as a thief: a small-time rock shop- I was hoping for more. I admit to myself that I am coming down fast. My sights were set higher than to be a petty thief, and my idealized 'saint' was becoming a man.

"It will let us eat for a month. Close your eyes now and concentrate." And I call up my powers, piercing the glass with my gaze…

"Well, is it worth it?"

A moment is passing as I'm working it out- like a mathematical equation that I saw in my head. "Yeah, it will do- for the moment."

He hands me the gun and I cover him, while he's picking the lock. He opens it quickly and I back in behind him. I block the safe with my body, sticking my butt out, exposing the lock between my legs, trying to keep the illusion: where is my mythical lover? I am asking the Mother. "Try 33 left- 66 right- 21 left." He turns the lock through my legs, but he isn't seduced. Hears the click. Can't believe it, and I spread my legs wider. He tries to ignore it and opens the safe, and, as if witnessing a miracle, looks at me with reverence.

"Well, Magdalena, how did you do it?"

"I doubled 33, the year of the death of the Son, and the time, 6 o'clock- the time he was crucified… but the third is a mystery." I kick the safe shut, dropping my pants. "Fuck me first. Fuck me, Leonardo. Pretend I'm a beautiful boy and that you're a soldier."

He tries to reason with me. "You know our… uh… lives are at stake."

"Yes, I know."

"And you don't care?"

"I like it that way. I want you to love me more than your life, more than what's in that safe, more than all the money and jewels in the world."

"But I do."

"Then fuck me, Leonardo, fuck me," tempting myself to break my vow.

"A good thief--"

"I want it."

--"Is able to resist temptation."

Stroking my butt, I moan like an animal, but still he empties the safe into the getaway bag. "I guess I was wrong. You're not cut out to be a thief."

"Anyway, I've changed my mind. I'm going to be a wicked woman." I give him the wanton look, but I'm crushed by his coolness, and he packs the jewels in the bag as I begin to remove them. I look in the mirror, adorning myself, as he stares at my body, which by now is quite tantalizing; I am mesmerized by my image, reflecting the light of the jewels, but he doesn't seem to want me, and I am wondering why.

It seemed that life now depended on breaking him down, corrupting my saint, so I could live in this world- in a corruptible body that burned with the fire, but my incestuous fantasy was not igniting his own. He struggles with something- something more than myself, and I want to know what, as he binds me to earth; puts my toys in the bag, picks me up in his arms, and escapes with the wolf girl into the poor winding streets.

In his old rundown shack on the docks that was once an old whorehouse, the house where Leo grew up, he has fallen asleep. It's filled with trinkets, and anchors, and parts of old ships, with pictures of the Virgin, the protector of sailors. I am lying beside him, in the bend of his legs, wrapped in the muscles of his arms and his leonine strength. I try to pierce his unconscious, to find a clue to the past. I'm still dressed as a boy, and find it strangely familiar. It's as if I am living something out, something locked like the safe, and I am trying to crack it, as I listen close for the click... But how could I know what was hidden inside it: his erotic obsession with Lupo... my wolf of a father: that the clothes I was wearing were the clothes that *he* wore, robbing the churches at nine... that he was reliving his love... I fell asleep in his arms and didn't awaken till dawn, as the Lupo inside him took me in his sleep- in a dream of the past, disguised as the present: a fact I repressed that changed the course of my life.

Something had happened, but I didn't know what. I had a foreign feeling inside me and I would never be the same. I went out on the balcony and saw the American battleship. It was anchored in the Bay of Naples, in the Tyrrhenian Sea, and was tied to the dock not far from our shack. It was an ominous presence, and it had the same feeling... something made of the past... as I returned to my darkness. Then I talked to the Mother of some of my illusory notions...

"I know now, Mother, that Leonardo is human. I tempted him tonight, so he would fall like a mortal, and though he was able to resist me, like one of God's saints, he was afraid of the beast in me and of my feminine body. I knew in my nerves if I was a *real* boy, he'd want me, and I know something else- that he was repeating the past."

There was an American sailor on the docks, who kept looking up at me, giving me the signal: come down, it was saying. I ignore him at first; then I get the idea, and become the whore in the Magdalen of the myth they created. I would use the senses as a weapon, to avenge the Fathers who tormented her- who made her a sinner, to redeem the whore in the saint. It was convenient 'cause America was warring with Italy, and sailors and soldiers were coming in droves. But I was still unaware of turning the trick on myself, as I developed the illusion of leaving my body. I tried to look like a woman and to dress like the feeling, and I was becoming more earthy when Magdalena was guiding me. It seemed perfectly natural to use my body as a sacrifice, and I got in the mood and went down to the docks. I headed him off on his way to do battle, and I began my experiment with the sin of the senses...

"Do you want it, sailor? It's cheap, real cheap. Thirty bucks for a virgin" (a black one to myself).

"Make it ten, kid, and you got a deal."

"Thirty, sailor- thirty or nothing."

"Fifteen, that's it, and a pack of American cigarettes.

I'll avenge it, I thought, pushing the hate down, betraying myself, and the workings of love. I wanted to hurt him, my thief, for not wanting my body, and I thought I could do it by turning the light into shadow.

The sailor is leading me to a cheap hotel on the docks, where I learn to pretend and make it realer than real.

"The money, sailor."

"Later."

"Now."

He searches through his wallet, stuffed with American bills, and hands me a ten and a bar of chocolate.

"I don't have change."

I give him my hardest look. "You just lost your deal. Sixty or nothing."

"What will you do for it?"

"Anything, sailor," getting into the role. "Like I said, you're the first."

"Well..." He hides his excitement, but I'm on to the sucker.

"Let's compromise, forty-five."

Hands me a twenty and a five and a pack of American cigarettes.

"Do you want it or don't you?

Hands me a ten and a five. Good thing I learned how to concentrate. "Ten more, for conning me."

"You sure drive a hard bargain."

"So does the devil." I get naked, while feeling that strange ancient feeling; stare at his dick till it's hard and make him come with a thought.

"Well, I guess that's it. The next one's ninety."

He looks confused.

"Thirty times three. It's simple- real simple: one for the Father, one for the Son, and one more for the Holy Ghost."

He gives me the money. It seems to be working. I commune with the Magdalen and some invisible force. Then I concentrate my will, until it gets hard. Are you listening, God? This is your miracle- dead flesh rises up, and I can make it fall, too.

But this time I couldn't and he rams it inside me. It went on for a while and I'm down in my darkness. Bite my lip till it bleeds, for the pain is intense... till I knew what she suffered, and why she had to do penance.

I sit in the alley, barefoot, surrounded by money, and I weep to unknowing for betraying my thief... Why did I sin against love? Why did I want to destroy it?... And was it my fate... for breaking my vow?

Three months had passed and I am clutching my womb, screaming a scream that leaves Leonardo trembling. Then I fall to the earth in passionate prayer. "Help me, Mother of Shadow! Help me, Dark One! Kill this thing growing inside me, a thing born of hate, and I will serve you, my Mother, for the rest of my days."

He paces like a beast that is locked in a cage.

"Help, spirits! Help me! Where are you, my thief?"

"It's too late...It's too late!" unable to act. Now he is pulling me up by the roots of my hair.

I look him straight in the eye. "Too late for death? I am always ready for death. Death is my Mother. I was born in Death's spell."

He tries forcing it out of me, the hatred of love, slamming my face, but I give it back with more hate. It is growing inside me- like the thing in my womb...

"Once I thought you were the lion, come to rescue the wolf girl, but I was wrong, you are weak, and it will have your weakness inside it. I will have the cursed thing, but I swear before God not to touch it. I swear before God."

I fall to my knees and implore the Mother of Darkness...

"Let it not be human... Let it not be human!"

Was this the soul of a child? Leo questioned his God.

CHAPTER 5
'DO YOU RENOUNCE THE DEVIL?'

Leonardo enters the perpetual twilight of the cloister, holding the newborn child in the shadow of the crucifix. The Reverend Mother is kneeling before it, with hands clasped in prayer, the Son nailed to his Mother. Leo stares at her image and knows why he fears her. The child is swathed in her darkness in the infinite silence. Leo looks down at him, knowing his fate. The Reverend Mother is torn from her God, aware of a presence, ending her mid-day meditation; returns to this world and goes to Leo and the child. Looks into his heart...

"And whose sin is this one?"

"Mine. I thought I was dreaming, but my dream was reality. You say you believe in the impossible, Mother. Though it was born in a dream, it is realer than real, and I have come to believe that what is real is impossible. Can you forgive the impossible that you say you believe in?"

"Only God can forgive it. I am nothing but human. I suppose you want to leave it here?"

"I don't know what I want, and it doesn't seem to matter."

"Let's believe that it does, so it doesn't happen again. Well, what is it?"

"A boy- born on Good Friday."

"What is his name?"

"He doesn't have one."

"Then we will call him Christo."

"It's a lot to deal with, and he'll be needing a bit of the devil in him to survive. How about Terzo- the third-you know, a bit of both- like his mother."

Sister Gabrielle, acting as the infant's godmother, is holding the boy child above the baptismal font. The Reverend Mother is acting as priest. There is a column on either side of the font, supporting a gold and a silver vessel. The sisters are chanting a Mass for the mystery of death, while invoking the spirit of rebirth in the name of the Son.

"*Receive the sign of the cross*, Terzo, *on your forehead and in your heart*,"[36] said the Reverend Mother, cleansing the child born of sin, in a dream that was trying to come into time."

The Mother pauses transfixed and crosses herself. Sees Snow, 'Lupa's' mother, in the shadowy nave-forty-five, but like 'Lupa', timeless. Her wild red hair tamed into a knot. Her eyes, like green water, wash over the rite. The long body encased in a severe black suit and hat; lifting the veil, the sleepless eyes that are lost. The pale face that is bruised shows a submission to suffering. Stares at the crucified Son hung on the shadow of fate, with the eyes of a ghost that seem to mirror her own... remembers her flight from her mother, as she stares at the shadow...

Snow, seventeen, struggles through the wind, fighting the darkness of night that is blacker than black. She pounds on the door of the cloister and passes into unconsciousness, wasted and bruised, face pale as a wraith. The massive door opens and the Mother carries her in, laying her weak broken body at the foot of the cross. She opens her eyes, red with fear, and stares at the Mother of Night.

The Reverend Mother whispers to a nun...

"It's her mother, she's mad. She will kill the poor

child. The woman's a monster. She belongs in an asylum."

Like a wounded animal that has come home to die, Snow listens with senses sharpened by fear.

"*She* is your Mother now and the church is your home."

Snow, twenty-one, in a white wedding gown, a crown of thorns on her head, moves towards the shadow of the Mother, renouncing her own in her marriage to Christ. The nuns chant the litany to the 'shadow of God',[37] as she kneels down before it and drinks the blood of the Son. The Brides of Christ seen in shadow 'in endless approach' pass into the Mother and cease to exist.

She returns to the present, the Mother performing the baptism, 'cleansing' the child- making the flesh incorruptible.

"*Do you renounce the devil?*"[37a] the Mother is asking the newborn child.

"*Abrununtio, I renounce him,*"[*] Sister Gabrielle is saying, answering for the infant, who is stunned into silence.

The terrified child stares at the shadow, more terrible than any devil- it looms on the walls and dominates the rite, as Snow is drawn to the thing, she is trying to renounce.

"We attract what we fear," Snow whispers to herself.

"*And all his allurements?*"[*] recites the Reverend Mother.

"*I renounce them,*"[*] said Snow.

"*And all his works?*"[*]

"I renounce him," Snow murmurs... "my wolf man

… my devil…"

The Mother makes the sign of the cross on the heart of the infant: words baptized in blood. "*Be opened… be opened, but you, O devil, depart,*[38] Snow mouthing the words… the heart like a tomb

'Lupa' watching the baptism through the eyes of her mother, immersed in her memories, as she straddles the bidet, the water flooding its bounds, feels the knife in the heart.

"Hey, what are you doing in there? I don't like it *too* clean."

She kneels, as if praying, between his unsightly thighs, opens her mouth on his dick, like the stump of a tree. Leaving her body, till he forces her back.

"Hey, where are you? I was just gonna' come"…

Pushing her head down: sinks her teeth in his dick: '*Depart from him unclean spirit'.*[*] He comes from the pain. I did nothing at all, but to conjure the devil. He has no idea how it happened- but they never do, do they? She slams her stiletto into his balls, gags him and binds him, and goes through his wallet; removes his money and credit cards: "That's for pushing my head down. *It* has a great sense of direction. Swallow that if you can. So long, sucker."

"The three whores are still out there. Leonardo still watching; reliving that day on the docks when he watched through the window: 'Lupa' trapping her trick, while living the myth. Leo remembers his dream that turned fate into dust.

The whores begin closing in on her, Leo transported in time.

"What are you doin' here, bitch?" asks whore #1.

"I've asked myself the same question."

"Well just get off our streets, or we'll fuck your face up, and it'll be the last trick you ever turn."

I smile at her graciously, as if she asked me to tea. "That would be nice. My greatest fear is that I'll be hanging around for *another* two thousand years, working some corner. But I mustn't get my hopes up. If time can't fuck my face up, I doubt if three dirty whores can, unless you're the Three Fates in disguise."

"Try one more night, and see if you survive it."

"Hmmm... maybe you're right. Another night of this would kill me. There's nothing worse than a cheap trick. Tell me, how do *you* feel about it?"

"What are you, a reporter?" asks whore #2.

"A detective?" asks whore #3.

"An undercover cop?" asks whore #1.

"Just a medieval mystic caught in the Industrial Revolution, trying to fit in."

They stare at her dumbfounded. Try to recover their veneer.

"Well, whatever you are, you wanta' work the pavement, you gotta' pay. Some things don't change. You know what I mean, bitch?" says whore #1.

"I know what you mean, but I can't say I agree. Change is the secret of life- the greatest secret of all. Do you want to grow old and ugly and lose your power over men, or master the forces of nature, and free the spirit from the flesh?"

"An activist?"

"A social worker?"

"Nature? What has nature got to do with sellin' pussy? Look, let's get one thing straight. You can't even pretend here without protection," says whore #1.

"Oh, but I *am* protected- by my primordial instincts.

I don't need a pimp."

"Who're you kiddin'? You ain't no whore."

"Sure I am and a good one."

"And you don't have a pimp?" asks whore #2.

"She's lyin'," says whore #3.

"No, really. I'd sell my soul to the devil, before I'd let a man make me his slave."

"Hey, watch your mouth, slut," says whore #1.

"Slut? (laughs). No man ever used *me*. It's you that's fucking for nothing. I could show you how to make money- real money, and still have your freedom; how to train the flesh to assume any form it desires, so that it can survive in any element, no matter how foreign or hostile; how to make men beg you to take their money. *Disguise is necessary to the mystery.*"[40]

"I get it now, the bitch is a madam. What do you want, half?" asks whore #1.

"I'll do it for nothing- for a little experiment."

"Oh, yeah, well experiment on yourself."

"Oh, I do, all the time."

Their pimp pulls up to take their money, dressed to the nines in a flashy car…

"Excuse me, ladies, while I deal with this slime, and show you what your man is made of."

He tries blocking her path. They give each other a conspiratorial nod, waiting for him to desecrate her.

"You better pray, bitch. This is the end," says whore #1.

"Sometimes I wish life were as simple as that- that there was a beginning and end. In the next life, I'm going to remember where I stashed the money. I'm perfecting my memory- the next one will be the last."

"It will be this one, if you continue workin' my

territory," says the pimp.

"You see this animal body, prick? It's made of dense matter, and the empty space that it occupies is automatically mine. Besides, it's the cheapest turf in town, and the only reason you have it, is 'cause no one else wants it."

The whores can't believe this wolf girl's balls. He slides like oil from his car, his killer instinct aroused, as she's daring him on with her fearless eyes...

"You're gonna' pay for it, whore, or they won't recognize you."

"They never do- that's the art. But it's not recognition I'm after. I promise you: you'll get what's coming to you. I'm just getting in the mood."

Leonardo is watching, his hand on his gun, but I'll be damned if I need him. The danger excites me.

The pimp lifts his hand up to strike her. 'Lupa's' sharp eyes are concentrated: focused on his with an icy intensity. Now his hand is suspended as if turned to stone, while the whores look on astonished at their mesmerized pimp. Though I have learned the mysteries of the mind from the Mother of Shadow, and have learned how to use them, how to freeze or to move it, it was not without consequence, and I have suffered the art. But it is only through suffering that we make it our own. This devil's minion of a pimp, who had lived on the sufferings of women, had lost his natural defenses against the secrets of her lore, and my will and desire came together to reveal him to his whores. I knew what it felt like to be robbed of your dignity, and I felt the pity for her Son, and wanted only to protect them."

If you remember, when Perseus, the hero, had to confront the Medusa, he reflected her image back to its source, by using his shield as a mirror, to return the projection. In short, he mirrored the face of the unconscious and turned her to stone, using her powers against her, so he could cut off her head. This is the key to survival in the underworld of shadows, and I have learned it from her- from 'The Dweller of the Threshold'. It was the Terrible Mother inside me that I called on to teach me, and the pimp who abused it was petrified from within."

His hand slowly falls, reaching into his pocket, and hands her his pimp's roll, which she slips in her own. The loss of respect in the eyes of his whores. Now he kneels at her feet in a puddle of water, gazes at her reflection and crosses himself; prays to her image, as it merges with the Virgin...

"Hail Mary, full of grace, blessed is the fruit of thy womb."

"Are you thinkin' what I'm thinkin?" says whore #1.

"Yeah, I'm thinkin' of all the money I wasted, while I was workin' my pussy to the bone," says whore #2.

"Yeah, 'the fruit of my womb"- from now on I keep it," says whore #3.

"Hail Mary, Mother of God, pray for us sinners, now and at the hour of our death."

"Now repeat it three times, until it sinks in. And when you return, you will remember everything.

The rain has washed her face clean- as pure as a virgin. The ironic smile on Leo's face. It conceals the conflict within: she had developed her talents from the things that he taught her, but completely surpassed him, and was now in the teaching position. She winks at the whores, having sated her strange sense of justice. Gets into her Porsche and revs up the engine.

"Hey, wait a minute. Can I call you some time?" asks whore #1.

"I'll be in touch. I have your number."

"But I ain't got no phone."

"You'll hear me."

And moved by the trickster, she escapes like the spirit in the bottle.

The Mother is holding the silver vessel, pouring the Water of Life on the boy-child's head: "Terzo, *I baptize you in the name of the Father, and the Son, and the Holy Ghost.*"

Sister Gabrielle is staring at Snow, who seems to belong to the world and the life of the senses, with the bitter envy of one who has not dared to live... What would it feel like to be beaten by love; to be searched for by Leonardo; have a child out of sin; to taste the forbidden and rebel against God? asking herself in the secrecy of her soul.

Poor sister Gabrielle, if you only knew what you aren't missing, so you can give yourself to God in peace, Snow thought to herself, knowing she suffers her fate.

The Reverend Mother, holding the boy-child, 'freed of sin and the devil', approaches Snow, who is spellbound. Stares at the face of her fear at the Mother of Shadow. Bows to her holiness, kissing her hand...

"It was like she sent for me, Mother...It was like it was long ago, the wind calling me back, always drawing me to her. I needed to know if I was still afraid of her."

"And are you?"

"Of course. Who is not?... But I am ready to bear

it."

"You've been given the chance to find out." The Mother hands her the child...

"With a stranger's child?"

"Yes, your daughter's. Born on the day of the sacrifice."

And Terzo grew up thinking that Snow was his mother.

CHAPTER 6
PIETÁ

'Lupa' speeds by the tracks to the gypsy camp, made from nothing and nowhere, a place for the archetypal outsider. Drives through the goats and chickens, and the dismal tarpaper shacks. The primitive feelings rise up and they strip off the mask. The gypsies mourn by the fire, waiting for death- cross themselves when they see her, who brings the dead back to life.

Young Toto, nine, is swathed in shawls, eyes white slits through half-closed lids. Esperanza, his mother, draped in black, is rocking the boy, stricken with grief. 'Lupa' is stuffing the pimp's roll into her cleavage, embraces her closely, so that the others don't see.

The gypsy is holding her dying son in her arms. "We were hungry, me and Toto, and we went to the city to beg. I found this picture. It made me weep, 'Lupa'." She reaches into her dress, over her heart, for a wet wrinkled postcard of *The Pietá*, the bitter sorrow of the Mother, holding the corpse of her Son. "Maybe if Toto and me pose like this picture...maybe it will make others weep, too, and this hunger will go away...'He is dying'," I said, my son is dying'."

"And then it came true."

She nods. "You've suffered, 'Lupa'. You know many things, but you don't know the pain of the mother when she loses her son."

'Lupa' lowers her lids, "No... no, of course not."

"When he dies, I will die, too."

"He won't die. We won't let him.

'It's too late...it's too late'. Leo's words long ago... when she rejected her son...They burn in her blood.

45

"Shhh... the Mother of Heaven will help us," pressing her finger to her lips.

"No... not this time... She is going to take him... Three days have passed... Three days and three nights. I have killed a goat and three chickens... no answer... no answer... She is punishing me, 'Lupa'."

"No, not punishing. She is telling you something-that words have power: that words can heal or destroy. Now wait for the wind of the Mother, and for the spirit to heal him," grasping her shoulders, holding her close... taking her suffering... taking it into me... till the god enters my body and his death is my own. I pray to the Mother, "Make me your vessel." The wind howling its call...

"Listen, Esperanza... Listen, can you hear her? Listen to the wind, to the voice of the Mother"... She listens a moment. The wind grows stronger...

"I hear her, 'Lupa'. What is she saying?"

"She is saying, *Love is stronger than death... Love is stronger.* Help me, Esperanza, to bring life out of death. Help me to imagine the life force filling little Toto, and bringing him back to his mother the earth."

I press my forehead to hers, our souls joined by the breath, till we are one single being, the spirit of life rushing through us. I breathe my life into Toto. I am breathing it into him...

"You see, you don't have to pose, she is coming right through you," placing the hands of the gypsy over the heart of her son. I cover her hands with my own, as I gather his life, projecting the god-image into him, who rose from the dead.

The sun is rising behind him, surrounding his head, the god burning inside him, transforming death into life. Toto opens his eyes. Looks up at the red burning disc. Struggles out of the shawls, as if from the womb, gazing at the face of his mother, as if at the Mother of God...

"I dreamed I was dying... and that I was trying to find you... I heard your voice call me back... but it was the voice of the wind...

The wind has stopped blowing and the gypsies pray to the sun, 'Lupa' bowing her head to the Mother of Shadow. The gypsy kisses her hand, her tears flowing over it...

"I remember the day that I found you starving in the gutter; waiting to be crushed by the wheels, like you wait for a lover."

"And you swung me up in your arms like a big black angel, and I was sure I had died and had gone to heaven. Then I looked in your eyes, and I was touching the earth."

"Well... almost. You were like a hungry animal turning away from its mother."

"I still am... Nothing's changed...There is only one Mother... the Mother of Shadow, who takes us back into her... to whom all things return."

'No more, you were saying, I am ready for death' ... "Only twelve years old, and so in love with death. But I rocked you in my arms and sang you songs of the earth."

"And you gave me my life and the longing to live. It was you who taught me how to catch the light, and to cast it back like a mirror, to heal the heart and the flesh."

"No, it can't be taught. It's 'the stars in the blood'. Remember, 'Lupa'? Remember your words? 'Go inside, Esperanza. You will find him inside'... 'The stars in the blood'... I saw them today... Today when I listened, I went inside, like you said... You belong to the god, 'Lupa'. He is burning inside you. You burn with the god, with the fire of life. Now dance for me, wolf girl. Dance for me!"

Toto howls like a wolf, and plays a dark haunting tune on his flute, the old man beside him playing the violin. Her eyes are closed, as she sways to the dirge, her face like a tragic mask, mirroring the music. Her movements slow, hypnotic, as she starts to dance, the mournful tone of the music becoming enchanted. The gypsies watch, transported, as 'Lupa' dances for the god. The beat of a tom tom. Another drum answers. The beat in the heart building in rhythm and intensity, as she whirls round the fire, her eyes reflecting the flame. The gypsies wild, ecstatic, beating the pots, while Esperanza is howling and beating the earth like a drum. She spins like a dervish and falls to the earth: kisses the earth, and the music suddenly ceases.

The laughter of Snow rings through the silence, frenzied, intoxicating, a maenad possessed by the spirit, devouring the flesh of the god, as she offers her own. 'Lupa's' hands to her ears to shut out the sound, the moans of pain mixed with pleasure, and the wind is singing its song.

CHAPTER 7
GHOSTS DON'T RIDE HORSES

1950. Leonardo buries Snow's body in a pit by the thorn tree, in the forest of Snow House, where 'Lupa' was conceived. The house, wrapped in mist, can be seen in the distance. Leo is mourning her death, looking down in her grave: stares at the inscription on the stone- a common stone from the forest. It was painted by Terzo in back-slanting letters...

1896-1950 THE WOLF TROTS TO AND FRO
THE WORLD LIES DEEP IN SNOW[49]

Terzo was nine when they buried his 'mother'. He undresses Snow in the pit and removes the white wedding gown (the gown that she wore in her marriage to Christ: it is slashed at the heart and stained with blood). He dresses her body in the black suit and hat- the same suit and hat that she wore at his baptism; his trembling fingers are touching the wound in the heart; veils her face that was bruised and makes a cross on her lids: 'Be open... Be open'. Leo covers her with earth.

The boy never questioned that Snow was his mother; that his father was Lupo... who murdered his 'mother'... and Leonardo?... the hero...a wish from one of Snow's myths...the father he found in her books- a myth of the mind? He never dared ask the question, always hiding his fear, that by asking the question the wish would dissolve.

He hides in the forest with Pale Lady, her mare, both on their knees, as if calling her back; the mare neighing in mourning, as she longs for her touch; the boy longs for it too, the only touch that he knew; a beast of a boy, but a sensitive like Snow, weeping in silence, alone in his fear. Leo has found him and kneels down beside him. He would have called him his son… but was unable to do it.

"Come, Terzo, let's go back to the house."

"I'm not going back."

"Oh? What are your plans?"

"Mother told me, when she died, her soul would live in Avalon, the Land of the Grail, where death has no name. She promised to wait for me there. I'm going to find her."

"You know what they say about Avalon, don't you?"

The boy's questioning eyes search for an answer.

"They say it's a floating island, as transparent as glass, and that there were knights who spent their whole lives searching for it: that when you're ready to find it, wherever you are it appears. That's why they call it, 'the Island of Fate'.[50]

The light of delusion leaves the boy's eyes, and with it the hope. Lowers his lids in despair.

"You'd rather search for it, wouldn't you?"

He doesn't respond.

"It won't be easy to find, but it would be harder alone. I'd like to go with you. I would be lonely. Do you mind? The knights protect one another from the forces of evil. We will ask the Grail to guide us, while we search for her soul. The soul does not die. It wants to be found. We'll ride the moors of Cornwall and the forests of Wales, searching the wild places, where the knights fought for love."

The boy's face darkens in conflict.

"Wait for me here. I'll get our things."

The white mare digs at her grave with her hoof. Terzo is lying on it, dashing his head on the stone....

"Forgive me for not fighting for it," staining the stone with his blood.

The French Renaissance manor house in Lower Normandy, with a high baroque touch, is a rough and imperfect pearl, with a flaw in its heart, built in layers of time; it seemed to combine all the myths that they lived. There was a timeless splendor about it that transcended its style and was tinged with a lushness and a lack of restraint, infusing the senses like an opium dream- in which a second door to the manor seemed to shadow the first: the door of the dead for the return of its mistress.

It was a whore of a house, mixing the lowest and highest, tending to either extreme, that could destroy or revive you, and which it was a mystery- till you returned to yourself. But for Snow and her 'son', the dream was unending, and they would live it through 'Lupa', who would make the myth real.

Back in 1950, Leo paused at the steps. He summons his strength and slowly climbs to the house; passes his image at nine, as it slowly descends. Both stop at the same time, looking over their shoulder. He pushes the fear down as he approaches the door.

Fatima, Snow's servant, a barefoot Berber, crosses the chessboard floor like a piece on the board, a savage queen that was moved by an invisible hand. She opens the door, her head crowned with rags, and presses her gnarled old fingers to a mournful heart. It was as if she were saying in words made of sand, that like djinns in the desert disappeared with the wind: I only serve who

I love, but I knew what the ending would be.

"We're leaving, Fatima, pack our things. Tell Guy to sell the horses."

"All of them?"

"All of them."

"Not Pale Lady, monsieur, madame would not like it."

"Madame is dead, and ghosts don't ride horses."

She nods at him disapprovingly with her old Islamic eyes.

"Keep her then, if you must. Just don't look at me that way."

"I look what I feel-... This Guy... I know… it is not my business--"

"No, Fatima, it's not."

"Business or no business, I will watch every move, and I will hide all the feelings and the money for the horses."

"I have a better idea. Why don't you split it with him? My gift to you both, for your loyalty and discretion."

"It's too much."

"It's not enough. The house is yours- stay as long as you like. I'll send you money to keep it- wherever I am- or am not. I won't forget you."

She presses her hand to her heart."

"How *is* the boy?"

His eyes cloud over... "I don't know how to help him. He thinks he killed her. Why does he think that? Why? I don't understand him...I wish I understood him."

"I do. The boy has lived in a world of knights and magicians, where the magic prayers that she taught him would protect him from evil. All night long she would read to him, till the fear left his eyes- the fear of the beast in the boy: the fear that the wolf man had put there. Like the moon who is holding the light of the sun, she prayed to his shadow to not swallow him up... like his mother she prayed... for the life of her 'son'. They were more than just stories: they became his whole world- a world where he was her hero, and he could save her from death. Last night, when the wolf man returned for his prey, he was forced back to the real world, where he was only a small human boy: a boy with no god-like powers and no magic sword...where not even love could protect her from the black evil knight."

Leonardo has realized he's wounded the boy even more...

"I've *never* known how to help him. Tell me more of my son."

"In his child's mind, he betrayed her, and for a child to betray is to kill."

It was simple, really. His son's problem merely reflected his own... "Not able to act was a sin worse than murder... and looking through the eyes of the killer, he became what he feared. He believes that he killed her, who he thought was his mother. How can I help him?"

"You must tell him the truth: that she was a mother of dreams, not the mother he needed, but a mother of myth; that she was more than a mother, but not on this earth- not the real one, monsieur: not the mother that made him. You must take him to 'Lupa', who gave him his life."

"I can't... I know what she is... and I made her that

way."

"You have asked me and I have said it- what you do not want to hear, and my answer has come from a woman's heart. He needs his real mother now, so he can be born to this world."

"It's a world he does not want to live in. He lives in *her* world... the as-if world of dreams... like 'Lupa'... a dreamer."

"Will you be coming back to this dream?"

"Someday...maybe."

"We'll be waiting for you, me and Pale Lady... poor creature... It is said that beasts can die of pain."

"Then *I* am a beast."

Her eyes fill with compassion. "I will pray to your god for you. Have faith, monsieur."

"I just buried my faith, and the god doesn't answer. And as far as prayer goes, I have more luck with the dice."

CHAPTER 8
SHADOW WOMAN

Terzo, twenty-one, in the thrall of the mother, is still trying to find her in his visions and dreams, in the lonely world that he lives in, where he communes with her shadow. He is inturned, cerebral, his room cell-like, monastic: except for some magical objects, ancient animals and gods; Snow's books on the Grail, mixed with physics and astronomy; his paintings of death, since the day that Snow died.

His nature is raw, his body lithe like an animal, with classical features, as if carved out of stone, that mirror 'Lupa', his real mother, who he shaped in his soul. Like Nola and Snow, of the airy realm of the spirit-*disembodied* by spirit, but the instinct of a beast.

He is startled awake by the fourth dream of the night. Gripped by his fear. Writes it down in his notebook. The same back-slanting letters: a knife marks his place; on the black onyx hilt, a cross studded with rubies; uses his pen like a knife, engraving the words on the page...

Fourth dream, same series...
Mother's house. Chessboard passage. No doors. No way out. Her earthbound spirit hovering over me. The woman walking behind me... the shadow of Death? The click of her heels on the stone are like nails in my flesh... She is wearing stilettos... that clash with her image.

After leaving the gypsy camp, and the disillusioned whores, Nola slams on the brakes in the Ile Saint-

55

Louis, at an elegant Arco Deco building on the banks of the Seine. Dawn is still breaking, the red sun still rising, the rain beating down, looks like she's been on a bender; she is still wearing stilettos, her feet caked with mud; still the wet clinging dress, the second skin of disguise, veiling her secret identity, that she pretends to expose. She ascends to her lair, shedding the red of the dress, washing the men from her body, infected by their touch. The god of thunder is beating the drum of her fate, and before passing out, she imagines the face of her son: the brooding boy she rejected, who drives her need to escape.

Terzo, naked, unguarded, hunched on his bed, is recording his dream with a painful precision, as if engraving the words into his flesh...

Fifth dream: same series...
It's like I'm one of the players in the game of my fate. The veiled image of Death like a piece on the board. I'm walking the chessboard passage, making my move, but I know I'm alone- that the other pieces are dead...I know that soon I will join them, and that only *she* will survive. She follows me at a slow but relentless pace, draped in black, like a shadow, her face masked by her shroud. The click of her heels on the stone are like nails in my flesh. I am facing the door with the cross on it, painted in blood... caught in her shadow that looms on the door... I can see my own end, my body nailed to her image. 'Be open', she says, her voice like a knife. I am frozen with fear, unable to move, but my hand reaches out and responds to her will. The door is locked, as I left it, and I feel a wave of relief. 'It's locked', I am saying. 'Open the door', she repeats. I remembered

hiding the gown Snow wore for the Christ...for the death of the *Self*... on the day of the sacrifice... I tried to remember plunging the knife in her heart, but there was a dark empty space... and only she had the key.

Leonardo is standing in the driving rain by a limo, yelling up at the window of Terzo's apartment, while talking to Guy about a dubious deal, his shifty chauffeur and bodyguard, who would kill for a sou- his twisted psychopath smile, faced scarred by a knife, revealing a scarred inner self, as if seen on the surface. He is blowing the horn in the father/son ritual, as Leo fends off his fear and calls to his son...

"Terzo, come down!"

Terzo ignores him, continues writing his dream, tracking his thoughts, as if that's all that there is...What else could there be?... He tries to remember...

I turned to confront her... No! that's a lie... My lids were like stone... like the one I placed on the grave... The door was locked, as I left it, and there was nothing but fear...

What if I'd looked in those eyes, and given myself to her darkness? Would it have freed me? Would I have learned how to see?

"Come down, Terzo! Come down!"

Terzo ignores him..

I will remember, till my thoughts are as sharp as my knife, and every image is carved in the stone of my mind...

What is the meaning of the sacrifice? Did he die for us or himself? What does it mean that he rose on the third day of his death?

He cuts a cross on his heart with the point of the knife: looks at the symbol in the mirror; tries to discipline the pain. Pressing the wound to the page, covers the dream with his blood; continues to write... and to question the *Self*...

What does it mean to be hung on the arms of her cross?... Her voice cutting into me...

'Look at my face'.

Leonardo is knocking. "Terzo, open the door."

Terzo, opens it, naked, with an air of indifference.

"There's someone I want you to meet (overcoming his fear). More like a twin than... C'mon, get dressed."

"I'm not in a social mood."

"She won't be either."

Nola, asleep, is grabbing the phone... "Yes? (pause) It's too early (pause). How *much* more? (pause). Alright, thirty minutes."

She opens the door with an air of icy serenity, to a repressed British masochist, too clean for a trick, conservative, handsome- in a clean kind of way. Her look and manner have changed, matching his closet case fantasy. She wears an ivy league suit, the same as his own; the button-down shirt; the striped tie; the boy wig; the boy shoes; the school ring (like his own); the light gray contact lenses, matching his eyes and his suit: the mirror image he longs for.

"You've been avoiding me, Nolan," he says, as if to a mirror."

"Yes. You bored me the last time. It's easy to bore me (in a thick British accent that matches his own)."

"Too personal for you?

"What are you drinking?" Pours him a triple.

"I missed you," he says, breaking the code.

"Be careful- you might begin to believe it."

"I couldn't stop thinking about you."

"Ice?"

"You could drive a man to his--"

"Must you? Let's skip the rhetoric, shall we?"

Pours a drop for herself- just a thimble of poison, to take the edge off his face... the dark thought that keeps rising. A slight sip- just a drop, to begin the wrong ritual.

"I had a fantasy that--"

"One more word, and I'll charge you. Every word will cost more."

"I--"

Gives him the look, leading him into a bedroom. He unlocks his briefcase. Removes two thousand pounds. Locks it again.

"Triple it- it's too early."

"But it's usually a thousand."

"Don't bargain with me. Triple or nothing."

He unlocks the briefcase and gives her three thousand...

"Only a madman would come back for more."

"Only a masochist, who wanted less than the whole."

She stashes the money in a drawer with a dildo and crystal ball- a little joke to remind her that matter and spirit were split. He gets undressed, folds his clothes with an anal precision. She remains in the suit and straps on the dildo, inserts it straight through her fly, controls his dick with a thought...

"Turn over." She mounts him...

It won't take long- if he's lucky. Fifty minutes at

most: ten for the words; ten for the act; five for a cigarette; ten for more words; five for the bargaining; two to open the briefcase; three to bargain for dinner; and five more for the ending. I'll skip the double. I don't have the patience.

It's over. She dismounts, lighting a cigarette.

"Was it good?" he asks."

"Aren't you confused? I should be asking *you* that question."

"Someday, I'll find *your* weakness and use it against you."

"That would take years and you won't be around that long.

"Do you get any pleasure at all from tormenting me?"

"None."

"I pay you to lie to me."

"No, you pay me to pretend, and to believe you can bear it. And if what you wanted was to give a man pleasure, you wouldn't come to *me*- now would you?"

"How do you know what I want better than I do?"

"That you want to be hurt and rejected? The same way a fox knows that chickens taste better than men."

"Have you ever been hurt and rejected?"

"Twice. Once at conception and once at birth."

"And you've been avenging it ever since?"

"Do you really think it's as simple as that?"

"Yes."

"And you who thrive on rejection- a mother who wouldn't let go? That's why you're obsessed with me, why you feel safe with me: safe with a wicked, immoral, and dangerous man, so you won't be unfaithful to mother, who understands what you want;

and if you're tempted for more, he will punish you- like she did, soothing the guilt of disobeying the command,"

Breaking him down. Eyes cold and direct. He tries to save face, to regain his composure...

"Who are *you* punishing? It wouldn't be your father would it?"

Her touché smile...

"Much too simple. Besides, I never knew him."

Both reach for their drinks- she for a third of the thimble. They break into laughter. But still he is trying to get her- knowing he'll lose, which is part of the game...

"I couldn't sleep last night. I was cruising around. I saw you on the street. You looked like--"

"A common whore? (impervious). "You feel cheated, don't you? But don't worry. He paid more- in the end."

He gives up. He's no match for her- just curious now....

"I don't get it. You have the best clientele in Paris. You're rich. And still, you're stalking the streets, looking for victims."

"A man needs fresh air and exercise. Some people take up tennis."

"Take the mask off, Nolan- just for a moment."

She takes a drag, drains the thimble...

"I was reminiscing- reliving a childhood memory. It's the only way I can feel the pain...It's a pleasant change- when I'm not in the mood for skiing. That moment is up. Leave me now. The truth is beginning to bore me (stubs out her cigarette)."

"Lie to me then. Let's do it again- just an ordinary

fuck. That's what I wanted in the first place- remember? Just a little pleasure- before I let you convince me that what I wanted was pain. I'll give you another thousand."

"I don't feel like it." Gives him the wounded look. "Shocking isn't it, that a whore can have feelings."

He looks at her in wonder...

"What are you, Nolan?"

"What do you want me to be?"

"You could have any man that you want."

"I don't want a man."

"What a puzzle you are- selling your flesh for your freedom, and yet, we all own a piece of you."

"But no one man will ever put the pieces together."

"What *do* you want?"

"What I want doesn't exist.

He looks at her for a moment, trying to fathom her.

"Well, I better get out of here, before I sign my will over to you (getting dressed). When can I see you again? How about dinner tomorrow?"

"Dinner costs more."

"I'll buy a few more pieces. It's more expensive than a shrink, but much more amusing."

That injured look, again. He's hooked. "Sorry that was in bad taste." Tries to touch her. She flinches... "You can have as much money as you want. I don't care about the money. Four thousand. No questions. I want to know what's inside. I'm more than just curious."

"They all are: as if they could find it."

"Getting too real, again?"

"There you go, kidding yourself again, with this relationship business. You're as incapable of it as I am.

I'll have to shorten your sessions. You've been 'on the couch' too long. Make it nine at Le Grand Vefour."

"Do you always have to be in control?"

"I'll make the reservation. What was your name again?"

"You're shameless. Just make it in one of yours."

He goes to his briefcase. Opens it (two minutes). Extracts two thousand- half in front for dinner. They've done it before. Tries to kiss her goodbye...

"Not on the lips, please."

Nola is bathing, steam rising off water; having a vision of reality, as though it were part of a dream...

Sees her trick exit and cross the street to the Seine. Guy driving the limo is cruising right towards him. Points out her window to Leo. Terzo in back; unaware his unconscious is beginning to merge with reality, his face flooded with light, his features indistinguishable. In her vision she sees it. It mirrors reality. Now can't see his face: eclipsed by the sun. Submerged in the water. The tension grows by degrees...

Sees a vision of two fishes, floating on the surface of the Seine. They lie in reverse, head to tail- like the two fishes of Pisces. The water is tainted. The fish are dying. Their mouths and gills cease to move. Nola gasping for breath... Gazing into the water, as if into a crystal, eyes open and concentrated, hair spreading Medusa-like. Sees the image of her face- the image of beauty and horror. Her face turns to stone as it reflects the unconscious.

She bursts through the water, trying to breathe. Goes to the window and stares at the limo. Mind racing relentlessly. Back to the wall.

Twenty-one years she's been running. Fate catching up with her. It slowly moves down the street. Eyes search for his face. Hand pulling the cord. Drapes shut out the light.

Begins transforming her image through the eyes of the complex. Making the mask in the image of Snow. The articles of disguise arranged in an obsessive order: eyebrows and lashes according to color and thickness, glass contact lenses of every color and hue, slap simulating every pigment from the fairest to the darkest, wigs that mock every style from the most outlandish to the most conservative. Her dusky skin whitened; eyes lose their intensity, turn to the coolness of jade, like water reflecting the moon; the red wig, fits it on- ties it into a knot...Gazes into the mirror at the ghost of an image. Traces the lines of her face with her long thin fingers... like a far-off memory... in a black suit and hat.

Frantically pacing and packing. The bell rings incessantly. Shuffling through passports. Recoils as the bell rings more urgently. Lowers the veil. Escapes through the rear door. Leo picking the lock. Knows that he's lost her. Terzo is watching through the rear-view window.

Sees 'Lupa', his real mother, like an apparition of Snow... just as he dressed her, when she was lain in the grave. His face through the window, like a terrified boy, the same feeling of terror that he had in his dream... under the spell of the *Shadow Woman*... like when he stared at the door. The cross painted in blood. Her arms like black wings. Hears her voice in his head: 'Open the door'.

Tries seeing her face... but he knew he could not... knew that to see her was death... that to know her was life... willing to die for her love... to return from the dead... willing to live in her soul... willing to cease to exist.

CHAPTER 9
SHADOW WAY

Nola, in her Porche, screeches to a stop; sees a 'FOR RENT' sign in the window of an elegant townhouse: presses the bell: knows it is hers. A myopic Russian, with horn-rimmed glasses, peculiarly introverted, comes out on the balcony. Stares at her strangely, as if seeing a vision. Opens the door, as if he tried not to close it. Reaches his hand out, while taking it back. "Leopold Archipova"- something desperate about him. Her glove is a shield: "Marie du Vallee." Takes her in with his eyes, as if absorbing her soul. She knows that she's got him. They enter 'her' house...

"Your house feels perfect for me. I often go with my feeling." She leads the way to the drawing room, as if he were the client. He follows behind her. Manic depressive, she's thinking- a depressive phase on the verge- about to plunge into mania (accurate, as always, in her study of men). I really should have been an analyst. I'm wasting my time as a whore. She makes a gesture for him to enter, inviting him in. He likes it that way, but tries taking control...

"Let me show you around."

"Don't bother, I want it."

"A woman who knows her own mind- a rare thing in a woman."

"Even rarer in a man."

She sits on the chesterfield, as if she's been there before. Her all-seeing eyes scan the high-ceilinged room. It is surrounded by frescoes of the opera composers- Wagner, Verdi, Puccini, Bellini... Eyes rest on the bookcase, scanning the titles. The books he has written, to know more of her 'patient': *Mask of the Moon; Water of the Moon; Ice Woman; Bound Woman; Totem Woman; Taboo Woman*: Leopold Archipova is *anima*[66] possessed. His Russian name is in the feminine- identified with his mother, continues her diagnosis, as he continues to stare at her...

Mary of the Valley, he muses...the dark version, no doubt... Good title for a book- the next one on death... Death becomes more appealing... Looks away, more self-conscious... Eyes find her, again... she lets him look, for a moment...

"What is it? Do we know each other?"

Finds her strangely compelling... "Excuse me, I don't mean to stare. It's just that- Tries to be more objective but resorts to a cliché... "I... feel like I've known you... but... not here... in this world... Can I get you a drink? I'm... not used to company."

"Just think of me as a tenant. I'm not used to it, either- except for my patients. No, I don't touch it. I find it interferes with my work."

"You are a doctor?"

"A hypnotist."

He's intrigued and perplexed...

"I'm certain it's no accident... Are you French?"

"My father is Swiss- a brain surgeon- and my mother's American. I was born in New York. I live there at times- when I'm not in Umbria at my vineyard, or doing research in Zurich, teaching in Italy, or on a lecture tour in Germany. I just arrived here. I'm giving a lecture tonight."

"What is the subject? (beside himself)."

"The Disease of Fantasy. I'm writing a book on it- from an analytic perspective."

"Fascinating"... Stripping her with his introspective eyes.

"Do you think so?"

"Yes, I do. I'd like to come- if you let me."

"Next time- it's a professional seminar," still scanning the room... Such a relaxing room. Just right for my sessions. You don't mind if I see my patients here, do you?"

"I don't see why not." He wants to be one of them.

She writes down some references. "My bank in Geneva, my stockbroker in New York, and some personal references in Mont Blanc, where I like to ski and go mountain climbing."

"I'm leaving for the Orient for four months. I had given up renting it. None of the applicants pleased me."

"Do I please you? (deadpan)."

"Yes... You're just right... (he's obsessed)."

"Then it's settled."

"But you didn't even ask me how much the rent is."

"I want it."

"It's steep."

"I said I want it (hard-edged). When you want something, Monsieur Archipova, do you ask the price?"

"I guess I never really wanted anything- until--" He is unable to resist, hypnotized by her suggestion, and under the spell of the unconscious he has already lost what he possessed.

"Tell me in dollars."

Forcing himself to be practical, he calculates for a moment... "It's four thousand, four hundred dollars a month- in advance- and a security deposit of eight thousand, eight hundred."

She removes four rolls of bills from her bag, in mixed denominations, and, at an amazing speed, transposes them into dollars, interjecting off-handedly: "You don't mind cash, do you? I haven't had time, yet, to open an account."

He watches, incredulous, as she continues to calculate... "So, thirteen thousand, two hundred dollars, and enough left over for lunch and a shopping spree." Hands it to him...

He trembles... "To tell you the truth... Well... I'm writing a novel... and-- well, I'm stuck... (pours himself a stiff drink). It takes place in Shanghai, and I thought if I lived there for a while... To tell you the truth, I'm beginning to change my mind... I have this recurring problem. I keep writing the same book. Maybe a little hypnosis...How much do you charge?"

"Three hundred dollars a session."

"Would you consider taking me on as a patient? I'm not as good at calculating as you, but how about three times a week for four months? And you can move in today." Hands her back the money.

She slips it in her bag and calculates. "You owe me twelve hundred."

He goes to his desk and writes out a check.

"I prefer cash."

He goes to his safe (she records the combination). Gives her the money. Stares at her as she counts it, "But what about you? (the tinge of a smile on her face). Where will you stay, Monsieur Archipova?"

"I'll stay in a hotel. I need a change of perspective... maybe a change of mind"...

"You are staring at me, again. Do I remind you of someone?"

"Yes. Someone I invented that I chase through my novels. If you were not so complete, you'd be her incarnation. It's as if you stepped off the pages to bring her to life. I'm not even sure that you're here, or if I imagined you into existence."

"I like to think I imagined myself. But I have no doubt you will be a good subject."

Later that night, in the red wig, in white, she is sitting on the chesterfield, still manipulating fate. Three gentlemen sit facing her, also looking for change. They are hung on her words...

"It's a rare treat, gentlemen- very rare. They're from a strict Catholic school that's run like a cloister, and have not been exposed to the strange world of the senses, so be gentle with them- until they get used to it."

"How much is it, Lily?" asks one of them.

"Three thousand francs each- for the first time, that is."

They take out their wallets. "Give it to *them*. They will appreciate it even more. They really should get accustomed to the crude rewards of this world. Afterwards, if you're pleased, you can give me a gift."

"That's very civilized," said another.

"Knowing Lily, the gift will be more than the girls," said the first.

"Lily is worth it, but whether the girls are--" said the last.

"They're well trained."

"By you?" asked the first.

"Not exactly. More by fate. They're made for it. Believe me. It will be a novelty."

"I'll give you six thousand to join us. I still think of

you with Lulu, and how you seduced her. I learned about women that night," said the other.

"You need to learn more."

"I'll never know as much as you do about a woman's body. You are a master," said the last.

"Well, I've devoted myself to it. Nature wants to be perfected. But tonight, I'll just watch. It should be amusing."

"Will you have dinner with us after?" asked the first.

"We'll see. One can't know how one will feel after- can one?"

"Don't you ever get hungry?" asked the last.

"Often, but I like to hunt for my food."

The three street whores enter, looking like innocents: like tamed adolescents in school uniforms: starched white blouses with medals of the Virgin Mary, navy ties, navy skirts, black sensible oxfords, white knee socks. They're heads are bowed with downcast lids. "Claire, Jean Claude; Elise, Jean-Paul; Madeleine, Phillipe. On second thought, perhaps, Claire will join me, when she's finished. Will you, Claire?"

"Yes, madame," said whore #1.

"Lily, Claire. Call me Lily."

"Yes, Lily (submissively)."

"Wait a minute, I want to get in on that," said the first.

"And me," said the last.

"Count me in," said the other.

"You can bid for it, gentlemen (starting a price war). The highest bidder can watch me work on her. How do you feel about that, Claire?"

"I think I'd like that," said the toughest, oddly

excited; the others are jealous, feeling rejected, as they fathom the mystery of their profession.

"The following morning, under her influence, Archipova lies 'on the couch', as Nola sits at his desk, taking detailed notes of his dialogue with his *anima*...

"She's more like some evil spirit that inhabits my body: an evil tyrant that dictates my every thought. It is she who writes my books."

"What is this one called?"

"*Shapeshifter*. The theme is always the same. It's about a woman who shifts her shape like the moon, and is trying to escape 'the ring of recurrence'.

Her body contracts. She does not want to hear it.

"It's trash- pure trash, but best-sellers, every one of them. It's her little joke."

"It's a good joke, but you're not laughing."

"Her jokes are driving me mad."

"There's a woman hiding in every man, of which the outer woman is only a mirror reflection. Some men turn her into a servant or pet and insult and humiliate her, others grovel before her like slaves; some fear her, some worship her, some are envious of her, but all are confused by her. You have made her your whore, and are blaming her for your third-rate work."

"That's what she would say."

"That's what she is saying, only you don't want to hear it. You want the fame and the money. You want it, and yet you can't come to terms with writing those terrible books. You see what you've done, don't you? You've projected the guilt onto her, and are trying to drive her out of your body."

"What am I going to do?"

"You're going to write a great book. But first you

must surrender yourself to her, and she will grant you the thing that only she can grant."

"What thing is that?"

"Immortality. You see, she wants it, too. You want the same thing."

"But I can't write a word. I don't have an idea in my head."

"Good. That's what we're working for. Close your eyes, Archipova. Make yourself empty... open."

He closes his eyes, but his face and body remain tense.

"You are trying to control her. Stop. Control is a form of resistance. It is foolish to think you can resist such a creature. Surrender yourself to her... surrender... and with your inner eye see the sun sinking into the warm dark sea... The sun is your consciousness... sinking... sinking"...

His body goes limp, and he gives himself up to her.

"The boundaries dissolving... the boundaries between the upper and lower world dissolving. These worlds are within you and they are becoming one, and as you sink into the darkness it is gradually illumined, with all the sparks of ideas that have ever existed, and those that have not yet been born."

He slips into a trance...

"She is with you now."

"Yes."

"She is going to tell you the story, the theme of your book, and you will tell it to me in her words."

She waits for a moment, knowing he will tell her.

"She is communing with me... She is changing the title"...

"What is it?"

"*Lady of the Beasts*- it is the story of the Huntress- a contemporary myth: a whore with two selves, who turns men into beasts... a woman who is guided by the shadows of the underworld; who reads the minds and souls of men, but who doesn't know her own heart: who reveals men's fate to them, but is fleeing from--"

It's going too far. Has to break it, the transference. "Return now to the upper world," snapping her fingers.

"From--"

"Return!"

He comes out of the trance, reluctantly comes to the surface.

"That's enough for today."

"But... I was just--"

"I said that's enough. Leave me."

Later, in Archipova's bedroom, a trick, blindfolded and gagged, and wearing her underwear, is tied to Leopold's bed, flinching in pain, torso arched, face contorted, as Nola, in a black rubber suit and high black boots, beats him relentlessly with a riding crop: possessed by her father: the spirit of Lupo. Her face is masked. Only her eyes are visible.

Unshaven, shaking, with blood-shot eyes, Archipova, undone, is enslaved to his typewriter, reduced to a seedy hotel room, in a manic episode. His desk is chaotic, ashtrays piled with butts, empty bottles of vodka, wads of paper- three versions in conflict for each page of text. Shaking hands shuffle through them. Trembling, he chooses one, writing 'THE END'- the end that he fears. He calls her to tell her, unable to restrain himself...

"It's exactly as you said. I've finished *Lady of the Beasts* in exactly four months. It's inspired, it's beyond me, and I can't write without you."

"We have had our last session. The timing is perfect."

"But I have no more money to give you. What can I do? I can't even pay for this crummy hotel room."

"You won't have to. I'm leaving on a lecture tour. It's called The Invisible Woman. You can move in tomorrow."

"Please. I need you. I'll give you the royalties. It was you who wrote it. I'll give you everything I have. I'll give you the house. You can have it- all of it. I am completely in love with you."

"Not with me. You are in love with the *Shadow Woman*, who guided you to the source. But where does science end and fantasy begin? Ask yourself, Archipova. You are completely possessed."

That night was the last, and she had a dream of her son. He dreamed of 'Lupa'... his mother, for they were bound by their fate, and by the mother/son transference, with the Lupa in Nola. She knew his dream was the same, but for five different elements...
In his dream...

A Black Virgin statue appeared in her image... the image of 'Lupa'... his beast of a mother... Her hand is extended as if for an offering, as she bears her son's death, mourning his life. In his, the signpost was missing that was pointing the way. But in both, the dreamer was passing through the tall iron gate, moving toward Snow House, as if moved by the god. The third that the wind swept him on, as if he were called by the spirit, with no choice but to follow... though he knew he would meet his own end.

In her dream…

She approaches the tall iron gate. Snow House looms in the distance, covered with ice. She walks down a long narrow road, passing the sign, like a cross, with 'SHADOW WAY' written on it, in Terzo's childish hand, his back-slanting letters, like they were on Snow's stone. Leo's voice from a distance: 'It's too late...it's too late'.

She enters the round room in Snow House, like a miniature chapel. Its oppressive darkness is illumined by an unnatural light. It focused on the Black Virgin statue on an archaic stone altar, her hand reaching out, as if for an offering. Three swords pierce her heart, and there is blood on her breast. The bitter sorrow is rending her time-worn features, bearing the death of her Son, as if his death were her own. 'Lupa' stares at the image with a chilling melancholy. Then the light goes out and the room is in darkness. Buried alive in his tomb, the walls closing in on her... unable to breathe... gasping for breath...

She is awakened by the image with a stabbing pain in her breast. Her eyes go to *Bound Woman*, the book on her bed. She opens the window for air and sees Leonardo. He leans on a street lamp, the full moon behind him, looking up at her window, eyes fixed on her shadow…

"Leave me alone, Love… Leave me alone."

CHAPTER 10
THREE FACES

She circles the *Rond Point* and stops at the Hotel Crillon. Still in disguise, almost unrecognizable: wears a chestnut wig, in a thirties bob; the blue eyes have a candour that reflect the cool light; a tweed suit; camel coat; and sensible walking shoes, revealing the taste of the author, as opposed to the whore. She enters the sumptuous lobby and approaches the concierge...

"I'd like a room for three days (with an American accent)."

"All we have are two suites."

"One will do."

"Your credit card, madame."

"I'll pay with traveler's checks. How much in dollars?" She throws an American passport down, signing the registry in a bold direct hand: 'Amanda Trent- 300 Central Park West- New York, NY 10024, USA.' She begins signing traveler's checks. He calculates: "six thousand, three hundred. Suite 969." She signs sixty-three checks and hands him a C-note. He gives the bell-boy the key and she follows him to the elevator. Leonardo, leaning on a pillar, still watching her moves, listens to the gossip of the clerk and the concierge...

"That woman is a notorious whore," says the clerk.

"Are you sure she doesn't look like one?" says the concierge.

"Do I look like a clerk?"

"Yes." Studies her photo. "Do you think it's real? Is she American?"

"No one knows." Looks at the picture. "It looks like

her, doesn't it- or does it?"

"Yes, and no."

"That's what I mean. You can see it in three different ways. Strange, isn't it? She's a legend in Paris. They call her 'The Woman of Three Faces'."

Leonardo musing, the three faces of the moon.

"Well, she can't stay here." Leonardo goes to the desk. "Leave the lady alone, and you'll be taken care of," passing three C-notes (one for each face.) "And I'd like the second suite." The concierge hands him the key. "It's below the lady's monsieur."

The two elevators arrive, an American man is in one of them. She sizes him up, and hands the bellboy a ten. Thank you. I think I'll go to the bar. Leave my bags in my room and the key in the door. I'll be right up." The bellboy gets in one elevator, and she in the other. Looks the man over and pushes six...

"I'm going down, madame," says the man.

"No, I am." She takes his handkerchief from his pocket, spreading it on the floor, and down on her knees, unzips his fly. "That will be three hundred dollars," holding her hand out. He gives her three bills. Slips her hand in his fly. He instantly comes. She hands him his handkerchief. Exits on six, ascends to the ninth in the other.

Later, bejeweled in a black cocktail dress, Nola sits in the dining room, studying the menu. Three men stare at her from three different tables; Leonardo at another, watching her work. The headwaiter arrives (he, too, is taken by her): "Have you decided, madame?"

"Yes, I want three dozen oysters and a bottle of Cristal. And would you take this note (dashes if off behind the menu- Suite 969- 10:00 tonight), to the man with the black tie, the one behind the plant- discreetly, of course," slipping it with a C-note. "On second thought, also, one to the red tie, the one by the flowers (dashes it off behind the menu- suite 969- 11:00 tonight), again, the C-note. "And one to the green tie, the one by the tree" (suite 969- midnight) slips him the C-note. He looks her over, impressed: "My pleasure."

"The pleasure is mine", she replies. "And I'll have a chocolate souffle' for dessert, with a glass of chartreuse."

They all read their notes. Their eyes never leave her. Leonardo's eyes burning into her as she is eating an oyster...

I return to the past and the way that he looked at me... how I needed his love... and the pearl that he gave me.

"But the Son *is* the pearl."

"And the Mother?"

"The oyster."

Washes his love down, as she sips her champagne... eats an oyster... another, as the three men watch hypnotized. Leonardo observes her, as she tastes the eroticized flesh. Lost in her solitary pleasure, she soon forgets they exist... till the last, in the center. Finds his note, beneath its shell...

Magdalena, its time (how it turns on itself.) The snake is biting its tail (can't you feel it?) and you cannot escape me.

The following morning, disguised as Snow, as she heads for the exit, she is recognized by the concierge: "Madame Trent." She ignores him. He cuts her off at the exit, blocking her way.

"You will come with me, Madame Trent. I would like to talk to you in the office."

"I have no time for nonsense."

"Your suite has been reserved. You will be out by noon. This is one of the finest hotels in Paris, and you have turned it into a whorehouse."

"That's what fine hotels are for. And I'll be out when I'm ready," thrusting her way through the door, and leaving him outraged.

She enters Angelina's, an old-fashioned tea room, a jewel box on the Rivoli, frequented by seasoned ladies. Their eyes follow her as she passes. Something curious about her... but what they couldn't tell... something wholly indefinable. She goes to the powder room, removes the red wig, the jade lenses: to be only her self for a moment- to remember she has one. They look with the same curiosity, as another self passes. Seasoned, they thought, but another breed than their own: something that triggered the shadow, and brought up unnameable fears. They had only *one* self- what would another self bring? but kept sipping their tea, knowing they would never find out.

She sits at a table by the window, as Terzo is passing. 'Time turns into space'[79], as their eyes meet through the glass- bound by a spell, as when they meet in a dream.

Terzo, naked, hunched on his bed, gripped by her face, remembers his dream; draws her image with eyes closed, carved in his soul. Tries purging it from his mind, but it's engraved in his nerves. The full moon through the window is surrounding his head- the moon reflecting her face, as it emerged from within. He looks down at his drawing and is completely bewildered. He has drawn a boy who is sucking the teat of a she-wolf. Eyes close as he stares at it. Falls asleep to forget. Wakes up, grabs his notebook, turns the knife to the page- as if carving the words in his flesh... recording his dream....

Her face through the glass, as if she were looking inside me. I try passing through it as if it were space. Watch her image fragmenting, as it shatters inside me, cutting me open, till the pieces are mingled... till we are one single creature, made of shards of the self...The unknown woman has captured my soul.

Nola is leaving Le Grand Vefour with a trick. They exit the rear door of the restaurant on the Palais Royal, walk to the street on Rue Beaujolais and pass Esperanza, still begging, at the door of the restaurant.

Again, the black suit, the red wig, the jade eyes, like still water. Wears high black stilettos, like knives on the pavement. Guy in the limo across the street, talking to Leo, still hunting her down. Nola, knows she is hunted as the huntress of men- her impossible fate that she has written herself.

"She's leaving now with a trick."

The trick hails a taxi. "Give me some money for the gypsy," she asks.

"Why?"

"Do as I say- five hundred francs."

"Five hundred francs? Are you mad?"

"Of course. Isn't that why you want me?" Pulls him in with a look. He gives her the money.

She gives it to Esperanza. The gypsy glances at the

limo. "Be careful tonight," trying to warn her.

"Don't worry, I'm on to it."

"Maybe someday you'll learn. You are only half wolf, 'Lupa'- the other half's human."

"Well, half a chance is better than none; only the wolf has a chance- the human half knows it doesn't." The gypsy tries not to smile, but her eyes are full of foreboding. "I said don't worry. Now get off the streets. What did I tell you about begging? Go home to Toto."

Nola gets in the taxi. The gypsy's eyes are on Guy. He follows with Leo at a distance, tracking her moves. The taxi pulls up to a 'high end' hotel by the hour. Guy parks the limo with Leo. The two watch and wait. Archipova bargains with a whore at the cheap hotel down the street...

"I only have fifty francs. I'll make it up to you the next time."

The whore laughs at him shrilly and yells up the street: "Hey Marie, did you hear that? He wants to make it up next time."

"Tell him there is no next time in hell."

Their laughter distant, distorted... like a scene from his book... the book that she wrote as she mined his unconscious. Guy watches the sideshow with Leo, as he turns to escape: stares at her image, as if at a phantom, as she's leading her trick to rooms by the hour. Guy observes his remains and waits for his move.

Terzo hunched on his bed, reflects on his dream. It is lit by the moon, like a lonely island in space. His pen is poised on his notebook, as he tries to decipher the symbols...

My back is pressed to 'the door', the cross replaced by

her shadow. I am hung on her darkness... conceived by a memory... Her arms are extended like great black wings... I'm engulfed by her darkness... until I cease to exist.

Ten minutes later, when her work has been done, 'Lupa', steeling her nerves, slinks through the corridor. Now pressed to the wall, she stares at her shadow: like the cross of the Mother that she sees in her dreams: her eyes like an animal alerted to danger. Moves through the corridor: feels the eyes of her death...

Archipova is watching her from a room in construction. The click of her heels on the stone as they echo inside him. He grips her neck from behind, as she rushed to the door. "*Nolo ma tangere*! Don't touch me! Don't touch me! You are trapped in the cliché of your prostitute *anima*." He stares at her through the numbness with fascination and horror. Drags her into the room, as she tears at his flesh with her teeth. "I want some, too. After all, I paid for it." She laughs in his face, "Why don't you write about it, instead?"

He clamps his hands round her throat, "I'm going to kill you." She smiles. "Are you? Still trying to make me immortal?" Looks into his shadow. His hands loosen their grasp. They caress her, instead, stroking her long pale neck (the made-up neck of her mother, who tempted the god). She conjures the thought of defeat. Looks him straight in the eyes. His hands weaken their grasp, as if under a spell...

"No... not this time. No...I won't let you." His hands encircling her throat, slowly increasing the pressure, but, somehow, she's no longer struggling... '*Please*', she is whispering... '*Please*', she repeats...

in the thrall of her mother, begging for death.

Leonardo, in the limo, looks nervously at his watch. "She's been in there too long. Take a look, will you?"

Guy enters the room as she sinks to the ground. Points his gun at the Russian...

"Which way do you want it?" Looks up at the rafters and at the ropes on the floor. "You can hang yourself, or I can blow your brains out." Archipova is mute: trapped in his novel. "It's a rough decision. Why don't I make it for you."

Leonardo carries her through the chessboard passage, laying her down on the bed of her mother.

Dawn breaks and he knocks on the door of his son. Terzo opens it with that furtive look, Leo brushed past him, and enters the cell of a solitary. Feels like a stranger. He produces two documents...

"One is the deed to the house."

"Burn it," says Terzo.

"If you like. Or you can sell it. It's worth three million francs- six hectares of forest and farmland, and another sixty for the wild life sanctuary. You can do what you like with the money. That's your affair."

"That's very generous of you, but I don't want it. The house is a tomb. I'll--"

"The other's my will." Terzo masks his reaction. Grows suddenly still. His eyes lose their coldness...

--"Get along. I always do." Leonardo hands him the papers. "Please... Take them."

He doesn't. "Stop punishing yourself. She chose her own fate. She wanted to die. What's your choice, Terzo?"

"Nothing. I've chosen nothing. Is nothing too much to ask?"

"Yes. It's too easy." An angry silence. "What have I done to hurt you?" Terzo turns away. Won't respond. "Answer me, damn you!"

"You have given me life."

Does he know? No, impossible. He didn't mean to be literal. I've tried meeting him like a father- but I know nothing of that... missing the moment... unable to tell him...

"You can always join her. But until you make that decision--"

"It's all so simple for you, isn't it? You belong here. You belong in your body." Sneers with contempt. "What does it mean to be human?... even a beast is closer to God."

"But the beast in the man stills longs to be known. We are not born human. It is an act of will to be human." He throws the papers on the floor and walks towards the door... Turns... "I have always loved you... but then you know that...don't you." Turns in the heart, but walks through the door.

Terzo struggles with love, for the father he longed for... "Leonardo!" He stops. "I... I do."

"Then why can't you accept it?"

"Because I'm a coward." Leonardo studies his son, sees the flaw in himself. His yellow eyes penetrate him. It's time now to tell him... but the moment will pass like the others... I will leave it to her. She's braver than I am... but she doesn't know, does she?... She would know if she wanted to... but she lives in her dreams... like Snow... like her son... "Come with me, Terzo. I'm going to the house."

Terzo goes passive, relents... as his will dissolves in his dreams.

Passes Guy and the limo and goes his own way…

"I changed my mind," over his shoulder to Leo.

"You'll never be free of it, Terzo, unless you go back." Terzo doesn't respond. The two fend off their fear. Guy knows the outcome. It's happened before…

"Still want to go to the fence, Leonardo?" Leonardo feels broken by it... as he was with 'Lupa'... with Snow... with Lupo... his mother...

"Of course, we don't do business with the heart- do we Guy?"

Guy's crooked smile, "No, Leonardo- unless the heart is a whore."

Dawn: Terzo is drinking a bottle of cheap red wine. He steals a baguette off a truck. Breaks it in two: *"This is my body."* Drinks: *"This is my blood."*[85] He hands the bread and wine to a beggar. Shoves his hands in his pockets, and whistles *The Messiah*. Sings: *"And"* she *"shall live forever and ever."* Then with a careless gait, he approaches his victim. The man is opening a small cafe. Terzo grasps his tie, holds his knife to his balls: *"E equals Mc squared."*[85a]

"The man doesn't hesitate. Hands him his wallet. He continues whistling the Mass, and disappears down an alley. He sits on the bank of the Seine, staring into the water. Looks through the wallet. Removes the money and counts it. "Three thousand francs- not bad." He folds the bills neatly, puts them back in the wallet, and tosses the wallet into the river.

Hands in his pocket, whistling the Mass, as he escapes from the ritual that he repeats every day... the work of a street thief, since the death of his 'mother'- the 'mother' he stole from the god, and believed was his own. Guy cruises by in the limo, looking for trade, passes him on the street, who he thinks is a trick. Terzo avoids him. Walks faster to lose him, but Guy catches sight of him; follows him slowly; tracks him down like a beast, as it tries to escape. Listens to the news as he follows him, and smiles to himself...

Today, we will focus on the tragic death of Leopold Archipova, the best-selling Russian author. His body was discovered early this morning in a hotel frequented by prostitutes. It was a prostitute that found him. Archipova had hung himself. I interviewed his editor, who spoke to him three days ago and had what he referred to as a 'disturbing conversation with him.' He said that Archipova was convinced that his female protagonist, a Fata Morgana figure, had taken charge of his soul, and had promised him immortality. Well, it seems her promise has come true, but Archipova did not live to taste of it. In keeping with the strange circumstances that surround his death, the reviews of *Lady of the Beasts* came out today, and was hailed as a masterpiece, both here and abroad.

Nola Troppa's review seems to have stirred up some controversy, not only in the literary world, but amongst several of our leading psychiatrists and physicists, some of whom are with us this evening to analyze the work and the review. But first, I will quote Nola Troppa: "The novel explores the shadow side of mind and the writer's seduction by archetypal forces, as he enters the fourth dimension- the inner space/time continuum- and loses himself in the great unconscious: 'the spirit of gravity', like a magnet, pulling him down to the Mother, to the source of all life, indistinguishable from death. Whether she is the soul of the creative process, or whether she *drove* him to death, is a mystery that only the *Shadow Woman* knows.

"Critics agree that *Lady of the Beasts* seems unrelated to the rest of Archipova's work, and, if it were not for the *anima* woman, who shifts her shape with the moon, it would not be credible that it was written by the same unfortunate man."

Guy follows him at a distance, always tracking his prey: "Hey, Terzo! Get in," as he pulls up beside him. Terzo looks at him wary, but goes to the window. "Still working? Why don't we go for a ride?"

"If that's what I wanted, it wouldn't be you, Guy. Save it for Leonardo. He's a sucker for a pretty face."

"He just likes the threat."

Terzo's relieved.

"You know, Guy, you're much more appealing as a devoted servant.

Guy's dubious smile. "Watch it, kid. Watch it." Plays with his gun. Terzo observes it. The crooked smile turns malicious.

"I'm used to psychos- I grew up with one. Haven't you wondered why he keeps you around? You're not that good. You're just a stand-in for Lupo- that's all."

Guy makes a pact with his darkness. This Terzo is hot, but he has just sealed his own tomb.

Terzo, turning away, moves down the street: 'The hero continues'[87], repeating the words of his poet, as he reflects on his dream... and the death of his 'mother'...

CHAPTER 11
SNOW HOUSE

Nola, unconscious, as if under a spell, is asleep on Snow's bed, still disguised as her mother: the red wig, the pale skin, the black suit she was buried in. She dreams...

'Lupa' is holding the corpse of her son (in the Pietá image Esperanza was in), and is watching his soul depart from his flesh. It has taken the form of a body of light, a translucent spirit that will endure after death. 'Death is not the end. You will return when she's ready', 'Lupa' said to his spirit, as it fled from the earth.

Fatima, sure that her eyes are betraying her, looks through the doorway in disbelief, as if seeing the ghost of her former mistress, Snow. Nola, as 'Lupa', is splitting again, gradually coming to consciousness in the bed of her mother. Feels the same chilling melancholy that she felt in her dream... Is she 'Lupa' or Nola... or is she her mother? Her arms feel empty that held him, as she tries to remember... the ascent of his soul... Her eyes look upward to find it... Above the boat-shaped bed is a child's drawing: a corpse in shadow, in the sign of the cross; a dove hovers above it, surrounded by sword-like rays, contained in a vessel, so that the soul can't escape. At the bottom is written in back-slanting letters, the ink blurred with tears...

MOTHER'S SOUL LEAVES HER BODY

A nail plunged through the paper, like a stake

through the heart, a rusty key hanging on it, to 'open the door'. Her eyes shift to the swan cradle, by the bed Snow was slain in, its gilded wings spread for flight- sees her son as a boy.

Feels Fatima's eyes and is thrust into time... her two warring selves still trying to merge. Fatima stands on the threshold, bridging two worlds. "She comes home... I have waited for you... thirteen years I have waited for you," talks to her mistress, the earthbound spirit of Snow, captive to fate, and to the yoke of the flesh. Now Fatima knows what she sees..."No... you are 'Lupa', his mother... the mother he needs," counting her beads, as she prays to her god. "Thirty-three years, I am counting... the year of the death of your god... 'Lupa'... his real mother... the mother who gave him his life"... Sees her son in the cradle, as he stares at Snow's corpse- the knife in her heart... that is marking his dreams: sees Leo beside her, asleep with his eyes open: the trembling nine year old boy, her ruby clenched in his fist. 'Lupa' sees him through Fatima, and the transference with Snow...

Nola closes her eyes, the feelings breaking her will.

'Lupa', they call me'.

"Madame must be hungry."

"Hungry to know. ''She' would eat from the tree of good and evil and converse with the snake... who it seems is my father... and 'she' admits she is tempted. But is 'she' dead or reborn? And you? Who are you?"

"I am Fatima."

"Fate... funny how names become real. How did I get here? Am I in a whorehouse or church?"

"This is Snow House. She has invited you. She must want you to eat." Bowing her head, she exits the chamber. Nola as 'Lupa' takes the key to the drawing…

She goes to the armoire, to find the piece that is missing. The key doesn't fit, but the door is not locked; the clothes have revealed a significant clue to Snow's character; her wardrobe is divided precisely in half. The left side is black the other side white: eyes are fixed on the hunting habit that is stained with Snow's blood: a hunt that can kill for the taming of fate, linking 'the warring of opposites', the past with the present: slips on Snow's habit: her spirit guides her to the stable. Pale Lady, Snow's mare, is strangely excited, hooves stomping the earth, sniffing the habit, the old blood of its mistress, who conceived in the pit.

"You know, don't you, White One. Show me. I am ready." And with no saddle or bridle, she climbs on her back, grasps the mane with her will, for the key to her birth. The spirited mare rides through the forest and carries her secret to the foot of Snow's grave. The mournful neigh of the creature and the voice of the wind, as it blows the thorns from the stone and reveals the blood of her son. Written in the same back-slanting hand…

1896-1950 'THE WOLF TROTS TO AND FRO THE WORLD LIES DEEP IN SNOW'

Goes down in the mind, to the pit she was made in, where Snow was the game, and the hunter was Lupo… (his spirit in Leo, who fathered her son… Does not want to see it… pushes it down to the darkness, drives it down to the shadow, to the pit in the heart). Still, she sees the betrayal through the eyes of her thief... her thief of a saint... sees the shadow of love: the red hair stained with blood, the dead fox at her feet as she weeps for its life... as the thorns pierce her flesh: Lupo is taking her... She is wearing the habit: her two selves confounded... that are needing to split: is she Nola or 'Lupa'... or is she her mother?

I will not remember... I will try to forget... Hangs the red wig on the thorn tree... the voice of the wind... But she vows to destroy him, to avenge the betrayal... pushing it down in the grave... with the will to forget.

She gallops to Snow House, hangs the key on the nail- it pierces the heart of the shadow... the knife... in her mother's... Goes to the swan cradle, lifting the pillow...beneath it, a big blood-red ruby that glows like the chalice: the blood of the god of the Grail, when she prayed in 'The Mother'. There was, also, a book with a hand painted cover: a boy on a white horse, holding a lance: the title, *Parsifal, the Boy Knight*, in a back-slanted hand... She remembers the story: he must ask the right question. She opens the book to the frontispiece and sees an inscription from Snow:

> Good Friday, 1950
> For my son on his ninth birthday.
> Ask the question. Mother

The question below in the same backward hand...
What is the meaning of the sacrifice?

It was stained with his blood...
But why would a young boy of nine ask such a question?

She lies on Snow's bed, reading the tale of the hero, who redeems the she-devil, Kundry, who tempted the knights, and whose second self was held captive under the spell of the shadow. She drifts into sleep with the book in her hands, and dreams of her son... the boy she abandoned at birth...

Terzo is nine. He is trembling in her arms. She lies on the murder bed, and tries healing her curse.

Leonardo, in the doorway, is watching her sleep. He is holding white calla lilies and red wine from the cellar, two rose crystal glasses, and a rare black diamond necklace. The past entered the present, as the dream became real... He throws her the necklace. She catches the stone: a black triangular stone, shaped like the head of an arrow: the apex points downward and poses the problem: the secret of extracting 'the light in the darkness': the black stone is connected to three strands of seed pearls: in her dream, she is searching the seed of the *Self.*

She returns to herself, and sees her thief on the threshold: "Trapped like an animal, like a wounded beast."

He throws her the lilies. "Happy birthday. How old are you?"

"My demons and angels are conspiring against me," counting under her breath on her long thin fingers, checking Fatima's calculations..." Thirty-three- thirty-three years of torture... the year of the god... who was hung on the Mother."

"Do you still drink blood for breakfast?" pouring the wine: *Sangue di Guida-* the blood of the be-

betrayer...Hmm, 1941- the year you tried to rape me."

"Get out."

"But this is my house."

She glares at him like an animal- the look that he needs: the same look as his brother... but from 'Lupa'... his daughter. Comes to terms with his shadow, in the guise of his twin- the beast in the man, who destroyed what he loved. Hands her a glass, and presses his own to his heart. "To the mystery of the human heart. Please don't feel obliged to be polite. You are free to go."

She drinks up the pain, trapped in her thoughts. "Am I?... not yet. Not till I put all the pieces together."

"And then?"

"I never want to see you again."

"Then I better be quick about it. Knowing you, it won't take long." He throws a handful of pearls on the bed. Keeps throwing the stones, till the bed is covered with them...

"I insist on paying for it, like everyone else-" taking his clothes off.

"How do you want it? Like this?" He takes her like a beast.

"Just pretend you're a woman- instead of a wolf."

"I'll tell you a secret: I don't know how. But I do know the secret of the theater, which began as an offering to the gods. It is unfortunate when women are the offering, and pretend to be the muse- the muse of men's sins, and, in the spirit of the drama, end up taking the hit. That, my dear Leonardo, is how the species originated."

"Which would be extinct, according to your sinful philosophy: if women controlled men as you do by making them sinners in their drama, and who must be bled at their altar, until they are satiated."

"But that is precisely what is happening. Can we survive love, Leonardo?"

He clasps the black diamond choker on her swan-like neck; and his will is submerged in the delirium of the senses, while she plays the muse, so he will return to the source- knowing she would learn her own history, by reading his memories of the past.

It was 1929, the year 'Lupa' was born. The brothers, in Snow House, are cracking Snow's safe. They are a beautiful pair of 'warring opposites'. It is the high point of their career. It is full of precious jewels. In the four corners of the room, as if guarding their mistress, are four looming angels with wings outspread. The walls are lined with religious art, but furnished with priceless antiques of a decadent splendor. The room mirrors the struggle possessing its mistress- the ascetic and libertine at war in her breast. The safe is concealed in a great carved wooden chest.

Snow is the same age as 'Lupa'- thirty-three years of torture. The unidentical twins have turned twenty-one- the same age as Terzo, but they pass for late twenties, seasoned by thieving as the sons of a whore. Lupo, dark and primitive, with an easy roguish manner, but with grey wolf eyes that are cold and ruthless; Leo gentle, more tranquil, his yellow eyes catch the light. Lupo begins extracting the treasure, finds the blood-red ruby with its hidden fire; Leo the black diamond necklace, with its triangular stone- mined from a pit in Perdue, the place of Snow's birth. The stones mark the beginning of their triangular drama that would lead to her death, and 'Lupa's obsession to kill. Both lost in the stones, forget where they are (it reminds us of 'Lupa', when she first learned the 'art'). Leo is restraining his mystical impulse...

"Let's go, Lupo. We're late." Covers him with the gun.

Lupo is gazing into the ruby. "It's got the fire of the blood in it."

"It's a cold fire- like yours."

"It depends on the angle. From mine it's too hot."

"I only wish yours was worth as much."

"Yeah, so do I. Take care of it for me. I'm claiming its fire. And hold the gun, like you mean it."

"The black diamond is mine...Fascinating isn't it... It's the depth of the stone- its darkness in contrast to the whiteness of the pearls, that makes it irresistible...that makes it what it is."

Lupo's wolfish smile. "Sure, Leo, sure, if you want to get precious about it," tempers the passion of Leo's, to temper his own. Snow enters, half sleeping, in a white dressing gown. Has the wildness of 'Lupa', but more otherworldly. Cool green eyes look them over, and a lower trinity is formed. Lupo, still at the safe, doesn't bother to look, mesmerized by the jewels. Throws them into the bag.

"We got company. Take care of it, while I finish packing." Leo moves in on her, his gun pointed at her. There is a slight smile on her face, almost amused. He moves like a wildcat, with slow de-liberate steps, stalking her in a circle, like a lion its prey. He's never seen such a creature. She likes being stalked by him. He sticks the gun in her guts, to remove the smile from her lips. She seems to be mocking him. He tries to seem dangerous. The smile still persists, as she falls for this fabulous animal.

"You're not afraid?"

She gently pushes it away, as if rejecting a lover. "Of that? I've had the finger of God pointed at me."

His yellow eyes are ignited. He wants her. "Who are you?"

"Snow," extending her hand, "and that's my ruby." He kisses it, giving it back like a gift.

"And my necklace?"

"Please," hands her the gun, "hold this for a moment, would you?" clasping the necklace round her pale white neck.

"Thank you," jamming the gun in his balls.

"It's nothing. It belongs there." His ironic smile. Somehow, he's won her, as he strokes her pale cheek. "Snow..." he muses... "so cold and white." Lupo's cold rage, as Leo takes her on the floor, as the wolf in the man jealously watches.

Night turns into day, but Leonardo won't leave her. They are playing roulette in the gaming room. All the jewels are on the table. "*Rien ne va plus*." Lupo calls, already hating her, spinning the wheel till it stops. He moves the horde towards him.

"So be it", she says, as if accepting her fate, but removes the red ruby from the moving horde. Leonardo's dry smile, in contrast to Lupo's malicious one.

"I don't like playing the victim" she says, with a tempting smile.

"You will," says Lupo, under his breath, spinning the wheel, with the same cold rage.

Snow and Lupo are sitting above an abyss, on the edge of a cliff, the house in the distance, enveloped in shadow, in an illusory light. The wind blows in the

97

dusk as the darkness encroaches.

"How do you do it?" he asks. "All those things. How do you live?

"Men- I do men. And you? Besides being an amateur thief, I mean

"Right now, I'm doing you."

"But you can't live like that- so haphazardly. One must perfect one's art."

"I intend to."

"Is it me that you hate, or just women in general?"

"Both."

"So, we have two things in common. We both hate our mothers, and we're both in love with your brother."

"Be careful."

"I'm afraid I can't. I don't know how. But I'm bored with talking. Let's play." She takes a bottle of vodka and two scarves from her bag. "It's a Russian game. Half my blood is Russian."

"And the other half?"

"Shadow- the dark side of French, as dark as this stone," as she rubs the black jewel; his eyes black with hate, fixed on her beautiful neck.

She takes a swig from the bottle. He takes a bigger one. Snow goes even further. He defies her. Snow dares him on. Lupo goes even further. She drains the last drop. Hurls it into the abyss. They watch it twist in the wind, in the jagged gorge far below; watch it dash on the rocks, and imagine the end. Snow blindfolds them both, and they balance on the edge. Their bodies sway in the wind...

"Do you have a limit?" he asked.

"It exists to be broken," daring him on, as she forges the break...

They feel the quickening rush of a compulsive gambling with the odds, trying to resist the mournful desire for death; but the resistance is weakening, the desire is mounting.

Leo lies on her lap by the pit of thorns Snow is buried in, as she reads from *The Most Holy Grail*, against the trunk of the thorn tree. Leo looks up at her, trying to fathom her mystery...

"I'm not enough for you, am I?" Snow is silent. "Nothing is, is it?"

"Yes, the nameless terror of being suspended between life and death, balancing on the threshold, not knowing which way it will go."

He shifts his eyes. Looks away. "What is it?" she asked.

"I just realized my mistake. I should never have let you trust me. Too safe for you, isn't it? Too predictable."

"I wouldn't go that far."

Her dangerous smile as they look in their eyes... really look, till it hurts... she pretends that it doesn't...

What happened to you, Snow, that you have to drain every drop of blood from every moment?" She lowers her lids, wanting to hide in her darkness. "It's not death you're in love with- it's the fear of it." He studies her in the silence "Why? Why are you in love with it?"

"I'm addicted to danger, and the thrill of escaping it. The escape lasts only a moment, and then there's the--"

"Crash? How did you learn this game?"

"I was made for it," veiling her eyes, so he can't penetrate her. Returns to the book. He covers the page with his hand.

"Where? Where were you born?"

"A town called '*Lost*'... a mining town in the Pyrenees." Eyes go to the book. He covers the page...

"Tell me about it." Again, she retreats into silence, but he won't let her go, holding her gaze, slipping the veil from her eyes.

"There was a black cloud above it that blocked out the sun. The wind never stopped blowing: it was covered with coal dust. There was a legend in '*Lost*' that the wind was the voice of 'God's shadow', the Mother who ruled from the top of the mountain- that she swallowed the sun, and was the source of all life. The miners called her *the shadow of the Trinity*, and they would appease her with offerings, to return from the pit. They weren't allowed in the sanctuary, but left alms of coal at the door, and prayed it would heat up her soul, so she would allow them to live. The few black diamonds they mined were the sacrifice to her shadow. The one that you stole was mined by my father. He died for that stone... buried alive in the mine... and left me alone... with my crazy mother."

"So you blamed him for dying- while you gamble with death."

"He was weak... like myself... and lived in fear of her madness. He would sleep in the mine... hiding from her hatred and violence... till he died in the pit... I still can't forgive him for dying."

"Can you forgive me for loving you?" stripping her soul. He is getting inside her. She tries to forgive him... but she knows that she can't... and takes refuge in shadow.

"So, you tried running away, but you were drawn to your fear... drawn to her shadow... the Mother of madness and death."

"Even the terror was a kind of relief, for she made my own personal mother seem small, insignificant. This was the Mother that lived in the dark of the mind, and all mothers were patterned after her. She was the original tyrant, the great devouring bitch. Her face was masked by her shadow, like God's executioner. Her Son nailed to her shadow, his Mother the cross. It was she who demanded this cruel sacrifice, a sacrifice that never ended. She took it back, her strange gift."

Leonardo looks up at her. She seems high above him... in love with her madness and her terror of love: as if the Mother of God were a magical formula that was controlling her destiny and could be cracked like a safe.

"And you wanted to know why?"

She nods. "I found a medieval inscription carved in her back. It said, *For what in the end is the Son without a shadow*? The words were simple, but I was mystified by them. I asked her the meaning."

"What did she say?"

"She said, 'Until the light has descended into the darkness, it does not know itself'."

"You can get lost down there."

"That's what she said... She said 'the gift must be given as if it were being destroyed... to give up your secret claim to it'[100]... but the real sacrifice is in the journey back- not till then is it ours to give."

"*Are* you able to give?"

"Not yet. I can only play at it. You see, I don't know my own shadow.

"Does she?"

"She knows it through us, her creature... But I've gotten carried away again- where were we?" She hands him the book. He reads…

"And the knight saw two women come forth from the chapel. One was dark and the other pale. The dark one held in her hands the most Holy Grail, and the pale one the lance and the point of it bled."[101]

He looks up from the book, and conjures the words:

'The knight gazed in the vessel and saw their reflection, and between the two women was a young boy in armour. The knight asked his soul that was twinned and was torn into two: what does it mean to be two- to be no longer one? And she told him the mystery of the son and his shadow.'

She smiled at his conjuring: Not as simple as he seems. Do I know him? she thought. Do I know him at all?
Mystified where it came from, he continues to read from the transference, looking into her soul, till she can't look away...
He hands her the book, and she reads of her fate…

"Then three drops of blood from the lance fell into the cup, and the pale one spoke to the young boy's reflection: 'My son, I shall not live much longer, wherefore I am sorrowful of heart, but still more sorrowful would I be if it were not for your coming. This castle is yours, and the land that surrounds it... only bury my body here when I die.'"[*]

She looks up in his eyes with a sense of foreboding,

and a shadow passes across her face.

"It's only a myth," Leo said.

"If the myth isn't real then what is?"

The three are on horseback, playing the hunting game. Snow House, in the distance, with its illusory beauty, wrapped in the mist, as if it were part of her myth. Snow is stroking her fox. She is wearing the habit. "I prefer you to both of them," whispering in its ear. She kisses its eyes, tapping its hind. "Let her go," as if freeing herself, breaking the spell of her love.

"Run little one, run." They give it time to escape. "Remember, don't scare her," she said to the twins. "She's a fragile creature- for a beast. I've played this game often, and she knows it so well: this testing to tame the animal passions that drive us, to know if the will can be stronger than death. But how can she know what it is to be at war with the instincts?"

"What are we playing for, and are we testing her or ourselves?" asked Leonardo, watching her play with her shadow.

"Why don't we play for the ruby?" asked Lupo

"Let's play for love," she said. "The ruby can't be replaced," sealing her fate. She blows the horn and takes off, setting the rhythm, as they gallop at a relentless pace; follow the fox through the forest, as Snow cracks the whip, blurring the boundary between life and death.

Pale Lady, in front, loses the brothers. Pricks up her ears and changes direction.

Lupo is steering the fox into the thorn pit, butting against it, till it falls to its end. Its cries from below as it's caught in a trap- hidden below the thorny branches, the thorns rending its flesh, as it tries to escape. Snow climbs down to free it. Kneels weeping beside it. Lupo jumps down behind her, and stares at the whimpering creature. He takes out his gun. Snow grabs his arm...

"No, Lupo, no!"

"It's better this way."

He shoots it. Its cries suddenly cease. Snow weeps like a child, presses her cheek to its fur, her hair the same redness, like one single creature, its blood in her hair, its blood on her lips. "Come back, little one, come back!"

She beats him with a branch of thorns. He throws her down on the thorns. She's trapped like the fox. The thorns catch her hair. He licks the blood from her lips. She is weeping and moaning, the dead fox at her feet: the spirit that guides her, both hunter and hunted.

"Let me go, Lupo. Let me go!"

"Not till you get what you asked for."

Leonardo is leaning against the trunk of the thorn tree, looking down in the pit and hearing her words: "I don't know my own shadow." And now he knew what she meant- that he did not know his own... and he would know it through her.

Lupo takes her like a beast. "Don't tell him, Lupo.... don't tell him," moaning like an animal, no longer fighting.

"No, it would kill him."

"Swear by your eyes."

"I swear by my eyes. I will not tell my own shadow,"

Leo is seeing his own. He closes his eyes. But the gift was destroyed, and he gave up his claim to it.

"Lupo?"

"Yes?"

"How did the trap get there, Lupo?"

She stares at her hands, stained with the blood of the fox, and somewhere she knows that it is also her own. The nameless terror of being suspended between life and death, and, as she comes to herself, she knows she is done. She has lost the game to the beast and is caught in its net; feels the fear of the love that she tried to renounce.

CHAPTER 12
THE WOLF AND THE LION

Later that night, Leo, alone, in despair, lies naked in bed, still hearing their words: "Don't tell him, Lupo"... "I swear by my eyes"... "It would kill him. Don't tell him... don't tell him... don't tell him"...

The words repeat in his head, repeat and repeat...

Lupo entered his room and lay down behind him, pressing against him, as he did as a child. "You want it as much as I do. Why can't you admit it?" Leo is silent. Stares at the wall. "Are you afraid, Leo?" Silence. "It's as close to ourselves as we'll ever get," stroking his thighs, pressing them to his own, slowly thrusting inside him, the way he imagined he would. "We belong together: no woman can change that."

Leo returns to a day in 1918, in World War I, to their room on the docks (the room 'he' took 'Lupa' in-the room Terzo was born in). Three battleships are in the Bay of Naples. One shoots a bomb near the shack. Their mother's whorehouse is shaking. The twins, nine at the time, are trying to bear it. They are naked in bed, in the exact same position.

Young Lupo is trying to awaken his brother. "Leo, Leo!" Leo's eyes are open and full of fear. "Leo, wake up, Leo! I gotta' talk to--" Leo bounds out of bed, shutting him out. Picks up his clothes from the floor and quickly gets dressed. "Last night, something happened last night, Leo... something- Leo, listen!"

"Leave me alone, Lupo! Leave me alone!" Lupo recoils like a wounded beast.

"C'mon, get dressed. We're late for work."

They run from the house, jump on a tram, and walk

through the alleys to a small simple church. They pick up two jagged rocks, and break open the padlock, dashing the poor box, stealing the chump change. Leo looks up in fear at the face of the Virgin. She seems to be judging him. He is flooded with guilt; mocking him now, her mouth smeared with blood...

"Yesterday, when I heard mama laughing--" Lupo was saying, trying to tell him...But Leo is lost in the image, as if he didn't exist. Lupo watches him in the troubled silence, then in a black rage slams the statue down, smashing her face with the jagged rock. Leo judges him with his eyes and leaves the church. "Why won't you listen to me?... something happened last night". Lupo buries his face in the broken pieces.

The whorehouse is arranged like a clinic or train, with twelve curtained cubicles on either side. Most of the curtains are partly drawn, out of a chronic indifference, and the need to save time. On one side of the corridor, in front of the curtain, six hooks with six uniforms of American soldiers; on the opposite side are six hooks for sailors: a system that simulates a kind of order in the chaos. The cacophany of the groaning and moans are like beasts in a cage. The boy Leonardo walks down the row, glancing at all of them with a feigned mood of indifference- till he comes to the last and lowers his eyes. His mother, Pietá, is straddling a soldier. She continues to hump him as she talks to her son. Her mouth is swollen and bruised. Her eye is black.

"You're late," she says.

"Late?" Leo asks.

"For your American lesson. You forgot, again, didn't you? Where were you?"

"Working."

"And Lupo?" he shrugs. "Well, you have to make it up. That's sailor's got blue balls waiting for you. You wanta' get somewhere in this world, don't you? You won't get nowhere without American, isn't that right, soldier?" The soldier humors her as she continues to hump him, thinking he's getting away with something. "Nowhere, boy. You won't go nowhere." Leo, eyes still lowered, walks away. "And wash your face first, it's dirty." Her proud look at the soldier, "My son, I got two of them, Leo and Lupo. How you say it in English?"

"The wolf and the lion," repeating it to herself, as she casually dismounts.

"Hey, wait a minute, I was just gonna' come."

She gives him the knowing look, "Don't take advantage of my good nature, sailor." Yells for the next.

"Pietá, have some pity," clasping his hands, on bended knee.

"Pieta's pity is expensive." The next soldier, standing there awkwardly, holding his uniform, waits for a hook.

Leo, lying in bed, remembers last night. Hears her moans and her laughter; tries to shut out the sound. Clamps his hands to his ears, buries his face in the pillow. Lupo was crouched in the waiting room, shooting dice with some sailors. It was four in the morning, only three of them left, all waiting their turn to fuck Pietá. All the whores have gone home, and he hears Pieta's mocking laughter, mixed with the anguish of the womanish voice of a soldier.

"It's that queer, again. C'mon, let's get a peek," says

sailor #1.

"What's a queer?" asks Lupo.

"Come, I'll show you.'

"I think I'll pass," says sailor #2.

"Me, too," says sailor #3.

"Well, I ain't stayin' in this dump alone," says #1. The three tip Lupo and leave the house.

Lupo, parting the curtain, peeks in the cubicle. An effeminate boy is trying to fuck Pietá, as she taunts him relentlessly, mocking his manhood. "If there's one thing I hate, it's a soft dick up my cunt. Get outta' here, soldier. I don't have what you want. What you need is a man- a real man with a hard one." She laughs in his face. He punches her in the mouth. Blood spurts from her lips and she spits in his face. Pietá passes out, as the soldier pulls out a knife. Leo watched through the curtain as Lupo lunged at the soldier, gripping his wrist, to wrench the knife from his hand. The soldier scoffs at the boy. Throws him down on the floor. Takes out his dick and starts jacking him off. Pulls Lupo's pants down, and throws him on top of her. Leo, secretly watching, frozen with fear.

"C'mon fuck your mama. Hard enough for you, whore?" Pietá is unconscious. It's like talking to a corpse. "Or do you prefer it this way?" running his thumb on the blade. "C'mon, boy, kiss those filthy red lips." Holds Lupo's head down, his lips pressed on his mother's. He chokes on her blood, and swallows the fear. Her mouth, like the Virgin's, blood smeared on her lips; her face dead as the statue on the altar in the church. The soldier presses the knife to young Lupo's throat. Pulls him up by the hair and begins sucking his cock.

Leo, still watching, unable to move. Wants to protect him, but unable to act. Lupo comes in his mouth, and faces the wall. "Fuck me, soldier, fuck me," like 'Lupa' to Leo. (It was clear now, she realized, still in bed with Leonardo, that she re-enacted the transference with Lupo, his brother, when she tried to seduce him that night on the job; was it the spirit of Lupo that took her through Leo the night she conceived of a son born of incest… who she abandoned and cursed… but it still wasn't conscious)…

The brothers return to 1929, the year 'Lupa' was born, after Lupo took Snow. They remember the day that fate became destiny, as Lupo pulls out of Leo, crouched on his knees, "Fuck me, Leo, fuck me. Why can't you admit it?" Leo enters his brother, his eyes filled with fear. Sees the broken face of the Virgin: sees Snow's face smeared with blood.

Snow, draped in black, in perpetual mourning, has that lost broken look, as if the light had gone out, compulsively snorting cocaine and drinking red wine. Her body emaciated, her sleepless eyes ringed and hollow. The lower trinity seated at a 'last supper table', Snow sitting between them, the two thieves at both ends. There are three bottles of wine on the table-*Sangue di Guida*, and a round loaf of bread. Terzo's knife that killed Snow is lying beside it. Lupo raises his glass, "To the blood of the betrayer." Snow and Leonardo lower their eyes; both are immersed in their own dark thoughts.

"What do you think, Snow? Will it survive your motherly instincts?" There is an unholy silence in the room.

Snow, unable to bear it, takes a blow of cocaine.

"You've had enough. You haven't slept in a week," said Leo, drained of spirit.

"Still trying to protect her, Leonardo?"

Her eyes dead, expressionless, see her reflection in the mirror, hazy, distorted, unrecognizable. Leonardo looks into her, and she lowers her eyes. Fatima enters with eyes that miss nothing. She carries a platter of two fishes that lie head to tail (like 'Lupa's' vision), the symbol of Christ and the betrayer. In a barbarian gesture, with the knife that kills Snow- the cross on its hilt, she cuts off the heads and the tails. The brothers stare at the fishes, as Snow takes a drink and a blow. Fatima serves her...

"I told you, Fatima, I'm not eating."

"Given it up for Lent?" asked Lupo.

"Lent is already over. It is already Easter, and madame hasn't eaten since Christmas," said Fatima. Bread and wine for four months. Poor innocent child, how will it live?"

"In our religion, Fatima, if you eat of the flesh and drink of the blood, it will live forever- if it doesn't starve to death. Of course, madame is extremely religious, so she might not have thought of that."

Fatima is putting a severed head on his plate, and with a dignified bow, she exits backwards, crossing herself, looking him dead in the eye.

"What about you, Leonardo, are you still a believer?" his grey wolf eyes, drunk on the blood. "What no game? Why don't we place our bets? I say it's a she-wolf and will outlive us all. Let's call it 'Lupa, the wolf girl'- after myself." The silence is chilling. "Not playing, Leo?" his insolent eyes mocking his love.

"But the wheel is spinning, and you're playing alone."

"I'm used to it. It's you I'm worried about. She really fooled you, didn't she? All that romance and mystery."

Snow rises from the table, staggers and tries to escape. Lupo rises in hatred with an icy composure, performing the ritual, like an unpleasant task. Grips her arm in his fist, forcing her into her seat. She wrests her arm from his grip and plunges the knife in the bread, her eyes fixed on the symbol of the body of Christ... Feels the knife pierce her heart: covers her face with her veil: Lupo, ripping it off, exposes the guilt. Feels the victory of defeat, as he observes the effect. Feels Leo's despair and that he killed what he loved, knows he will lose him, and there is nothing but death.

Leo slowly rises. "Love has burned itself out."

Snow sees his strength and for the first time she knows him- as if the loss were the means to grasp what she loves. "Don't leave me, Leonardo... don't leave me... I need you."

He turns. "It's too late. You'll have to live with your take."

Lupo buries his face in the broken pieces. "What's the matter, Snow, afraid to be alone with me?"

CHAPTER 13
MAGNETIC MIRROR

'Lupa' continues to rape his unconscious, using the senses to spark it, to discover the past. Linking the fragments of memory, while Leo is fucking her; they assume every possible position during the following dialogue...

"So Lupo won," she says.

"Is that the way you see it?"

"How else?" She moans.

"Avoiding her masochism?"

"Yes, why deny it: and yours, Leonardo? What about yours? He is your devil, like I am, but he wasn't as easy to resist. How I hated you for it, even before I knew why."

"What did you know?" he is careful.

"That even God's saints are tempted."

Is she spinning again? Has she repressed only that?... that I fathered her son... and destroyed both their lives? "And now that you know?" testing her wiles.

"I forgive you for wanting you."

He didn't... for wanting me, secretly relieved. She doesn't know what she knows... But it won't take her long.

She comes like a beast. He takes her again. "How could he? You were fused like a *monstruum*. Could you forgive what he is... and yourself for forgetting?"

She does not want to know. She can see all but the heart. She has locked it away from the light in the Mother of Shadow; constructed a world with her will that she could destroy when she wished.

"You mirrored his weakness. He cast it back, you

received it... Imagine...I have a father. I was not born by divine intervention, like the vultures."

"Disappointed?"

She nods. "I liked it better that way... Maybe it is as simple as that... why I was born hating men. I didn't know, till I wanted you. It was a real revelation- that desire and hatred are closer than twins. How could I know I wasn't the reason that you were able to resist me, and were in love with your brother? And now I know why- you are in love with your shadow that you tried to deny." She mounts him and moans. He comes like a beast.

"You know too much- but not enough to be free of it. You are imprisoned in the flesh, like the rest of us mortals. While you were reading the runes, you could have broken the chain. You could have been happy hating me, without turning men into beasts." He fucks her from behind.

"How else could I learn it- this art of the trickster, but by using his blind spot to survive the betrayals? Besides, it would have been a mistake to concentrate all my hatred in any *one* man. After all, you were just serving your purpose by making me conscious of it, and teaching me to express it- more fully than I wished."

"I wouldn't want to waste your time," licking her like a beast.

"Why not? You paid for it. But let's look at my fate that has made you my uncle... and my son your great nephew, the mythic son of my mother, your unattainable lover- who you still look for in me. What am I but the daughter of your wolfish shadow... your brother... your lover... who would kill to possess you."

She moans.

He studies her a moment, in awe but amused. "If I was an archbishop in the Middle Ages, I'd have you burnt at the stake."

"I can still feel the flames." She comes. "To think I really believed I was evil, when I was only possessed by the shadow of my father- the killer *I* that he gave me that is unconscious of itself." He penetrates her. "So, it follows that you are the good twin. How boring. I'm fucking your goodness."

"You have no humility. I'm fucking *you*."

"You certainly are. You've run out of pearls."

"I'm fucking more of you than you know: your darkness, the core of you, that you are able to penetrate more fully when I am inside you."

"So then, it's not me that you're fucking- it's my unconscious. It's been so long since I've been fucked that I'd forgotten what fucking is about. Did you ever name him- your son?"

He stops. Looks into her. Do you mean yours?"

"But it was you who created him- through your resistance... His name?"

"You mean you don't know?"

"I must have blocked it out."

He looks deeper inside her. Her two selves are coming together. She'll be more terrifying, he muses. "Terzo", he says.

"Terzo... the third... I like it. Not one or the other."

His ironic smile. "Tell me, these visions, what are they like? What form do they take? Can you see our faces, hear our voices? How real are they?"

"As real as you fucking me in this bed- the same bed you fucked my mother in. They're like shadows passing before a mirror, which from time to time are illumined."

"Tell me more about what we are to you, and how we are serving your purpose.

"You are the substance of the magnetic moment that reflects the unconscious through the magnetic mirror of the psyche, and 'the dependence of the state of a body on its magnetic history'."

"You can't get away with it, you know- not suffering your story. You're afraid of love, aren't you?... just like she was... afraid of weakening your magnetic shield, of living the tragedy you have written, in which you are playing all the parts."

"And what part would you play- if I let you, that is?"

"I *am* playing it, but in spite of you. It's the one you forgot to write- the one you had nothing to do with: the part of making you suffer your false sacrifice- of making you *feel* what you did." She tries to confront it. She knows that it's true. "While you're trying to come to terms with your shadow projections, and for making us suffer what you don't dare to feel," daring to say what he is doing himself... or how would he know? he is asking himself.

"Where did you take him- to 'The Mother'?'"

"To the source- where you were born."

"And Snow suffered it for me... and got caught in my story."

"And you in hers. Someday, you will know what it is to lose what you love: that without it, nothing is real- nothing matters. Someday, something will get to you, and it's going to be terrible- till you learn how to suffer your drama."

"I never doubted it. So, Terzo grew up thinking that Snow was his mother."

"And that--?"

"Lupo was his father."

Again, he was relieved- the deeper truth still concealed (he wants to believe it... still can't believe it).

--Wanting it to be you," she continues. I wouldn't be surprised if it was, and you took me in my sleep."

Inside he was trembling, while shutting the door of the tomb... "One more shadow passing before a mirror?" he said, pretending he could bear it... changing the thought... "When I returned to Naples, you were gone. Where did you go, by the way?"

"I turned a suicidal trick and continued my journey to the underworld... I didn't *want* to go to hell."

"What *did* you want?"

"To hurt you... for not wanting me... Strange... I never thought of it that way."

"You didn't have time."

"Did *you*, with your double obsession- while you--"

--"Searched for you in every alley, in every whorehouse in the world?"

"And when you couldn't find me, you went back to her?"

"Now you're jealous? Would you have preferred to be replaced by a stranger?"

"*One* stranger could never replace you. But please, go on with your magnetic memories. I'll just fill in the gaps."

His smile saddens. "Twenty-one years had gone by, and I went back to Snow House... It was a tomb... They were gone... Only Fatima was here. Like a nomad in the desert, she was waiting for death. Not even a beast could survive it. It was like a dead planet that had lost its magnetic field."

He stops telling the story and gets lost in her body, as she tries to unbind the chains from the ghost of the past... "Tell me, it's not the same when I'm doing it myself."

1950. He walks down an alley in Paris in the driving rain. "I believed in nothing, in no one... Time turned to stone. The gun in my pocket got heavier and colder, and I went to The Door, where the boys hung out." He enters the gambling room, filled with schemers and thieves. His eyes meet Lupo's- he looks away. "Our eyes cut through the crowd, but he couldn't stop playing: shooting craps, copping dope, and making life and death deals. He rolled a double three, and the dealer took his chips. Cons some smack from Slime, and tries to forget".

"Pay up, Lupo."

"Tomorrow, Slime." Smiles that crazy smile that I was a sucker for."

"It's not that I don't trust you, Lupo. It's myself I don't trust."

Leo approaches him, Lupo averting his glance."I missed you, Leo."

"Strung out, again?"

"It's just a chippy." Leo judges him with his eyes. "Still can't forgive me, can you? Always judging me."

"It takes time."

"It's been twenty-one years."

"Ask me in forty. Did you ever love her?"

"You must be joking. You may be surprised. It's not

that she's aged- she hasn't. It's just that there isn't much left of her. She's more like a ghost than a living thing. But you can see for yourself."

They walk in the insolent silence through the slums of Paris, as 'Lupa' continues the story in the dark of the self; sees Lupo in shadow, as he avoids Leo's eyes, make a sweeping gesture at an abandoned building; only a flickering light in an upper storey, the exterior crumbling, like an ancient ruin. Their fear mounts with each step on the crooked stones to the top, both in fear of the outcome, the split in their being; bear the alien feelings, knowing the end. 'Lupa' sees Snow in shadow; she's in her room with young Terzo. The stub of a candle is burning, her image gradually illumined: has that lost jaded look, her eyes red with weeping; still mourning for love in a gaunt fragile body; the rotting wall behind her, like a faded fresco, won't let her forget what is lost to the past. The boy lies in her arms as she reads *Parsifal* to him, while they listen to the footsteps and his eyes fill with fear. He escapes to the tale and is part of the myth- the trick that she taught him to protect him from Lupo. She reads…

"And Kundry anointed his feet with her bitter tears"-[118] The footsteps cease. The sound of the key in the lock. "Don't stop, mother, don't stop."

--*"Drying them with her tangled hair"** The footsteps get nearer. Their eyes dart to the doorway, resting on Leo, like some mythical hero that's come alive from the tale. As it was for young 'Lupa', so it was for her son, for whom Leonardo was playing the role of redeemer. Snow is reading by heart, weaving him into the myth... *"And the pure fool redeemed her, with one simple word, 'Believe'…sprinkling the Water* *of Life on the she-devil's head."*

Leonardo, reaching out of the past, tries touching the boy, but he cringes with fear. Expects to be struck, shielding his face with his arms. Leo's eyes burn with sadness and fasten on Snow. She breaks from the room, unable to bear it. Lupo grabs her arm in the hallway as she is trying to leave, takes off her coat, like a gentleman would. "I thought you liked surprises. What of your love for the game?" She takes the gun from his belt, and kneels at his feet. Hands him the gun, and begs him for death. "*Please*," she is begging..."*Please*," as if praying ('Lupa's' words to Archipova, when her mother's spirit came through her). Lupo's eyes fill with hate, "No, not yet. You're going to live for a while. That's part of your punishment. We will wait. You're too willing."

Leonardo sits on the bed of the trembling boy and continues reading the story to his broken son. They can hear Snow weeping, and the crack of the whip... He reads...

"And he received her into the holy realm, who had tempted him and cursed his path."[119] Lupo drags her to Leo by the roots of her hair, shoving her body onto the bed; as in the legend of *Parsifal*, she weeps at his feet. Looks up at Terzo, as if seeking forgiveness, but wants to imagine the boy could protect her. Terzo cringes in terror, unable to be what she wants.

Leo's eyes pierce his brother's: low and controlled: "Let's talk," burning inside, wanting his blood. Drags Lupo out and boxes his ears. "And now for the real test: can evil thrive on itself alone?" slamming his brother into unconsciousness.

Guarding 'Kundry' from 'Klingsor', the evil

magician, the boy holds Snow protectively, his eyes on the door. Leonardo enters, like the hero of his vision; wishes *he* were his father... Why can't it be him?

"We're leaving," said Leo, throwing their things in a suitcase... hurling it through the window... controlling his rage. "And Snow, that Mother of Sorrows mantle of mourning, it doesn't suit you. Wear something white, like you used to."

Terzo will not take his eyes off the man. Who was he, this stranger: the mythic father he imagined? Who else could he be?... It can't be Lupo... Don't let it be Lupo!

"There's nowhere to go," said Snow.

"We're going to Snow House."

"It's gone. I lost it."

"I know. I bought it."

She bows her head. "I'm afraid I have nothing white. I've been in black since you left me."

"No, *you* left *me*, but enough of repenting for love."

He opens a chest and pulls out the white wedding gown: the one that she wore in 'The Mother', in her marriage to Christ. "No, not that one. I took my vows in that one."

"It's time to take a few more." He takes Terzo's hand, as he once did young 'Lupa's', when, in her magical world, he 'set her free from 'God's prison'. "C'mon Terzo, all you need is some love and adventure."

Leonardo and 'Lupa' are still watching the past...

"And so, you tried to redeem her, still playing the saint; tried to father the boy, born of a trick - like your own."

"Tell me, Magdalena, why do you bother selling

your flesh, when you've been given these amazing powers: when you could just witch their money away? Why--?"

She moans like an animal, for he knows how to touch her... "Besides revenge, I mean."

"I'm a compulsive gambler. 'It's in our blood'- remember?" repeating his words from long ago. "And if I'm going to play, I want to take my chances."

He takes her. "You don't really think they're amazing, do you?"

"Yes."

"Why amazing? Everything that's ever been or will be lives in the darkness of the unconscious, and appears in the glimpses of light in our visions and dreams. If we trace the image to the source, to the core of the complex, and translate its magnetic resonance from the image to the word--"

"It never stops with you, does it? It's relentless, isn't it?"

"So is nature. But your question is interesting. Why do I bother selling my flesh, when I've been given 'these amazing powers'? You may as well ask me why I bother to live. Why do I bother fucking you, when I could fuck your curious mind and learn my magnetic past? Why dally with your mortal flesh to extract the poison of memory that can free the mind from the body?"

Yes, he is thinking, her two selves are coming together. She is more dangerous now, a warning to guard his unconscious. "That was my next question," he is saying aloud.

"It is also mine. But let's get reductive- let's say I'm fucking you for the art of it."

"The art of seduction?"

"The art of the impossible."

His eyes penetrate her. Her own lose their focus... She drifts into a trance, and responds from the unconscious... "Why do I live?... for 'the unknown third'[111]--" He smiles to himself. It worked: he penetrated her psyche, as she penetrated his. Yes, he was learning from her, but it was a dangerous game. -- "That rises up from the god," she continues... "from the death of 'the warring opposites'."

His face darkens. He looks at her strangely... Both have a dark premonition, not knowing who thought it... while 'Lupa' drifts back to consciousness... both feeling the loss... "Where did that come from?... Did you think it? You did, didn't you? Stop putting thoughts in my head."

"Just getting you back for invading mine."

She smiles and reflects on the name of her son... Terzo... the stranger, invading my dreams... puts the dark thoughts aside... and is lost in his image...

CHAPTER 14
THE TASTE OF THE MOTHER

Terzo is searching for 'Lupa' through the window of the tea room. Did she really exist, or was she a vision? His hungry eyes look for her. Tries to conjure her image; an *ordinary* woman is sitting at her table, obscuring her face that is more like a dream: the dual mother image is warring within, and is blurring the boundaries between fantasy and reality; sees 'Lupa' enthroned in the fresco of angels above- the fresco on the ceiling, as if in a church.

A suave American woman, early fifties or so, looks the boy over and likes what she sees- an unattainable object, a rebel of chance; alienation and hunger and a moment of danger. He pretends to ignore her. Imagines the pastries; reaches into his pocket: hungry but broke- why should that stop him? More, immune to all pleasure... The wolf is nursing the cub, and he imagines her taste, as he sucks at her teat for the life-giving potient: it would be wild but subtle, dark and bitter, mixing his fear of the shadow with the fear of the light.

He sits at the table, by his vision of 'Lupa'. The woman fixes her gaze. The mythic face blocks her out. The waiter wheels out the tray and he studies the tarts. The waiter is wary. He looks like a vagabond. "That one, that one, and--"

"Try that one," she says, pointing to the best one, far right, "I've had them all" she is saying, interrupting his intense concentration: tasting the tart, the way he tasted his mother. "And that one," he says, pointing to one on the left. A difficult number: she liked them that way. He tastes of the last. It doesn't please him at all, aware of his childish rebellion and wondered why it appealed to her.

"Would you like to taste mine? It tastes better."

"Please. You're distracting me."

She is completely unscathed, thrives on rejection; her interest is mounting the more he ignores her. Shameless, she watches him eat like an insatiable child... the taste of the mother... as if nothing else matters. Looks up at the ceiling at the fresco of angels, devouring the pastries, as he conjures her image.

Signals the waiter. "Two more, like hers, and a double expresso." When he has finished: "I want to speak to the manager."

"Is anything wrong, monsieur?"

"Not a thing. They were perfect."

The waiter looks perplexed. Terzo patiently waits. Her eyes are on him, sipping her tea, prolonging the ritual, and observing his moves. The manager arrives. "Yes, monsieur?"

"I have no money. Arrest me."

"The woman is riveted. "Please, allow me." She pays, and leads him to the Hotel Meurice, not far from the tearoom: "Why don't you come up?

"I'm late for work."

"What do you do?"

"I'm a thief."

Her jaded smile. "I admire your discipline, but why don't you take the day off? I'll match your day."

"I'd rather steal it."

"Are you good at it?"

"No."

"I thought not. I'll double it. If you prefer, you can take it. I'll pretend not to notice, if that's what excites you. Besides, it's safer than the streets."

"I don't want to be safe."

"I know what you mean."

"No, you don't. What do you want?"

"Don't you like women?" Silence. "Have you ever had one?" Silence. "I wouldn't expect you to do anything that's against your nature. I'll do all the work."

"What's involved?"

"I want to devour you, the way you devoured those pastries."

"How long?"

"Just an hour."

"Don't expect me to touch you."

Like 'Lupa', his submission defied the strength of his will, while he challenged his feelings and his own human needs- a rebellion against nature and the Law of Attraction. It was in this sense that the act seemed an act of pure freedom, while being *bound* by the needs and demands of a stranger. In other words, it was the stranger within them that finally claimed them, by subjecting them utterly to the desire of the senses- the desire they both tried to master, to be free of the flesh. When it was over, there was the reversal of values, in the compulsive style of his mother, while tailing her shadow: first, the triumph of spirit, and then the plunge into matter...

He looks in the window of an exclusive men's shop, directing his gaze to the perfect disguise. He enters and is approached by a skeptical salesman, who senses his animal nature that doesn't belong there. "I want that brown tweed suit in the window, the cashmere camel's hair coat, those dark brown shoes, the burnt sienna socks, and the brown and yellow plaid shirt."

The salesman stares blank-faced. "In what sizes, monsieur? Let's begin with the suit."

"I don't know, never had one." He measures him. "I'll wear it." Enters the dressing room. Throws his torn leather jacket, torn T-shirt, worn shoes, and ripped socks into the garbage, over his shoulder. "And the brown kid gloves," holding his hands out for size. "And I'll be needing that crocodile wallet," as he peers through the curtain. "The brown belt, eggplant scarf, and bring me that underwear." Sticks his bare butt out. "That size." Throws his jeans and his underpants into the garbage. Closes the curtain and reads the book that he holds: Spengler's *Decline of the West*, on the struggle for the unattainable- the mother he longed for that he sees in his dreams.

"What should I do?" asks the salesman to the manager.

"Bring him the things. I'll guard the door."

The salesman and tailor are sitting on either side of the curtain and, as if in a theater, they wait for the end. The curtain is parting. Terzo transformed. "How much in dollars?"

"In traveller's checks?"

"Cash." The salesman arches his eyebrows, calculating a moment. "Make it an even thirty-three hundred dollars." Terzo counts out thirty-three hundred's, handing it to him and heads for the door. The salesman and manager exchange paranoid glances. "You'll have to wait, monsieur," says the manager, holding a bill to the light.

Tries blocking the exit.

"Out of my way, or you won't know what hit you."

He quickly stands aside as Terzo exits, and strolls down the street, beside the vision of his mother.

CHAPTER 15
THE PEARL AND THE WORM

There is a hunger, a compulsion, to return to the source, as he walks through the Palais Royal towards Le Grand Vefour. Esperanza and Toto are begging by the door: they are playing the Virgin and Christ in the Pietá pose: the Mother of Sorrows holding the corpse of her Son- like the night Lupa healed him, when the myth became real. They are barefoot and hungry and dressed in rags. Terzo looks at the menu and pretends to ignore them...

"Have pity, have pity, my son is dying." The boy opens one eye. Terzo catches it- winks.

"Yes, I can see. He's covered with flies. That's not a good sign, especially in winter.

"The winter of the heart."

"The flies must be hungry."

"Dying, monsieur, dying of hunger," says Toto.

"Try changing squares- make a move on the board. That's what I do when I'm hungry. The queen is taking your knight. Why watch the rich stuffing their faces and getting drunk on expensive wine, when you're dying on 'queer street'?

Toto is unable to restrain his curiosity. "The queen?"

"The Death Mother."

"Queer street?"

"British for broke," his eyes still on the menu.

"Pity, have pity," Esperanza is moaning.

"I don't believe in it."

Why wasn't it working? It always worked. Toto sits up and changes his approach. "I'm not really dying- not this time, monsieur, but I feel like I am."

Terzo shrugs, "Same thing."

"This is worse- worse than being dead. At least, when you're dead, you can't feel it."

"If I could be sure of that I'd kill myself."

"It can't be as bad as being cold and hungry."

"Nothing is, except being lonely."

"What do you know about pain?" asks Esperanza, fooled by his cynicism and perfect disguise.

"Oh, I imagined it once."

"You can't imagine pain. Pain comes from the heart, not the head."

"Somewhere they meet and that's when the real pain begins."

"What do you know about real?"

"You're right. I know nothing. I know more about dreams. But be quiet a moment, I'm imagining dinner. We'll start with oysters. I do know one thing: if you eat three dozen oysters a day, and reflect on the pearl and the mystery of its birth, you will learn the mystery of transformation."

She scoffs at the boy in the man, who can believe such a myth; almost laughs in his face, who was taken in by a mollusc, and by the pearls that she worked for, like a slave of the sea. "Some mystery. It is born of dirt. There is the mystery of the gutter. If you are born in the gutter, you will die in the gutter, and I will die before I eat oysters."

"We used to work in the oyster beds, three years, nine hours a day, six days a week. We lived on oysters," Toto explains.

"Then you can have caviar."

The boy is bewildered. Who was this madman? His

thoughts dwell on his words. What could he mean? Or was it a game men play to torture the poor? Esperanza is sure of it, cutting him dead with her eyes.

"What makes it a mystery?" Toto asks," 'cause it is beautiful, or 'cause it comes from dirt?"

"Both- but that's only a part of it. The best part of a mystery is the part that is hidden. The pearl is like us, in a way. It is made of flesh and *born* of pain."

Toto looks puzzled. "Can an oyster feel pain?"

"Sure. Everything that lives is in pain. You don't think we're the only creatures that suffer, do you?"

The boy is quiet and thoughtful... "What does the oyster's pain come from?"

"It comes from the devil invading her flesh... and yet, it's her devil that is moving her will for the change. You see, the pearl is its tomb, but it is also her Son. For the alchemist, who was a kind of magician- who turned the filth of the gutter into the purest gold, the perfect pearl is the tomb of the lowly worm."[129]

"How does that work?" asks Toto.

"Let's think of the devil as an impure particle of matter that invades the Mother's secret mantle. She protects the purity of her nature by building its tomb- a tomb made of layers of mother of pearl, as she imprisons her devil in the pearl that is Christ. *

Esperanza looks at him strangely. His words were familiar.

"How does it work for *us*?" Toto asks.

"It works the same way. When the shadow part of our nature invades our thoughts, we disguise it in layers of our own psychic substance, and imprison our darkness in the dead part of self."

"The dead part of self?"

"Yes, we don't want to see it, and try to cover it over. But if we dare to look at the part that is dead, we see the flaw in our nature, the devil inside us, that produces the mystery of the perfect pearl. Do you know what I mean?"

"No."

"Let's look at it from another angle. In some way, you are playing both Christ and the devil, for you are both lying and telling the truth. And in this way, you are learning the mystery of life and death, and having the experience of both. My own 'mother' used to say: 'that's what I call myth': you are disguising the truth to protect the secret inside it: 'disguise is necessary to the mystery'. Each truth contains its opposite: the lie, the truth: the truth, the lie. Know what I mean?"

"Yes... and no, but keep telling me." Toto can't take his eyes off him. What did that look remind him of? It was the same way he looked at Leonardo, the night that he rescued them.

Esperanza is trying to fathom his words, and hears 'Lupa's' spirit in them that brought her boy back to life. *Is* it a mystery, she wonders, and if it is, why do I deny it? "I heard that same story once. Who told you that story?"

"A man with yellow eyes." Must be one of her tricks, thinks the gypsy, repeating her magic words.

Terzo studies the menu. "And then maybe some lamb and some great red wine, with the blood of the god in it. But I insist you dress for dinner."

Again, her dark gypsy eyes fill with suspicion. "You are laughing at me. I hope you choke on your dinner. Hunger is real. Death is real."

"Let's think about life. Come, we're going shopping."

"I am old and weak. Let me die in peace." She lies on the pavement.

Terzo picks her up in his arms. "You just need an hor d'oeuvre. The dying god needs one, too." He carries her into a chocolate shop.

Toto follows, immersed in his thoughts. Is he a con or a hero... or maybe both? He is learning fast from this stranger, who lived his life on the streets.

"Twelve truffles, and hurry, it's a matter of life and death- or worse," Terzo says to the chocolate man. He feeds Esperanza a truffle and sets her on her feet. Gives the truffles to Toto. "Don't eat too many, you can die of truffles."

He buys the gypsy a bunch of violets, and opens the door to a fashionable dress shop. Esperanza is in a daze, as if some angel had dropped her in Paradise. The shop girl gives her a contemptuous look. The boy reacts, cringes with shame. "We'll get her," to Toto. "See anything you like?" With the eyes of a child, she points to an extravagant red dress, while the soulless eyes of the shop girl are fixed on her rags.

"Sorry, monsieur, but we don't serve--" Terzo ignores her. "This subtle black one is more elegant. Yes, this one will complement your beauty. The other might draw too much attention to it." The shop girl rolls her empty eyes. Esperanza nods in agreement. "Are you going to leave, or shall I call the--?"

"The lady wants it. And those black suede shoes- with the ankle straps, that coat, that hat, that bag, those long black gloves, and the black silk scarf- the long one," draping it over the gypsy's head- like the mantle of the Virgin, veiling her black tangled hair.

133

The shop girl's sneer is replaced by greed. "She won't be able to try--"

"The lady will be wearing them," containing his rage.

"What size is... the lady?"

"I have no idea, and neither does she, so you better get it right- hadn't you? And be quick about it. We're late for dinner."

She suddenly changes her attitude, powerless, subservient. "Yes, monsieur," holding her breath as she measures her on bended knee.

"Queer thing, human nature, isn't it?" aside to the gypsies. They take up his attitude and observe her objectively, as if performing an experiment, like watching a rat in a labyrinth. She has quickly gathered the things he has chosen, which are the dearest, most splendid- for he has the eye of his mother. "How much in dollars- cash?" She nervously calculates. "Speed it up."

She's rattled. "I'm going as fast as I can."

"Go faster." She's crazed.

"Let's round it off- four thousand dollars."

Terzo counts out forty hundreds. "Take the lady's things into the dressing room. And wrap her rags: be careful with them, they're extremely delicate."

"Yes, monsieur," forcing a smile. "Madame?" leading the gypsy into the dressing room.

"Wait a moment," slipping the shoe on her scarred primitive foot. "It fits. You're lucky."

"You'll need some black-seamed stockings and some slingshots to hold them up. Why don't you get dressed? We'll be right back." He exits with Toto, as Esperanza transforms.

When they return, Toto is shoed and dramatically altered, wearing a cashmere blazer and well-cut pants. He slips her stockings and garters around the curtain. She appears, transfigured, unrecognizable. Terzo sprays her with a musky scent, combining the animal and human in a subtle fusion.

"Do I look like a lady?"

"More like a dangerous woman, but only a trained eye would know the difference."

The maitre d' meets them at the door, giving the gypsy woman an admiring look. "You were here for lunch, weren't you, madame?"

She lowers her lids. "It must have been someone else. I had lunch in Madrid."

"Such beauty is hard to forget. I'm sure I've seen you."

"I've been here before."

He's pleased with himself. "I remember your perfume. May I ask what it's called?"

"Hunger."

"Ah, (straight-faced), I thought I recognized it," leading them to the table. He exits bowing.

The gypsy shoots Terzo a wise old smile. "And only this morning, he wouldn't give me one franc."

The waiter brings her a bottle of *Eau de la Vipere* with a dead viper in the bottle. "Something special for madame, compliments of the house. When the viper has drowned in the hypnotic liquor, it expunges its venom, making an irresistible aprodisiac." The waiter pours for Esperanza and Terzo.

"He is saying that poison is the essence of love," says Terzo, pouring a glass for Toto, "To the mask," toasting the two. He orders. "Two ounces of Ossetra caviar, and a dozen oysters. Lamb for three- pink, and a bottle of *Sangue di Guida*- the blood of the betrayer."

"A sinful wine, monsieur" says the waiter.

'Lupa' and Leo are still in Snow's bed. Fatima dares to enter with three dozen oysters. The two disentangle. She pours the same wine, sensing 'the third', and suppresses her fear.

"Thank you, Fatima, the three of us appreciate it. Did you know you can live on oysters?" 'Lupa' asks her.

The third must be Snow, thought Fatima. "No, but if anyone can bring her back, it is you, madame."

"Call me, 'Lupa', Fatima." Fatima presses her hand to her heart, and quickly exits, before Snow's spirit appears.

"I didn't know either. Then I will live forever," said Leo. He devours her. "It tastes like the unconscious, dark and deep. I can see why they're afraid of it, and why they pay to survive it."

'Lupa' is eating an oyster and swallows a pearl, as Terzo is seeing her face, the face of his dreams, dark and foreign, like the shadow of night. Searches his roots for 'the philosophic wine', eating an oyster... longs for its essence.

"My third father, mama's ninth husband, was a pearl diver. He taught us to hunt for the pearls in the depths of the sea... It was cold down there... cold and dark.", putting his thoughts into words (the ones he kept to himself).

"I know, I've been down there."

"There is a woman I know, who talks just like you do... the same way as you. She gave me this pearl... the life of my son... *I* have nothing to give- only my body, but you can have it, if you want," says the gypsy woman.

"That's very kind of you- very kind. But I don't indulge- never have. Why don't you keep it for someone who really wants it."

"Then I will read your fate for you."

"I have banished my fate. It no longer exists."

"Your will is strong- but not that strong." She takes his hand and studies the lines in his palm. 'It's too late', she is thinking... Leo's words coming through her... like when Toto was dying.

How do I tell him, what I do not want to say? I see nothing but death... I do not want to see it. This boy who brought life, will die the death of the god... She traces the lines of his fate, engraved in his palm... "Look at the cross- the cross in the line of your life... See where it stops... and returns to the earth... how it continues to live through the soul of the mother. Look... it is written, not banished- just hidden by shadow. You will never banish it, no matter how hard you try. 'Love's silent poison'[135] will mix with the blood." The gypsy is silent. She will say nothing more, pouring the wine like a stream of blood.

His face darkens in conflict, "My mother is dead."

"No, not dead, only sleeping... and only her son can redeem her."

Esperanza leads Terzo up the steps to a church- the sister church of 'The Mother' that 'Lupa' was born in, where as a child he was baptized in the lonely peaks of the Pyrenees. He is listening to the Mass, the somber chords of the nuns, who are chanting the litany for the mystery of death... remembers the moment (that no one can remember), when the Mother baptized the child- it

137

still lived inside him, invoking the spirit of rebirth in the name of the Son... bathed in the shadow of the Mother of God... Bathed in her shadow, he prepares for his death. Looks up at the statue of the Black Virgin in mourning. She is holding her hand out, as if for an offering; three swords pierce her heart... like it was in his dream... like the knife in his 'mother's'... as he watched on the threshold.

"I don't like churches. Some other time, when I've risen and I have time to kill."

Esperanza is moving him towards the statue of the Mother. "This one is different. You can feel God in this one." He follows her slowly, as she is guiding him towards her. What is the meaning of the sacrifice? he continues to ask himself. What does she want me to give? Does she want me to give up my life... the life of a dream... that I am willing to die for?

He kneels on the pew between the boy and his mother.... Looks down a long narrow passage, like a tunnel of time... He is nine, Toto's age, and is crouched on the threshold, looking at Snow and Leonardo in a drunken sleep. Leo sleeps with his eyes open, as in 'Lupa's' *Child's Book of Saints*, his head on her breast, as if tracking her heart. There is an empty bottle of vodka, surrounded by broken glass, and an arsenal of shot glasses lined up in a row. She is wearing the white wedding gown in her marriage to Christ, and dreams of the Mother of Shadow, a dark smile on her face... Terzo sees Lupo's shadow- it looms on the wall, the knife clasped in his fists, with the cross on the hilt. His shadow seems to be praying, mocking her marriage to Christ, plunging the knife in her heart, the ruby clenched in her fist.

"Unlucky stone," Lupo mumbles, as he watches it fall.

Leo and 'Lupa' are asleep in Snow's bed. She dreams of Snow's death. The ruby falls from her fist... 'Unlucky stone' she is mumbling, 'Unlucky stone'... as Leo dreams of the murder through the eyes of his son: how he slept with his eyes open, unable to see; his hand on her heart that no longer beat; the knife in the fist, the fear in his eyes: unable to act... like he was on that night: remembers how Lupo protected his mother, and how unable to act, he watched his defeat. Watches Lupo, her killer, crossing the threshold, passing the trembling youth, his hands in his pockets: hears him whistling the Mass, Terzo's theme as a thief- the rite he repeats every night, as he watches her death.

Terzo is watching, trapped on the threshold of time, as Leo is dreaming his dream, through the eyes of his son: how he crawled to the ruby, and lay in the cradle, curled like an embryo, clutching the stone in his fist; humming the Mass... as if it were he who had killed her...

But again he moves into time, as he kneels on the pew: the nuns are chanting the Mass, as on the day of his baptism... It was the wolf man who killed her...It was the wolf man... not me. I would have died to protect her... or would it have been a false sacrifice?

CHAPTER 16
HOW, TELEPATICALLY?

'Lupa' gazes into the blood-red stone. Leonardo observes her, as she puts the pieces together... "My father murdered my mother... My son identified with the murderer... My son grew up thinking he murdered his mother. You never told him she wasn't his mother. Why? Why didn't you tell him?"

He tries to escape, to avoid it... "He escaped like you into a dark silent world... an inner world I couldn't enter... I didn't know the magic words."

It was your own fear, not his, that kept you from entering that world: not the fear of a hero or saint, but the fear of--"

His fear turns to rage. "You mean, while you were getting fucked in some cheap hotel? What are you now, the compassionate, all-embracing mother? You would have let him die in the gutter!"

"But before I did, I would have been straight with him. I would have told him how it was- exactly how it was."

"How, telepathically?"

"I could have talked to him in any world."

"In any world but this one! You abandoned him in this one!"

"While you were asleep? Does it excite you to fuck me in the same bed he killed her in; this tomb of a bed you trapped me in... knowing it would--?"

He explodes. "Rip you open? That it would open your heart that's as cold as that stone? You are lost in your visions, blinded by them, and with all your goddamned magic you can't accept what you made-that he would never be perfect, that he would be flawed, like yourself. He still lives by your curse, a myth of the mind that's inhuman!"

I am seeing him now, the fallen saint I created, the real Leonardo, who I sacrificed to the depths. He is more than the myth... more than a saint who was perfect... more than the god-man I worshipped that I tried to make real... I see the heart in the rage, and the soul of the man, that was split in two by his love, knowing it would never be whole- like the son that I cursed... that I renounced for a myth.

His rage is replaced by a great sadness. "But you're right. It was my own fear that kept me from entering the world you both live in. My shadow was stronger than me: its merged with my soul and split into two."

"What is it like, fucking a ghost?" Is it her that you're fucking- or him?"

"You *are* jealous, aren't you?" He takes her like a beast. "You're all of them- man, woman, and beast, in one single creature- your own lower trinity. What about you? Are you pretending?"

"No. I've forgotten how."

And they devour one another, lost in their dreams.

"I think I'm in love with you," she says, as if it were perfectly natural.

"What is the real riddle of the Sphinx? Let me give you a clue. She walks on two legs, has a tail, and acts like a wolf." Who is she? he asks... My Magdalena, my saint- the whore who is not. I am in love with a wolf, who is bringing the dead back to life. I was dead. I'm alive. She has given me life.

Terzo exits the church. The gypsies are waiting for him. "I just remembered, I have something to do. You know that tomb we were talking about that the oyster builds for the worm? Well, I have to help her to build it."

He empties his wallet- the last of the C notes. Gives them to Toto. "Protect your mother…protect her."

They watch him disappear in the night, as if they had witnessed a miracle. "Did we imagine him, Toto?"

"No... he is real. He's the realest thing I ever saw- besides 'Lupa', I mean'. Do you think the Christ sent him to us?"

"He's like a Christ, himself."

Leonardo and 'Lupa' continue to ravage each other, as she hears Esperanza and sees her son through her eyes. Like some dark pagan Christ, she says to herself... "Where is he?" she asks.

"Lupo?"

As always, her answer is secretive, concealing her real thought... "Yes... Lupo."

"He's in the joint- Wormwood, in London. I'm breaking him out. I'll need your help."

"I knew there was some other reason. What a sucker I am. I really fell for it... this tale of love and redemption... the Magdalena redeemed."

"So you think I'm using you? Why, because I need you? You're as perverse as she was, who reversed every thought, every feeling.... a trickster... like you... like your son, who makes me doubt my own heart."

"You must have a weakness for them. He's going to betray you."

"I can handle him."

She gives him the fateful look. "You can't handle the trickster. It's an archetype, not a man. Your brother is gone. What you think that you love is an empty form with no soul."

"How could *you* understand? You never loved anyone."

I swallow my feelings... "No... no I haven't"... but her eyes contradict her, and she is splitting like him.

"His prison is mine. So is his freedom."

She remembers the words from her *Child's Book of Saints*: *This Leonardo sets all captives free... and causes every other beast to stand still in their tracks...* "Not now, Leonardo, now that I found you."

"No. I found you. You've spent your whole life running away from me, and now that I found you, you're afraid of losing me? Can you make any sense of it?"

"No, not yet. But I will make it make sense. I'll change it- the pattern of fate."

"Can we change 'the stars in the blood'?"

"If we can't we will die."

CHAPTER 17
KILLING THE PAST

Lupo in solitary is caged like a beast. He kneels in a straightjacket, mumbling indistinguishable phrases.

Stares into oblivion, lost in his darkness. A key turns in the lock. A ray shoots through the door. A rat scurries into obscurity as two burly guards enter.

"You got a visitor, wolf man- a real one this time."

"You could've fooled me. She's more like one of them bloody hallucinations. Did you see those eyes? Got the look of the witch. It's those eyes that got him outta' this hole."

"Yeah, those eyes, but did you see the body? Those legs reach down to hell."

"The high head up to heaven."

They undo his jacket, and he wraps his arms round himself. "Well, *he's* gone. It's just one more way to go over the wall. If you're gone, you're gone. He won't know the difference if she's real or a dream." They drag him out of his cell, down a long empty corridor.

"Odd, isn't it. He's killed a guard and a con, and broke outta' max, and he's goin' back to his cell with three squares and a recess. Since I been in this joint, thirty years in all, there's only three cons been balmy enough to kill a guard, and all of them died in that hole."

"Hullo, it's like you said, she's a bloody witch. I took her into the warden myself. Watched her workin' on him. It didn't take her long neither. Besides, who else would visit the likes of him, 'cept for that rat, and even he don't trust him when he's not in his jacket." They drag him past a row of cells, as the prisoners, like beasts, howl in their cages...

"Wolf man, wolf man, wolf man, wolf man."

"There's our girl. Too crazy to fuck- and that's all she's good for."

"Not so pretty anymore, is she? Lost her looks with her mind. Rotted inside- nothing left but the husk."

"How do you figure it? The wolf man outta' the hole, after killin' a pig?"

"C'mon, did you see the bitch sweepin' in here, like she's queen of the hole? Just doin' my knowledge. It's the bitch got him out."

'Lupa' is disguised as her mother, Snow: still green eyes like water with the empty stillness of death; the black suit fits her body like the sheathe of a knife; the black hat with a veil that serves as a shadow; the red hair like a fire, the vengeance that lurks in the heart. Her back is rigid against the wall. The shattered glass in the window, a hole in the center- as she planned it with Leo, her own secret plot. She turns to face him. His eyes glazed with madness. Blind from the dark and the darkness within. Sees the masked face of 'Lupa', replaced by her mother's- ghostly, transparent, like a mad waking dream: a dream of betrayal, in which he murdered his soul...

"I've been waiting for you. I knew you would come."

She smiles strangely- knows what he sees. She made it that way. It always worked, what she made....

"Kiss me. Kiss my frozen lips," lifting her veil. Her eyes, the eyes of a killer, have an icy intensity- like the frozen water of death, as she wills what she wants; eyes suspending his breath, thought racking his brain. Compels his unseeing orbs into contact with hers;

moves his lips to meet hers, thrusting her tongue through the hole, passing a note through her mouth with the plan for the break. '*Evil is only unconsciousness*',[144] as if through the lips of a corpse…

'Lupa', father, 'Lupa', remember?" Wipes off her mouth with the back of her hand, seeing the end with a grim satisfaction. A shutter comes down, like the blade of an axe.

Terzo, on the banks of the Seine, stares at the river: the water is tainted: two dead fish head to tail: the mouths and gills cease to move- like the vision of 'Lupa', who remembered the future- mixed the past with the present: it comes to pass as she saw it.

The brothers are shooting craps at The Door. The dealer is placing six stacks of chips before both. The table is hot- all high rollers. All are betting on Leonardo. "A double three," Lupo calls, "For Leo and me." Bets half their chips. Leo's eyes shift to his: the pupils have swallowed the doped-up eyes; sees him scratching his arm, nodding out as he calls. The dealer is placing their chips on the six. The players observe them, betting against them.

Three men at a table, with dead fish eyes, are also observing the brothers. They signal to Guy. Leonardo is watching- eyes fill with suspicion. The dealer takes half their chips and is paying the gamblers. Lupo gambles the rest. Takes Leo's as well. Leo is fuming, grasping his wrist.

"Stake me," says Lupo. "A double three."

"What happened to last night's take?"

"I invested it."

"In your arm?"

Lupo tosses the dice. Nods out on the roll. One of

the men gestures for Guy to sit down. Looks over at Leo, who shifts his eyes to the men...

"What are his weaknesses," asks man #1.

"Look again," says man #2.

"He's got four of them. One of them's dead. Two are... strange," says Guy.

"How strange?" asks man #3.

"Too strange to fuck with. And then there's his brother, the junkie, playing dead with the powder- a suicide pact. Guilt makes you blind. It made Leo a sucker. I'll take care of Leo-three kilos for Lupo, nine for me,"

"Can he be trusted?" asks man #2.

"No, isn't that the point?" replies Guy.

Leo pulls Lupo away from the table. "It's finished. It's done. You don't exist."

Always judging me- my whole life judging me. I almost preferred to rot in prison than to see your sanctified face again."

"You *never* saw it. It's your other face."

"No, Leo, it's you who wouldn't look. It drove me mad, but I looked."

"Try looking inward. Maybe you didn't look deep enough."

Lupo shoots up in the filthy latrine. Jabs at a vein. Can't get a hit. Obsessed with the act, arms scarred from abuse. Repeats it more roughly, compulsively boots it- pumping the blood back and forth and prolonging the rush. Squirts the blood on the wall, and slips into oblivion, numbing the thought of his brother, and that he killed for his love: that he still doesn't have it, that he destroyed what he had, and feels more secure with the paraphernalia of death. Looks at his watch as he comes to the surface; his dealer three minutes late. There's a knock on the door...

"Slime?" He opens the door, slamming it shut. "What do you want?" shoving his props in his pocket.

"I got an offer for you" says Guy, with his insidious smile. Lupo narrows his eyes. Guy pushes the door in. "Where's your hospitality?"

"Get to the point. I'm busy."

"So I see. Some junk came in from Marseilles- hasn't been stepped on yet."

"How much?'

"Three kilos- for nothing."

"What do they want, my soul?"

"Your brother's. Tell him to meet you in the back alley at exactly 3:30, then go to the side alley and I'll give you the dope."

"Make it six, and you got a deal."

Guy tenses up. Looks at his watch. What time have you got?"

"12:36."

"Mine says, 12:33. So does the clock. Change it," says Guy.

Terzo climbs up the step from the tainted river, as Guy cruises by, stopping beside him...

"I was just thinking about you," said Guy.

"While you were jacking your gun off? No, Guy, I don't want a ride."

"Lupo's out," baiting him. Looks at him sideways with his devious eyes.

Terzo lowers his own. "Oh?"

"Yeah, I just saw him, at The Door."

"Let's go for a ride. I'd like to see him. It's been a long time." Terzo gets in, Guy mentally masturbating.

Death becomes real. He takes off down the quai. "I'll make it easy for you- if you wait your turn. I also have business with him. Be in the back alley at exactly 3:30. Check your watch. What time have you got?"

"2:30."

"Change it to 2:33." Terzo changes his watch. Pushes the fear down...

Lupo works Leonardo for an illusory deal, as Guy watches the two and looks at the clock. Lupo goes to the latrine for an anxiety fix, preparing himself for the final betrayal. Then goes through the door into the back alley. Terzo hides in the shadows and watches him exit. The bouncer changes the clock as Guy watches the hands. Leo looks through the mirror, changing his watch to a three. Feels the fear in his soul, unable to act. 'Lupa', in Snow's room, is mentally moving the numbers, and, like chess pieces, they seem to be playing their parts; works on the hands of the clock to change the hand of his fate- to alter the pattern of having no choice. Leo looks through the mirror, reflecting the games of The Door, as the hands of the clock seem to move of themselves- sees the hands on the six: the hands move in his head...

A double three... six o'clock... the hour of the crucifixion... when Christ died on the cross... Magdalena, you witch... The hands move to the three. He sees 'Lupa's' face: there's the trace of a smile: 'It worked. Watch the game.'

He looks at Guy through the mirror, anxiously checking the clock. Leo goes to confront him. Looks him dead in the eye: "Looks like you're busy, Guy."

"Why, do you need me?"

"Not really. Just curious." Hears 'Lupa's' words:

'Not the fear of a hero, or saint... but the fear of a--'
Tonight I will act- change the course of the stars.
Shoots dice at the table. Guy narrows his eyes.

Lupo waits in the back alley: tries to follow the plan: was it the back alley or side alley... as they merge in the mind...Tries killing his conscience by snorting some dope.... Slips into darkness... into unconsciousness... Terzo slinks up beside him, holding the knife to his eye... He is frozen with fear... unable to act. 'Lupa' summons her will- moving his hand with her will. Opens the eyes of her father, as she moves Terzo's hand: he pierces his eyes with the point: 'Lupa's' will thrusts it deeper. Lupo is clutching at cold empty space; hears Terzo whistling the Mass and feels the rage of the god... 'Lupa's' voice as it echoes through the image of Snow, ripping the veil from the face of the shadow of God: '*Evil is only unconsciousness*', till time and space are as one. Hears Snow's voice from the pit: '*Swear by your eyes*'. Hears his voice in his head: 'I swear by my eyes'. His blind eyes see Nothing, where love is a void, and, as he thrashed in the dark, he knew what his blindness had wrought.

In the side alley, Guy is stroking his gun. Terzo sinks to his knees as he's shot in the groin. Hears the voice of his father, calling his name. '*The special power is in it*, as it said in the myth: and *every other beast stood still in his tracks'*. Three times for the father, the son, and the ghost of her mother, and the word 'struck the stars'[148] as it rang in her blood. Leo holds him in his arms and embraces his son, curses the moon- the three faces that mock him. The real time is 3:30. A double three on the dice.

He shoots Guy in the face. And goes to the back alley. Blows Lupo's brains out. Then blows out his own... Sees young 'Lupa' ecstatic, lifting her up on his horse: *'Nothing lies'*, she is saying... *'nothing lies... nothing lies'*!... 'Can we change the course of the stars? If we can't we will die'.

CHAPTER 18
GHOSTS DON'T HAVE SHADOWS

'Lupa' is shielding her ears, as the sound of the gun echoes through her. Her scream pierces the night, as Snow's ghost gallops towards her, the mare, white as the moon, as she rides through the window. The ghost enters her body, and she and her mother are one. Eyes lose their intensity, growing cold and remote. Looks up at the drawing of the corpse seen in shadow. The shadow is lying in the sign of the cross. A dove hovers above it, surrounded by sword-like rays. They are contained in a vessel, so that the soul can't escape; Terzo's child-like letters slanting backward in time: *MOTHER'S SOUL LEAVES HER BODY*, as 'Lupa' is dying Snow's death.

Her two souls are confounded, as her shadow merges with Snow's. Takes the key from the nail that pierces the heart. Rises up from the murder bed, to find the door that it fits, and, possessed by Snow's spirit, moves like a ghost through the corridor...

Crossing the chessboard passage, in the trance of death, she stops at the tall narrow closet that Terzo saw in his dream. There is a cross painted on it: it is painted in blood. Turns the key in the lock and opens the door. Sees the white wedding gown stained with the blood of the heart; it is nailed to the wall in the sign of the cross; she pulls out the nails, slipping into the gown; then returns to the bed of the murdered mother within her; places the key on the nail that pierces the heart; looks at the swan cradle, sees the nine- year-old boy. He is curled like an embryo, the red stone in his hand: "Unlucky stone," and she prays to the Mother: "Tell your Son to come down. Make him human... like I am..."

Terzo lopes through the gate like a wounded beast and staggers towards Snow House, leaving a pathway of blood. 'Lupa' lies in the murder bed in Snow's wedding gown- like the drawing above her, in the sign of the cross. The moon casts a shadow on the face of his mother, and he is frozen on the threshold, as he was as a boy: "Ghosts don't have shadows," he says, as he moves towards the bed. "You're only a phantom... a trick of the devil... but the devil is blind, and I'm going to outwit him. I'll lure your soul down to earth... *Love is stronger than death.*"

The moon illumines her face... "The face of my fear."

"Do you know who I am?"

"No, dark one... but I have always loved you. We are of the same spirit."

"Yes, our spirit is one."

He died on her body, as if nailed to her shadow. Her bitter tears bathe his face, as his soul leaves the earth.

CHAPTER 19
CROSSING

Nora is absorbed in her psychic ritual with Nola and is analyzing the transference to analyze herself, recording her thoughts to keep Nola alive, as if the life of the *Self* were sustained by her shadow...

A month had passed by since I read her obituary and I finished her book the following week. At times, I was certain that her death was symbolic, so she could live with the guilt of the death of her son. Her guilt seemed to double, as if it rose from the grave... or was it my own... as if she were buried inside me. Her past crossed with mine- a complex of opposites, as if our sons had been twinned- or was it their shadow? What I thought was delusion, I was convinced was reality, for she taught me to live in the ambiguity of myth. I was tormented by the thought that I might have prevented her death and preserve the life that I valued... as if her life were my own. The book she had written had its roots in the past, and it was more than a fantasy, though it was only one session.

I opened the door for Samara.

"She's alive. I saw her."

"Really?" veiling my reaction, bordering on religious- the elation and fear... as if her death were my own... as if we died it together... How many more deaths to die? "What were your thoughts?" I inquired.

"That I could find her in death, but on earth she would never belong to me."

"So, you can live in the underworld what you can't live in life, instead of tapping the unconscious, to live what you imagine?" using the transference to understand her obsession, while understanding my own, and my neurotic immersion… It was as if Nola were writing of her obsession with mine… as if our shadows crossed paths through the ghosts of our sons. Was it the end of the book that 'opened the door'… her son hung on her cross… while mine was hung on my own? As if the book had continued, and she wrote from the grave, the session continued in the dark of the mind…. as if she were living inside me… in the fourth dimension of mind… in a timeless session inside me, where we met in the dark…

She presented my problem of living the imaginal life, like a tale we were weaving from the mythic unconscious: and why did I need her, but to find a way to come down. What I called acting out, Nola called living. What I did to protect myself, she did as a challenge. She was my erotic obsession to come to terms with the dark side- with her Mother of Shadows and the son I denied. Just as she was identified with the sacred whore of the patriarchy, I was identified with the Virgin as the untouchable analyst. As a pair of 'impossible opposites', we were more alike than we realized, for as Jung said, *the extremes meet in the unconscious*, and now they were meeting in the ego.

"Have you been stalking her ghost again, to confront your obsession with death?" I was asking Samara, gripped by my thoughts...

We were woven together by the death of our sons, for both were hung on the mother and nailed to our will. I had been traveling with 'Lupa' into the medieval past, in which the disembodying was followed by a relentless urge for incarnation, expressed by the ritual of Communion that we saw in her dream: the renouncing of the body, followed by the consuming of the Son: denying the body for the spirit, and the 'bulimic' appetite for wholeness, as if the Holy Eucharist was the symbol for the stone of the philosophers.

"It was just 'synchronicity', said Samara. I was reading *Shadow Woman*. It's gripping. What she writes simply happens."

I ignored the remark- it was a quote from a review. "What were you thinking while you read it?" I asked, as if I were neutral, but, like her, I was lost in the transference and under its spell.

I'd become as passionate as 'Lupa' about the medieval saints- the women who crucified their flesh by identifying with the Christ- the feminine body of the god, while despising their own. Like Nola, I was healing the mind/body split, by the feminizing of the Son, who grew breasts to feed his starving saints, and who were nursing on his flesh. The Virgin Mother was cleansed of her feminine qualities, transposed to her Son, the feminine Christ; and while 'Lupa' identified with the whore of the Fathers, Nola redeemed her by playing with flesh: freeing the Magdalene, she projected the curse on her son... while mine stole my identity and died in my place...

"Are you listening to me, Nora?"

"Yes, I'm listening," I replied, "you are speaking of your mind/body split, and how you have spawned a second self, that is personified as 'Lupa' and stolen her shadow, so that the whore and the martyr do not appear to be in conflict- as in your dream in the marketplace, where you are hung on the hook. In what way do you think you are *hung* on her shadow?"

"I was thinking that she knew herself, but is just as compulsive as I am, and yet, both selves are communicating, while it is obvious that she is splitting: thinking, now that's 'turning a trick' and I wished I could turn it."

"Maybe you can."

"How?"

"By *using* the complex, and not being used by it."

"I had a dream that I did, but it never works in the day world."

"How did it work in your dream?"

"Lupa' and I were turning a double together, and were about to go down on each other for the trick, who was watching. What about *my* pleasure, I thought? Why are we doing it for him? 'Let's think it over, 'Lupa', let's do it alone,' I said to her shadow... that was also my own"...

I couldn't help smiling. "What did she say?"

She smiled at me- just like you're doing. 'But you can't afford me,' she said, and I was angry at the truth. 'I am much richer than you think, and I am willing to spend it,' I argued. Then I turned to the trick and asked him for change. He looked at me puzzled, and I lost all my patience. 'Never mind,' I said, 'I'll change it myself.'

This one doesn't need interpreting. She's changing me, Nora: my relationship to men, to myself, even to whoring. I still hate my mother, but I'm not throwing her up. I can say no to her now, without starving her out of me. I hate to say it, Nora, but it's like 'Lupa' is my analyst."

"What am *I*?"

157

"My imaginary mother. What do you make of it, Nora?"

"I would say that you are trying to unhook yourself from your mother- the mother in *you* that has sold you in the marketplace, merged with the Mother as trickster, who reverses the opposites, confounding the ego, and who has compromised your identity. You have been playing your image through the masculine eye, and have victimized yourself, while you pretend you're its master.

"But the master is 'Lupa'... and I am the victim."

Your envy of 'Lupa' is the urge to be free, because in your fantasy she lives for herself. You are trying to enliven the deadened feminine, by merging the mind and the body to heal the split in the psyche, that it seems you've personified with 'Lupa' and Nola, 'the third' as the analyst, the *soul* of the mother, who stands apart as the witness, to make the experience conscious. In your dream, you are *hooked* on the *Death Mother,* who has a devouring quality and is selling off the potential for *transforming* the self- your hatred and fear of her that you have sold to the mob, for you have merged with her image that you think is your own, that *belongs* to your mother, who has used you to live."

"The potential in being the victim is in making more money."

"What if by merging with the Death Mother you were attempting to build a bridge- an *unconscious* attempt to find a descent to the underworld- one from which you could return and to bring about a separation, instead of being *devoured* and *identifying* with her? Of course, Hades is known to be terribly rich, and may be trying to separate you from the *merging* with your

158

mother.

But Samara returns to the projection, and to being the victim. "The real problem is that I'm in love with a killer, and I want to hold 'the wolf one' in my arms, to bring my body back to life. I was dead till I found her, and again I am dying for her. But just as you learn all her secrets, she slays you again."

"Sounds like you're setting yourself up for a mythical suicide."

"I want to be deathless, like she is. She has the secret of immortality. When I thought she had killed herself, I didn't want to live. But when I saw her alone in the mob, like a wolf in the marketplace, and I knew she had the courage to live with her darkness, it made me feel stronger to be alone with my fear. I was dying from anorexia, but I felt the hunger again. In my fantasy, this time *I* was the woman, and 'Lupa' was hunting me down and was lusting for my body. She was 'the false door' of the tomb that was painted in the murals of the underworld, so that the pharoah could come and go as he pleased. She would know how to free me, how to open that door."

"But those doors are deceiving and are always opening and closing, and whether you are entering or leaving is always a mystery. It seems that she is the threshold experience that you are trying to sustain, for the she-wolf is the symbol of the union of opposites. She is bloodshed and death, the devourer of life, as terrible as any devil, but the great protector of shadow that roams in the dark places and that wants to be known. Try living in both worlds at once. Try to 'open the door'. Try to find her inside you, instead of looking for her in the marketplace."

"Inside she betrays me. Inside I'm alone."

"Let's look at the betrayer inside you- the mother who sold you to the mob, and how being alone is experienced as being abandoned by the *Self*."

"My mother is my cross. She's my depression, my eating disorder, my isolation and loss. She keeps me from living and being able to love. I don't even know what I feel, or who it is that is feeling it. It is only through 'Lupa' that I am beginning to know, and why I live with the fear that I won't be able to return. It is only her image that can bring me back from the dead. Why do I feel that I don't exist without 'Lupa'?"

"The wolf-headed soul that you want to hold you in the underworld is the Lady of the Beasts, who is both instinct and spirit, and is able to link the two worlds that you have divided in half. When you use the false door, so you can transit from the underworld, she can instruct you on using the shadow as a bridge, rather than splitting and dissociating, and dismembering the self. But she won't let you cross over, until you are willing to make the sacrifice."

"What does she want?"

"She wants you to sacrifice the narcissism- to stop the false sacrifice."

"Isis, my *real* mother, will gather the pieces of my body, and put them together, as she gathered the pieces of Osiris- 'The Awakener of the Dead', who is 'The Lord of Two Worlds'."

"I imagine she'll be needing your help."

"That always confuses things. She never found the penis. I am looking for it, while I'm whoring. Do you think I'll ever find it... or will it always be missing? The myth tells the secret of why I became a prostitute. As a whore I awaken it and conjure up its mythic power, but I am not able to do it for more than a moment. I guess, like me, men are suffering from psychic castration. It must be what brings us together in the alleys of the underworld."

"Think of the phallus as symbolic, connecting the conscious and unconscious, instead strapping one on and making it literal."

"I see your point, but if you mean it is a metaphor for my analysis, and that it is either too hard or too soft, I am aware of the problem- that I want to be what I'm not."

"You are beginning to sound like Nola. The book is altering your personality." That sounded sadistic- I must be more careful... for I, too, am missing the wolf-headed soul... to bring my body back to life, by coming to terms with my darkness.

I lead Samara to the door, and see Nola in the waiting room. I contain my reaction, and assume an air of neutrality. I must stay more alert to her devilish workings, I say to myself, as they ignore one another- Samara holding 'her' book, stealing the shadow of the heroine.

Nola enters the room, but does not lie 'on the couch'. "While I was waiting, I had an imaginary session. I was angry that this borderline was identifying with my shadow: angry that you colluded with her and gave her my session, instead of spending it in communion with my disembodied spirit, talking to my ghost in the empty chair that I abandoned."

Somehow, I kept my composure. It was exactly what I *was* doing. She would never know the effect that her psychic wanderings had on me.

"My shadow said," she continued, in her maddening style, 'I came at the time of my session, and like a gentleman I waited, while she pretended to be me, and you pretended not to care. There is a 'reversal of opposites' at work and I was tempted to yield to it, but I want to know why, and why it appeared in that form."

"We will look at it," I said, trying to bear it. "What made you decide to come back?"

"I was going to kill myself, but decided to write about it, instead. It seemed more to the point, so I'll be needing my hour- the one that you gave to that devouring woman."

"I see death hasn't changed you. I was wondering if you had the courage to stick around on the earth, or if you submitted to what you think of as a negative fate."

"I was curious to see what would happen, if I didn't try to control it."

"That must have been humbling, rather than trying to end the world with a thought."

"I'm a primitive, so it ends and begins every day with the setting and rising of the sun: meaning, it ends when I forget what I know, and begins when it rises to consciousness."

"You are only half primitive: the half that kills what it loves. What else did your shadow say?"

'It's not that I need you', it said.

"What did your ego say?"

"It admitted it did."

"Well, that's progress. Did you have to die to accept it?"

"And to return from the dead to finish what we started."

"You mean, to do it on earth's surface, rather than in

hell? Did you have a dream last night?"

"I dreamt about that Egyptian whore"…

"We were turning a double together, and she was trying to make it real. I winked at her and said, 'Try to remember where you are.' 'But I am where I am,' she was saying, and my shadow is *real*. Where are *you*?' "

"This hit me in a deeply emotional place."

I veiled my reaction. "How did you answer?"

'I'm in the hell of the body. Where else would I be'?

"What did it mean to you?"

"Well, like she said, my shadow is real, and my body is shadow."

I tried not to tremble, not to idealize her.

"I tried to accept it, and tried coming down, but I knew I still wasn't here. Then I suddenly realized that I wanted to be. I vowed to turn the body to a vessel for the *Medicina,* rather than a prison, or a tomb, and decided to live; for the first time, to inhabit it, and not hover above it... like my mother. And then I wondered, why was *she* in my dream? She is the last person that could make me conscious of my mother."

"Why, do you think?"

"I imagine she has a compulsion for death that is more extreme than my own; that like me, she is under the spell of the Devouring Mother; that she has a *literal* eating disorder- not metaphorical, like mine, and is subjected to matter in a literal way- the lust for the body, instead of the soul; that she is a masochist in her whoring, and loses herself in the act; and I imagine she has a martyr complex and is resisting incarnation, and like the Son of the Mother, she is hung on her shadow."

My fear at that moment is that she would tell me how to cure her... "Tell me, if you were her analyst, how would you cure her?"

"I would take her down from the hook and expose the wound to the light, so that the animal soul that is living in the realm of the dead, could enliven the body and inspirit dead matter."

I swallowed hard. She was a better analyst than me. And I knew that I loved her, with the kind of love that transforms. "Tell me more of this wound," I asked.

"It is the wound of love, but not the kind that transforms- the kind she is wanting from me that I have for you."

I felt the chill in my soul. "How is it that you brought Toto back to life with that kind of love, but couldn't use the same love to resurrect your own son?"

"The Mother of Shadow was demanding a sacrifice. She took my vision, my power, and brought me down through his death. I was possessed by the ghost of my mother, and the compulsion to escape, and yet, by mourning them both, I wanted to live. It was at the moment of death that I embodied his spirit... but still, there are moments when I would join him in his tomb."

"What keeps you here?"

"The dead live through us. I will wait. The spirit of the wolf will bring the dead back to life."

I controlled it, the trembling. "And your experiment?"

"With the killing of desire? I have extracted it from the shadow, but I am still making it conscious. How? By going down to my darkness, but being the witness of my death."

"How do you see *our* experiment?"

"I was unable to give myself to it, until I *suffered* love's death. In our experiment, we will reanimate it, and will suffer its birth."

I am already there... She was bringing me back... the dead parts of the self were returning to life. I tried to contain it. "And the 'psychic bulimia/anorexia'?" I asked.

"I am ready to work with the trickster, who 'juggles with halves'.[163] It was not till the death of my son that death became real. The masculine spirit in a woman's psyche needs to be embodied through a whole mother image, but when this spirit is androgynous and closer to the feminine, it is more easily lost in her and caught in the *shadow* of the mother. It is this kind of shadow that escapes from the mother to the heights, for it fears coming down and being trapped like a beast. It is the hunger for becoming, this 'psychic bulimia/anorexia', the *fear* of the hunger, and starving it out of me, because the need is too great... almost greater than I can bear."

What could I say? She had analyzed her core complex, 'destroying her claim to it', in a symbolic suicide. I was identifying with her son... and my own... and was caught in her depths.

"Why are you looking at me that way, Nora?"

Why not say it? "Just feeling like your patient, and trying to come to terms with it."

"There is more to come to terms with. But we will try not to go there. Funny, I just had an image of you with the head of a wolf. We were down in the underworld, and you were holding me in the dark... The door of the tomb was opening and closing... and we were surrounded by shadows... the shadows of the

165

dead... When it closed, I couldn't find you. The wolf had swallowed the sun. I wanted to live on this earth... but it was empty without you... Funny... the desire for life took the form of your body."

I tried being an analyst, but my shadow was laughing at my terror: 'What's funny about that?' asked the ego as she strung the pearls of the past, while sorting them out from the stones of the future.

CHAPTER 20
MARTYR COMPLEX

I dreamed of her that night ... or was it a vision... a portent of the past... or a healing of the future?

She was giving me Communion and I was devouring the god, but it was 'Lupa', not Nola, who was acting as priest (the animal spirit acting as analyst, and myself as the patient, who needed to transform). I was kneeling before her: 'Be opened'! she said, and I opened my mouth, for the blood of the sacrifice. It poured from her breast from the wound of the Son... but the wound was my own... and was buried in shadow.

When I awoke, Nola arrived for her session. She was silent as I continued to analyze my dream, and I watched her imbibing my thoughts, like the wine of the god... What was clear in the dream was that I couldn't get enough, and like an addict I was feeding on the antidote to death. I confronted the martyr in myself and the lust for Communion.

She responds, as if I had spoken aloud: "We have the same problem. We are both addicted to spirit. It's a defense against mortality and the death of our sons."

She invaded my unconscious, and I knew my thoughts were at risk...

"I had a dream of you last night- after our session," she said. "It was a 'big dream' of how we change one another: how it continues in the dark and is beyond our control."

She was reading my shadow: she had opened the door...

We were in the coal-mining town, where my mother was born, at the base of the mountain of The Mother of God. You were my priest- my awakener- my only means of transformation, and were placing a rough piece of coal on the palm of my hand. 'Taste it," you said: *'it is the bitterness of love, the eating of God by the self, and the self by God.'*[166]

"The mystic words of the sainted medieval poet, looking inside me, like she could see in my soul... Hadewijch, the martyr, and the tasting of the shadow."

I had written those words in my notebook, as I drifted to sleep, and they inspired my dream of 'Lupa' as priest. "Let me quote," she went on, "from *Love's Seven Names*, the words of Hadewijch, the mystic, who inspired my dream (and as if she were inside my brain, she repeated my thought): "words like the inner relationship between analyst and patient... but, somehow, her words were coming from you"...

"The heart of each devours the other's heart, one soul assaults the other and invades it completely, as who is Love itself showed us when he gave of himself to eat. By this he made known to us that Love's most intimate union is through eating, tasting, and seeing interiorly. He eats us, we think we eat him, and we do eat him, of this we can be certain.'"*

'Taste it again, you were saying' (delighting in my conflict), "as I emerged from my dream, as if I were having it with you"... 'It's the taste of the spirit,' you said, 'when we are finally one- when the bitterness of shadow will turn into wine,' "and I opened my eyes, and I knew it was so."

The words I was writing, as I emerged from my own. Somehow, I knew it was coming and I tested myself, as I tried not to tremble and wondered how far it would go.

"This mutual transformation," she continued, "is a metaphor for the analytic process, and for the love in the transference between patient and analyst: the analyst, as the Eucharist, must allow herself to be devoured, and must suffer Love's wound through the wound of the patient. It is through 'Love's most intimate union'[167] that the healing takes place, and, unless the healing is mutual, the patient will suffer love's sickness.

"I want to believe it, and I pray it is true: that in the mutual process of the great transformation, we will turn the shadow of love to an indestructible light. It's 'the rejected stone', isn't it, Nora? 'The stone of little worth', the philosopher's stone both 'found and made', by suffering the darkness of the *Self* at the breast of the god. It's the alchemical poison that wounds and heals, the mystic love of the god that we are trying to bear… the next stage of my dream of Holy Communion- the dream that I wanted to keep to myself… when I was protecting the compulsion I was not ready to sacrifice."

I tried hard to separate us, to turn the coal into fire- to psychically transform it, and give her back just a part, for it was too much to receive... too much to hold: "Yes, you made the sacrifice of pride when you let me look at your shadow- your darkness that kept you under its spell. In this dream you are breaking it, and are tasting the difference."

Nola nods in acceptance and contemplates the difference- how the past and the present were mingling in the pattern of the weave... "They complete one another, as they must, and they will. Your interpretation of my first dream confirmed that I finally found you: the one person who was able to look in my darkness: who could not only look, but who knew what you saw...

"What complex was that? I was asking my shadow. 'The martyr complex," it said- 'the non-transformative side'. And I knew it was ours- that we'd transform it together, the poison of love that nearly destroyed us. In *this* dream, its twin, you *are* my 'Last Supper'."

The beginning of Communion, I thought... that foreshadowed the betrayal...

"What is the difference," she asked, "between the true and false sacrifice?"

I watched her reflect on the mystery in her uncanny way, and I am hooked on her magic and hung on her cross.

I looked at the martyr complex and its non-transformative side, and saw the particle of difference between submission and surrender. I thought of Catherine of Siena, who starved herself to death, while devouring the Eucharist in an excessive Communion. But again, she was listening to my thought and delighted in tormenting me.

"Let's look at the difference," she said, "between submission and surrender- the same difference that exists between the true and false sacrifice, and why my own martyr complex could not lead to transformation. *What about* Catherine of Siena, who starved herself to death, and who replaced earthly food with an excessive Communion? I was asking my shadow, "What makes the complex a non-transformative' one?" And it said,

'It's the *literal* nature of asceticism that's the devil in the mix'."

"Catherine devoured what she denied by 'gorging on the Eucharist'-[169] the feminine body of the Christ, that she denied in her own, who, in her vision grew breasts to nurse the starving feminine. I looked at my own self-denial, to my submission as a prostitute- the 'psychic bulimia/anorexia' as a means of disembodiment. Was Catherine psychically contaminated by the *literal* nature of the patriarchy- repelled by the feminine body, while she lived in Mother Church, in the body of the Mother that she continued to deny? I, too, was born in her body- while my own was denied, and, in my vision, my son was the feminine god."

Again, the same complex, and we were both 'on the couch', while we were being reborn, and were *devoured* by love…

"Let's define the martyr complex," I said, "and its relation to the *devouring* aspect of the Mother."

"Let's," she agreed (I almost wished she refused): "The Christian martyr, or mystic, on the transformative side, surrenders to the embodied god, and is willing to work through the negative veils by surrendering to the spirit- not in an act of submission, in which one gives oneself up. The particle of difference in *submission* is the *resistance* to the Mother, who personifies the unconscious and the transformative side. But when we try to control it, we attract her *devouring* aspect, breaking us down, until we blindly submit."

"Say more," I said, dreading it.

"More... On the shadow side of the martyr complex, by disembodying the self, we are crucified on her body that is veiled by her shadow. I see now that I exiled my son to protect the ideal... disembodied him... and myself... for a perfect   Christ-like *animus*... while I was trying to escape the torture of love... How I tried to bear loving you, and blindly submitted, and disembodied the 'Virgin' in an idealized transference: re-enacting the split in Mother Church between the Virgin and the Magdalen- the whore of the patriarchy, and the symbol of redemption. I projected the sinless Virgin onto you, while I played the rebel whore, and, like the nuns in the cloister, I was spellbound by the Fathers."

"And so, you were renouncing my shadow. What would have happened if you succeeded?"

"I would still be a myth. You made me real to myself."

More real than I am, I thought, seduced by the martyr complex, but intent on using it for the healing. "Let's go further with the shadow side," I said, overcoming my resistance.

"Yes, always further... until we can no longer bear it. Well, in the Christian myth, the Greek word *martus* signifies a witness, who has spiritually grasped the life of Christ, from the baptism to the crucifixion. To be conscious of the martyr complex is to *bear* the shadow of the god, till an unconscious content rises to consciousness. The saint and mystic, who *identify* with the god, endure his torture and death by *submitting* to the death, the body rising with the spirit and abandoning the earth. The act of witnessing ceases when one is possessed by the mystery… as I am… sacrificing the body for the spirit, and the *incarnation* of the *Self*."

"In other words," I added, "yours was a *literal*

crucifixion, as it is in addiction, and the *desire* for death- in a *literal* way, as opposed to the symbolic that comes through 'the third'. What you experienced is a compulsive *imitatio Christi*: the martyr complex in its *non-transformative* aspect (I almost said we). This was ritualized in the 'psychic bulimia/anorexia', in a purging of the flesh and a *dissociative resurrection-* that is, leaving the body out of the equation, by turning matter to spirit: turning the trick by *becoming* the shadow. And so, the cross of the Shadow Mother, so you can suffer your destiny, while the Mother takes on a devouring quality. Let's look at how Hadewijch reflects your experience."

"Yes, let me quote her"...

Clearly, she memorized the mystic writings of the female martyrs, who recorded their passions and sufferings, and their submission to the god. Nola was addicted to her complex... as I was to mine... in which human love was the shadow to the transcendent, or divine.

And she quoted the mystic, who renounced body for spirit... as Nola had done... I had tried it myself...

"There is nothing Love does not engulf and damn. As Love turns everything to ruin, in Love nothing else is acquired but torture without pity, forever to be in unrest, forever assault and new persecution, to be wholly devoured and engulfed. In her unfathomable essence to founder unceasingly in heat and cold, in the deep insurmountable darkness of Love. This outdoes the torments of hell."[171]

"She also said," I added: *"Let one who is held captive by these chains not cease to eat."**. So, you renounced love," I continued, "rather than being engulfed by it, and yet, were engulfed in the renouncing- like your mother."

"Like my mother... playing both sides of the game, while both sides of her nature were being played by the trickster: by identifying with it, one is crucified on the shadow. The body is broken, like the bread- like the broken body of the god- like she was... like I was... like Leo...and Terzo."

How would *I* break the spell of the father that had broken my body, for I carried his sickness: it nearly had killed me... We transferred it to our sons... the ghost particles inside us... that were charged through the transference, as we confronted the past... and how it ended in death... the death of our sons, that were dying inside us.

I thought of Saint Catherine, serving the Fathers ... and how body as shadow had finally killed her... as if renouncing the body was freeing the self: 'destroying the gift', as we 'gave up our claim' to it'... but kept it in secret, to redeem what we killed... the broken sons of our fathers...the rejected stone of the *Self*... how they live through the transference in the hell of the heart... as if without one another, we would die another death...

She continued to taunt me, confirming my thoughts: "the spirit of our sons extracted from body as shadow... *redeeming the devil*...that invaded the flesh...

"Catherine extracted the feminine spirit of the Christ, through the sickness in the flesh that she 'condemned as a dung heap',[172] representing the devil, or shadow, as the lowest property of matter- *mater*, or mother, excluded from the masculine Trinity: 'the fourth part that is missing'-* the dark side of the *Self*: the part that is 'exiled to hell', and that must be redeemed- like the whore in the Magdalen that took the projection."

"How does Catherine's experience of the feminine relate to your own?" I asked, as I wrestled with the question of the shadow of the father.

"Like Catherine, I felt imprisoned in a feminine body, as I was in Mother Church, under the spell of the Fathers…"Let me quote Raymond di Capua on Catherine's compulsion for Communion and the consuming of the feminine body, to sustain the body of the god"…

"Catherine's longing for frequent Communion was so intense that when she could not receive the body of the Son, her body felt the deprivation."[173]

"As I deny mine, as you deny yours, for we live in our head and need 'Lupa', the beast."

How *could* I deny it- that I needed her, too? How precise, I was thinking… like my longing for you… like a sickness in the body, I was thinking at my peril. But was it I that had thought it, or was it 'Lupa' who was thinking it?

She continued mercilessly…

"And yet, when she did receive it, she could no longer assimilate earthly food"*… I sometimes wonder," she reflected, "if *I* can no longer receive it- not in its literal form, but as the food of the Mother… replaced by the feminized Son, who hung on her body of shadow. Catherine's repulsion for the feminine body may be traced to the Immaculate Conception: for how can a god be born of a human mother? a question I am working on, while deconstructing Christianity. Matter must be spiritualized, if we are to survive its betrayal, or worship the spiritual body that is no longer flesh. When the body is shadow, one chooses death over life."

She might have been analyzing me. "Yet, your shadow has kept you here, for by hating the flesh, it forced you to earth by your whoring, by making you submit."

"Yes," she admitted, "I have almost come down. The submission was unconscious. I will try to surrender… to know the real difference between the true and false sacrifice."

Where could I take her that she had not been?

"You can let me love you," she said, as if I had asked it aloud.

I'll try, I was saying… but only to myself.

CHAPTER 21

NOLA/LUPA

Nora lies 'on the couch' and becomes her own patient. I am finally alone... quickly reversing the thought, as the Lupa in Nola invades the core of her defenses.

'She' wears seven veils that she gradually sheds, confronting 'Nora, her patient', with the self she denies, and reveals that the Salome figure, in Nola's Communion dream, was Nora's shadow personified, defying reason and intellect. Nora begins taking notes, as 'Lupa' intrudes, taunting 'her patient' to break the projection...

She is in every dream now, even the waking ones...Now 'she' intrudes on my thoughts in her usual way- as the voice of the shadow that I am forced to confront: the animal soul driving me into my beast. It takes all my discipline to record what she says, for I am merging with Nola, and want to escape from my body.

'When there is a despising of the body', 'Lupa' says, quoting Jung, *'and a belief in the spirit exclusively, the self desires to die.* It seems you are familiar with the problem, but you prefer to think of it as Nola's. What you call the transference, I call obsession'.

'Lupa' rips off a veil, as I try to deny it. "It's like talking to the devil."

'The devil is an analyst'.

"It would be more practical to be an exorcist."

'Is there really any difference? Remember your Jung, Nora: he says that *Every split in ourselves is eventually personified.* The split in the medieval church was personified by the devil, or *diabolus*, meaning, *splitting apart*. How? by the feminine identifying with the masculine spirit of perfection. You recognize it in yourself, but you prefer to think of it as 'hers'. Now let's eat the god, so we know who we are'.

'She' rips off the second, tossing it in the air.

Like the devil, itself, 'she's' invading my body, but I continue my notes, trying to be more objective...

'Dance for me, Nora, the way you danced in my dream, rending the veils and exposing the wound'.

Again, I have tricked myself by shifting my complex to 'her'. And I return to the projection and continue my theoretical speculations...

'Lupa's' manic defense is personified by the trickster, as in Nola's dream of the priest, who profaned the meaning of the sacrifice- 'her' masochistic fantasy of the annihilating of the feminine.

'*My* manic defense'? 'she' asks, and rips off the third.

"Enough *diabolus*, for the moment," trying to contain her" (I meant to say constrain, but I was afraid it would excite 'her').

'Tired of confessing'? she asks, trying to mock me.

I try to ignore 'her' and continue to write...

It was through the archetypal underpinnings of the Magdalena and the Holy Virgin that 'she' linked the whore and the saint through the medieval church... I try to remind myself... possessed by 'her' shadow.

'You forget that in the core of the martyr complex', 'Lupa' intrudes, 'where the sacred and profane co-exist, that the whore becomes the Virgin, and the Virgin the whore- the whore of the church, who must be 'redeemed' by the Fathers. But it takes a masogynist to make a woman divine, as they continue to disembody her to perpetuate the myth, so she can bear the death of the God, suspended between matter and spirit, who has made her inhuman- like Nola and yourself'.

'She' rips off the fourth, and continues to plague me, calls me one-sided, and points out the whore in me... the whore I was trying to redeem by living in my head. I, too, was under the spell of the Fathers, and was still denying that part of me that I was living through 'Lupa'.

'You have finally understood'. 'She' rips off the fifth.

I am feeling enraged, but force myself to be objective, and continue recording my notes, as 'she' watches me like a ghost...

The anorexic is starving the mother inside 'her', that threatens to consume 'her', so as not to be consumed. In both states, the renouncing and consuming of the poisonous substance is experienced as the destroying of the mother, and the simultaneous creation of her- the act of destruction and creation being utterly confounded.

'You are afraid of the whore in you, Nora. I know why you need me. You have buried the beast in the shadow, in the cage of the past. What are you afraid of?

I am annoyed by 'her' arrogance, but have no choice but to listen. Why don't I ask 'her' to look at 'her' own fear? I thought.

'She' rips off with the sixth. 'I am afraid of loving you, Nora. The intimacy is killing me, and so, I'm conjuring the whore... but I'm not able to find her. I

179

don't want to pretend any longer, and there's so much I haven't told you'.

I could feel a tinge of defensiveness and was afraid to ask what. I could no longer write. I had run out of theories.

'Are you afraid to go down there, Nora- afraid of being devoured? Afraid the pieces won't fit the way you constructed them? Let's talk about the betrayal and why you're so interested in mine. There's the split in the father who defiled you, and who you had to be perfect for: the tyrant who robbed you of the mask of the feminine. You became like a nun, scourging your body for the Virgin, while healing the mind/body split through the communion of analysis'.

For a moment, I hated 'her'.

'Dance for me, Nora, and let's eat what we suffer. Let's eat the god of the spirit, who has the breasts of the Mother. Let's talk about your castrated son, who remained a mother-bound boy, who got fucked by your lover, while he was wearing your clothes, and, dressed in your image, hung himself above your bed'.

'She' strips off the seventh, and I am finally naked-stripped to the core, to the instinctual base... Now, like Herod, 'she' mocks me, but in the voice of the Salome, asking me what I want for dancing the dance... the dance of the shadow that I was trying to repress. 'What are you lusting for, Nora? Is it the head of the saint or the betrayer'?

"*There is no saint without a betrayer.*"[178] But it was a good question, really, and I couldn't make up my mind. I was 'Lupa's' first patient, besides the men she had slain, and she was exploring my shadow side that I once called dark. I represented the Virgin that she tried

to bring down, and how we changed one another is the
mystery of love.

PART TWO

CHAPTER 22

HAWK BOY

Going into Samara's was like entering a tomb. The small room was dominated by a vertical sarcophagus. On the gilded lid of the tomb is a carven image of Horus, revealing his boyish identity that belonged to his mother. The winged Hawk boy, a sun god, presses his finger to his lips, in a burning sun made of hieroglyphs, the symbols of immortality. Behind the sarcophagus is a mural of the underworld, a giant phallus in the center, which is worshipped by the dead. They bow to its power and pray to what's missing. Dismembered body parts encircle it: the ritual offerings to Osiris; a circle of the mummified, like shadows behind the worshippers: vessels of *the Medicine* that contain the secret of transformation.

'Lupa' takes off her clothes and lies on the bed. Samara, naked, is waiting for it, and gazes at her body, as Nola gazes at the image of the god on the tomb. "Tell me about the Hawk boy," knowing she's found what she was looking for.

"Horus, the boy god, has avenged the rage of 'The Red Man', who has killed his father- Osiris, who can awaken the dead. Seth, his envious brother, has dismembered the god, and Isis, his mother, has gathered the pieces, but the phallus is missing, the power of change. Let me fuck you with that missing phallus, to awaken the dead."

"Tell me more if you want it. You must work for it first."

"You're treating me like a trick."

"Of course. You're acting like one."

"I am playing the victim as you act out the myth. Do as you wish, mistress. I will pay for my lust."

"I want more. Give me more. I want the key that will turn it."

"Isis has brought Osiris back to life, so he can give her a son, who will slay the betrayer, the spirit of evil and chaos, who turns life into death, who scattered the pieces of the god on the banks of the Nile. The Mother, the river, is flooding the starving earth, that drives her to death until she awakens the dead."

"And the missing phallus?

"It is eaten by a fish and is more like a rather large clitoris. And now, I will devour you, as if I were that fish."

"*More matter, less spirit*,[180] before you can have me."

"You are difficult to please."

"Even the illusion is expensive."

"I am willing to pay, like the trick that I am. The Hawk boy has dwarf legs to signify his youthfulness, a motherbound boy who will slay the betrayer. He is holding a taut bow and arrow and is surrounded by beasts... Strange, it's like you're writing it in my head; it's as if I am reading it. Do you think that the book will come true?"

"Doesn't it always? We are her creatures, created by the Mother of Madness, who wrote all our myths- a fusion of tales to amuse her, as she scatters our pieces, confounding the mind, until out of the chaos, we create a new order. Now you may fuck me with the missing piece. It will be included in the book."

"Knowing the end, is it worth it, when I know I will lose you?"

"It would never be enough. Perhaps, it would be wiser to imagine it."

"What choice do I have?"

"Are you sure that you want one?"

"I would rather have it and lose it," tastes the fear like a child, lost in the dark. And even while fucking her, Samara was jealous, competing with the dead boy and the son/lover myth. The animal soul was invoked, and the descent was complete, and the eye of Horus was watching as 'the unknown third'.

"It's like Nora is watching," whispered Samara to Nola, who under the spell of the Hawk boy was pressing her finger to her lips. 'Out of the third' was emerging 'the Awakener of the Dead', bringing her boy back to life, who she would nurse to a man. He would be contained in her lover, and reappear through a son, and, as the spirit of 'the third' would bring the dead back to life; while in each incarnation, he would become more complete.

"We better get dressed, we'll be late for the opera," said Samara, more obsessed, after feasting on her flesh (as if 'Lupa' would awaken her and bring her back from the dead). "You will see why I'm taking you. It reveals all your secrets. It's *The Woman Without A Shadow*[181] on the descent of the soul. Like you, she is trying to come down, but she is under a spell," confounding Nola and 'Lupa', and not aware who she fucked.

CHAPTER 23
AFFINITY

They sit in the first row orchestra of the old Metropolitan Opera House- Samara *wooing* her with opera, a kind of emotional blackmail. In a vision, the flute player appears in the image of her son, playing the theme of the Hawk, guiding the hunter with his bow, and is gazing at Nola as the house lights are dimmed; as if drawn by a magnet their gazes lock in the dark. The curtain rises on the likeness of an enchanted waking dream, the empress flooded with light in the body of a white gazelle. The flutist, a Greek androgyne, reminds her of the boy god- trapped in the memory of a boy, avenging the shadow of the father. Terzo seems to be peering through the eyes of the flutist, guiding his mother down to earth, while the Greek plays on his flute, as her son enters his body, to be close to his mother. She sees his reflection through the image of the boy-man, and is irresistibly attracted to what is ancient but new.

Who is she, this woman, who I seem to be playing for? She has the nostrils of a beast, but the royal nose of the empress... the lithe illusion of an animal, but the noble nature of a higher being. Is she the woman in the opera on the mountain of the moon, who my song of the Hawk is guiding on for the descent, as she searches for her shadow, and sees my own in my face?

Nola could feel Nora's eyes, and Samara's fear that she'll lose her, jealously guarding her treasure from the flutist and analyst. Nola turns to the box that Nora is sitting in, where the current is coming from, and their eyes meet for a moment; turns back to the flutist, veiling her feelings, as Samara follows her eyes and mentally stalks her. Meanwhile, the flutist is observing their opera, a drama more spellbinding than the one on the stage: their manner of being and dress in sharp contradiction: the conservative woman in the box, so neutral in demeanor, in contrast to the masculine attire of the foreign woman escort- her mannish suit and black tie, clearly flashing her jewel…

The elegant creature beside her, so apart from the crowd… the black diamond necklace, with the inverted triangular stone, that seems to carry a tale on her dark swan-like neck; her black sheathe of a dress on her angular body; the legs, slightly bowed, releasing the arrow of her will; the high tilt of the head; the mane of dark hair; the strong graven features; the dusky face, like the earth, so ancient but here… and yet… not really at all: so foreign by nature, from another time than our own, and who, unphased by the mob, belongs to herself.

Who could he be, with his Greek god-like self? the charmed androgyne boy-man, who has brought Terzo home… but not really like him… more here in this world… the knowing hands on his instrument; the dark hair knows its way; his suit knows his form, something made of the earth… and yet, a stranger… like I am… guiding me down… as he tells the tale of the music and I receive it inside…

The hunter, led by my Hawk, with the voice of my flute, is tracking the empress, who has taken the form of a beast, and is spellbound by spirit on the mountain of the moon. Her magical talisman is lost, her only means of transformation, and, under the spell of the uncon-scious, she is without a 'human shadow'…

She's like the empress in the opera in the body of a white gazelle, the boy-man is thinking, as he is playing his flute

Like Snow's ethereal mare... like the mother within me... who, in the thrall of the beast is caught in a spell. I hear the voice of the Hawk invoking the god, gazing into my soul... in the guise of my son...

He continues to send her the song of the Hawk on his flute, and the tale she is watching, like a waking dream of her own... She remembers the story… as if the tale were own… on the mountain of The Mother, trapped in the body of a beast… the soul of her mother… like the empress on the moon…

The hunter is trying to bring the empress to earth; his red Hawk perched on her forehead, striking her eyes; the wound of love that awakens her, brings him back from the dead. The hunter tries to protect her, striking its eyes with his dagger, and the Hawk weeps tears of blood that she must suffer her shadow. She must make the descent and accept being human, for 'she is the bridge across the gulf, over which the dead return to life.[184]

His hooded eyes like the Hawk are striking at Nola's, and they are transported through time, as the two women watch. Samara is steeped in self-hatred for having arranged it, as Nora had done, and they knew they would lose her.

Nola, alone in the Russian Tea Room (as it was in '63, a haunt for dancers, musicians, singers, and writers), sips a pepper vodka with caviar, while writing her book. It is coming right through her- the descent of her son. The flutist watches from his table, across from her own, but he is also inside her, eyes searching her soul. She is thinking of Terzo, how 'time turned into space'; how once in a tearoom in Paris, they met between worlds…He's reappeared in the flutist- she sees her son in the man. Her eyes fasten on Philos, who is watching her write... his eyes like her son's as he looked through the window...

Just as it was, it is happening now, and, as she unravels the plot, he composes a song. Now she is writing the lyrics, as if she can hear it, and orders more vodka and caviar for him and herself. The waiter follows her to his table, and she hands him the lyrics. He hands her the score, and they study their shadows: it's alive in the notes that are haunting the moment...

"You have given yourself," he says in a heavy Greek accent.

"What would you call it?" she asks.

"I was going to ask you."

"I would call it *The Huntress and the Hawk*- the spiritual companion of the hunt." And they knew the gods were in the mix, who had interceded for the catch.

"What were you writing before the words to our music?"

"I was writing the Hawk boy, when you enter the tale, and began the chapter called Affinity. Funny, it seemed like your name."

"Yes, I am in it. It's not strange- it is I: Philos: affinity. The gods must have told you."

"Yes, they are in it, and it's beyond either one of us. My affinities are in the spirit realm, and earth has been nothing but shadow. But the hunter made me hungry, for the spirit is at work. Let's dine and we'll talk, so we can know who we are."

"My thought exactly. And yours?

"Nola Lupa," as her two selves come together, his spirit healing the split...

"Nola Lupa... It sounds like you. Let's go to the opera house first, so I can play you *The Huntress*, and enchant you with my flute- the voice of the Hawk that is coming through me."

"Yes, we will hear it, and hold our hunger together. I have learned when one is hungry, one must wait till it's unbearable, for it's important to appreciate the power of the instinct," striking each other in the eyes with the tale of two selves, that have met in the dark and are stricken with light.

"Come, I will play it for you, and you can tell me if it's ours."

Philos opens the stage door of the old Met Opera House. They enter the stage through the wings, and he plays the song on the piano. She drinks his spirit through his eyes as she listens entranced, her son crossing the bridge between the living and the dead.

"It sounds so familiar- it's like the voice of my soul, and the words that I wrote with the blood of my eyes... the pure extension of the notes that have come from inside you"...

She incants the words as he plays, and they wander through time...

> You found me broken in the gutter,
> my splayed and broken limbs
> earthbound
> to the turning wheel of chance,
> mended my wounded wings
> and carried me home,
> setting me free in the forest:

but like the Hawk that returns
to his master's wrist,
you clasped me with your talons
and gave me strength
for further flight.
Borne by fate you lured my soul
back
that abandoned my lifeless body,
and with the self-same poison
that had slayed it,
you healed the failed and closing heart
with the magic draught of love
and made it human,
nursed my will
back
to the wounded earth,
until you won me
and it bowed before you,
my friend and savior,
my believer,
who redeemed and blessed me.

And so, in their dinner at the Twenty-One (as it was in '63), during oysters and Cristal, drinking her in with his eyes: "Who are you, my soul, the Huntress or the Hawk?"

"I am the woman who is trapped in the body of a beast, but the three are as one, and are a kind of 'lower trinity'."

"We will work together and tour the world. You will write the words, and I the music, for the form and the spirit have finally met. "

"To Apollo and Dionysus- the form and the spirit."

They toast.

"And to the goddess of the hunt, disguised in human form," he says to her soul that is listening to his own.

CHAPTER 24
HUNTRESS

1941. Philos, a prodigy of twelve, studies a score he has written, and waits for his father, the fear in his eyes. He knows what is coming, and he tightens his nerves. His father enters the room and takes the score from his hands.

"Take off your clothes, Philos, and lie face down."

"Why papa?" asks the boy, pretending he doesn't know.

"Do as I say."

The boy tries to bear it as his father molests him; as he conjures his mother, a virtuoso violinist... playing his flute with his mother at her concert in Athens; how she was praised and adored and received a standing ovation; he remembers how he loved her... as his father forced his way into him... When it is finally finished, the boy grabs his flute, and runs through the vineyard- it belongs to his father. He sinks to the earth, crushing the grapes in his fist, passes out in the vines and dreams his revenge:

A wild boar in the vineyard is eating everything in sight. Artemis the Huntress, the Lady of the Beasts, 'aims her arrow at its heart'[188] and it dies a violent death. 'She rips its heart from its breast and' feeds her wolf, who 'devours it'*, as the image of the boar changes to the image of his father.

When he awakened, he seduced a beautiful shepherd, the one he watched every day as he was fucking a sheep. He makes love to him in a frenzy, getting drunk on his father's wine. Then they romped with the goats through a field of red poppies, singing the old peasant songs that had turned into myths.

He jumped on a sheep truck on its way to the harbor, and stowaways on a cargo ship, from Piraeus to Le Havre.

A year and he is playing Bach's *Partita in A minor*, at the Paris Conservatory, a demanding piece for solo flute; it is far beyond his years, and he is the youngest to be accepted, and is praised for the mastery of his penetrating instrument. The male musician, who is teaching it, watches his performance with interest. Later, Philos seduced him, and they are kissing in the dressing room A year later, in Paris, he is playing his flute in a salon, charming the dilettantes, who are fascinated with the boy. A woman painter of thirty takes a fancy to Philos; and, as she poses him naked, he seduces the woman. She keeps him for a while, until he tires of her love, and goes on to the next like an insatiable child. At eighteen, a famed virtuoso in the Vienna Philharmonic, he seduces his female analyst, as she interprets his dream. But it was never like Nola-only Nola was enough for him.

CHAPTER 25
MUMIA

Still 1963, they perform in a theater in Paris. The fans are calling for Nola. She keeps them waiting a moment- listens in the wings, till it builds in intensity, and appears on the stage as the audience swoons. She bows to her adorers and Philos enters beside her. They go even wilder, and they bow to one another. He plays the theme of the Hawk, Nola incanting their song. In Rome and Madrid, a full house of converts. Now back in New York, they perform in Carnegie Hall. Nola can feel Nora's presence, as she watches from a box; Nola incanting *The Huntress*, her eyes fixed on Nora; closes her lids and imagines a life without Nora.

After the performance, on a dark premonition, Nola goes to Samara's. There is a stream of blood from the tomb. It runs through the threshold. She opens the door. Turns the head of the Hawk on the lid of the sarcophagus. A dagger extends from the left 'eye of Horus': the mythical moon eye that is wounded by Seth- the god of betrayal and chaos that pierces Samara's, a stream of blood flowing from it, staining her palm. Hung on a nail in the tomb is a small ancient Hawk mummy, and clutched in its talons, a suicide note...

> I leave my body to Nola, who abandoned me in the underworld.
> I will wait for her there, until she is ready to receive me- Mumia, the mummy, who loved like the Hawk.

Nola goes for a session, with the Hawk and the note. It was the time of Samara's that once was her own. She throws her arms around Nora at her Patchin Place door, holding her close, while Nora pretends she can bear it.

"I have come for her session. Samara is dead."

Both struggle with their conscience, coming to terms with the shadow.

Nola lies 'on the couch', holding the mummy. Its left eye is pierced. Nola's left eye is bleeding. Nora sits in her chair, holding the note. A moment passes, till she is able to speak: tells Nola the myth… to put it in context…

"In the myth, the eye of Horus, like the phallus, was a symbol of power. During the dark of the moon, Horus was blinded by the Red Man- stabbed in the left eye, the moon-eye…the eye of the moon…"

"The shadow of the moon- the eye of the unconscious. What sense can we make of it? I want to find meaning in it."

"In Jung's words: The unpredictable behaviour of Trickster, his pointless orgies of destruction and self-appointed sufferings are a gradual humanization, and are just the transformations of the meaningless into the meaningful- but it also works in reverse."

"Again, I helped the trickster to reverse it, to turn life into death. Without me, she may have been able to live… If I hadn't been tempted by the trickster… and helped him turn the trick."

"In alchemy, 'The Red Man'- the opposite of 'The 'Red Man' in the myth- is the reordering of the elements, so they are no longer in enmity, and like the Hawk mummy, a symbol of transformation and immortality: *Mumia*, the Medicine can bring the dead back to life, and is also a play in the note on the Mother of death and transformation."

"So, the *Mother* is the trickster, and is behind the trickster *animus*: a cunning aspect of *Mercurius*, who escapes prematurely from the bottle... and is so hard to contain: so hard it consumes us."

"He is the spirit of the thief, who reverses the play of opposites, but he steals what is necessary for the new to appear, and again, she reversed it. When the son's eye was wounded and miraculously restored, it became the symbol for the reunifying of Upper and Lower Egypt, signifying the renewal or resurrection after the darkness of death."

"And so, the Hawk mummy is a talisman for a new order that is deathless."

"If one doesn't turn the trick," Nora replied...

How will I work with it, Nora wondered, when I am so attached to the result? I must remind myself that my own part is happening within, that I have not acted out my fantasies, that the relationship is still intact. "We should talk about your regression," Nora is saying, "and how you fled to the senses," sparing her nothing: "how in the compulsion to escape, you tried to destroy the analysis, and carried out your experiment outside my door."

"I was, also, escaping the fear of loving you, Nora... and how I destroy what I love, but the fear was displaced: I destroyed Samara, instead- by tempting her love- the perversion of love, I was unable to return. Can I forgive myself, Nora, instead of asking it of *you*?... But why escape the second question that is already taunting me? What is the worst fear of all? not being able to leave you, and how it would be if we were free, and we were outside your door?"

"I would say that all three questions are relevant: but the fourth even more so, as you are leaving it out- whether by design or repression. Why leave your shadow at the door of your analyst?"

"Are you asking, was it the fear of being earthbound, without my compulsion for flight?"

"The fear of the binding of love, and so the *compulsion* to destroy love, and, yes, that it binds you to earth- the earth you are trying to deny; the fear of the analytic death that precedes throwing light on the shadow- the fear of losing the compulsion that you have managed to survive- the fear of making it conscious and being unable to re-enact it."

"The eighth fear, that you have got me, and that it is only you who can do it- the number of infinity with its infinite impossibilities... the fear of love's shadow... of *drowning* in the *Self*... the fear of loving you, Nora. But isn't that nine?... three squared like the moon with its impossible phases. And what would we *do* if we were outside your door? Would we be able to sustain the intensity, without burning it out?... Would we finally know our own shadow... or want to dissolve in the Mother? And are we already writing it, while we are trying to deny it, and believe we can renounce it, and can *bear* the renouncing?"

"Isn't that twelve- one for each saint?"

"Fourteen for the pieces of Osiris that were dismembered by 'the Red Man'- that were searched by the Mother in the Stations of the Cross.

She gives the Hawk mummy to Nora: "And the doubling of the trickster, turning its poison to love: the *fear* of the poison of love, and not being able to heal it."

CHAPTER 26
'THE *MEDICINE*'

1966. Nola is lecturing this day at the University of Padua, before a recital with Philos in Venice that night. She alluded to their trysting place as the *Isle of the Dead*- a somber landscape by Bocklin, where she could be with her son. She crosses the Grand Canal in a gondola at the Danielli, and enters the basilica of Santa Maria della Salute', where once the saints were protected in the church from the plague, and prays to the Mother for the souls of the dead, and that the plague of the heart would be banished by love.

On the boat from Venice to Padua, Shelley's *Alastor* came to mind, the 'evil genius' that was guiding him on his journey to death, who sailed to infinity, lost in his visions and dreams; and she saw the image of her son as the disappointed poet, driven by the mythic Alastor towards the tragic ideal... and Terzo... his death... the mythic hero of his mother.

Her lecture in the medieval university on the *anima mundi* was based on the work of Marsiglio Ficino, the Renaissance priest of the Florentine Cathedral- a Christian scholar who taught theology at the University of Padua, and who was one of the fathers of Neoplatonic Hermeticism, condemned by the Inquisition and nearly burned as a heretic. She explored it in terms of linking all opposites, and bringing the irreconcilable into a mystical unity: psychology, alchemy, the Kabbalah, and Gnosticism, combined with the philosophy and polytheism of the Greeks and Egyptians, the understanding of the stars, and the dynamic principles of the universe.

She began with a question in her usual way: "So. What *is* the *anima mundi*, and what is its function?" But not a soul dared to answer, and she doubled the question: "What is this universal soul linking spirit and matter that bridges the Word and the image in the heart of Hermes, or *Mercurius*- the god of medicine, wisdom, philosophy and the mysteries, who allows us to go down to the underworld and to return to the earth? In Neoplatonic Hermeticism, the dead become gods and spiritualize matter through the life of the soul. Their spirit reanimates the dead parts of the self, for 'the stars in the blood' are linked to the dead stars in space. In the reciprocal relationship between spirit and matter, the dead and living are one, for each is transforming the other."

There was a pale fragile creature, with a translucence of skin, who was hung on her words and mesmerized by her presence.... The slavish look in her eyes... It had the look of Samara's, and, in truth, they were twinned, for Samara had entered her body, whose desire had driven her back to the earth. She saw her face coming through her and then disappear, but continued her discourse, containing herself...

"It was a linking philosophy that receded into silence, during the terrors of the church and the Holy Inquisition, reaching its climax in the Renaissance with the burning of 'heretics'. Its teachings reappeared in the 17th century, despite the grip of orthodoxy and the teachings of the church. It lost its spiritual influence with the ascendency of materialism and the rational methodology of the literal sciences in the Enlightenment, which denied the life of the soul and the reality of spirit."

The girl continues to stare at her with an unnerving intensity. Now she is clasping her hands and seems to be praying, seized by the spirit of Samara and her unrequited need.

"For Ficino, *the anima mundi is the cosmos, and is itself an animal, more unified than any animal, the most perfect animal, linking the symbolic, material, and spiritual*.[196] Here, it is the animal soul that carries 'the instinct for meaning',[196a] expressed in the primal emotions of the religious experience. Ficino's words remind us: *We are not only the passive recipients of the* influences exerted by the *anima mundi*, but we can also influence the universe. *Let no man wonder*, says Ficino, '*that the world soul can be allured by material forms, since she herself has created baits of this kind, and willingly dwells in them.*"[196b]

The girl swoons and faints. Nola passes a vial under her nose. She had experienced such reactions when she had lectured before. She immediately revives her, who pretends she's inside her: but *who* is inside *her?* the question Nola is asking.

"Do try to control yourself," whispers Nola. It seems you are needing attention."

'Yes mistress', says Luce, who responds through Samara. "Luce," says the girl. "My name is Luce.... like the light."

Nola blanches. Steps back. And returns to the podium. She continues her lecture, as if nothing had happened, voice steady and concentrated, her thoughts directed and controlled, *using* the conflict, which she almost has mastered.

"We can see why Ficino was almost burned at the stake, though, in essence, this is the mystery of the

Immaculate Conception, for what we are talking about is 'bringing spirit down to matter'[196c] How would we do this, we ask, but my making the unconscious conscious? for it is not the feminine that needs redeeming, but the *concept* of matter- 'the devil' personified by the *fear* of the feminine, in conflict with spirit, as it was in the medieval Christian church.

"It is said that *Adam was created a lifeless statue,*[197] like the Virgin Mary, 'sinless,' who must be re-animated with spirit. And why does she need to be re-animated? Because her image has been split by the fear and envy of the patriarchy, and emptied of libido by the masculine projection- a projection *we* have taken of a 'woman without a shadow', till we have become like the statue that must be re-animated."

They know what she means and they burst into laughter. Her satiric smile has incited it, but she is now deadly serious, and continues relentless to sharpen the point. "When a woman has no shadow, she is merged with the shadow of the *animus*, the masculine spirit that is driving it out of her, and, in the name of redemption, makes 'the devil' desirable. This medieval problem still persists in the unconscious, for women are looking at their reflection through the masculine eye. Yet, this problem allows us to discover the profoundest mystery in alchemy, combining philosophy, religion, mythology and mysticism, and most important of all a psychology that links them...

"When the lifeless statue receives the idealized projection, as it does with the Virgin, we see the basis of art; the secret inherent in the philosopher's stone, and with it the secret of bringing the dead back to life: and so, the Son of the Mother, who rises to consciousness: the resurrection made possible through the *anima mundi*. Alchemy tells us, 'the Water of Life that comes from the hearts of statues may have been Egyptian sarcophagi, or portrait statues. An Egyptian alchemist was reported to have removed the mummies from Egyptian tombs that were meant to possess medicinal value'...[198] that could make the dead rise... and inhabit the living."

Nola sees Luce's face, again reflecting Samara's, and again, the girl faints, Nola feigning indifference. A group of girls crowd around her. "Leave her alone," Nola says. 'She will return when she's ready'... 'Lupa's' words from a dream... the dream of her son... the dream she returned from when she awoke in her mother's house... the dream of his death... the death of her son... her son who inhabits the body of Philos... In my dream...

'Lupa' was holding the corpse of her son and was watching his soul depart from his flesh. It had taken the form of a body of light, a translucent spirit that would endure after death. 'Death is not the end, you will return when you're ready', 'Lupa' said to his spirit, as it fled from the earth.

"For this reason," she continues, *bits of corpses were sold in European pharmacies*, known as *mumia, and were used for alchemical purposes as the poison and antidote*,* the spark in dark matter that arose from the union of opposites. *Mumia balsamita*, or *Medicina* was the elixir of immortality- the revivifying poison of the *anima mundi*: the mediating or uniting agent, and the *Mercurius* itself, both masculine and feminine, the sun and the moon, each hidden and revealed in the sacred substance of the other.

"The pagans made statues of *Mercurius* who kept changing his form, from the primeval nature of chaos into the stone of the philosophers. Plato tells us that *inside these statues was a hidden image of the god, who often held a pipe or a flute,*[199] symbolizing the spirit in matter, known to be a symbol of transformation, and that contained all the opposites... as if they were one," lapsing into the present, as she watches it happening.

The class is re-animated, but Luce is unconscious. She wants Nola, not knowledge, and Samara knows how to get it.

CHAPTER 27
RETURN OF THE DEAD

Later, in the Danielli, when they were resting for the recital, Nola had the dream of the Huntress that he had in his youth, with other elements included that roused a dark premonition...

She is standing in the ruins of an ancient Greek temple, surrounded by the vineyards of his father, with the purple grapes of Dionysus. Artemis is in the distance in a field of white poppies, stretching her bow to an extreme as she aimed at a boar.
Philos is sitting on the roots of an ash tree, playing his flute as a Hawk circled above him, and began its descent to the earth for its prey. The shepherd was slitting the throat of a sheep, its blood staining the poppies to give them their redness.
Terzo and Nola are watching the sacrifice, as the blind prophet, Tiresias, is telling Philos his fate: that he'll murder his father, like Oedipus, and marry his mother (confounding his fate in a fusion with Terzo's). 'Two snakes are coiled at the prophet's feet- the symbol of incest that he separated with his rod'.[200] The boar changes its form to the father of Philos, as "the arrow of Artemis strikes at his heart. Like a savage she devours it,"[*] wiping the blood from her mouth.

Nola is coming to consciousness, knowing that Philos is the sacrifice; as Philos is fucking her into reality, and she prays for his life, knowing the end. "No one's ever fucked me like that, except--" But I felt guilty for comparing the living with the dead.

"Except?" he is asking.

"Well, I've been fucked by the spirit, and some things are beyond us," wishing as I said it, it was not as it was.

Philos is suddenly vulnerable. "I couldn't bear to have a *human* rival."

"If I wanted to be fucked by a human, it would not be you that I found. You don't have to worry: no human can have me."

"Neither do you. No worry there... but just the same, it feels dangerous to need you like I do. What if I joined them, your spirits, and abandoned my body? Would you be able to tell me apart from the others?"

I was feeling the danger that my darkness would claim him... like it did all the others... and was already mourning him. My son and his spirit were like one single being, and the door of the heart seemed to shatter as the gods tossed the dice...

"What did you dream?" he was asking, sensing his fate.

"I dreamed of the labyrinth of psyche, and was lost in its turns... while the bulldancers of spirit were tumbling as acrobats, and had become one another on the backs of the bulls. The bulls were the gods, and we turned on ourselves- and we were the dancers- you, me, and Terzo...

"In my dream you were fucking me into reality. I never loved you as much as I did at that moment, but I was drunk on the blood... the blood of the god: the blood of the sacrifice, and the gods were as one: the god Dionysus, who was devoured by the instinct, disguised as the maenads, who could not get enough, and the Hawk in the boy, who descends for his prey."

"You love the boy in me, Nola, and were dreaming of my boyish reality, but you have made me a man, and I will always be with you in spirit," as if he were living the real dream and knew how I changed it. I smiled at the boy in him, but inside I was shaken, as he played at his innocence, like he did as a child.

"Why do I never stop wanting you? Not even death can destroy love," as if he were playing the flute for an opera he wrote.

She was dressing for the performance, while he was stripping her clothes off. Throws her down on the bed, and was taking her like a beast...

He infused me with spirit, while he was fending off death, and the door of the tomb was opening and closing... for it was already written... and, somehow, we knew.

They were performing in the garden of the Palazzo Ducale. The students from the lecture were awaiting her appearance, along with Venetian society, for whom Philos was their darling. They enter the garden to a standing ovation; Luce, mesmerized in the first row, possessed by Samara; she is focused on Nola with the same manic intensity.

Nola makes an announcement, changing the program, Philos masking his terror, like she taught him to do.

"To begin, I will write a song in the moment, inspired by the spirit of Venice, where the dead are investing the souls of the living."

She rips up the music they decided to play and throws the pieces to the wind that disappeared in the dark. It was always uprooting, though he was used to her changes, while the mood of the audience changed with her words, their aura of fear woven into the piece.

I will call it *Return*, for the dead are with us tonight. They are in the room and it's a dark song, for those who wander in the depths. She begins to incant it from the ninth circle of hell, and the depth of her voice reflects the mournful tone of the dirge. It is coming right through her and is linking the worlds, while she is trying to vanquish his death and to keep him on earth...

> Again, the call in the night
> that awakened the dead
> and coaxed the stars
> into being,
> till the dust became flesh.
> The world was deaf and dumb
> but it listened and trembled,
> and watched with its blind eyes
> as the god descended,
> the wind parting like a curtain,
> baring his broken body
> that once had been whole
> and was dismembered by love.
> Again, the call in the night
> as he dies to be born,
> in us
> who are lost
> and are alone on the earth.
> Again, the call in the night,
> for the dead have returned.

A chill ran through the audience, ripping right through them, as the fear mixed with longing, and the longing with pain. And the dead bowed to the living, and knew they existed.

She has done it, thought Philos... They are coming for *me*...

They were there. He could see them. Only Terzo was missing. And why was he missing?... 'cause he was living inside him.

CHAPTER 28
HEART OF THE STATUE

Nola lies 'on the couch', broken by grief; her words shatter like glass, as she weeps to unknowing, passing into unconsciousness, as in a dark waking dream. Nora, lucid, lugubrious, waits in the silence, as Nola emerges from some unnameable place... reconstructing 'the dream', till she is able to speak... fitting the parts to the whole, like a story she wrote... as if she could still change the ending... and bring him back from the dead...

"I returned to our house on Campo di Fiori in Rome, while Philos was touring, and was alone with myself... At last I'm alone... but why am I thinking it? I was planting the calla lilies on my luxuriant roof garden- the part of the roof that was facing the square, when I suddenly realized I was feeling ob-served. I looked down at the marketplace, as if in a dream, and saw the girl from my class, holding a hundred white calla lilies, her eyes raised to heaven, as if she were praying... Other followers came to mind that I had attracted through the years, but I continued planting the lilies, absorbed in their beauty... in the death of my mother... and son... the white flowers of death...

"The obsessive ritual continued for three endless days, and had begun to get eerie... but there was something erotic about it. I tried to justify the urge, and to put aside the guilt... Philos was playing in Prague, why not have a fling? I need a distraction... something meaningless and light... something to take me from the darkness and transplant me on the earth. It had been several weeks since the dark dream of death...   a projection, I thought... but something else was at work. I performed an exorcism on myself: the compulsion to escape, and looked down from above... it was like a waking dream. She seemed to beg for my body- what I was always a sucker for... and I asked her to come... followed by a moment of dread...

"Still, I invited her to my study for what I thought was an interview. Yes, I needed a secretary... for the bookings... and arrangements... They had become overwhelming and I needed some help... I tried not to realize that she was part of the plot, and like my dream of Communion, I defied what I knew: acting it out... as if it were already written... written by what?... when it was I who was writing it... Her name was Luce... something light... as light as a ghost... a spirit stranded in space that was seduced down to earth... It was only after I hired her that I remembered the interview... the one I forgot... and had held in the senses: a fatal mistake that would change the course of my life...

"She was rather beautiful, in a way: pale skin and blue eyes, the ethereal body of a wraith that was waiting to be defiled; something delicious about her, with a lost look of hunger, as she stared at my breasts like a young starving animal. It was the kind of fantasy I am prey to, when I want to escape."

"Have you ever been with a woman, Luce?" I heard myself asking.

"Only you, in a dream. I had to make the dream real."

"I'm going to show you what it's like, until you beg me to stop," and I laid her down on the couch, as I slipped off her underwear; studied her genitals like a scientist, testing the theory of light: teasing her thighs, till the girl was delirious"...

Samara's voice interrupts as her spirit enters the session: 'It was the contradiction that excited her, between the animal and physicist. It made her feel more important, like it was recorded in history'...

'Please never stop', begged the likeness of Luce.

"I don't intend to," said 'Lupa'. Not till you beg for your life," turning her over and smacking her bottom. And so, it began, with the delirium of the senses. I showed her what to do and she learned how to do it. She also answered my fan mail, and was doing my proofreading, tended my garden, and served every fantasy. What did *Luce* want to do? She really didn't know, besides being my slave, and learning to *be*. Soon she was calling me 'Lupa' and had a touch like Samara... hung on my words... like Samara..."

"And still you didn't stop," Nora said.

'She couldn't', said Samara. 'I was counting on that. She was caught in the compulsion, romancing the dead; escaping from love, but obsessed with her son; escaping from Philos... could only *find* him in Philos'.

"I did *not* want to find him," said Nola... I couldn't *bear* not to find him..."

'Still splitting body and spirit', Samara was saying.

"It was tearing me in two."

"And 'the third'?" Nora asked.

"It was lost in the dark... only found in the dark... found in the shadow of Philos... When he came back from Prague... Luce was jealous and possessive, and was compensating by attending him. I taught her to suck him (I was bored with it from whoring); to iron his shirts; be his page turner; arrange his life and his music. When we had business meetings for recitals,

Luce served the guests. She made reservations in restaurants, for the opera and theater; booked the rooms, boats, and planes, and was running the house, and with occasional glitches things seemed to run smoothly."

"Did you ever wonder," Nora asked, "why you needed a slave?"

"I was the slave of my will, while I was playing the master... caught in the game, while I was tossing the dice... He couldn't bear her obsession with me, and that she was serving his needs. I gave her a room on the roof... where she would pretend to be alone... and feed the Hawk in the aviary with the doves that she bought... the Egyptian cat I was spoiling... that belonged to Samara."

Samara, in a lotus position, descends on Nola's hips, where she pretends to be meditating, and gives her version of the tale. Nora studies the spirit- as if she still was a patient, and nearly asked, like she used to, if she had brought in a dream.

'You began to ignore me', said the spirit, 'as you ignored me in life. I was your instrument of pleasure when Philos was away, but when he was there Luce would wait until bidden. This way, *things* seemed to take their allotted place in the universe, as you and 'Lupa' conceived it, by the god of the moment- for *things* had mutable boundaries, and those that didn't you tired of. But how did Philos conceive it, this *thing's* obsession with Nola? Though Philos was used to her acolytes and to others serving his oral needs- and, for that matter, Nola's, which were becoming excessive- with his finely tuned intuition, he felt Luce's envy, and was aware that she hated him, despite her talent for hiding it. But he also knew that without Luce, she would be searching the alleyways, and that being bored with her slave was his only security.

'Though Luce was a self-denying masochist', Samara continued, 'like any girl in her position, she got her power by serving, and knowing the needs of her mistress, she began to believe she possessed her'.

"I was not unaware," Nola said, "of the Samara pattern of the martyr complex, but Luce seemed more benign, more accepting of her passivity... and again, I denied what I knew and began to believe it. Philos could not imagine such evil- an almost natural malignancy, for his father dominated the shadow side, and there was little room for *other* demons."

Samara's etheric body lies 'on the couch' next to Nola, and tells how she mastered her mistress, who believed she controlled her...

'Luce had been playing the flute on the roof and was trying to emulate his style, as he played the song of the Hawk, trying to block out her notes (what was worse, Luce was tone-deaf and hated his talent). He spoke to Nola about it, who refused to listen to reason, as if Luce was appointed by the *Self* to create a new order. But my cat was found dead and he knew Luce had killed it, for my animal hunger was arousing her own.

'When 'Lupa' no longer wanted him, he got one of his boys to 'amuse' him, but it was Nola he longed for, who now was distant and withdrawn, wholly absorbed in her son and her fantasies of death. He was arranging their tours to have her all to himself, but the more obscure the destination, the more women she seduced. There was a growing fear taking hold of him that he could not compose without her words, could not breathe without her breath, who was the force that gave him life'.

The voice of Philos intrudes and continues telling the story...

'Our venues were packed with the fans of her book, that became a bible for women coming out of their cage. Armies of lesbians followed, to every theater, in every town, and though I no longer doubt-ed she loved me, my rivals were relentless. One night on our tour, I had a dream of my death'...

'There was a horde of Amazon women that were going to kill me, and a procession of mourners lamenting my love. A life-size statue of Nola, shrouded in black, was standing on a platform that was drawn by four horses. My open coffin was behind it and I could see my own corpse, while my shadow was playing the song of the Hawk. Then from her heart rushed a fountain with the Water of Life. I wanted to drink but the women kept fending me off, and, as they mumbled a prayer, the leader cut off my head. She thrust a pole through my neck, a sign of her victory, while the horde worshipped the statue and drank from its breast'...

'Nola was dreaming my dream'...

'Don't let them take you, Philos! Drink! Drink the Water! Don't let them take you'!

'She said in her sleep. And she woke up in terror, and woke me from mine'. "Why are you weeping, Philos?" 'she asked, in the way that she had, pretending death wasn't happening, as if she could alter my fate. I didn't tell her my dream- she was already dreaming it, already dying my death that she knew was her own, and that I loved her too much and had lost her to Terzo (his jealousy consumed me... he wanted her all to himself)'.

"I know that it's true, she was saying... but something else is at work."

'Only then did I realize, she knew that her son had invested me, and that 'the incest taboo' had won out in the end- for what was taboo was alluring (she was never able to resist), and her incestuous feelings were at the heart of the attraction.

'Do you mind if we cancel our tour? I have a strange premonition', 'I said'.

"So do I," 'she replied', "I had a dream of my death."

'She was not letting on that the death she dreamed of was mine, and that her own was a psychic death, as real as my own.

'Promise me, Nola', 'I said', 'that you will fire that false pagan you converted, who can't make up her mind whether she wants to be me or yourself'.

"I promise you, darling. I thought the same thing. We must have had the same dream. She will be gone tomorrow, I promise."

'I tried to believe it- that I was escaping my fate. We returned to Rome, to the house, but Luce was playing the flute. I slept deeply that night, but I never woke up, for Luce, moved by Samara, put three drops in each ear- the poison of envy that had taken her life. In my sleep, which was endless, I knew I was deaf, and Luce knew Nola would leave me if I was unable to play. Just to be sure, Luce slit my throat like a sheep, and Nola awoke in my blood and prayed in my essence till dusk. Then she called the authorities and told them she killed me'.

Nola arrived for her session the following day, throwing the paper on the analytic couch. Nora glanced at the lurid headline in the Roman arts newspaper...

TROPPA WRITES HER OWN END AND MURDERS HER LOVER

"And Luce?" Nora asked.

"She was arrested for murder and admitted to 'a crime of pure passion'; she confessed that the pieces of corpses known as *mumia* were the poison of love that influenced her and the universe: 'that 'Lupa' taught me to extract it from the god with the flute, *for the world soul can be allured by material forms, as she herself has created baits of this kind and willingly dwells in them'*, adding: 'My soul was allured by the soul of my mistress, but I cannot be a pagan, like she wanted me to be. An invisible being is not *always* exempt, and I was the sacrifice, protecting my mistress from the Hawk', confounding the authorities with her philosophical contradictions. The psychologist reported that she had three distinct personalities: a Christian martyr, an Egyptian whore, and a psychopathic medium."

"It seems she had a fourth personality- yours," said Nora. "And in your own martyr complex, you believed you killed him, again... the son you rejected that returned in your lover. Tell me, do you still believe you are responsible for everything that lives and dies? That an unconscious thought has the power to kill?"

"Of course, I believe it. It happened again. I did it by influencing the uninitiated and seducing the dead."

"And now you are mourning your freedom?"

"I am mourning his love. It is madness to love me. I *kill* for my freedom... and to free my lovers from my will, who are like doves in its cage, and are sacrificed to the Hawk- the boy that *feeds* on my love, and wants it all for himself... that he never had in his life."

'Love is death', said Samara, 'but the verdict was life'. And her spirit dissolved, bringing the session to an end.

CHAPTER 29
SAINT OR SINNER?

Three years passed with Philos: it was 1966, and I returned to 'The Mother' and the lonely mountain I was born on: renounced three years of my life for each life I had taken (my father didn't count- I could go to heaven for the act).

Today, I entered the church and communed with her darkness, and laid the black diamond necklace at the foot of her cross. I spoke in the fusion of tongues that I conceived as a child, when I was hiding the secrets that her shadow revealed...

"I've returned to you, Mother, to take refuge in your darkness. Death has taught me to love, with no one left to receive it. Permit me to find you and to be in your presence a while, to know the soul of all things, and to live an interior life."

The Reverend Mother, now close to death, enters the church. I am kissing her hand. "I am ready now, Mother, to give myself to God, but I'll be needing your help to accept my own vows; naturally, they can *only* be mine, and not those of the church."

"Naturally. I know something of your spirit, and in what way you will need me. Come, Nola Lupa, I will show you your cell. It once was your mother's. You were nearly born in that cell, but you refused to emerge, till your mother was laid at her feet. She has accepted your offering and the vow you have made."

I look up at her face that is veiled by her shadow, and her Son who is nailed on his Mother the cross.

Then I go to the statue of the young Magdalena, where I played hide-and-seek with my thief of a saint, and enter the cell of my mother- nothing there of the senses. Only God and a pen: it is enough for me now. My pen is my analyst, fused with the image of Nora. She is all that exists now… only Nora… and the dead. I sit at the desk and write her a letter (why write to the dead- they are already inside me).

> Dear One,
> I am at the Mother of God 'taking the veil'. Our work has prepared me for it. Without it, I would not want to live. Nola Lupa

The bells begin ringing. Nola exits her cell. The nuns are all leaving theirs and enter the Reverend Mother's, as the priest gives the last rites and makes the sign of the cross. The Mother is asking for Nola, and she goes to her bed. Kneels down before her and kisses her hand…

"Your mother gave me a message for you, the day she took Terzo. 'Tell Nola', she said, veiling her wounds, though I never knew her, I pray for her soul every night, and I hold her in my dreams, as I never held her in life; that I have always loved her as much as I hated myself, and in my heart she and Terzo will always be one'."

And she dies in my arms… as I die to myself… while the nuns bow their heads and whisper their prayer. Alone with my God, my prayer is my own…

Teach me how to draw the poison from the tortured mind, and to hold your death within my heart, as if it were my own, Lord… as if it were my own….

Then I gallop down the mountain through the black rolling clouds, to the mining town of *Perdue*- in the

Biros of Ariège, where my mother was born, who tried to renounce what was low, that she confused with the lowlands that she tried to escape; but she died at the hands of what fathered my flesh- what could have been lower? and I am here to redeem her. Now her spirit was driving me down to the town, 'carved with the blows of a hatchet', the wind at my back. From the height of the mountain, it looked like a graveyard, sunk in the Valley of Death as I make the descent.

I walk through the ancient stone town that is blackened with coal dust, and wander through time by the old tomb-like houses, Snow's spirit inside me, guiding my steps. Pass the women in black, in perpetual mourning: dead fathers and sons, husbands and brothers, all buried alive in the cold black earth; and offer myself to the Mother of Shadow, willing to suffer the *Self* in the dark night of the soul. Veiled by the past, the women pray by a hovel, the daily ritual of death, casting a pall on their lives.

A woman was dying in childbirth, and I approach the crone in the doorway, "Can I help?" I am asking in the old primitive accent.

"How?" asks the crone, filled with suspicion.

"Death is an old friend. I was born out of death. At times, she allows me to sway the dark course of fate. Please, permit me to try, and to change her mind for a while. It is the reason I live, to try breaking her spell."

The crone was struck by her words and the magnetic look in her eye, and led her to the bed of a woman in the last throes of labor. She was gasping for breath, and coughing up blood...

She placed my hands on her lungs. "She has consumption. Be careful. She has black lung, as well.

221

She worked in the mines."

"I don't believe in being careful. I never learned how."

Nola places her lips on the lips of the woman, and gives her the breath of the Mother and the life of the Son: the breath coming right through her, as the crones watch in wonder, and the woman's breath becomes steady as she returns to the earth. 'Give me her death, Mother, as if her death were my own.'

She pulls the child from her womb, cutting the cord with her teeth, breaking the spell of black death and slaps the child into time: How long, Lord... how long? she is asking the God.

The women are kneeling in prayer, while they are watching her work. She gives the mother the girl child, who has been blinded by fate. "I will return with some food and some medicine, if you will allow me to help. My mother was born in this town, and I was born in 'The Mother'. I am staying in the cloister, and I will come to see you every day. What is your name?"

"Luba...my name is Luba."

"The nuns call me 'Lupa'... only one letter difference. What will you call her?"

"Lupa', I'll call her, so I can remember you always. You have given me faith, when I lost it... and the breath of life... for a moment. What are you a saint? Do you really exist?"

"Not a saint, just a 'sinner... but do I really exist? That's a difficult question. I do and I don't. I am here for you now. That's all that matters on earth."

The women, still watching, were struck with the silence of God. Not a word passed between them, and their faith was renewed.

Nola gallops on horseback to the nearest big town and buys food for a feast; then dismounts at a doctor's; follows him to a wet nurse and lifts her up on her horse: lays the child on the nursing breast, and prepares the feast for the women, who eat with their hands on the floor, while the doctor fears for his life...

"Get out,' Nola says. "And don't come back. We don't need you."

Again, she breathes her life into Luba, and feeds her by hand...

"I have hired a cook and a messenger. The nursing mother will stay here. She will feed little Lupa, while we nurse her on spirit. Pray to the Mother that she will give you more life."

Now she kneels at the feet of the Mother of Shadow, and the ruby red chalice is glowing with an unnatural light.

A year goes by quickly. The thought of Nora sustains her. She is surrounded by death and the souls of the dead.

My Life,
A year has passed by- one lonely year. I come down every day from the top of the mountain, healing the miners, coaxing them out of Death's arms. I have taught their children to write, so they can put their dreams into words; deliver parables from the Scriptures for the numerous burials, mourn with them, feed them, and hear their confessions, and, in the most unorthodox fashion, I've become the first woman priest (the old priest died of black lung, another died of consumption). You will laugh at me, Nora, but they call me 'Saint Lupa'- the saint of the

Mother, who can awaken the dead.' They say, 'if consumption can't kill her, then she must be immortal.'

> Yours,
> Nola Lupa (the two are now almost one)

Nora blanches and shivers, reading the letter: "If consumption can't killer her... but will it kill me?"

The blind child is lying on the shrunken breast of her mother. Luba clings to the child, but both are dying their death. "It's no use, 'Lupa'. We can't fight against fate... Can we, my saint?"

"We will try, little mother, and if we can't we'll surrender. I will sing you the song of the gypsy, who mothered my soul, and taught me to be almost human, when I wanted to die." She rocks the blind child in her arms and sings them a lullaby. The spirit of Philos is playing the flute.

Nola, in her cell, is writing to Nora...

> My Strength,
> Two years pass without you. Death's spirit is hovering. But always closer to God and the souls of the dead. I am teaching the children of Lost to explore psychic mining, guiding them down to the pit through their dreams and dark fantasies, dispelling their fear of being buried alive. The lessons begin with a prayer to the Mother of Miners, to protect their fathers and brothers in their descent to the darkness. They live in the terror of death and I teach them to look at her image, to put their fear into words and confront

their resistance to depth. But what could I give them, without the gift that you gave me?
Nola Lupa

CHAPTER 30
MINING

In a primitive hovel, in the clothes of the dead, children nine to fourteen sit in intense concentration. Nola is teaching them to confront Death through their dreams; most of their brothers and fathers have died in the mine...

"Your turn, Didier (he is 9), will you tell us your dream?"

"I dreamed of the Mother of Death... I *think* I was sleeping. I was down in the earth, in the mine, and she was walking behind me, and when I came to the end, Death put her hand on my shoulder. I wanted to run, but my legs were like stone."

"What can we do when we have such a dream? Anjou (she is 10), do you have any thoughts?"

"I would ask Death, are you sure it was me that she wanted, 'cause I have a dream like that sometimes, but Death makes mistakes."

"That's an interesting approach. What do you think, Didier? What if it *were* a mistake, and it *wasn't* you that she wanted?"

"It didn't feel like a mistake. It felt like the truth. And if it *were* a mistake, why would *I* have the dream?"

"An excellent question. What are you thinking, Anjou?"

"I think Didier's right. Death knows what she wants... I think I want to believe that Death is not real... or I can make Death go away, if I think the right thought... and she will think she believes it, and leave me alone."

"My own thought" Nola says, "is that you both have a piece of the puzzle. Anjou would try to confuse Death, and change Death's course with a thought. She has discovered a secret: that a thought can change fate. She would make Death believe that she is mortal, like us: that she thinks like a human, and makes mistakes- just like we do. There are times, no matter how far away she is, that Death seems like our own, and we must ask the right question, while we are learning the difference. Is Death calling us home, or is she calling a stranger or friend?

"Didier's question also has insight: why would he have such a dream, if it were not meant for him? Our dreams are an image of our hopes and our fears. His question can help us to realize the wisdom of a dream, and how to ask Anjou's question to learn to change our own minds. There are all kinds of deaths, not just the death of the body."

"What other kinds are there?" asked Didier.

"The kind we imagine. Death plays with us sometimes, to try changing our thoughts. So, Didier has a point: the dream was meant just for him, and we can see by asking the question that the meaning is double. There is the *fear* of the thought and the *hope* of the change. 'Change your fear with a thought,' Death is saying to Didier, 'change is the secret of life,' and Death is the secret of change. We will remember Didier's wise way of looking at it: why would he dream of her image, if he couldn't learn from the dream, or someone else would be dreaming it, and Death would be playing her game. Death is not without humor. She knows what she knows- that we are *hooked* on our fear. '*Play* with your fear,' Death is saying."

"What about you, Chretien (he is almost 15), what does the dream mean to you?"

"To me, it means Death has told Didier he is at a dead end, and he must turn and confront her to find a new way of seeing."

"So, you are saying that Didier has a choice. What way do you imagine? Try to see it inside, as if you were Didier in the mine."

He takes a moment to imagine it, like she has taught them to do...

"I look inside, like you said, but I can only see one way to go. There is a secret passage going down... but I do not want to take it. I am afraid if I do, I will be buried alive in the mine... like my brother... who died there by going too deep... But down is my chance, and I follow it down... It gets darker and deeper, and I can no longer breathe... I don't know where I'm going, but I follow it down... I have given up hope of surviving and I am lost and afraid... When I have no more hope, I see a circle of light, and the path starts to turn, and is leading me up... then the circle gets bigger, and the fear turns, like the path."

"What do you think, Didier, about turning the thought, the way that Chretien is telling us, of turning darkness to light?"

"I think he is brave, but I would not dare to go down."

"Why not? What if going down to the depths were the only way up, and if you refused to go down, you would be trapped in your fear? I think a good exercise for all of us is to turn the image in the mind- to go down through the image to the depths of the mine- to imagine the way to the light when we think we are trapped. Of course, when you believe you are trapped, it can feel just as real, so try to remember the secret of change. Death changes her mind and she can free us from fear. You see, 'it's a universal law that the reverse is always true.'[224] That is the law that I live by- that we can reverse every thought. Death curves with the light, when you change the *meaning* of the thought."

"Aimee,' (she's thirteen), how do you see it? What would you do if you were Didier, and you were trapped in the mind?"

"If I was Didier, I would ask Death *why* she was calling me, or was she hearing my thought that I wanted to die?"

"What if Death asked you why? What would you tell Death?"

'So I don't have to fear you and feel more dead than alive.'

"And what if she said, 'I only came 'cause you want me. Are you sure that you want me'? What would you tell her?"

'If you give me three questions and I can give you an answer, will you let me return from the dark, so I don't think I want you?'

"What does Death say?"

'You must all answer the first question. Do you want to live or to die? It is a question you all have to answer, but I will give you two more.'

"Aimee has discovered a truth- that changing the mind can change time. So, the first question, Manon (she is 11 or 12)? let's learn the three questions, for Death is testing us all."

"Death asks: 'What would you want most of all if you wanted to live?' "

"It seems she is becoming more human: Death asks what you want. What would you say to Death's question?"

'I want to see through the black cloud that is always above you, and I am asking for light, so I don't have to fear you.'

"What does Death say? You are making it hard for her."

"She is angry, she says, 'cause I am making her work. She says, the black cloud is her sign, and it reminds us she's here."

"Death is sharp. How do you answer, Aimee?"

"I say, 'you will not be so hungry, if you do what I ask.'"

"So, you have challenged old Death. I am sure we can learn from it."

"Gustav (he is twelve), can you tell us her next question?"

'How will you feel, if you can't answer my question?'

"What would you say to her, Gustave?"

'I will feel like I'm dying.'

"So, you would give yourself up, Gustav? What is another way?"

"I could say, 'I will not have the answer, 'cause I am not ready to know it, and I am asking you, Death, to give me a chance, and let me ask *you* the question, 'cause you are smarter than me.'"

"You are learning her game, Gustav, and turning the tables. Outwitting Death is no small matter. What is the question you ask her?"

'What do I fear more than you?'

"And what does Death say?"

'There is no name for it, yet,' "but she is trying to fool me."

"Death is sometimes amusing. How do you answer her joke?"

'How does it feel Death, when you don't know the answer? Now you must give me my wish.'

'And what *is* your wish?' "Death is asking."

'That you will not make me a miner.'

"What does Death do?"

"She gives up."

"So instead of giving *yourself* up, you have turned it around. What is the *real* answer, Gustave? I am sure we all want to know. What do you fear more than death, besides the fear of the mine?"

"That I don't believe in the light. I don't believe there's a God, and if there is nothing to believe in, how will I return from the dark?"

"Can you give her a name that you fear more than Death? What do you think Death would say?"

'Her name is Life,' "she is saying," 'and I am her Mother. I am Death and afraid of the thing that I made.'

"It seems that you have the same fear. You have won this round, Gustav, by using your wits. You have told Death her secret, and given Death back her fear- the fear she created, and you gave it a name."

"And Death's third question, Magdalena (14 on this day)?"

'How does Christ rise from the tomb of the mine?'

"I have asked that question myself. Why not ask Death for the answer?"

"She says, 'Ask 'yourself, Magdalena, if you dare such a question.' "

"Your answer?"

'You can only rise up to heaven, if you go down to hell.'[226]

"What if she asks if you've been there, to know such a thing? What would you say?"

'I am practicing, Death. I am practicing every day.'

"What does Death say to that?"

'You are trying to trick me, Magdalena. You have been talking to my Son.'

"It seems we have all been talking to him today, and we will continue to talk to him tomorrow. Write your thoughts down tonight, after your dialogue with God."

She walks through the town, passing the widows in mourning, who are crossing themselves, as if she were holy. Nola enters the hovel. Luba is dying. She breathes her life in her lungs, invoking God's secret names. But it was time to release her and the child died on her breast. They were led down to the mine, into the dark heart of matter, where the black diamond was formed as an offering to the Mother of Shadow.

The mothers stood weeping by the grave for the death of the mother and child. They tore at their hair, while the miners were digging, and the dead ones were guiding them through the invisible veils. Nola acted as priest; her dirge rang with the bells, for Luba and Lupa, who were baptized in blood: and she delivered herself-the symbolic child of her birth...

> You were screaming for alms
> as you rocked yourself numb,
> howling like a blind beast to a black sun,
> caged in a vacuum with invisible bars.
> You tore at your eyes like empty graves
> that mocked your face

and were robbed of their treasure,
and called to dead stars,
to an impassive and unyielding universe
for some simple proof of your existence.
The dead and living were indistinguishable
and you threw a ball into Nothing
that never returned,
but you waited for its message,
for the symbol of its roundness,
and begged it in secret tongues
for wholeness of form and for light.
You scattered the photons
with your flailing hands,
unaware that your prayer was unanswered
and grasped at the void of inverted space,
at the shadow
of some nameless thing,
lunging at it into frozen time, as you pleaded
for some sign of grace.
A teasing God smiled at your childish courage
and at his strange creation,
at his silent and withholding world,
reflected on it
and judged himself:
a world of tortured children,
a warring and polluted world,
poisoned by hatred,
ravaged by murderers and madmen,
and he frowned awhile
and grew quite grim.
But you without eyes,
could you be sure I even existed,
or yourself, dark child, or yourself?

Yet with perfect faith you knew
I was there for you
and your arms engulfed me
as if I were your world.
I gave you a sound that confirmed you,
an image you clutched at
and tried to believe in...
laughed...
as you held it on your empty palm,
so alone in the dark,
like an island in space.
But the world existed,
it existed inside you, invisibly there…
There were no boundaries to tell you:
'this thing stops here,
here another begins,
you begin and end here.'[229]
And so, you dissolved into things,
into me,
never knowing your limits,
but in this fact we were one.
I never knew them myself...
and when you reminded me of it
they obtruded again,
wrenched me from inseeing
and coerced me to acknowledge them.
How suddenly sacred those boundaries
that I had sacrificed for the depths,
for the dark was my refuge…
and in this we were different:
you were trapped in your darkness,
it was your prison and home,
while I was trapped in a world

that was unable to see.
But for a moment, I was your light,
I was your eyes
and your mirror:
I reflected the forms of the earth
until you could find yourself in them…
and for a moment… you were all of them,
your orbs burning, alive with the vision.
You were my black queen
and I set you on God's throne,
boosted you high above me,
kneeled before you and praised you…
but I knew what I knew...
that the need was too great,
knew it would swallow you up
and that I wasn't enough:
I knew, 'though you were small
on the outside
that you encompassed our pain,' [230]
carried it for us,
and your small heart was as pure
and as open as heaven,
'a heart for birds to fly in,'*
and yet, in your few grief-stricken years
you were completely alone.
Abandoned by God and his Mother,
unable to walk, you stumbled from the primal
urge,
drawn by my voice, clinging to me...
Alone...
Mouth seeking object, hungry mouth at my
breast...
Alone...

Hand reaches for toy, but in your blind eyes,
you hold the seed of your death,
bearing the sins of a world you would never
know,
an empty world, clutched in your little fist,
as you beat at yourself with the blind certainty
of it.
And I?
You made me rejoice in my limits,
almost celebrate them,
as I mourned for your boundlessness
that was so nearly mine:
I who could only pray for you and hold you to
me,
embrace you in your innocence
and ask God to crown you with it,
and to bless your child's soul,
knowing you would not live to find it.

And the living and dead bowed to the child, and the mother that bore her, who returned to the pit. The wind was singing her song, the bells ringing the call, and I saw my mother and son, who were watching the rite. Was I trying to redeem them or the child in myself?... Was it I who was blind, and unable to see?

CHAPTER 31

CONVERSION

When the new priest came, love came with him, and when he saw her, he knew that his vows were at stake. In fear he'd betray them, he extended his hand for a kiss, a foolish gesture to remind him that he was a priest. She kissed it all right but looked right in his eyes, with a satirical smile that put what he knew into question. He tried looking away, but was unable to do it: a look that challenged his nature and had the strength of the called. He was a man of God with real faith, in the truest sense she had known, and she would have thought it impossible but her own was restored.

They taught the children the Scriptures, and examined their meaning, reconstructing God's stories in the light of their dreams. He began sitting in on her classes and listening in awe, for they had learned psychic concepts that would have daunted most men. Meanwhile, she was teaching the nuns the hidden texts of the *Apochrypha*: the heretical texts that were banished from the church, as she delighted in taunting him with her heretical teachings.

The new Reverend Mother was transferred from Paris, from the small sister church of the Mother of God; where Terzo, her son, had reconstructed the past, and designed his own death, deconstructing the future. The mother, a renegade, embraced Nola's work, for it was time to alter the doctrine and break from the dogma, that was confining the nuns to a patriarchal prison, and by combining mysticism and myth, Nola converted them to Gnostics.

She was supporting the church from her royalties-her books were a bible for the nuns, and was working with their shadow and interpreting their dreams, while the priest worked with the miners in the depths of the earth.

Nola and Ambrose loved like pagans on the mountain, infusing the feminine mysteries and the ancient gods with new life, while giving the peasants and nuns the desire to live. Meanwhile, she read Roman myths at High Mass and changed the meaning of the rites, transforming the Virgins, who were spiritually starved, and whose faith had been tested under the patriarchal rule.

On a day in her cell, when she dwelled on the past, she looked up Saint Ambrose in her *Child's Book of Saints*...

"Ambrose comes from *ambra*, an aromatic spice, for he was very precious in the eyes of the church, and spread a pleasant aroma around him by his speech and his actions. Or Ambrose comes from *ambra* and *syos*: the amber of God, for through him God spreads the healing scent. It also comes from *sior*, small, for he was a father in conceiving spiritual children"...[233]

And so, she sainted her lover, as she had sainted Leonardo, who, like a jealous father, was chiding her for confounding religion and myth, for she had made his love holy and he cherished that place in her heart, when as his spiritual child she confounded the father and lover. His jealous presence inspired her as he was trying to intrude, making love more illicit by inducing her dead lover's shadow, and she returned to the book, still avenging the past...

"Saint Ambrose was a light in his interpretation of the Scriptures, rousing a heavenly aroma or taste of

Christ."*

'Christ, my ass, tastes more like the devil to me', said the spirit of Leo.

She pretends to ignore him, as she continues to read of his rival...

"Ambrosia is the food of angels, an *ambrosium* is a comb of heavenly honey, as Saint Ambrose was a divine odour by the perfume of his good renown; he was a good taste by his interior contemplation: a heavenly honeycomb, the food of angels by his glorious fruit of good works."[234]

'Enough! I have had it. Enough of this glorious fruit'! Leo was raging, like a commonplace ghost, rustling her papers and using the cliché to irritate her, while jarring the senses she once thought she 'renounced'. Like the wind of 'The Mother', he was blowing her notes round the room, to forget that he wanted her, and that it was no longer possible.

"Needing attention, again? I haven't taken up necrophilia... Well... not completely.... But really, it's exhausting, these jaunts to the depths of the underworld. I need a break for a while. I'm tired of being a nun."

'You're tired? What of *my* endless journeys to ancient Egypt and Greece, while I follow your pagan diatribes on Ficino and the distant stars, the subtle influences of the furthest planets, as you try to unify your gods; and feast on the archaic vestiges of every god that was consumed. And as far as change goes... well... to be honest, I've never seen such a change... Okay, so you've changed. I admit it! It's a miraculous change. How I regret being dead! Can one change after death? It is a question for philosophers, but I refuse to follow you into alchemy: your experiments with the devil as you deconstruct Christianity, and romp with the clergy to reanimate dead matter'.

"If I didn't know better, I would think you were angry at me."

'Angry? I'm beside your self. If it wasn't for you, I'd still be shooting craps on the earth, instead of having to transit the worlds like a ridiculous psychopomp, tracking you like a beast, as if I were still in my body. *You're* tired? tired of turning the nunnery into a whorehouse'?

"Please go back to hell. I'm tired of death." And they laughed like they used to... wanting him like she used to....

CHAPTER 32
HOW LONG?

Ambrose was confessing to Nola in the garden of 'The Mother'...

"I never told you how I strayed."

"But somehow I know. I had a vision of you as 'the prodigal son', working for your father in the vineyard of the heart; while his heir, your older brother, was vying for his love, who never questioned his faith that he blindly embraced: the *literal* path of the father, rejecting the feminine Christ... Your brother was favored by your father for his lack of reflection, while, with the passion of the mystic, you gave yourself to God."

Ambrose was in awe of her...

"You are a devilish sorceress, but I will tell you my story, for my soul has heard its own secret, it was unwilling to hear. He gave his love to my brother, who was unable to love. When I hear it through you, it gives me another perspective, a new way of seeing my shadow through the eyes of the *Self*."

She could feel Nora inside her, for it could not happen without her: this new way of seeing that allowed her to love... It was Nora who taught her to bear the shadow of love, without the need to destroy it and escape to the stars.

"It was a repeating theme with my brothers in the monastery in Rome: the spiritual envy of the so-called disciples of God; the ones who had chosen the *literal* path. I had one friend to confide in and we retreated to mysticism. We were exiled together for being heretical, but it was a self-exile, really, as we fought for our freedom. I loved him completely- well, almost completely, but sex and eroticism are not always related."

"How did you become a priest?"

"When I left the house of my father, I was given part of my inheritance, and, like 'the prodigal son', I squandered it in the gutter. He cut me off and disowned me, and left the rest to my brother: the vineyards in Umbria (my imaginary tale as a whore), and the remains of his fortune... which I decided to renounce. I tried to escape him by becoming a priest... and lived in a cell that was *ruled* by the Father."

The vineyard again... Something clutched at her heart... She wondered if Philos was in it, who turned the wine into blood...

"Tell me, how did you find me in the vineyard of the heart, when I live in my thoughts, in the vine of the mind?"

"I find you where you are, when you aren't trying to transcend it- as if the heart and the mind were not one and lived in two different beings. How else would I find you, when you are so far above me? I can only drink you like wine in the heart of the Word."

"How else? I have been crushed in the winepress, and I am here to be drunk by you. I thought we might work on *The Prodigal Son* for the nuns, so they can know what it is to be lost in the gutter, and to return to the God, without leaving their cells. The Reverend Mother conceded. Are you with me, my saint?"

He smiled. "It is you who are sainted, and who they think is the devil: who act out their projections, to completely confound them, like the devil itself, who has taught you its secrets. The Mother of Sorrows is being transformed. Yes, I am with you. How would I not be?"

"I knew you would see it."

"What *don't* you know?"

"I don't know if I can live without you."

"Why would you have to?"

"Just a thought"... But she felt a chill in her soul, and again, she knew it was coming, for the world had stopped spinning- the one that they lived in. His face, etched by shadow, charmed by the spirit, his wild hair, so unpriestly, tossed by the wind, and she knew he'd pass into it, like all the others she loved... But he was here for the moment, and she'd drink him in through the senses.

"Your heart is too busy making the wine, and your tears are mixed with the blood of the crucified god. Let's not think about death."

How long, Lord, how long?

The sick came from the village and she continued to heal them, and he resurrected a god who accepted their shadow; took their sickness right into him, till he could no longer breathe. She kept him alive for six months by invoking the Mother and Son, and when he died, she died with him, writing the book in his blood; and so, the three years of sacrifice had come to the end.

'When God came to the Biros, said a shepherd, it was night then, and he carved the land with blows of a hatchet. But as he left, he was seized with remorse and threw over his shoulder a handful of ore.'

I felt the axe in my heart, and threw my pain with the ore: tried throwing my love over my shoulder, but could not let it go... held it tight in my fist...

In her vision, she walked through the mountains

243

with Ambrose and Leo, and they were having a dialogue on the immortality of the soul. She could see Terzo in the distance, sitting on a rock, but was distracted by what Ambrose was saying to Leo: that 'the soul's delight was to cross the threshold between the immortal and the human realm'.[239] When she looked back, her son was reading with Snow. She was wearing the white wedding gown as the Bride of the Christ- the gown that she died in and that symbolized immortality- the gown she was wearing, when Terzo died on her body, like the image in 'The Mother' of the Son and his shadow. Snow was reading an alchemical interpretation as an addition to the *Scriptures*, and she asked her the secret of 'the albedo', or whitening'- the gown she was wearing and the purifying process, which prepares the initiate for the marriage with the *Self*- while hidden in the Christ is 'The Red Man' of alchemy, the 'Universal Medicine', healing the wound of the shadow.

Snow spoke of 'the nobler *Mercurius*, who alone is the shepherd',[*] the true spiritual Christ, who is the secret in matter: the rarified spirit in psyche that penetrates all solid things, as it goes through the stages of suffering, in which its substance is tortured, flayed to its essence, and whitened in the great transformation. She could not make up her mind to listen to Snow or to Ambrose, but now their words were interpenetrating, and she heard 'a third' version more revealing.

What she finally deciphered was a parallel to her lecture on Ficino, for Snow had a purpose and was intent on achieving it. She said that with *The Thought* of the philosophers, the dead are revived, lighting all living things, and that it was the essence of *Gnosis*: the unfathomable light of an interior god, and in this work of 'the whitening', 'the illumination takes place.[*] This is the Mother of the art and in the Water is the hidden fire- the hermaphrodite, or the mystery of the sun and the moon, both male and female, in all its parts'.

Somehow, her mother had returned to the cloister, to give the wolf girl instruction and what Nola had asked for, and the three came together in the spirit of the lower trinity. She understood that her mother was inhabiting her body, and that the Lupa in Nola was taking back the projection: Snow was within her for the next transformation- to initiate the nuns into a new rela-
-tionship to Christ. "In what language would she do this," 'Lupa' was asking?

'Why in the language of the philosophers: the double god is coming through you. Purge 'the whore in the metals'.[240]

"How?" I was asking.

'Teach the nuns at 'The Mother' that the flesh is not a prison, and to free themselves from the spell of the shadow of the Father- and tell yourself, while you're at it, for you sometimes forget'.

She taught me many secrets on the mountain of the Mother, and, without the usual resistance, I was able to receive it. I had learned how to love… such a simple thing, really… but to learn how to love, one has to learn how to die.

'Who are you talking to'? the spirit of Ambrose was asking.

"My mother. She was telling me a secret."

'Can you tell it to me, so I can hear what I know'?

"She was telling the rite of return that is talked about in the Scriptures: 'the missing fourth of the Trinity'- the part that's left out: how the conscious and unconscious transform one another: *It was always there from the beginning, but appears only at the end.*"*

That morning, before the nuns rose, I stood in the water of the fountain, weeping with the young Magdalena, as I talked with Leonardo, as I had done long ago, in what seemed another incarnation.

'So, Magdalena', he said, 'can you bring me back to life'?

"You will live in me, in my spirit, as I am dying my deaths, and I will live more completely, now that you are inside me."

CHAPTER 33
THE LOW PLACES

She began the class for the nuns beneath the Mother of Shadow. "This class will be dedicated to Father Ambrose, who found 'the light in the darkness' by mining the shadow, and came to know his own heart by going down to the low places. Like 'the prodigal son', he found the way to return, serving the God by *not* renouncing his darkness: not the way of his brother, who served like a sheep.

"We will also be looking at the myth of the Magdalene as the patriarchal 'whore', or the devil in matter- 'the missing fourth of the Trinity',[242] and the problem of body as shadow. Of course, taking the veil, does not make us exempt, for whether a nun or a whore, we *take* the projection, and are acting it out in the gutter of the soul."

She catches Sister Gabrielle, running her eyes down her body, lost in the projection of the taboo feminine.

"This projection reached its high point in the Christian medieval church, and we are still living the myth of the sinless Virgin, who was 'cleansed of her shadow' that we unconsciously worship, her feminine qualities transposed to her androgynous Son, who was missing his dark side and *nailed* to her shadow."

"And, yet, they call her 'Saint Lupa'," Sister Gabrielle whispers. "How does she get away with it? She killed Father Ambrose, by breaking his vows, made him believe in her magic, and turned him into her slave."

"It seems Sister Gabrielle would like to be teaching the class," she said to the sister, who is shaken to the core, nervously working the beads of her rosary. "Let's pray that the gossip does not interfere with our work.

"To continue: what is hidden in the parable of '*The Prodigal Son*'[243] is what is denied by the father and *projected* on the son, who must come to terms with his shadow, as he makes his descent. In other words, the son must go down to the low places- to find the spirit in matter. In the parable- known as *The Lost Son, or Two Brothers*- the son is lost in the gutter and has wasted the gift, and *confronting* his shadow returns to the father. To honor his return, the father 'kills for him a fatted calf',[*] and, is envied by his brother, who never made the descent.

"In *Luke,* chapter fifteen, verse eleven to thirty-two,[*] *we see that the father had two sons, and the younger asked the father to give him the portion of 'what falleth to him', and took his journey to the far places, wasting his gift with riotous living. When he had spent all he had, there arose a mighty famine in the land, and he began to be in want and was perishing with hunger*[*]... as I am, I thought... as I am...

"I knew what Ambrose had felt when he strayed from his God, while I watched Sister Gabrielle who was tortured by lust, and I knew I'd be helping the sister to come to terms with her shadow... and I returned to the text and tempted my saint into time.

"And the father, who we know is God, asked his servants *to bring forth the best robe and put it on him; and put a ring on his hand, and shoes on his feet, and to kill for him a fatted* calf... *for 'my son was dead... and is alive again. He who was lost has returned.*"[*] The older brother, who had never stopped working, was angry at his father's sacrifice, for he had made no sacrifice for *him*, who did not stray from the path and go down to the low places."

Sister Gabrielle, my shadow sister, was burning with envy, and wanted my body, but was a slave to her God- or was it my shadow she wanted, to receive the gift of the Son?... But you, my dear saint, who went down to your darkness and who were given the gift, has your God not betrayed you? And the spirit of Ambrose appeared and was trying to reason with me, but I was in no mood for reason. He was gone, and I was here. All four of them gone, and I was ready for a bit of blasphemy (and yet, I was only obeying the spirit of my mother).

I'd be damned if I spend my whole life mourning for him. Not one of them would I mourn, and I ripped off a veil. It was time to inspirit dead matter and to bring down my son. And so, I eroticized the flesh of the least erotic thing I could imagine- Sister Gabrielle repenting, since 'the wolf girl' was twelve, who fell in love with my darkness and believed she was burning in hell. And I played out the image and went to her bed, to free the nun from the shadow and to languish in 'sin'.

The sister was sure she was having a vision, when I went to her cell and took off my clothes. How many animal fantasies had she masturbated to, while 'the wolf girl' was watching through the walls of her cell. And now it happened as she saw it, and she was *gripped* by her fear.

"Don't be afraid. I know how you want me. Come and lick me, like you used to, when you were alone in the dark. I am 'the wolf girl', not the devil- just a beast, like yourself. Come, forget your vows for a moment, and dare to do what you want."

And the sister licked her and fucked her-more like the devil, himself, and was possessed by the madness that she feared all her life, while the wolfish spirit in Nola was tempting the dead to return.

CHAPTER 34
THE STARS IN THE BLOOD

'69. She was reading *Shadow Woman* in the waiting room when she was gripped by a force. She wondered who Nora was dissecting, while she was diving for pearls. Then he opened the door in his mythic proportions. He observed her a moment and drew an interior map, tracing a rogue constellation and charting the course of its stars, and whether two rebel forces that strayed from their orbit could survive one another and return to themselves. Then he looked at her picture on the back of the book; drawn to the danger- an irrepressible nature, a beast of a woman and the peril she posed. As if drawn by a magnet he was moved towards its source: her enigma revealed in the book and her 'complex of opposites': an impossible creature who could never be tamed.

The white mountain of hair seemed to spring from his thoughts; the deep indigo eyes that mirrored the night; the strength of his features and uncompromised character, as he confronted the challenge with a gaze free of fear. His fixed sense of direction... to what end, she was asking?... what was its nature and breadth, and the force of attraction?... the force in her limbs that bound her to earth, while she was pressing against it to return to the heights. And if the will worked its way in the course of her destiny, then this was the mystery of how the design came to be.

He was quicker than she in enacting his own. It was the first time it happened, and she forgot to resist...

"I'm reading it, too. I see we're both fans of yours. I would be honored if you'd dine with me after your session. Do you find you still have an appetite after you've fed on your soul?" "It can go either way. I'm either starving for fauna or lusting for the impossible, and renouncing it all to feed on the stars. But let's imagine the former, so we can meet in two hours."

"It seems we have something in common; the bar at the Hotel Pierre. Do you tend to do doubles?"

"Yes, if it isn't a triple: it seems the hungry beast of the soul can never quite get enough. If earthly food could only satisfy it."

"We will try the impossible, knowing the beast whets the appetite."

Nora opened the door and knew that she lost her; he hit the earth when he realized he'd broken the analytic boundary. He nodded to Nora in deference, but knew it was necessary; that in that moment of transference something of fate had occurred. A lower trinity was being formed in interior space/time and would chart a new course in the path of their stars.

Nola entered the room and was at a loss where to start, for three years had passed by and love was a trickster of time. She had lived one more life, and one more had been lost. But Nora's love and her own still burned in the brain... Still the question remained: what to do with this love?... And then, in the space between moments, she knew something else: Nora's love for the stranger... and the wound in the heart.

Nora sat on her throne: "I see you've seduced another patient."

"It was one of those things."

"It always is with you, isn't it?"

"Not always, but often. In any case, let's not waste our time talking of matters of 'synchronicity'. Since

I'm not a theoretical astrophysicist, I'm not able to explain it. I only know that it happens and that I'm an animal in the desert; that I move in a dangerous orbit, and am destined to collide with dead stars."

How does she do it? Nora thought. Indeed, the stranger was an astrophysicist. "Another death?" she was asking. "Is more death what you need?"

"I came 'cause I must. But there is always another... Am I an unconscious killer, or an 'awakener of the dead'?"

"Why one or the other? You are both- always both."

"And where is 'the third'? Am I splitting again? Trying to integrate the opposites, by killing off what I love?"

"Perhaps, they are stages of wholeness- but who will be left when you're done? Who will be there to see this impossible wholeness?"

"Last night I had a dream that there was only you and I"...
"We were lying on an ancient Turkish carpet that had the pattern of eternity: a geometric pattern of the archetype of relationship. In the dream, I knew what it was.... but I wished that I didn't. In every triangle and square were ancient formulas and secret writings, and we were conversing about love and all its possible combinations. I said there was one I couldn't translate, and you agreed it was hard, but you were reading the ancient symbols, and held the key to the mystery."

"What do you imagine I would say?"
"That it was the way we were combined... that it was hard... but not impossible, and was just a problem

of gravity, and, of course, there's the fear of being consumed."

"Perhaps, you are fearing that only I could survive you?"

"Perhaps. Or the fear that you won't, and that the pattern reflects it."

"Why did you come back?"

"Do you wish that I hadn't? I came back to find you... and myself in your depths... and to try to realize what has happened."

"Why don't you tell me about it?"

"Well... I have been communing with the dead, and always death follows love... It's an impossible pattern."

"Not impossible at all. It's an *archetypal* pattern, for dead stars want to live."

"Three years means nothing, when you are working the vineyard of the heart, but I have learned how to die and return to the earth. Still, I am asking the question, and the *Self* hasn't answered: is it because I am identified with my shadow that they are caught in its orbit, or am I a 'woman *without* a shadow' that must come down to be human?"

"To be identified with the shadow is the same as not having one, and I think you have found it. It be-longs to you now. But you are still identified with consciousness: your sun is too bright, and as Jung says: *the more conscious you are, the bigger the shadow.*"

"As big as the shadow of death? My last lover, a priest, died of consumption... consumed from within... all that was left was his spirit... How I prayed Death would take me, but she spared me again... Why does she spare me?"

Nora veiled her reaction... Her father died of

consumption; he had given it to her... Was it the transference that magnetized it? The disease nearly killed her. She was consumed, like the priest, by the shadow of her father... And still, there were nights that she spent with his spirit, unable to breathe, when death appeared in the dark... nights she spent with his shadow when she died to herself.

"Have you questioned your shadow- why it leaves you alone on the earth?"

"It said that I value my freedom more than the bondage of love. Is that why we are sitting alone on the alchemical ground of our being, with only each other to confirm our aloneness?"

After the session, they met, and it was harder than she thought. What was it her shadow did not want to know? It fought for a while, but she was able to tame it."

"I want to know who you are," she was asking the stranger.

"Yes, it isn't quite fair. I know so much about you. But so does the world. Do you find it a disadvantage, to be known by a stranger?"

"Not really. The world stage is only one way of disseminating ideas. I like using them all. You might be surprised that I'm an extremely private person. My books are compensatory to an extreme introversion. I don't expect you to believe me- until you finish the book."

"I also live in the shadow of ambiguity and of what is impossible."

"I'm relieved to hear it, or we would not be able to converse."

"Conversing will not be the problem. It's really a

question of survival. I have an idea what I'm up against."

"You are not up against it yet."

"I am aware of the odds. I am an explorer of odds, but in space, not on earth. As a theoretical astrophysicist, I am here to observe them. If it were not for the odds, the earth might not exist, and if it did not, how would I know the unknown and your odd aggregation of atoms, that prefer the disguise- as if you might cease to exist if they were balanced on earth. I have lived in space far too long. It is time to return. I spend all my time with the stars."

"So do I. I am also trying to come down: the dead ones are... consuming."

"Maybe we can come down together. It won't be easy to do. It is against my better nature to be bound to the earth."

"So unnatural, isn't it? Such a cold, distant planet- compared to Mercury and Pluto, which are so ego- near."

He smiles to himself, for he knows what she means. That was important, for she needed someone to know. She was wondering if fate would allow it- and Nora, of course, who would be trying to accept it... the shadow of fate.

"We will be needing some oysters, if we are going to descend," Nola said.

"Our formulas are similar."

"What is your name, by the way?"

He gives her his hand, "That's what I mean. I sometimes forget that I am not one of my theories- an abstraction that explains the magnetism of the stars: Sergei: Sergei Gobosky- Gobo, they call me. I already know yours."

"You know only two of them. You might be learning a 'third'."[251]

"I have no fear of your shadow, and will be learning 'the fourth'."[252]

CHAPTER 35
DEAD STARS

Sergei is lecturing at Yale on 'theoretical physics', linking the dead parts of the self with the dead stars in space. He assumes by combining mysticism, psychology and the science of the stars that the Law of Attraction confirms that life arises out of death. His theories expand on his father's, a conservative physicist, acclaimed for his work on the electromagnetic field, and the force of gravity and its effect on the electrically charged object. Sergei goes further, like Maeterlinck, and concludes that 'gravity is God',[253] for it can enliven dead matter, and bring the dead back to life. He presumes that an unconscious content magnetizes the field and can change both subject and object by making them conscious. Nola, contained, in a tweed suit and hat, is taking fastidious notes with intense concentration...

"If dead stars, which consume their inner planets, are the souls of the dead, that the Neoplatonic Hermeticists believed were the gods, and we try to explain this phenomenon, the next thought that comes to mind is that death is not immutable. Giordano Bruno, the Italian Renaissance cosmologist, philosopher, and priest, who was burned as a heretic, understood this, as did the Greek philosophers.

"As in the psyche, dead and dying stars create new star formations and constellate new possibilities of being, and as dead stars evolve, so do we on the earth, for heaven and earth are interpenetrating, as in the Kabbalah, physics, religion, and myth. We are exploring a deathless communion between above and below, and realize that the spiritual Trinity has a shadow, projected on the feminine as matter; that when 'the third' rises up from the 'tension of opposites', there is a *descent* of the spirit or consciousness that re-animates the dead, and what we conceive as dead matter becomes the substance of *Self*. It happens through the Law of Attraction, or 'the *spirit* of gravity' that has its psychic equivalent in what we call the unconscious, *magnetizing* the above to below and reconciling 'the conflict of opposites'.

"In Pythagorean terms, *Every triad presupposes the existence of an opposite triad*, that according to Jung is completed through 'the fourth';[254] each triad modifying the other to reveal an all-encompassing *Self*, a psychic entity that contains all opposites within it, and from the 'archetype of wholeness'* arises an image of God.

"In the Aristotelian view, *the celestial world tends toward perfection, and the earthly world towards imperfection.* The two worlds once seemed unrelated and mirrored the split that we see in the psyche, but we know now they are reflections of conscious and unconscious and are incompatible without a 'third'* that emerges as a symbol, bridging the opposites, and throws light on the shadow side.

"The dead stars in the heavens, as the souls of the dead, create new stars and permutations that inter-penetrate the psyche. Like death, the shadow is not immutable, but contains the potential for transformation. Is this always the case, regardless of the quality of soul, or the energy contained in a dead star or god? We could deliberate on this question, but why split atoms?"

Why indeed? He made sense; finally, someone who

made sense, besides Nora, who was weaving the symbolic carpet the three if us were on. Can I really bear to love again and to wait for his death, as I wander through time in the wilderness of space? How many deaths can I bear and wish to remain on the earth? How old is this star, this atomic particle of consciousness, who scatters my libido like so many photons?... And yet, I can bear nothing less as his voice 'strikes the stars', and while she mused on his theory, it was like being reborn.

"And so, the quintessence of dark matter has godly proportions," he continued, "the inherent implication being that, at the point of origin, the forces of creation and destruction are indivisible. Taking it one step further, at another point of the continuum, it is this mutuality that allows for the redemption of 'God's shadow', and our own, who reflect it, while the light and the darkness transform one another. According to Meister Eckhart's 'relativity of God and the soul': *As we become conscious of God, God becomes conscious of himself.*[255] We might say that when we know our own shadow, God becomes conscious of his own. Likewise, dark matter has the potential for its conversion into spirit, and we realize that by turning the current of the forces of destruction, we have entered the fourth dimension, or the space/time continuum, in which the living and dead can heal one another.

"This psychic fact makes us realize the potential-the inherent possibility, to transfigure both psyche and matter, and is the basis of the transference and of human relationship, producing a magnetic field through an 'unknown third'. It is the beginning of art and psychoanalysis. The disturbance or transposition of numinous energy that exists in the magnetic field is very the basis of alchemy, allowing the living and dead to hold an ongoing dialogue, made possible by the Law of Attraction and the unconscious, itself. Are there any questions?"

Nola raises her hand.

"Yes, Nola."

"Paracelsus, the medieval Neoplatonic Hermeticist and alchemist, asks the question- an impossible question, and I have been asking it too, a question we all must ask, as we die and return: *What does it mean to rot?*[256] In other words, what does it mean to be dead matter? What I am asking, from a scientific point of view, is there such a thing, either in space or in us, that *cannot* be regenerated by the Law of Attraction? If this devil of a shadow that is all the darkness of the universe, to which we are attracted, and is the potential for wholeness- the very means of transformation, does dead matter exist?"

"That is a very elegant question, but one for a philosopher, not a scientist. Is God dead, or am I? might be Nietzsche's question, if he had believed in something transcendent to the ego and its spirit. When we kill God off, the ego *becomes* God, says Jung. And if we succeed, does God still exist? To rot is to return to the *prima materia*, or eternal chaos. Dead matter is God's shadow, and has the potential for life, but it also contains the compulsion to annihilate the God.

"We might say, dead matter is the unconscious, till it is sparked by desire, and without it, body and spirit may seem like non-being. But can science argue that the death drive is the absence of God? What would be the meaning of the sacrifice? In Jung's words: *The sacrifice must be understood as the overcoming of uncon--sciousness, and at the same time the attitude of the Son, who unconsciously hangs on his Mother the cross.*[256a] When we reflect on his words, the question arises: Is the death of God the beginning of God in the psyche?"

"Thank you (jolted back by those words to her son and his shadow, masking her face, as she swallows the feeling). You have answered my question well, and if it is possible for dark matter to rest, I am encouraged that the spirit of Paracelsus, and my own, can stop wrestling with the question, which has kept me awake for many a night. "What does it mean to be endlessly awake, trying to fathom an answer to your unanswerable question," I ask him. 'Please, Nola,' he says sternly, 'You might as well ask me what it means to be dead, or to endlessly sleep?' "

He laughs with the audience, all aware of her work, and that she has a devilish reputation for being deathless.

"Don't worry, Nola," said Sergei, "You won't have that luxury."

A distinctive woman with prominent features, Christa Helden, a German Jungian analyst- the author of *The Black Hole in The Psyche: Or The Negative Mother Complex*- has been watching her with interest and observing her relationship with Sergei. "I'd like to ask Nola what she thinks Paracelsus meant when he said: *All things are poison and nothing is without poison,*[257] and whether she believes that."

"He also said that *Water can be deadly if over-consumed.** He was referring to the dosage and 'the poison that heals', but I don't think you are really asking me that. What are you *really* asking me?"

"You are right. I wasn't asking that, but was completely unaware of it. I think what I am *really* asking is a question that is keeping *me* awake at night, as I am reading your stories, disguised as fiction: why do all your characters poison each other with their love, and what is this compulsion to destroy love, to kill it off, as if it could rob us of our freedom?"

"Am I 'on the couch' now, or are you asking me for a date?"

The audience laughs uncontrollably.

"If I were an analyst" she continues, "I would interpret it this way: what you are *really* asking is, would I drink the poison with you? and I am flattered and almost tempted to accept, to know if it would kill me. You do realize that it is the self-same poison you drink with your patients: that is, the poison of the negative mother complex, and though I don't want to become one of them, I'd like to know your special recipe to get such a poisonous transference, such as you write about in your case material."

"Again, the audience laughs. Sergei is fascinated. But he will avenge the interruption at the appropriate moment- mythically, of course."

Nola continues, "But to get back to the lecture, I have one more question, Sergei, and please excuse the interruption. If a dead star consumes its inner planets, what becomes of them? Are we to see them as 'unborn children', screaming to be born? Would you call it an internalized Medea complex, when it occurs in the psyche, on earth?"

"That is very astute. But let's look at the myth. Medea, the sorceress, knew all the secrets of nature, but killed her children out of revenge for Jason's betrayal of her, after helping him capture the Golden Fleece: the winged ram, whose fleece was the symbol of renewal: the psychic equivalent of the alchemist's gold, or the philosopher's stone that is the secret of life. It was Medea who made his shield impregnable, while allowing herself to be vulnerable in love: this, combined with the fact that she betrays herself, and her father, the king- or her inner authority- and gives Jason power over her. It is her self-betrayal that does not allow her to use her transformative powers, as she is colluding with her be-traying *animus* and its lust for power. Are you thinking of Medea as the Devouring Mother, and as a dead star who compulsively sacrifices her children, drawing them into the black hole in the unconscious, to avenge her lover for giving up her power for love?"

"Yes."

Again, the audience breaks up. Christa takes up the problem, for, like Sergei, she is intrigued by Nola's writings- and its author: "It's a good analogy- the dead star as the Death Mother, or *prima materia*, who takes her own creation back into herself, as you describe in your stories, that black hole in the psyche that sucks us into negative matter."

"That date is becoming more ominous every moment," says Sergei, amused.

"You can always back out, Christa," Nola says, smiling.

"Not so easy. It's a challenge."

"Then let's hope for the right dosage," says Nola.

"I will measure it precisely. I am not suicidal."

He wonders if he is.

The audience is still. They are no longer laughing,

but tasting the poison.

"We all have an unconscious," said Nola, "and the black hole is its extreme. But it's best not to go there at lunch."

CHAPTER 36
THE WRONG DOSAGE

Nola and Christa are eating oysters excessively, as they play with dark matter in Christa's suite at the Pierre. Christa likes being close to the Egyptian tombs at the museum, so she can visit them often, in order to feel more alive.

"What I am saying is that this kind of mother complex is an inverted force field of gravity that is pulling the subject into its vortex," said Christa to Nola.

"Sounds irresistible", Nola said, smiling. "Let's go to the tombs first, and then we will try it."

"It's better at night. I'm having a fling with the curator- an Egyptologist who knows the secret that was buried in the mummies. She lets me in when it's closed, and we pretend that we're dead. We like it that way. Nothing like sex in the afterlife."

"Somehow, I knew you'd prefer the dead to the living."

"There is always an exception, and I think I've found it in you."

"I, too, court the dead, not for sex but for *gnosis*. That's how we're different. You may not know who I am." She devours an oyster.

"I know what I need. Do you *live* on oysters?"

"I try to, but I get distracted by the pearls and forget that I need earthly nourishment." She devours another.

"Let's do the tomb of the flesh, and explore the *mumia* within."

"So you want it now, do you, Christa? Yes, let's have it now. I like watching your lips take in the flesh, as though you had found the black pearl in the vortex

266

of hell; the way your hands hold the shell and devour what they hold. Yes, I want you to do what you are doing to the oysters."

Christa turns to a beast that is maddened by lust, as Nola is spreading her legs and ripping the silk from her cunt. Christa, kneeling before it, opens its shell to devour it.

"Yes, I need it now. I must have it," thrusting her tongue out to take it.

"Your hands know how to hold it. You've been named for this act, Helden. Spread it open and suck it, until you are drunk on its poison."

Sergei knew what was coming and that she would get to her first- this dead star of a woman, looking for the elixir in Nola... who already belonged to him... how presumptuous, he thought... He never conceived such a thing... it was compensatory to her resistance... to the dread of surrender... to the loss of the self... to the fear of love's death... that he knew was the end...She entirely agreed with Paracelsus: *Let no man belong to another that can belong to himself.* He had felt that way once... but it no longer worked.

And so, another lower trinity, with Christa poisoned by love- but Nola was already bored, and love turned to death.

And then there was Nora, who died to herself...

"In some way, Nora, I want to belong to him. What do you think has got into me? I don't understand it."

"Yes, you do. Why are you pretending?"

"Am I? Is it guilt? In some uncanny way, I want to belong to you, too."

"That's no excuse," Nora said.

"It wasn't meant to be: just a confession. It is you

who has woven his image into the pattern, and so we are in it together."

"This weaving business... it was completely unconscious, and I deeply regret it. How could I know that you would identify with Samara and sit in the waiting room, reading your book- as if you contrived it, like she did, and were identified with the dead? but a *psychic* seduction, which you are terribly good at, and which she was trying to imitate and that drove her to death. The problem seems clear: she is seducing you from the underworld."

"I'm insulted. If it were not for your magnetic field, charged with your fantasies, and whatever went on in that magnetic session with him, it never would have happened."

Suddenly, they are mortified, when they realize they are acting like lovers. Nora, always the analyst, even while suffering defeat, asks the inevitable question...

"And how do you *imagine* that session that was 'charged with my fantasies'?"

Nola, transported in time, is poised on the threshold, and imagines his session, the day that they met... "I imagine he was telling you about his own erotic fantasies, while you were having yours... but yours were not only of him, but were also of me, and he received it in the transference, and fell in love with your image of me... and so it was you and myself that he was falling in love with... That's all I'm prepared to say"... What she was seeing terrified her: the Mother shrouded in black: the dead star of a Mother, consuming her unborn children, and she wanted to die at that moment, but she didn't disclose it.

Why? Wasn't it why she was there- to disclose what

she wouldn't? It was a session, goddamn it, not a love affair... protecting her analyst from her unbearable feelings. Why couldn't she tell her what she saw? Because she could feel Nora's fear?... because her fear was her own?... for she had been entirely accurate, as if she'd been perched in the room... and had seen more than she wanted... what only the dead can reveal.

Nora was faced with her shadow. What more did she see?... She was unable to ask... and was asking herself: was she *protecting* her patient from love or her shadow?... Or was she protecting herself?... And now she knew that she was.

Still... the question kept turning, both eluding, both pretending...

"Why are you trying to protect me, Nola?"

"I might ask you the same question, but I know you won't tell me- no more than *I* will tell you- until I am ready."

"And then?"... And then there is no turning back, Nora said to herself...

"Let's try to stay in the room, Nora", Nola's wry little joke, 'reversing the opposites', while trying to return to the room. "Are we lost in our myth, in which we create one another?" smiling that unknowable smile that could kill a man- or a woman.

There was no answer to such a question, Nora was thinking... but that doesn't mean she won't try to find one.

She went to his West Village loft, overlooking the river. A huge room, so essential, that it combined the four elements: a bronze desk, two brown leather arm chairs- very old, very worn, facing a black granite fireplace- it was big, it was burning, the brown leather couch in between them, behind a bronze Arts & Crafts table: on it, his notes from that session, written in code, that somehow was focused on her, with a vase of white calla lilies. She watched the fire from within while she entered his world. In the center of the room, thrusting through a pyramidal skylight and trajected through space, was a steel rocket like a giant lingam- that fit the fantasy of his proportions and the contours of his body. Behind him on the wall were the star maps he drew, and he waited as she looked, as if she were peering in his soul. They sit on the couch, at either end, sipping a very old port.

"How was your session?" he sensed it.

"It was confounded with yours- not a good sign," glancing at his notes and arching her brow.

"Which one?" he said laughing- sharing her joke, as she was breaking the code.

And they knew it was true: true that their minds were as one. No, it was not a good sign, this fusion of sessions; and they were trying to bear it and to laugh at the odds.

"The one that we met in. What was your fantasy of me?"

He didn't want to tell her, but he did, and wished that he hadn't. "You were naked and mounted on that rocket like a pagan, like you were riding a giant phallus, with a whip in your hand. Your head was thrown back and you were laughing like a maenad, and when the rocket took off, the room shattered in fragments. In my fantasy I was thinking, this is my mind and my body... I didn't tell Nora it was you. I think she thought it was her."

"How did you know it was me?"

"From your book. I had been reading it in the waiting room, before going into my session- like you... and I hid it, for a moment. I didn't know why at the time. I was determined not to look at your picture on the back- until you were reading it, and couldn't resist."

"Why not look?"

"A premonition, that for the first time, I was faced with no choice."

"Funny, that's how *I* felt. How did she interpret the image?"

"She thought I was trying to escape the analytic container... and herself."

"What did *you* think?"

"I thought I was trying to escape into love... and that it was going to destroy me... I knew it was beyond me... and that I'd defy all the limits."

Nola wanted it to be her that was destroyed at that moment.

"What do *you* think it means?" he asked.

"I think that it's compensating for the need to come down, and that we have to be careful, so it does *not* get beyond us: that together we could generate a greater force than we can handle- that my power complex could destroy us and reverse time and space, but if we are conscious of it, we can try to find the limit, so when the stars of the dead are exploding in the blood, it is not as excessive as a psychic supernuova- when an *inner* constellation has too much energy to contain it. But the explosion can create new stars and constellations, new psychic realities... We won't let it destroy us. 'We *are* our own fate'." And she knew that she loved him. She even tried to contain it. But she knew that she couldn't. She tried but could not...

271

"What shape did I take?"

"That was the strange part- your own. I see now, by not looking at your image, I was protecting myself from being defenseless; I saw your interior self before seeing your face. I was wondering what kind of beast might have created such a book, to unleash such a force as the self you created. That's how it began... and how it may end, as I wonder what kind of beast could bear loving you as I do."

"We will change the course of the stars (Leonardo, again)... It won't end. We won't let it. We will do the impossible. She mounts him, as if she were riding the rocket; throwing her head back and laughing with an invisible whip. "And don't mind my lust, will you, it's just one of those things."

It was the biggest penis she had ever seen, like his body, his mind, the big thoughts that he had- the ones defying the odds- the ones that could stand up to hers: the best sex: the best talk: the best... what?... Things exploded... And then, as if thrusting through space, they continued to soar... It was not inevitable, she told herself. She would rewrite it, she thought. It would continue on earth... and they would come down together... Stars explode and build worlds... Dead stars could evolve.

"Where shall we have dinner?" she asked. "Let's stop thinking about death."

"I agree. There are things that taste better... but I wish I could think of one."

He devours her... "Tastes like death."

Where did she hear it before?... Of course... Leonardo...

"More like Pluto than earth: that fiery underworld

quality, mixed with the cold purity of space," Sergei was saying (as she conjured him up- or was he watching from the wings and pretending it was him?), while he fucked her to infinity, till they were *famished* on the earth.

They were dining at the Twenty-One, when Christa entered with a fling, knowing it was one of Nola's haunts, and it was obvious that she was stalking her; she'd been avoiding her manic calls, Christa obsessing on their jaunt. What was a moment for Nola, was a rejection for Christa, and, in her masochistic fashion, she fastened on that moment- the kind that Nola was so good at- and wished that Sergei was herself. She began to fantasize that she replaced him, and that she possessed the unattainable. She spied on their intense conversation that was becoming more impassioned, and her fantasy intensified as she witnessed her defeat; then was compelled to act it out- a compulsive pattern that remained unanalyzed; a perfect figure to project on, and loose the shadow that controlled her.

Her interest in her fling had immediately waned, when not a moment ago, she was fascinated with the creature- taken with her elegance and wit, and with her intellect that she eroticized... but there was nothing like Nola's... it no longer seemed remarkable. Throughout a disastrous dinner, while pretending to focus on Gaza- the Arab/Israeli, she picked up at a lecture, and who she'd been fucking for weeks, and would imagine was Nola; she continued to spy on the pair, and found a way to interfere. Sergei, with his back to her, was unaware of her presence, while Nola, with her sharpened intuition, was summing up the situation. Christa, wanting more poison, ordered some oysters, as she

273

projected her hatred on Sergei, instead of turning it inward.

When Christa finished her oysters, she sent them a bottle of Cristal, and followed it up with her presence, so they were unable to refuse. She asked if she could join them for dessert and introduce them to Gaza. "She's an authority," she said, "on the Ar-ab/Israeli conflict," as if she created her for their amusement. "Her ideas on the subject are fascinating- as she is. I'm sure you'll find it interesting."

As Nola said no, she could not, Sergei said yes, though reluctantly. "I'll go with Sergei," said Chris-ta, with the smile of the trickster.

Nola let it go for a moment, but decided to get her- politically, and when Christa brought Gaza to their table, Nola feigned interest in the conflict: So, Gaza, tell me your thoughts on the Arab/Israeli conflict (till feigning an interest became a reality). Christa was telling us you are an authority on the subject."

"Not at all. Christa exaggerates. I've been working on a three-state-solution, based on the axiom of Maria: the Jewish woman alchemist, who discovered a formula for projection, but as a process of transformation in the feminine vessel; Jung applied it to analysis, and I'm applying it to politics.

"I wrote a paper on Jung's exploration of it: how 'out of the third comes the fourth', and how to integrate the shadow side. The U.N. became interested in it as a possible solution to the problem."

"So. 'Out of the third comes the one, as *another*, as the fourth', as a means of resolving the 'conflict of opposites': Maria's axiom as a formula, for *integrating* the opposites: here, both Israel and Palestine as undivided states- but with a *relativized* separation, that can also function as a whole, by combining the two and *creating* a 'third'- and so, comes the 'one, as the fourth' that includes the shadow side of each- *transcending* the *literal* conflict, by making it conscious- rather than *killing* it in the fundamentalist way: in the compulsion to destroy what it is trying create."

Gaza agrees. "Yes, just as I conceived it."

"I would like to hear more, but it's too complicated for dinner. Let's do lunch here tomorrow; it would be my pleasure to take you, and *explore* the feminine vessel. Perhaps, I could interview you. I'm writing a paper on *splitting*," glancing pointedly at Christa, "and how interpreting the symbolic as literal is the basis of war- in the psyche."

"I'd like that," said Gaza. It might clarify my thoughts. I'm presenting it at the UN the following day- leaving Maria the Jewess out of the equation."

"Of course. We're in time. It will clarify things for both of us. Are you a Jungian analyst?"

"Yes, I practice in Jerusalem. I'm working with religious texts- mainly the exegesis of the Torah, and relating it to the Koran. My interest is in hermeneutics- the phenomenological interpretation of the contradictory texts, and how when 'the conflict of opposites' is interpreted as literal, the shadow is projected on the other- ending in war."

"Lunch will not be enough. Let's extend lunch to breakfast, to *understand* the feminine vessel, and how it is the crucible of change. I want to know more- so does Maria."

Christa was becoming increasingly nervous, compulsively drinking Cristal from the bottle she sent them,

275

losing control of her persona and her bait of the third. Sergei was watching Nola work and was rather amused; his ironic smile took the likeness of the smile of Leonardo- whose spirit had entered his body, like an imaginary number.

It took several minutes for Nola to accept it. You cannot fool me, Leonardo. I see you've invested my lover. How else could you have me? But please, don't make a scene. I'm confronting the devouring mother in the flesh, who is trying all the tricks to appropriate my soul. Try not to shatter her glass, while she is drinking to forget, or to pour an overdose of salt in her chocolate souffle'. No sooner had Nola transferred her will to the spirit than Christa *choked* on her souffle', and washed it down with champagne, but the glass broke in her hand, and her feminine vessel was shattered: it could not contain the projection- a joke of 'the fourth'.

"We'll continue to look at the phenomenon of *splitting* at lunch. Tomorrow at one- as *another*-slipping her a card. "Sergei and I were just leaving. Thank you, Christa, for the Cristal. It really worked, don't you think?" But Christa was numb with defeat.

"You realize, of course, that you were staring at her, as if you wanted to devour her?" said Christa to Gaza, as she recovered her voice.

"Was I? I thought I was looking, and that it was you who was staring. You are completely obsessed with her, aren't you, Christa?"

"Just curious. And you?"

"I am also curious."

"I had a fantasy of a kind of three-state solution," said Christa, trying to cover herself, and prolong a premature ending.

"And I had a fantasy of two- with an *invisible* 'third'. I think I'll go home and rest up for lunch. See you, Christa- around."

Christa ordered more poison, but it was not the kind she was hoping for, and was forced to accept her own dosage- which had always been wrong; and in-stead of attacking the two warring tribes in her breast, she directed her venom at Sergei (her 'rival'). She could not find 'the third', and could not fathom 'the fourth', and in a fit of desperation she hit on the waitress.

CHAPTER 37
SPLITTING ADAM

Gripped by images of death, Nola writes in her notebook...

I am dreaming of death, and the fear of losing him to it, but the more I escape death, the more I attract it. I hear Snow's voice from the past through the wind of 'The Mother': 'We attract what we fear', and I am a magnet for death. Then I hear Nora's words: 'the fear of the binding of love,' and so I eroticize death, as if it were death that would free me... and then... the compulsion to destroy love... and the fear of love's death...

I have been pulling away from him by eroticizing Gaza, who personifies 'the conflict of opposites' and the betrayal of both, and I am telling him of my trysts and hoping he'll leave me, but he has a high point of bearing, though not as great as my own. I must be more careful and stop trying his courage. I don't want to hurt him, but I have to know he can take it. In some ways he's a stranger. I know nothing about him. I know the year of our wine and the grape it was made from, but not the vintage he came from, and how he became what he is: how long crushing and pressing the wine of the truth, and tracking it down like a beast, as if pursuing my prey... He must be as old as Leonardo the year that he died, and who resides in his body to give him a taste of the earth... fifty-five years of rebellion, searching the secret of time... escaping death... and myself... in the timeless journey through space... But how long will he live?... how long, Lord... how long?

She still lives in the penthouse on Abingdon Square,

and, as if the room had absorbed him, it con-firmed his theories of time- his maps of the stars on the walls and above on the ceiling.

After writing her thoughts, she fell asleep and had a dream. The image mocked my Communion dream, in which my son was lying in his tomb, as the Salome was dancing for the head of my saint; and then the reversal of the sacrament and the profaning of the god. In this dream...

Christa's corpse- a perversion of the Christ- was rising up from her tomb, and was offering me the Eucharist, but the body of Christ was defiled, for it was literal- not symbolic. '*Abrununtio Satanae*'?[273] asked Christa, and this time I renounced it: 'I renounce it, I renounce it'... I said in my dream... but it was not my voice that responded... but the spirit of Snow... When I awoke, I was starving for the Eucharist... as in the dream of Communion, when the Sacrament was reversed.

I awaken to Gaza ringing the bell. She was clearly unnerved. I sensed it was related to the dream. I began to explore it, without letting on...

I gave her a glass of Chartreuse as a sedative for her nerves, as I listened intently for the clue she'd reveal. We sat on the Victorian couch (designed for a solitary, swooping down on the back- the two at extremes- clearly designed to prevent any gesture of intimacy).

"It's Christa," said Gaza. She's returned with a vengeance. She's becoming extremely possessive and it's beginning to frighten me. Now she pretends that I'm you and that she is able to control me."

"You are right to be frightened. She's capable of believing it."

"Can you imagine? The affair, if you can call it that, lasted only three weeks."

"Mine lasted only a day, and it's becoming a tragedy. She appears at physics lectures and restaurants and makes it appear like 'synchronicity'. She called me at dawn, and interrupted my dream: "What do you want?" I asked bluntly.

"It's nothing, Nola... nothing.... a psychotic episode... 'nothing more'."[274]

"A psychotic episode is not nothing, Christa," I blithely replied. "It was just an erotic moment, and yet you are 'tap, tap, tapping on my chamber door':* can you hear it, Christa? Listen closely, 'Quoth the raven, nevermore'.* And not wanting to be rude, which is so foreign to my nature, I hung up on her, hoping she would come to her senses."

"She's not *completely* psychotic: just a vampire who is splitting, 'Only that and nothing more.'* Just splitting your Adam- a case of *animus* envy."

So, the key to the dream, and again, the wine turns to blood... Communion reversed, from the symbolic to the literal; and, though it is not in the dream, a warning for Sergei, who could be entombed like my son, while I am dancing the dance. The psyche is making use of the first dream of the tomb, to inform me of the danger, but is rearranging the details: it is only revealed as a whole when the first is used as a blueprint. Like Catherine, I am starving for the soul of my son... who lies in his tomb... while I live in the fear of love's death: it was as if she was mocking the means to resurrect what I killed.

"Her daughter was anorexic," said Gaza, and

280

starved herself to death. She sucked the spirit right out of her- drove her to suicide... I can't help feeling I'm replacing her."

"How many shapes has the Devouring Mother."

Later, she was dining with Sergei and expecting Christa to appear: and again, Christa arrived with a woman, who she was using as bait. Again, the bottle of Cristal, followed by a visit with her 'fling', and Nola feigned interest, as in the visit with Gaza, while the Leonardo in Sergei was watching her work. When Christa slipped a vial from her glove and poured the poison in his wine, Leo was reversing the glasses, acting as the spirit of her will (he tried re-versing the cliché but was not as successful).

Nola was watching and silently thanked him, and Christa swallowed the potient and suffered a stroke. She was rushed to the hospital and died of complications of the heart. The subtle fluid she used was never detected, while Nola's dark premonition was suddenly lifted. She did not disclose what had happened, and that she protected him from death. And Gaza returned to Jerusalem, the place of the crucifixion and the tomb.

CHAPTER 38
THE HEART OF DARK MATTER

I have spent my life fighting love, but my real enemy is death. Like a death warrior I am fighting it, and confronting it from every angle: every complex, every religion, every belief system in the universe: from the pre-Columbian death cults, to the ancient philosophies, from Christian mysticism to analysis, from polytheism to unity.

She continues writing her thoughts on 'the spirit of gravity', having tried to come down through promiscuity and death. Meanwhile, her students were coming for private consultations, and she was known as a seer and an interpreter of dreams; an expert on depression and bulimia/anorexia, and the phenomenon of consuming and being consumed; consulted for fashion and film, and the opera and ballet. She worked with life-threatening illnesses, addicts and prostitutes, and continued to teach through the lens of Neoplatonic Hermeticism. She studied physics, astronomy, psychology, archeology, while she was writing a treatise on *The Problem of Gravity: or On Love and Death and the Art of Falling.*

Sergei had sparked it with his talk on Einstein's thought experiments, from which he had quoted: "*If a person falls freely, he will not feel his own weight,*" and she was applying this concept to the surrender in love. In the first chapter, entitled *Breaking the Fall*, she began with the question: *Why does love bring me down?* and attempted to answer it in relation to the Law of Attraction:

'Even the undying spirit is attracted to matter, while

knowing to embody its essence is to be crucified by love, for love lasts for a moment and is the beginning of death. Even the dead are subjected to the Law of Attraction, and, as the spirit is searching for a body, it is destined to die. Yet if it suffers its death for the life of the soul, by making the sacrifice, it will rise like the god.

'Question: if light is both a particle of darkness, a divided thought that bends the light, like the dead it will return on the curve of the wave, and so, the darkness is unable to destroy its continuity. As light curls for the return, we can outlive our own limits, and like 'the light in the darkness', the dead will rise and descend, and will continue their journey in the souls of the living, for by the Law of Attraction, *love is stronger than death*.

'Question: if light is both a wave and a particle, then how do I divide myself? If my devil of a shadow is but a particle of darkness, a divided thought that bends the light, like the dead it will return on the curve of the wave, and so the darkness is unable to destroy its continuity. As light curls for the return, we can outlive our own limits, and like 'the light in the darkness', the dead will rise and descend, and will continue their journey in the souls of the living.

That night Sergei was lecturing on Maeterlinck's 'romance with gravity': *What would* be *a universe devoid of attraction*? the master asks. *It would be a universe without matter, which is, after all, quite possible, but would mean nothing to us; it would be a universe in which not only could we not remain alive, but where we would be as inconceivable for it as it was* for *us. And in any case, even if we could exist, we would not be able to appreciate it.*[277]

Precisely my struggle, I thought...

A god who wished to annihilate the world at one stroke, Sergei continued, *would only have to deprive matter of its power of attraction. Instantly everything would dissolve in what we can no longer call space, for considering that only the movements and displacements of matter bring it into existence, there would no longer be any space.*[278]

These thoughts posed a problem, but I could not grapple with them at the moment, for Death hovered above us, and I wanted the form and the name—something wholly recognizable that I could place in the heart.

"Let us continue to look," Sergei was saying, "at the words of the poet, dramatist, philosopher, and scientist, and realize together that we are 'on the edge of the world',* and like Maeterlinck, never stop learning from the mystic drama of love's gravity, to comprehend its cosmic mystery through the spirit of tragedy. Any questions?

"Yes, Nola."

"Though Maeterlinck's imagination transcended the limits of science, he was unwilling to imagine crossing the threshold of dead matter. When matter is deprived of its spirit and its power of attraction, it can prevent us from turning death into life, but if we challenge the limits and *re-animate* the spirit in matter, and cross the threshold of the possible, we can find the way to return. Though he has crossed every boundary, Maeterlinck says: *As no one has ever come across matter that has no attraction, we cannot imagine it. And if we could, would it exist? We cannot know, for we, too, would be dead.**

"My question is: Is not the real tragedy that we are orphans of our own preconceptions, by believing that we have not encountered dead matter in the living, as it exists in the psyche? Why can we not raise the dead in us, and invest it with the power of magnetism? If 'gravity is God', as Maeterlinck says, then dead matter is 'God's shadow', and can we believe that this 'devil' is missing the power of attraction, when we are not able to resist our attraction to evil, and the urge to destroy what we fear, whatever form that it takes?"

"And your fourth question?" asks Sergei, "for I am sure there's another."

"If we confront our fear of the shadow and enter the realm of dead stars, by *re-animating* spirit can we transcend the limits of non-existence, by *creating* attraction, where we imagine there is none? And are we repressing the urge to turn death into life? By *creating* the force of attraction by desire and the will, to attract the spirit of all that has ever existed, can we not *inspirit* dead matter, by changing our relation to time?"

"Of course, you have hit on the problem. This is precisely what we are struggling with: that *gravitation creates time*.[279] In our construct of time all things die- yet we know through *The Thought*, that they are also reborn. Could you continue that 'Thought' that could allow us to transcend our own tragedy?"

"Yes. Time expresses the imaginal limit, but the very thought that our life is bounded by time can be reconstructed in the fourth dimension, in an inner space/time continuum. If time can be reconstructed and if gravity is the unconscious, then it is the *Mother* who personifies it, and if death is the *shadow* of the Mother, its darkness is the source of all life. If we have deadened the shadow through a lack of imagination, then we can infuse it with life, where we perceived nothing but death. If we can believe we killed God and then imagine his resurrection, it is hard to imagine dead matter cannot be revived. Yet, we know we can suffer the death of the spirit, for killing time seems to pose no problem at all. If we can crucify spirit on the shadow of matter, identify with its death, and create a religion from killing it, why is it hard to imagine transcending the limits of life?"

"Could you answer your own question?" asked Sergei.

"I will answer it with a question: If by crossing the threshold of space/time through the experience of death- which we may experience in a dream or an unconscious fantasy- and if, by the deadening of spirit, we believe that by crossing it we are dead, by not re-imagining it, are we hitting the limits of faith? If we are able to conceive that dead matter exists, it is hard to conceive that it cannot be sparked. When we experience a psychic death, and then return to reflect on it, we know it is possible, for what is not psyche?"

"That was two questions," he said, with an ironic smile. "Then are you saying that without re-imagining death, we cannot imagine resurrection, which we experience by becoming conscious of the shadow, or dark side of the *Self*, as the psychic equivalent of dead matter?"

"Yes, if we imagine dead matter as the basis of life, we can imagine that life comes into being through the process of destruction, and if gravity is life, it is also *The Thought* of our death, for 'The Law of Attraction' can always be reversed."

Sergei sums it up for the audience: "So then, how can we imagine it in a god and not re-imagine it in the self, and by not daring to imagine it, we make death immutable. But I am sure you have another question."

"Yes. Is death our projection of 'God's shadow', or our own? And if the spirit cannot imagine it, can matter really die? We imagine it does, and so we experience death. We know that with the death of attraction comes the desire for life; that there is a compulsion to resurrect it through the process of projection. Is this magical thinking, and a defense against death, or is it the basis of art and the desire to create?"

Both gravity and time had been my enemies, and my mother's prayer for my death at the moment of birth was just the beginning to both court and to challenge it. Though death was like a stranger, or an impersonal force, it was like an old lover, who you tried to escape, but who tracks you down like a beast, till the huntress is prey.

Did she see Leonardo's ironic smile, leering from Sergei, proving that dead matter lives, or did she only imagine crossing the boundary that Maeterlinck imagined has 'never' been crossed'? Was it the spirit of gravity or faith that 'brought spirit down into matter', and resurrected *The Thought* that we imagined was dead?

"Indeed, it is here," he continued, "that we must look at the limits of faith, and, by transcending the limits of science, continue to resurrect *The Thought*," said Sergei, agreeing (as if hearing her thought). "Maeterlinck also said: *From the time an atom comes into existence, and it has always existed, it attracts, it acts, it lives.*[281] In its psychic form, we may imagine that a dead atom- or the shadow of matter- is an essential part of an aggregate of the atoms of a soul, which have attained a degree of consciousness that resonates through the spheres.

"Here, he seems to agree with you, Nola, that from across the boundary of dead matter, a boundary he has crossed for us today, what has lived will always live. Something suffers: something dies and is reborn. And even in the darkness of doubt, when attraction reverses and turns to repulsion, when overcome by the shadow, or the dark side of *Self*, there are moments when we discover 'the light in the darkness', and we know death exists to transform what is living."

That night as they slept, he had a 'big dream'...
He was pulled into the vortex of the black hole in space. In his dream, he was unable to breathe, and his heart had stopped beating.

Nola awoke in a frenzy, calling him back. When he didn't respond, she entered it with him, and was willing to die with him in the heart of dark space: her greatest fear, which was Nothing, as she confronted the death of all meaning, and went into her terror, to find the source of all life. She would bring him back, or be Nothing; she would become her own fear- if that is what happened to negative matter. She placed her hands on his heart, and prayed to the force of attraction, by recreating the force with the will and desire, without which dead matter would be all that existed, and became the mother to his son and held him in her arms, singing a lullaby and rocking him to life, and, in the endless night, found the words as she fell through love's gravity…

> Like a starving swan
> with high-pitched cry
> too weak from love to dive,
> its feathers caught in winter's ice,
> will wait for death,
> knowing that its chance is spent,
> I wait for you with frozen wings
> that beat the heart
> to heat the chilling blood
> that still is rushing for you,
> my dark wings lifted by your image,
> borne up by your current,
> knowing there is no flight without you;
> for now, the cold north wind has numbed
> them,
> pinned them down in its embrace,
> holding me for the Communion,
> breaks me open for you,
> while the vultures cleanse my bones of
> flesh,
> drain the heart of all desire:
> the need to dash myself upon your rock…
> to die in you.

"I dreamed of my death," he was saying, struggling back in her arms, "and I used your heart as a compass, so I was able to return. I remembered Maeterlinck's words: *A god who wished to annihilate the world at one stroke, would only have to deprive matter of its power of attraction.* I was sure I had lost you, and was searching for you in the cosmic dust, pulled to the heart of dark matter, unable to resist... but I heard your voice in the void and it was calling me down... the voice of my soul... and I'm here in your arms."

"You know what Leibnitz said: *Every speck of this cosmic dust is both an atom and an angel,*"[283] she whispered.

"Yes, it must have been that... it had black beating wings... but it was more like a swan... and I was dashed on your rock and my heart nearly died. I knew that without you, my heart would stop beating: that you were my gravity, my life, and I knew you would find me."

"I found you where dead matter lives, but I am asking the question: I don't *want* to ask it but something else is at work."

"You are asking, was it your shadow that drew me into your darkness?"

"Do you still want to come down with me, now that you know what you're 'up against'?"

"How would I not? You have taken the risk with me and are the most heroic person I know. I have always attracted the most powerful forces, but I have not found their human form, until I found *you*.

"You are attracted to my darkness. You *want* to lose yourself in it."

"Sounds like love. By the way, I know you were protecting me from knowing that you turned Christa's shadow back to the source, but, as an astrophysicist, I've perfected my peripheral vision. I saw her switching the glasses, and how you played the cliché. It is too easy to be devoured when you are spacewalking through time, and I notice such things, which is why I'm still here. But I *also* switched them the night you stole Gaza. I was not as adept in the game, as you who attracted it, and she caught me, but I pretended it was a *private* game just for two- that she was *not* possessed by the trickster, but only playing its part. Her shadow was flattered, as I was watching you work. I know you didn't want to burden me with the shadow of death, but I have only one question: was it loyalty or guilt?"

"Why split atoms? Can you forgive my motherly instinct that wants to devour you, while trying to save you from being devoured? I am *jealous* of Death, who wants you all to herself. She becomes more possessive, when I take you away from her."

And they laugh till it hurts in the fear love would die.

CHAPTER 39
THE INNER COUPLE

Nola lies 'on the couch', lost in her thoughts. Nora is studying her, reading the silence.

"How can I put it, Nora? You are my gravity."

"And he is your spirit?

She is in love with both of us, thought Nola. "You are in love with him, aren't you, Nora? You can't fool me, you know."

"I'm in love with 'the inner couple',[286] that keeps the universe spinning: that is carrying the projection of 'the unknown third'.[286a] But tell me your fears."

"I am in love with both of you."

But *I* am unable to say it... "What do you not want to say?"

"That without either one of you, I would fall into infinity."

"You are afraid that without us the past would engulf you: that its shadow is boundless and you would drown in its depths." Like I am, I admitted, but only to myself... "What are we for you, who live for yourself, but the projection of wholeness, so you can be who you are."

"As we are to you. This 'inner couple' you're in love with that we have somehow made real- it must be torture for you, as 'an unknown third', who, as the keeper of secrets, are not able to be involved. How is it for you, Nora, this projection of wholeness, who can only be *witness* to the marriage of the mind and the body? I am as willing as you are to carry the projection, which could only be *real* through 'an unknowable third'. We are in it together, Nora, for only through you could it happen for me. Strange that this vision of wholeness was made manifest by the senses, and was able to be realized in mundane reality, while linking the three of us through the interior work. But it must feel like a betrayal through the very law of your profession: like I am living it for both of us, as I struggle with my love for you-while you will not tell me of yours, that I can only know through the transference."

As she dismembered my situation, I felt the pain in my lungs. There was no solution to my problem, and she was laying it bare: that both she and her stargazer were my imaginary lovers: more, that it was the work of the trickster, who was playing both shadow and *animus*. Was there a purpose to this madness, or was it simply an analytic joke?... an experiment on the analyst, carried out by herself.

And yet, we both know it's Sergei, thought Nola, who is going to be the sacrifice: that he will be suffering ours, as if it were his... while the three of us are attempting to 'marry the opposites', and either *anima* or *animus* is trying to escape from the bottle.

It was ingenious of Sergei, Nora was thinking, to equate the Mother with gravity, while he was he stealing her wisdom. In any case, she is bringing me down, and, yes, this lower trinity is unbearable, in which Sergei will be sacrificed...

"You have learned to stay with the projection and to then take it back," I was saying aloud, while I wrestled with myself. "Now you are able to heal others of the spiritual illness that splits the mind and the body, and you know it better than me. Love has allowed you to cross the imaginary boundary and to link spirit and matter, which are now interpenetrating. Do you really think you still need me?" I asked, still trying to be objective, but I was asking the impossible... for I still needed *her*.

"You mean, while I am searching for your shadow, so that I am able to complete myself? Or because you won't let me love you- a love that we know is beyond us? How do you see it, Nora- or would you not dare to tell me?"

"I see that you have a longing to complete yourself by internalizing your analyst"... I would have said tanta-lizing, if I hadn't stopped myself in time.

CHAPTER 40
THE BODY BETRAYS US

Nola and Sergei were having dinner at Sardi's. She liked luxuriating with him on her victory over death: not even the Devouring Mother could destroy him in her presence, and, by identifying with the trickster, she imagined it was so... But how long could she bear it, fighting God and the devil for him?... And why did she feel incomplete when not creating her myth?... when the myth became real, and she had to live what she wrote? She pulled out a thread from the weave, too subtle to analyze at dinner, and was trying to digest what she devised in the mind: that *The Thought* was the crucible for the souls of the dead, and by combining their spirits, she would produce an immaculate conception; while for Sergei, the challenge would be to make it more human. But only Nora could grasp it, the need to transcend the flesh.

She tried to reduce it to the simplest equation and to find the right dosage, so she would not poison him with it, but she had never learned how to measure; it was simply not in her nature. And as she resisted expressing the full weight of the thought, she resorted, instead, to splitting spirit and gender...

"Tell me, Sergei, why does it feel incomplete to be with either a man or a woman? Why do I always experience it as though the other is missing? Why do I always need both, while wanting to transcend the flesh, for the body betrays us and turns love to dust."

"I'd say it's the fear of not being whole, as you kill off your lovers, in your battle with spirit and matter."

"The fear I will be robbed by the body of the inner

295

experience. And yet, it is finally here, the union of both... so here I can't bear it. Why can't I bear it?"

"Why *imagine* your love, without taking the risk?"

Leonardo smiled at her through him, for he had asked it before. It was the same question disguised, and he reminded her of it.

"It's a real question, isn't it- the one I can't answer, for I am mourning the limits by indulging in promiscuity."

"In the fear of love's death, you defy the boundaries of love, while you are killing us off in the mind and changing the bodies at will. I am not really threatened by the wayward spirits of your lovers, for I know I'm enough for you, and, perhaps, enough is too much. Whether you are enough for yourself is another question entirely. I am willing to endure it, while you test my endurance. I know what you're doing: you are tempting me to leave you. But I would rather be tempted by you than--"

"Than who?"

"Than the Devouring Mother."

"Perhaps, I have fooled you, and she is using my body as a disguise."

"I've never been fooled by the mask. But, perhaps, you have fooled yourself, Nola, and what you want is a woman: then maybe one would be enough."

"I am not a monotheist by nature (a little joke for the god). Now you're imagining I'm a lesbian, instead of a hermaphrodite."

"I'm not as mercurial as you. But really, if it were one, what kind of woman would it be?"

"It could only be Nora."

"But what if it were possible?"

"I've wondered that myself. It is not that she's unattainable, but what she has attained."

"Yes, she is brilliant, and I am also in love with her."

"I felt it. And, somehow, I can accept it completely... only Nora, you understand. It can only be Nora."

"Then it's a deal. Do we agree?"

"Yes, I believe we can agree- which makes us nearly monogamous, as Nora's off limits."

"What will happen, do you think, to our multiple selves? Will they become dead stars in space that collapse on themselves, and will they try to devour us, or will we integrate our unborn children?"

"What are you thinking? By making them human?" But she was already thinking it... of bringing a son down to earth... already denying it... the symbol becoming reality... preferring the symbol... an immaculate conception, combining her son and her lovers in one single being. "Please, Sergei, you're scaring me. Do you mean... an unborn theory?

"Naturally, what else?"

"For a moment, I felt the fear I repressed, and I wondered if you were coming down further than I anticipated; the fear of being buried alive in the reality of earth. We must remember, we are dealing with not only particles but waves, and with the curving of space, not with linear patterns."

"I promise not to betray you with a thought that's not curved. And we will always have Nora- if you fear we're lacking a 'third'.

"There are only three things I fear: the linear pattern; the particle; boredom and monotony."

"Isn't that four? Then it follows that the fifth fear would be the death of our love. You find the antidote in promiscuity- and being 'Catholic' it's a sin. That gives it a kick, as it keeps you burning in hell. You can't get bored while you're burning- unless you 'imagine' you're dead."

"So again, what remains are love and death, and the splitting defense. Please don't cure me, and make me want to belong to you. Don't make my fear real by loving me more than I can bear, so I can keep my fear an illusion that love will tame my wild beast, and that Nora will spend her entire life analyzing it."

CHAPTER 41
'REVERSAL OF OPPOSITES'

It was at this moment in time that Nora became deathly ill. She was in a sanatorium in Switzerland and was dying of consumption. Nola believed that she carried it from *Perdue*, and had infected her analyst, who was contagioned by her shadow- a condition inevitable in every analysis, and, consumed by her guilt, she questioned her soul. It was called consumption, she echoed, because it consumes from within, by killing the breath of the spirit, and what Nora kept secret. But she did not have a choice: it was being revealed...

"It's the shadow of the father," said Nora, "who passed it to me. I know you are sure you've destroyed me, like a lover, but it is only your narcissism that you feel responsible for life and death."

"Will you allow me to heal the sick father in you, Nora, as you healed the father in *me* and have given me life? Will you let me give it to you, to re-animate the heart: to strip the veil that denies you the will to receive? I am here for you, Nora, because you gave me love's secret, and you must let me return it, and give you the key to the mystery. I know all of your complexes, like I know my own soul, and it can only be me, as I received it from *you*."

"We will not let the body betray us. It's time... I will let you... We will kill him together," said Nora, sinking into a trance.

Why had she suddenly contracted the illness again? What had infected her mind and was consuming her soul? She had been dreaming of her father, while Nola was 'mining' in *Perdue*, and what was killing the analyst, the patient would heal, who vowed that the tomb of the worm would be turned to the pearl of the *Self*.

'Help me, you thief of a saint, to transform the shadow of death,' and she was standing in the fountain behind the young Magdalena, as the tears streamed down her face like they did long ago.

Nora told Nola her childhood myth, as if their roles were reversed, and how the shadow of death made her into an analyst... Now she traveled through time to 1941, twenty-one at the time, during the war in Berlin, still incested by her father, a Nazi medical scientist, who specialized in torturing women in the Ravensbruch death camp. She was forced to take notes on his experiments with death, while she worked on her manuscript, to reveal his atrocities: *A Study on Fascism: the Betrayal of Self*:

"I am taking notes for my father as I watch the experiment, but I have wandered from his and recording my own. He called it assymetrical torture and designed it himself, to compare the limb that was crippled to the limb that was normal. I sit in the stark glaring room that heightened the atmosphere of terror; the naked Polish women on line who are waiting their turn. He injects a poisonous fluid into the leg of a girl, who stares at her limb now misshapen, distorted. She is starving, emaciated... like I used to be… Then he looks at her arm and tells me her number. I record it, methodically, as I was instructed to do, and it is like I am one of them… and am waiting my turn. Their souls have been driven out of their body and they look like an army of ghosts, who subsist in the shadow."

Nora was born in Berlin in 1921, and suffered the perversions of her father from early adolescence. She survived his violent molestations by living in a myth, replacing him with Wotan, the hunter and father god. She fused him with Zeus, who was raping semi-mortal women, as he played Wagner's *Siegfried*, the hero, to drown out her screams. He began his experiments in the camps in 1941, injecting the TB bacilli into the women he raped, and contracted it from his victims and passed it to her. He proved that on the verge of destruction, the longing for death turned to life: that before the extinction of will, the urge to live would return.

His sadism was considered a scientific form of vampirism- an act with no reflection that shunned the light of day. As his patients were infected, they were devoured from within, as he projected his shadow into the women he enslaved. His victims were thought to have vampire traits, such as 'red eyes tinged with blood, which produced a sensitivity to light; a deathly pale bloodless skin; and the chronic coughing up of blood; and were forced to attend nightly blood-letting rituals, wasting away from their sleeplessness', like the inmates of the camps; but the evil returned to its source and he contracted the disease.

Nora lived out the myth of the purge of the sleepless, and in her nightmares she attended the rites of the dead. He found it erotic that she resembled a corpse, while she continued to live by thinking of ways to destroy him. But while her will had been broken by disease and starvation, she carried it out in the dark of the mind.

In time, he tired of her 'corpse-like beauty',[295] for it

retained a kind of purity, as he raped his victims of 'the system' (that was lauded by the German Reich): that fear was a sign of a psychic imbalance that distorted the brain, while destroying the body. Convinced he had finally proved it by the torture he devised- that the real disease was the fear, not the poison in the vein, for the final proof of his theory, he shot a bullet in his brain, and was sure if he conquered the fear, he would achieve immortality. The experiment was successful for killing the brain, but, though he could not feel the fear, he died like a mortal.

Meanwhile, Nora took notes while he was going insane, on how sadism and masochism were not really opposites; how the sadist's power depended on robbing the will of his victim, and that the legend of the vampire was based on a dependent personality; but the blood of his victims was what finally killed him; as if the consciousness he feared was contained in its essence; as if his fear turned to blood as he was coughing it up; as if he tried to reject that it 'proved' what he 'knew'.

After his suicide, she gave birth to Siegfried: the son of her father, she named for the hero of Wotanism- the idol of the Nazis, who was almost immortal. It was a psychological paradox that the hero was indestructible, whose only weakness in the back was the part he couldn't see- the shadow, or unconscious side, that became the focus of her studies. She projected the heroic ideal on the innocent boy- like Snow's image of Terzo, to protect her from death. At nine, feeling dwarfed by the image, he seduced Nora's lover, a fascist and killer, to save her from death. Dressed in her clothes, he hung himself above her bed, and she was prepared for her profession as an authority on fascism: the part of the shadow that turned on itself, and that killing the God, like the fascists, who replaced it with ego, was like killing the self, turning the 'hero' to victim.

Steeped in the memories and fears of the past, she confided her secrets to her patient, as if relating her symptoms to a doctor. It seemed their experiment was working, and she began to believe: that by healing the shadow, the body would follow. All she had was their myth as she wasted away, and was told she had three weeks to live and to prepare for her death. There was no reason to doubt the fatal prognosis, and while Nora fought for her life, Sergei mourned for them both.

She was moved to intensive, where the blood was drained from her body, and given continuous trans-fusions, a cure for heroin addicts, which the doctor invented and applied to consumption; a morphine addict himself, who resembled her father, and the vampire syndrome in his blood-draining rituals. Meanwhile, Nola waited for her resurrection at the door of the tomb.

The delirious fevers brought her closer to death, and the dreams were revealing what was needed for the healing...

I dreamed that my father was transfusing his blood into mine. The tube was connected to his heart and was hooked to my own. The transfer was lethal and he was timing the beats, as if counting the seconds that would lead to my death."

"Strange, isn't it, Nola, how I discovered my

calling, which was to work with despair, and the wasting of body and soul."

Time escaped like the trickster as I began the transfusion, taking her sickness inside me- the wasting of body and soul. I place the Hawk mummy of Horus in her skeletal arms, and awakened her calling on the threshold of death. Nora would only allow me to heal her by a 'reversal of opposites' that I called into play: I as the patient and she as the healer: a *psychic* transfusion that took place in 'the underworld'. And so, I passed the projection in our experiment with death, that Nora was bringing me back from the realm of the dead. I begin our myth of transformation, to reverse our tale of life and death, and whisper our rite in her ear as she lies in my arms, the Hawk mummy between us as we descend to the god...

"My heart burns with the fever, as we circle down to the darkness, and descend through the veils to the ninth circle of hell, where you will be bringing me back from 'The Abode of the Dead'...[298]

"Down in the realm of the shadow, we sit by the waters of Lethe, and are watching the past as it dissolves and coagulates: watch while the snake is devouring its tail, changing to the shape of 'a woman bent back on herself'.* The Hawk boy appears, holding his eye on his palm- the wounded eye of the moon that 'the Red Man' has pierced, as Isis gathers the pieces of 'the Awakener of the Dead'.

"On the opposite bank, in the endless region of night, the dead are kneeling in prayer to the missing phallus of the god, the mummies standing behind them that contain the secret of life. We cross the black water, as they wait for an offering... I know that *I* am the offering to 'the god who is not'.[298a] Now the dead lay my body on the sacrificial stone, and you watch as 'The Red Man' dismembers it, and scatters the parts in the darkness. The Hawk boy instructs you to slay the killer of Osiris, 'the Lord of Two Worlds', and to mix his blood in the *Medicine*, and when you have danced the last veil, you cut off his head. Like 'the Black Goddess', who gathered the parts of the god, you are gathering mine on the banks of the Lethe, 'the river of forgetfulness', to change the memory of the past, extracting life from dead matter, and resurrecting my body, reversing the spell of your death with the elixir of life. '*Mumia,* you whisper, the Hawk in your arms... '*Mumia*'... '*Mumia*', and we rise through the veils.

"I dreamed of you Nola... I dreamed of your death"...

"We were down in the Land of the Dead... You were torn into pieces... the Black Goddess appeared, and I gathered the parts of the *Self*... I joined them together and was making you whole... mixing the *Medicine*... with 'the poison that heals'... You were wracked with the fever and were gasping for breath, and I gave you my life, mixed with the will of the god."

"It's like your dream of Communion, isn't it, Nola?... the black dust of the dead, down in the mine of the '*Self*'... the poison of love... that must be trans-formed."

Your body is burning, and you are sinking back into death... but I will not let you go: "Tell me, what do you see?"

"I am dancing the veils... You are finally here... I have brought you back, Nola... I have brought you back from the dead"...

"Yes, Nora, you healed me. I knew you would not let me die. *Love is stronger than death'*."

"Funny... his shadow is no longer killing me."

"Then your body grows cold and death swallows you up. Three weeks passed like this, as we journey to the underworld, from the chill of the fevers, to the fire of the god, as I wait by your tomb, till you are ready to rise...

"I had that dream of you, Nola... You were dying again.

"We were having dinner in hell, and you were stripping the veils. You were down in the seventh. You were receiving Communion... You were finally whole... *Love is stronger than death...*"

"How many Communions can one bear? Tell me more of your dream of reality."

"Again, we're in the Land of the Dead, in the depths of the underworld, and as 'The Red Man' dismembered you, I had to dance for your life. When we arrived in the world, I had the hunger of the beast, and, when we returned to earth's surface, we continued the feast of the Lamb. Sergei had joined us, and we devoured its heart... like Philos' dream... and your dream of Communion... There were nine courses in all."

"Why nine" I am asking. "Why not seven for the

veils?

"I asked the same question and the *Self* always answers: It said, that the lower trinity has been squared, and that the saints have returned. "Do we have to die to be conscious?" I was asking the god."

"It was a good question, really, and he gave me the image of the sacrifice. It was like I forgot to return for our feast... when you were dying your death... but I was returning for *you*... so we could celebrate life and bring you back from the dead."

"And you have, Nora... you have. I knew you would all along. This squaring of our trinity that is the feast of the soul takes several lives to achieve, and we are not finished yet. There is work to be done, and I can't do it without you."

And you gaze at the Hawk mummy, like a miniature dwarf, the one that I gave you, and that I placed in your arms- the one from the tomb of Samara, and you smile the smile I adore...

"*Mumia*... the *Medicine*. Did you conjure him up?" you were asking.

"We did it together," I said, "with the help of the god. 'The Awakener of the Dead' has accepted the sacrifice. The son of the transference is rising up from his tomb, for you have worked for it, Nora. You have worked for your life."

Sergei was leaning in the doorway, and he smiled like Leonardo: "What have I missed? You have returned from the dead."

"It seems it wasn't quite time," Nora said with her wit, "We have killed the shadow of the father and it has affected my appetite."

Sergei and I had been looking at her in wonder. She

was more alive than myself, but then it was she who had died. My own death was metaphoric and was not quite the same. She had suffered far more than myself, though we both took the journey for love. It was clear that to heal the inner father, we had to annihilate 'the real one'- he was a *psychic* reality in the shadow of *Self*. Death seemed like a dream that had given us life. But how long would it last? I was asking the god. 'Wholeness lasts for a moment *only*,[301] but we were here, in the moment, and that moment was now.

"Let's go to Rome" I said, "I know a great restaurant. I'll book the rooms and the flight. Why don't you check her out, darling. And pack Jung's *Collected Works*, while you are at it. You must have known you would live, Nora."

"I don't mind obeying her commands, when she is translating from the gods," Sergei is saying to Nora, taking the needle from her vein: picks her up in his arms, as if to seat her on his horse, as Leonardo once did, when he brought me down to the world. "*Death where is thy sting? Where is thy victory now?*"[302] he was whispering in her ear, immortalizing her death.

'Nothing lies', she was saying, repeating my words from long ago.

How could I deny that she loved him, and that 'the unknown third' was at work?

I had not been in Rome since Philos had died, and as I sat in our restaurant with Nora and Sergei, I remembered the words of Rimbaud that Philos quoted and lived: '*You have to separate and derange every sense, before you can learn how to see*'. "And we have been faithful to this formula," his spirit was saying to remind me, "putting our lives on the line, while we

308

honored Apollo and Dionysus: the form and the spirit, until they are one- though we longed for the form's dissolution in the madness of the god. This spirit," Nietzsche said, "comes from 'the heart of the universe',[302a] and without the gift of Apollo, and the *word* for the boundary, 'the spirit of music'* would rend us to pieces, as it dismembered the god whose spirit returned to the earth."

"Tell me, if I had not been unconscious, and possessed by his dark side, would you have lived?" I asked the spirit of Philos, as the dead pulled up a chair and joined us for the feast.

'A question *I* would have asked, when I awoke by the body of your mother', Leonardo was saying, as he separated from Sergei.

Nora and Sergei had gotten used to my dialogue with the dead, and they were learning to see and to hear them, when there was a change of the heart. The dead were looking at Sergei, guiding him through the inner constellations...How long, Lord... how long? I was asking my mother...

'Not long at all', Snow replied: *The angel has rolled back the stone*[303] *from the door of the tomb,* while the Magdalen is waiting, and '*on the third day he rose'.*[303a]

"In what form I was asking?"

'Why, in the form of the son. The stars will come down and reside in his blood, and you will ask the same question that you asked the spirit of Philos'.

CHAPTER 42
CROSSING THE THRESHOLD

1972: Sergei is lecturing on Einstein's *Finite Universe*, at the Science Congress in Paris, in the Hotel Crillon- where Nola escaped Leonardo in one of her many disguises, and turned 'one of the finest hotels in Paris into a whorehouse.' Science or mysticism, asked the mainstream physicists- more aligned with his father's theories than they were with his own, looked down on by theorists as spiritual paradoxes, with an arch of the brow, if not downright suspicion.

It was at the Hotel Crillon that Nola was exiled by fate- disguised as a concierge- when she first saw her son; and through the window of a tearoom, 'time turned into space'. She reserved the same suite, as when Leo was tracking her down, as if her escape was a fiction, when the huntress was turned into prey.

She is recognized by the concierge- now aware of her myth, as she checks in with Sergei and Nora, a trio too serious to tangle with. With her usual flourish, she signs her real name, producing a real American passport, without acknowledging the in-congruity.

The concierge signaled the clerk, rolling his paranoid eyes. "Do you recognize her? She's here again."

"Who?"

"That woman with three faces."

"It doesn't look like her."

"It never does. Don't you remember? That's the problem."

"Let us imagine the infinite in Einstein's 'finite universe', Sergei began his inflammatory lecture, 'that in the heart of each atom is a universe with no boundaries'. How can we live in a finite world without limits, but by exploring the boundaries of the archetypal patterns: the timeless forms of the psyche that give it meaning and depth; where the god-given limits seem to extend in infinity, and 'round on themselves, like the infinite stream of the stars.'[305] For as time bends the light, it returns to the source, where the opposites are joined in an infinite round.

"Whether what seems to be infinite has limits in space/time has created some controversy and the usual splitting. Though the mind is constantly reconstructing its finite patterns, it is born of archetypal principles that shape its existence. We ask, does the infinite mind create its own limits, or do we worship a limited God with an infinite imagination, who can't conceive his own death, but has imagined our own? We live in a maze of shapeshifting patterns and are sleepwalking through the universe in the four dimensions of space/time, and project our delusions, which attract an external reality, and are compelled to possess them as they move out of reach. Has God possessed our unconscious to come to terms with his own? Are we projections of a God who can't accept his own shadow? Is God responsible for his unconscious, as we are for ours, and does he punish himself, when we stray from our orbit?

"We may imagine our projections have created themselves, or may wonder if God has the same infinite fantasy- the problem of having no limits in an infinite universe; and when he denies them, is he destroying himself? like his limited creations, who are identified with their Creator, and who die the death of the Son on the cross of our shadow, but are *not* resurrected by God's infinite fantasy.

"Our psychological patterns seem to repeat in infinity, and like a recurring dream can become an accepted reality, and whether finite or infinite is a matter of perception. We can reconfigure the pattern but it has its combination of notes, and we are continually attracted and repelled by the same archetypal forms; while, depending on our angle of perception, they either create or destroy us, as we construct our own laws and begin controlling our destiny. Just as the archetypal forces that we project on the stars can produce psychic energy that can awaken dead matter, if we are willing to accept that space/time is curved, then the dead can return through infinite space."

Nola reflected, moved by 'the spirit of gravity':[306] if 'gravity tells matter how to move,'[306a] I invoke the *Mother* of gravity to call down my son. I will find a form that will suit him, and conceive a son by the stars, and, by undoing my curse, he will learn to be human...

And she whispers to Nora, clasping her hand: "I have an appointment with Terzo. I'll be back for the con-clusion."

She returns to the tea room, where he saw her through the window, when she removed her disguise and the black veil of matter, reconstructing the pattern in a finite world without end: when *time* as *the son and the mother as space*[306b] met in a deathless dimension, and the stars were the souls of the dead. Now the pattern was repeated at the same table by the window, when they returned to the source with the same subtle influence, and 'the stars in the blood' seemed to conjure the moment. Now she called him to join her through the window of time and his soul-image moved toward the spark of his birth. She studied his walk and his gestures, watching his spirit move towards her, looking into the heart as he sat down beside her.

She had invoked what she longed for in the years since his death, and though she had changed, he was still a boy of twenty-one- the fated number revealed, so Leo could open the safe, before she was cracking the mind and had realized her gift; finite time 'with no edges' from the moment time stopped, and with the same years when he died, time had curved like the light. When she tried to know him as separate, they seemed like one single being, and though he was just as elusive, they were of the same spirit. Again, they thought the same thought in infinite space, when finite time and the infinite met on the threshold of death, and he died on her breast in the sign of the cross.

"Do you know who I am?" she had asked: the question that warped time and space. And again, he gazed at his shadow mother, as they searched for the words. The veil of silence was rended after nine mystic years... how many dreams, since his birth from the wolf girl of twelve; he remained the same age as he was when he died; time seemed to stop, since that day (she even *looked* thirty-three).

'Twice, I have seen you', he said: when I was born and when I died, though you appeared every night in my visions and dreams'.

"I have wanted to tell you, it was not you I rejected, but the shadow of my father, I could not distinguish from my own. But now there's a 'third', for we have crossed the threshold of worlds. Though I can't change your death, or find your limit in a boundless universe, I am with you in the moment, for I have found the limits of my self."

'But I can't find my own, for I have died on your shadow. We have the same problem, and I was never able to define it. Not having a mother, I slipped the boundaries of earth, and under the spell of our fate, I was born out of death- it was already written; I just carried it out'.

"At least, you had Snow."

'Not really. She had me. I was only possessed by her'.

"I know what you mean- fascinating creature, but not cut out to be a mother."

'It was you that I wanted- but I didn't know who you were'.

"Neither did I. It was through your death that I knew."

'I thought I invented it, my alienation and loneliness'.

"You won't be lonely anymore, now that I know how to find you."

She returned to the lecture, and continued her notes, as Sergei was drawing his ineluctable conclusion: *It is inconceivable to wander outside the universe,* as Einstein observed, while he wandered outside it. But when we long for the eternal, while perceiving our limits, we can find the infinite in the finite in the archetypal image. Though the god forms are timeless, they exist in the mind, and when breaking the boundaries, when we search for the infinite, they return 'in endless approach' in more limited forms. It is only by accepting our limits that we can begin to transcend them; by confronting our darkness change the finite equation, and discover eternity in the fourth dimension of mind."

They had dinner in the dining room of the Hotel Crillon, where Leonardo had watched her turning three men into beasts. Now his spirit came to join them, instead of observing from a distance, having separated from Sergei, to be more objective, while Nora was beginning to get used to him, in his archetypal form...

'You made several good points', he was saying to Sergei.

"What were they?" asked Sergei.

'Your talent to transit the worlds of the living and dead through the spirit of the word is rather impressive, grasping the paradox of what it is not to be: to live in the boundlessness of non-being in the limited structure of the visible. It can be a problem in terms of interacting with the other. It's rather lonely on the shadow side'.

"Tempting me, as always. I almost feel I want to join you," said Nola.

"Having nearly lost my boundaries, I think I'll stay for a while," Nora responded. After all, I just got back."

"As I did", said Sergei. "I have no conscious inclination to slip into infinity, though my dreams contradict me, and it is often rather close. Do you eat, Leonardo?"

'I only imagine it'.

"I had the same problem," said Nora.

"And I," Nola said.

'I'll just have a dozen oysters and watch Nola eat them', said Leo. "My pleasures are vicarious."

"It makes me feel guilty for having them."

'There you go with your martyr complex', said Leo, winking at Nora, knowing she shared it.

"When you are born in a cloister for a womb, it has an effect on you," Nola said to her thief, who abducted her from God. I would not believe I

"I was born in outer space," said Sergei.

"They are not that different," said Nora. "I was born in hell, and believe me, they are almost indistinguishable."

The waiter came to the table and Nola ordered the usual. "We'll have three dozen oysters to begin with, and a bottle of Cristal."

"Calling up Christa? You *are* tempted, aren't you?" asked Sergei. "I thought when you killed her, you had given them up."

"Some things don't change- like the pearl and the worm. Just a play of opposites that I seem to be prey to"...

And she told them Leo's myth of the pearl that changed the theme of her life, and thought of their last night in Snow House... when he was still almost human... Somehow, she thought of Esperanza and her son, the only mother she knew, and she realized she missed her... and that she needed her touch: the touch of the earth, of the finite, to not get lost in the infinite.

In the early hours of dawn, Nola went to the gypsy camp, and was told by a grief-stricken Toto that Esperanza had died. Nola had given her money to take care of Toto and bought her an apartment in Paris, but she had given it to a thief. The heart of the gypsy had stopped on the street, as she was posing in *The Pietá*, to give meaning to their suffering, and, repeating the myth, it became a reality; the mythic motif was reversed by the trickster, for the *mother* had died, and the *son* was in mourning.

This day, Toto took Nola and Terzo, her ghost of a son, to the sister church of 'The Mother' and the three prayed for her soul. Nola gazed at the Virgin that she had seen in her dream, her heart pierced by three swords, as she mourned for her son. It's the *heart* of the statue that contains the Living Water, she thought... the heart of my mother that was pierced by 'the Red Man'... the Virgin's hand still extended, as if for an offering. As Terzo sat in the pew between Nola and Toto, looking up at the Mother, he felt the sword in his heart, and he longed for his life, so he could know her on earth.

Terzo was nine when he witnessed Snow's murder, the same age as Toto, when 'Lupa' gave him his life, and Nola would teach him like a son- whose spirit would enter his body- and in the near distant future he'd be a priest, like 'Saint Ambrose': a *pagan* priest, who was linking the past and the future, the son and the mother through his lady of the beasts.

Toto, kneeling in prayer, was kissing the feet of the Virgin, and now in the moment, the spirit of Ambrose appeared, and he removed the three swords from the heart of the statue, holding a bowl for the Water as it poured from the wound. Then he washed Nola's feet with the Living Water of the Word, reversing the fate of the Magdalene and the tragedy of the Son, who in time would be freed of her shadow and return to the stars.

But first: 'Your son will be finding a body, and will rise on the earth, and this time you will know him as human, while the curse is dissolved', he was saying to

317

Nola, and she knew it was so. She was awakened again with a new understanding, and it would grow in the mind and illumine the heart.

It was in this moment of awakening, when Terzo entered Toto's body that changed the course of the stars of the young gypsy boy. Now Nola would mother him and prepare her new saint, and made her offering to the Virgin, who was ready to receive it.

CHAPTER 43
PAGAN PRIEST

Two years had passed, since 'The Mother' in Paris, and Toto was bridging the split between Christianity and paganism, while Terzo inside him, was trying to learn to be human. Terzo had taught him to read and to write; Nola, philosophy, mythology, theology, psychology; Ambrose' Latin and Greek, church dogma, liturgy, hermeneutics, sacred Scripture, the Apocrypha, and classics; Philos, mathematics, ancient history, sacred music, and art: but no one could teach him logic, as not one of them had learned it. With the help of the dead, in a year, he was attending the seminary, and would travel from Paris to Snow House, two weekends a month. Nola helped him write papers, construct learned arguments, and to dazzle the Fathers with his rarefied knowledge.

During a break, he went to Abingdon Square, where Nola held a feast to exhibit his talents, which would have been humanly impossible, without the *gnosis* of the dead. The spirit of his mother was cooking for the living (Leo was grateful he was dead, when he saw the gypsy's chthonic menu): bull's balls, lamb's heart, and *escamole*- or ant eggs (it was a discipline to get them down- the unborn children of the queen: the excavators of the earth, who were working for the Mother- the architects of temples, and the tunnels of the underworld, built by her army of workers, as they dug through her bowels.

"It's really amazing, the ant eggs, said 'Lupa'. Your mother has proved, once again, that she is the great chthonic cook. It's as if we are eating our complexes, which always look better than they taste. She used to cook for me as a child, in the days I refused to eat earth food," as she watched her hand moving Toto's, and stirring the body parts, that Nola loathed but made use of, as she fed on her men.

Esperanza pulls up a chair between Toto and Terzo-whose death she predicted, and was fused with her son. 'Don't pretend that you like it. Just keeping you here. I have nothing to give you but the food of the Mother'.

But 'Lupa' looks deeper than her words, and can feel her bitter sorrow; remembers her words from long ago and knows her broken gypsy heart... 'the sadness of the mother when she loses her son'... and how she knew the same sorrow, when she was losing her own... the boy she renounced to be free... but free for what? she was asking.

'You have changed him, 'Lupa'. You are his real mother now'. But she longs for her son, who is mothered by Nola.

"*We* are his mother," said Nola, trying to redeem her.

'She is still trying to redeem me, by adopting a priest', said Terzo to the gypsy, who has separated from Toto.

'No, Terzo, not trying. She will turn your fate into destiny, so you can become what you must; it will give you something to die for, which you never had in your life', said the gypsy who loved him and knew what he suffered.

'I never thought of it that way', and he stopped resisting for a moment.

"What Esperanza is saying," said Nola, "is that you will finally live. We are using the body of Toto as a temporary dwelling place, until we find the proper vessel for you, for you are not meant to be a priest. In the meantime, you will be getting a good education."

Leonardo pulls up a chair, leaving the body of Sergei. 'It makes sense', he was saying, wanting to invest a different body, and divines his own conflict, existing in the body of the physicist- a body he doesn't belong in, while he is serving her complex.

Terzo reflects for a moment, still trying to see it.

Somehow, she continues weaving the threads, Sergei is thinking as he watches her work: weaving her pro-jections into the archetypal pattern, and I'm wondering if there's a limit to how far she will go... Is she talking to the dead or to one of her selves? adjusting his vision, so he can see the invisible.

"How is life at the seminary, Toto?" asks Sergei.

"I *guess* you could call it a miracle. Ambrose and Philos have instructed me every day, and I have learned the language of the dead rather quickly, Nola says."

"You mean the dead languages, Toto," Sergei says, smiling.

"Yes, Latin, ancient Greek, Hebrew, and high German. One can't really do it without an *anima* like 'Lupa', who tricked the archpriest at twelve and is making him repent- now a theologian at the seminary, who has exerted her influence."

"Do try to be discreet, Toto. Has he hit on you yet?" Nola asks.

"In a way, but he's careful. He knows that I'm on to him. He is very strict with the others and gets pleasure from torturing them, but he does what I wish- or what *you* are wishing through *me*. After I observed him for several months, discreetly, of course, Nola wrote a scholarly paper on the dangers of celibacy, and the sin of lust in the priesthood as a result of repression. He called me into his office to discuss it in detail, and reveal what is hidden by acting it out. I knew he was getting off on it, and that he masturbated when I left."

"You seem to be making progress," said Sergei, with an irony like Leonardo's. "The last time I saw you in Paris, when you *imagined* being a priest, and had a *fantasy* of celibacy that was more like an erotic deviation, you still were not able to read and to write- that is, in the language of the living, which you seem to have mastered. How did you do it? I'm curious."

"Well, after Nola brought the spirits down to instruct me in the arts and sciences, she wrote all my entrance essays, which got me a scholarship, and she advanced me to the third year, with only three years to go. Terzo taught me to read and to write, and by the time I wrote my first paper on *The Prodigal Son*, and the clergy's denial of the senses, as it related to pedophilia, I had internalized Ambrose, my prodigal saint. That paper by Nola promoted me to seminary. But when I learned Christian doctrine through Nola and Ambrose, which was much more advanced, I was ready for ecclesiastics. When it came to calculus and physics, Nola said you were better at it, and she taught them through you and the Mother of gravity."

"That was kind of her. And now?"

"I'm also studying classics at the Catholic University of Paris- the dean was, also, 'Lupa's' trick... and... well, I'm afraid of my pride, but I healed him of Lupus- 'the disease of a thousand faces', which 'Lupa' is familiar with. He had red marks on his face and said he was bitten by a wolf, and when I purged him of lust, the Lupus was banished. 'Lupa' taught me to do it, and to reverse the old spells. It was a miracle, really, disguised as reality. She did it for *me* once, when I was dying of blasphemy. She said that once you've been healed, you can heal someone else.

"In only a year, I've been advanced to sacred theology, and have been chosen as worthy of aspiring to the Holy Orders- the sacramental ordination, as a priest of Mother Church. 'Saint Ambrose' is interpreting the shadow of the Gospels, and Philos is tutoring me in Greek philosophy and mythic history, which with Ambrose, we are combining with the *Apochrypha* and Gnosticism, to know what is missing in the dogma, so I can be worthy of my calling. But mainly, I am devoted to healing the soul. The priests say I have a gift for it, and though in my heart I am a pagan, I want to find God, and he is beginning to talk to me. Nola says that the *Self* can be projected as the *anima mundi* or as the *lower anima* and she is only its instrument, but she is more than a projection: she is my *mediatrix* of 'the lower trinity'."

"That's how it is with the *anima,*" said Sergei. "She tends to change shape and to take different forms. I can only speak from experience, but she often appears as a wolf, and it is sometimes not easy to tell them apart."

"That's what *she* said. At the moment, I am writing a paper on the Immaculate Conception, in which the properties of the Mother are transferred to the Son, through the spirit of 'reflection, or the Holy Ghost'."[316]

"Sounds like magic"- (hers).

'Yes, it's a good argument', said Terzo, 'but not really Catholic. It's based on an alchemical idea that 'the vessel' of the Mother' is what it contains'.* I'm a product of that experiment'.

"I'm afraid we all are," said Nora. "She hatches us like thoughts, and we become what conceived us."

'If you are talking about *me*, you are projecting again', said Siegfried, sulking in the corner.

"What she is saying, Siegfried, is that we are *all* projections of the Mother," said Nola, "and it is hard to return to her, but even harder to separate."

'You taught me what it means to *live* the projection', said the gypsy mother, and the *mystery* of mothering, so my son could stay in his body, when I left it for the spirit world'.

'She teaches the world how to do it, but she's never done it, you know. And yet, she's perfected the art of mothering strangers- though they find it hard to remain in their human body', said Leo to the gypsy, missing his own; resenting the body of her lover, and feeling like one of her projections.

"I admit it's a problem. I can only mother metaphys-ically. But why are you constantly pointing out my limitations, Leonardo, as if you weren't one of them? Have some ant eggs, darling."

'I'm not willing to go to that extreme. It's just the frustration of not being able to belong to you- in a less limited form'.

"But you do belong to me, darling. It's one of the advantages of being dead. My limits are your freedom."

'Again, you are trying to justify killing me'.

"I'm alive, and she makes me feel just as limited. It's a gift," says Sergei."

"I have the opposite experience- the unlimited one," says Toto.

324

'So do I', says Esperanza. 'She taught me to listen to the wind, and to return from the dead'.

'What about you, Nora' asks Leonardo. 'What's your experience'?

"Both finite and infinite. Both- always both." But she still couldn't have her in her limits- now that Nola was her analyst. She couldn't have Sergei, her patient, who belonged to her completely. Who *could* she have? she asked herself. She was as good as a virgin. The presence of her son reminded her of it- her own immaculate conception, who had her feminine properties.

'You are beginning to see it', said Siegfried. 'As the son of a concept, it was the same way for me... always alone in my head, just a part of your self- just an unconscious content that you hatched with a thought... not your son, not your lover, but a theme in your son/lover myth', said the son of her father to Nora, who was acting as his analyst, and who was trying to be neutral, and to overcome the incest.

You are part of me, Nora... Can't you see that I want you? Nola was thinking, hoping they weren't listening to her thought... And yet, how I long for my aloneness. Will I ever be alone again?

She belongs to no one, thought Sergei, and yet, we all belong to *her*.

She doesn't belong to him... not to any man... anymore than she belonged to me, thought Leonardo, who lost her, before he could feel that he had her... for though she still has a body, she escapes the demon of intimacy... and still she believes that love is a vice.

But if I had known her, thought Terzo, would she really belong to me, and felt the ancient longing for the mother that would never be sated.

She's more like an imaginary lover than a living mother to her son, Toto thought, and yet, I'm *replacing* him, who inhabits my body… and is the reason she wants to develop my soul… yet, I can't be without her... she is the will that has moved me.

She's like the twin of my mother. It's disturbing, thought Siegfried, and yet, I'm strangely attracted to her... or is it the mother/son transference?

What can I do for her, thought Esperanza, but cook for her, for eternity.

"Please, Esperanza, don't cook for me. Promise you will never cook for me, and stop trying to reciprocate- it's a fatal error in love. These ant eggs are bringing me back to the past... back to an old frame of mind that I thought I transcended."

"I will mediate," said Toto, who Nola taught to read thoughts, getting the gist from 'Saint Ambrose', who was inhabiting his form- as if he were being unselfish- to be closer to his lover…

"I can hear what the spirits are saying- what they *really* are saying, not what they think they are saying, as they play with our parts. What is happening is that the trickster is blurring our boundaries, and we slip into other forms than our own."

He has been influenced by Nola and is confounding his parts, as he slips into hers, which he thinks are his own," Sergei thought.

"The worlds are coming together," says Toto, "and we must be careful of merging, for if we escape love, the need to return is too great. Something is trying to happen in linear time, so that things can move forward and not turn on themselves, for there is an unusual compulsion to return to the Mother. I feel it myself and I am trying to resist, which is why we need conflict and a sense of disunity. Below the surface is the desire for the danger of a mystic oneness, but the ancient gods are presenting us with the multiplicity of paganism, as unity in incest would be absolute death."

"You have learned to go down to the depths, and to mediate her wisdom," said Nola. Tell us what each of us is trying to grasp from the unconscious, and at the same time denying- not wanting to know what we know."

"Let's start with you," Toto said, "since you have always wanted what you don't. You would die for the love that you are trying to escape, and still can't accept your own need, though you need to feel you are needed."

"How precise. I must try to accept what I resist and to use what you say, for you are learning my shadow and reflecting it back to me"... I'm not entirely in this world yet, thought Nola to herself. I still need to come down. My fear is that love will consume me; the need feels like weakness; I still have to learn my own limits, and not destroy what I love. My gypsy priest can instruct me, for he has learned to mediate the infinite. He can teach me how to stay here, within the boundaries of the body. My compulsion to escape love only drives me to the death pole, and if I do not learn it now, I will be disembodied with the dead.

It was then she saw Ambrose, peering out from her priest, but pretended she didn't, as Toto basked in his wisdom- mixed with the primitive instinct that bypassed the ego. My two selves are coming together, my parts being gathered, she thinks to herself, hoping

327

the spirits can't hear her. This fusion of forms is a better idea than I thought, for the unconscious is creating a sense of wholeness from the dead. The ancients knew the secret and borrowed one another's qualities...

"Toto' is right. It's the pagan conception of multiplicity in unity... with the longing for a unified field that spans the three worlds," Nola is saying aloud.

"I want to know more about what *I'm* resisting," says Nora, "and how I put in my body what I can't come to terms with- how it gets constellated in the flesh, instead of the psyche."

"In your need to believe that the mind and body are one," Toto said, "you have created a mind/body fusion through the misuse of the unifying principle. Because of the mind/body split they are unconsciously merged, and by trying to heal it, you forget that each system has its laws. For example, you believe that love needs to be consummated, or that it doesn't belong to you: quite a primitive belief, really, that keeps love's spirit imprisoned."

"That's very accurate," says Nora, abashed. How many others had she helped with that problem?... The mind and the body are merged through the incest... and yet, each envies the other, for spirit and matter are at war... and yet, in a constant collision, they are trying to separate.

"What is *my* shadow in love, Toto?" Sergei asks with foreboding. "What do I know that I deny?"

"You want to possess love from the fear of love's gravity: the fear that if you cannot control love, love will devour you: that you will lose your will in its force, and be split into atoms. What you fear is that you are unable to measure the force of the feminine, the unconscious itself, to be lost in the infinite- not having the words for the concept that is abstracted in space."

"I see. I must work on it. I will try to personalize my theories." He didn't learn that in seminary. He's been spending too much time with the dead, and his mystic mother, who is recreating him... so she can live with the guilt; by mothering Terzo through Toto, she is trying to bring him back to life- in her usual style that resembles a tragedy- an impossible fusion of personalities, which get confounded with the dead. How will he ever put up with the limitations of the living?

'And your gypsy mother, Toto, or have you forgotten her? What does *she* fear'? asks his mother, Esperanza.

"She fears I will replace her with Nola, and not long for her love."

'You are right, I envy her, your lady of the beasts, who has changed you in a moment, but living or dead, I am still your *real* mother, Toto'...

And she entered the body of 'Lupa', reading the lees of her blood: 'There is more to this tale of the mother and son. Let's talk about *your* son, and how his soul came to earth, and why you are mothering mine, instead of your own. You know things Nola Lupa, but there are things in the shadow- things you do not want to see, but that you know in your soul. After you pulled your first job, wearing the clothes of the wolf boy, when you thought you were dreaming, Leo, possessed by the wolf man, took you in his sleep and gave you a son. It was this you were running from in the streets and the alleyways, look-ing for love in the low places and making your tricks pay in blood. Your son had a father, who was not a hero or saint, and you turned your son to a spirit, instead of a real human boy'.

Terzo was listening and could no longer deny it... and he was hanging his head, like he did as a boy. He had the father he wanted, and a living mother on earth...but he could only know her in death... and he wanted to live.

'Why didn't you tell him'? the Berber asked Leo. And the words echoed in space, as if she were 'striking the stars'. 'Why didn't you tell him, who his real mother is'?

'Lupa's' words were still haunting him, reverberating in space- the words that he tried to forget in his death, but now he knew he would not, and they would live in his soul.

'Really, Fatima, you know better, you old wily storyteller', said Snow. 'You know that our myth casts a spell on us that even a thief can't escape- not a spellbreaker like Nola, a dreamer like Terzo, a saint like my lover, a murderer like Lupo, or a nun and whore like myself... for 'we attract what we fear', Snow's words at his baptism.

'I didn't know how', Leo repeated, 'how to translate from the dark. 'Lupa's' words were her art... mine were the art of escape- she learned it from me... how to run from the heart'.

"This gives our dream of the shadow another dimension, what we were searching the street for, what we already had, but the flesh has been spiritualized by confronting the shadow of the father," Nola said to her son, embracing his spirit, trying to hold him on earth, knowing he would slip into space. She felt the wind in her hair, as he left Toto's body, and she longed to go with him, but she was willing to stay.

330

'The 'unborn children' are waiting to be given life in this world', said Philos to Nola, who was calling them down...

> *'Mother, mother, let us come home!*
> *The door is bolted and we can't get in.*
> *We are in the dark and we're frightened.*
> *Mother, let us in!*
> *Or call our dear father,*
> *to open the door for us!*
> *You are the bridge across the gulf,*
> *over which the dead come back to life'.*[324]

And so she prepared for the birth, to give the spirits a home.

CHAPTER 44
'AN UNKNOWN THIRD'

The Science Congress of '73 on 'The Unknown Third'[325] proposed that it changes the electrical charge in the shadow of matter, and the magnetic field as 'the third' of the living and dead. The most notable and conservative scientists of the day were at the Hotel Crillon to deride the idea: that a 'psychic fact' could explain a theory in physics was a ridiculous notion, casting aspersions on science, and on Sergei's late father, who was renowned for his work: electrically charged particles and their effect in outer space-denying the magnetism of the mind and its psychic effect: the conflict of conscious and unconscious producing a 'third'. His father concluded that electromagnetic forces and the bonding of atoms had nothing to do with the workings of the mind, with the bonding of thoughts in the transference and the linking of complexes; and the notion of the space/time continuum in 'the collective unconscious'-* in contrast to Jung and his renegade son.

The physicists concluded that Sergei's attempt, based on the theories of Jung- to integrate' science, and myth, mathematics, and psychology, mocked the memory of his father, who made *serious* innovations, and they were there to defend him against his heretical son. Nola and Nora were observing their cynicism, who were scowling at Sergei and his daring advances: that the transference of thought waves produce an electromagnetic field, that can change the dynamics of space/time, enhancing the Law of Attraction, not only in psyche, but the universe itself. And yet, they were curious and wished they could fathom its depth, and, while critiquing his theories, they were masking their awe, as they degraded their uniqueness in their imitative journals.

The two women watched as he carried their shadow, and was standing alone in his towering body: watched him bearing their mediocrity as they tried to destroy him, and he waited a moment, till they were ready to listen...

" 'The unknowable third' can be recognized as the divine child of our field theory, and allows time and space to be wed in the fourth dimension of mind. It allows dead stars to be born and to burn with new life. As Einstein said, 'a changing magnetic field produces an electric field, and a changing electric field generates a magnetic field'.[326] It is from the physical and psychic interactions of the forces that are generated by the Law of Attraction, in both the universe and psyche, and their archetypal underpinnings, transmitted by 'the third', that a mysterious other arises, by which irreconcilable entities will finally combine.

"As the 'unknown third arises from the tension of opposites',[326a] it changes the structure of the human psyche, and perhaps, the structure of the universe, by changing the nature of relationship to both the personal and archetypal; it changes the relation to gravity as it exists in the unconscious, and the magnetism of the field, in which the opposites combine. Jung's 'transcendent function', related to higher mathematics- 'the combining of 'real and imaginary numbers', creates an unknown entity, '*transcending* the conflict of opposites',[*] by *combining* conscious and unconscious in a new way of seeing. The beginning of change in interior space, causes a psychic disturbance in the magnetic field, as it is doing right now in the magnetic field in this room. The disturbance creates a desire for consciousness, or it attacks the new vision that leads to change and transformation.

"Your lack of belief in what is transcendent to the ego is *obstructing* the field and the interaction of energy, that creates new pathways in the brain and in the space/time continuum."

They fumed at his audacity for calling them out, as if the unconscious was not related to universal laws. A few left the room, while others were paralyzed with rage.

"All change is brought about by a disturbance in the field," he continued, "a crucifixion or dismemberment of the light by the shadow, but without the consciousness of the disturbance, the transformation will not occur."

How many times, Nora thought, was I dismembered by his light... and by the shadow of the woman that disturbed the substance of his thought. He has magnetized the spirit through her shadow and made it conscious through the myth, till the dead stars are alive and ignite her desire to live. But the darkness surrounds me and I am submitting to its lure. How many times have I died and returned to the earth, by extracting the elixir from shadow and making it conscious? And now? I am in love with them both, and it is made of 'the third', and I am under its spell that rises up from the grave.

CHAPTER 45
GODWIT

When Sergei finished his lecture, the three dined at the Crillon, and talked of a thought experiment with 'the third' to revivify the dead. Nora was disturbed by the talk and had a premonition of death, but most disturbing of all was that she felt like a third. Terzo appeared to even the playing field, but she sensed a disturbance of shadow that was coming from Sergei, fending off feelings in the transference that he changed into theories.

'It's a philosophical problem of identifying with the shadow', said Terzo to Sergei, who appeared in his soul-form, and dared to sit beside his mother, who was playing with the death drive. 'At bottom, the Death Mother is drawing us back to the source: a problem of magnetism, in which the negative charge is much greater. I have incarnated my spirit in a form that is foreign to me, seduced by her complex, which will not let me rest, playing the shadow that killed me, so I know how you feel'.

Sergei was always amused when Terzo was trying to be objective, and realized that Nola's son had idealized him as a new kind of father figure: that he tried to replace Leonardo- the primitive hero of his first life, as he evolved in the mind through his mother's affairs, by identifying with her lovers and dying their deaths.

'I understand your position, Nora, for I have suffered it myself', Terzo continued, always the outsider. 'I was baptized as 'the third' and was destined to endure it, but I know it is you she is possessive of, more than she ever was of me. It is as if we were only three characters that she has conjured in the vessel, while the others are trying to get into the act'.

Nora empathized with Terzo's tragedy, for she had almost died before she lived, and, like Terzo. had confounded the past with the present, till Nola appeared in her office and resurrected the heart. Nola knew he was looking through the eye of the complex, and was blocked by the memory of his birth, and her rejection in his first life. He would never believe that she could accept him as he was, and not abandon him again for not being as perfect as the god.

He remembered her dream, in which he took the form of a hermaphrodite, part woman, part man, and how he took her in the lilies; how he conceived of a son as 'the fifth', who would incorporate his gifts, so he could inhabit its body and complete his life in its vessel... Was it *her* desire I was acting on, or was it my own? I have *never* been sure, whether my feelings were hers... The feelings were always a problem. It was the way I was conceived. But I could never juggle them, like she could. The edges were always unclear.

The spirit of Siegfried appeared and took the seat beside his mother- the sons like psychic bookends, who contained the breadth of their existence,

'Why not take him'? said Siegfried, looking from Nora to Sergei, giving voice to her thought and seducing her shadow.

"Why not?" said Nola, with a mix of possessiveness and the need to give up her claim to him, while wanting Nora to have him- what she was unwilling to give, and felt like death to renounce, but knowing she must. It would complete her, she thought... Why not surrender him to her? But it was mingled with her need for her freedom, which he was always in fear of. "Why not take him, if you want him, to complete our 'lower trinity'? It's only natural, Sergei, to penetrate the vessel of your secrets. It might make them more conscious. I would not mind at all."

"You have an uncanny way of taking the kick out of it, darling- making it seem like a discipline. It's all that whoring," said Sergei, feeling the sting of betrayal, but hiding his feelings (he learned how to do it through her).

Of course, he's right, Nola thought. I still have the whore in me. But the need to possess him only weakens my soul, trying to reason with her heart, which would not let him go. "Yes, it must be the whore in me," she said in her off-handed way."

"Why not?" said Nora, falling into her shadow. "Tonight, *I'll* play the whore," turning it back on her.

"It seems my fate is decided," but inside he was fuming. Now he wanted to hurt her, by going along with it. "It should be interesting, Nora, giving you the secrets we never analyzed."

Nora knew Nola was confronting her shadow, and what felt like betrayal, though it was she who had thought it. But Nora wanted her to know it, to let her wrestle with her love...

"You can trust me to keep them," said Nora, taking the challenge.

"It's the *only* thing I trust," he said, wanting to hurt her.

It stung, but she took it, "I'm beginning to feel like a third" (a false sacrifice she thought, and wishing she could turn it).

Terzo knew how it hurt, but he admired her courage. He wished *he* could do it, and play the game with his fate. He forgot, for the moment, it was precisely what killed him, that he died from that trick and was forced to return.

And he heard the words of his father: '*It's too late... it's too late',* the words he heard in the womb and that formed his own fate...

He still blames me for his death, Nola thought, hearing the words of her curse.

'I'm trying to forgive you for my birth- my death was a miscalculation. 'We are not responsible for the unconscious'.[331] I realize you didn't *try* to kill me'.

'I think we can learn from this, mother', said Siegfried to Nora, 'knowing love and death are inseparable, and that a dark thought can kill'.

"*Who* shall *I* have?" 'Lupa' was saying, as she played with 'the third', scanning the room... and she focused on an elegant woman, who was dining alone, and who was watching her with interest- a match made by fate. Nola scribbled a note, like when she was playing the whore, and Leo, who was leaning on a column, was now as curious as ever: he knew what was coming; but how would she handle the situation?

"Waiter, give this note to the woman in black, the one by the column," handing him a hundred dollar bill.

"Remember our deal," Sergei said.

"What deal was that?" Nora asked.

'That the third could only be you', said Terzo indiscreetly, 'with the exception of myself, who was created for the role- but then spirits don't count, though they are moving the play'.

"So I'm part of a deal I'm not in on," said Nora,

perturbed. "No wonder I felt that I'm playing the whore," now caught in the part, and unable to reverse it.

Nola was beginning to regret it: that she had taught her trick to her analyst, and was trying to swallow what was mixed by the trickster. Dangerous, the transference... for what if she should lose him?... But to think it was unbearable... and she pretended not to care.

The woman was watching her with a subtle intensity. She looked strangely familiar, but Nola couldn't place it. She was blaming the feeling on one of her characters, but Sergei and Nora were trapped in her web. Nola asked her to join them, in her mind, and ordered another twelve oysters...

"Half of that deal that we made will have to be broken, for a moment," she said to the two, and swallowed her medicine, for it seemed 'too late' to refuse, though she knew it would kill her.

The woman introduced herself and was not unnerved in the least, though she was faced with six penetrating eyes, and with the eyes of the dead. Still, she focused on Nola and seemed to know what she wanted. But who was she like? Sergei wondered, and his discomfort was palpable... her distinctive features... familiar... as if cut into glass... the veiled eyes full of guilt... but the feeling escaped him. She wore a conservative suit, forties style, that was not unlike Snow's, and was meant to conceal the exquisite body beneath it, her dark hair framing her face in a Madonna-like swirl. Her name?

"Marlin, a big fish, or 'godwit,' by definition," she offered as table talk, enduring the holy inquisition. Yes, she had been at the lecture of *The Unknowable Third*,

"And one of your lectures in Berlin," turning to Nola- "the one on *The Incest Taboo*. It had a disquieting effect on me."

Nola was doubly intrigued. Strange, how the context could change it. And Marlin observed every gesture, like both a scientist and analyst. "Are you a scientist or analyst?" Nola was asking.

"A Freudian psychiatrist- or astronomer, who studies the stars in the head."

What is it, Sergei thought, while feeling completely uprooted. He had the same dark premonition that Nora was feeling, but quickly reduced it to being neurotic... So what if she did have a fling, and set him up with his analyst? So what if she played with his pride and betrayed what was sacred? So what if he belonged to a woman... not a star, or a quark?... but a shadow woman he idealized, and who liked to play with his heart... So what? said his shadow... but his ego was trembling.

"My sister was a Jungian- Christa Helden. Perhaps, you knew her?"

And the Sphinx seemed to smile, as it had the desired effect. The play of detachment was broken, and all three felt the fear.

"I met her- briefly," said Nola.

"It seized me- your talk."

"I take it as a compliment."

"As I intended it to be."

Where was she from? From Vienna, and she had a penchant for opera. But this was already clear, as she'd chosen Nola for the mad scene. The dead boys were deflated, for their *puer* games backfired. Again, they both lost their mothers, who they avenged for their deaths.

"Christa was also intrigued with your work."

"Yes, she was telling me- the night that she died," Nola said boldly, having more or less killed her. "They said it was a stroke," Nola tested.

"She had a weak heart," said her sister.

"A constitutional weakness, I gather. Perhaps, it was not as strong as she thought. Well, shall we?" to Marlin, "my friends have other plans," defying fate and the odds, and even her own intuition. And she guided her out, feeling a knot in her breast, leaving the living and dead to feel the dread of the godwit.

CHAPTER 46
LIGHT CURVES

In an immediate cohesion, like mercury and silver- an irresistible attraction in the crucible of *Self*- Nola and Marlin are discussing the dangers of fusion, aware of its seduction, but seized by its madness. The focus of their talk, in Nola's suite in the Crillon, is on Marlin's fusion with Christa and the Devouring Mother- on which Christa had claimed to be the only authority, but which was behind Christa's death, for what you know can destroy you. Still, for Marlin, a woman with the will of a child, the discussion was laced with the fear of the past, charged with the fear of the Devourer and the undead in her dreams. They took the form of her sister, an unidentical twin, who would not allow her to love, and invested her body as shadow.

"She was a terrifying fusion of a jealous lover and a mother, and she managed to convince me it was a neurotic fantasy we shared. Before your lecture on incest, it was more like the nightmare of a child, but she fed on my *animus* like a vampire, and allowed me nothing of my own. Her books were extracted from my journals, and every phrase was twinned with mine. She controlled my thoughts and my feelings, and I began to fear her in my sleep: that she would steal my soul in a dream and I'd awaken as a shadow. I became anorexic and feared that she poisoned my food. I know it's completely irrational, but I believe she poisoned our mother."

"Irrational, Marlin, or the intuition of a child?"

"Then you don't think I'm mad?"

"I would say you are close to the unconscious."

342

"So close that when she died, it was like my body was her tomb."

Nola, as always, was tempted to study the problem. She felt her despair and was aware of her own, but while she was completing her sacrifice, she would take her pleasure, as well... at least that's what she told herself, as she thought of Sergei with Nora...

"Enough of your sister. Let's pursue the unknown," and she began to undress her, slipping her skirt off. "You see, fear of madness, dear Marlin, is not something I'm prone to. A bit of madness is necessary for the unveiling of the mystery," removing her stockings and underwear, sucking her nipples and playing with her. "It is not possible on this earth to remain undisturbed, and if I encountered such a thing, I'd be convinced she was mad. But there is madness and there is madness, and we can't always know what we're fucking," licking her like an animal, until she's mad as the moon.

In Sergei's suite, just below them, he is fucking Nora, his former analyst, like she had never been fucked- at least, by the living. Sergei, tormented by his shadow, is beginning to feel like the sacrifice. For Nora, it seemed, it had to come through the body: the need to spiritualize matter, for the redemption of the feminine- so that it wasn't fused with the *animus*, a problem she had witnessed in Nola. Nonetheless, the compensatory separation would come in the form of a tragedy, and was another victory of the Devourer, though it promised a prospective integration.

Meanwhile, Terzo and Siegfried, still tied to their mothers, were watching the four, flitting from above to below, on a fragile bridge to the earth, and were

343

dissolving in the feminine.

'Your mother has become a whore. They are trapped in the transference', said Terzo, jealous of his mother, and projecting it on Nora.

'*Your* mother was right, or, perhaps, it was Plato: 'A change of lighting can turn a comedy into a tragedy'.

'This Freudian sister, a proponent of Freud's incest theory, who reduced all the myths to the Oedipal mother/son fusion, has manifested as the separator, a necessary element in the descent. And just as her shadow sister signified the mother/daughter merger, and her death brought about a separation from the shadow, this sister will be separating the shadow from the *animus*. But first, there is the sacrifice, and I am glad that I am dead', said Terzo to Siegfried, sounding more like Nora and his mother

'As your poet once said, 'We slide into the forms we create',[337] though it begins as a game', said Siegfried to Terzo.

What will become of us, thought Nora, now that the delicate balance has been skewed? Will it help us to complete ourselves, or will it rend us apart?

"What do you make of it, Nora, how she arranged us like chess pieces? And how she managed to escape again, like the spirit in the bottle. Clever, the way she picked up on your thoughts, through the spirit of your son, and used your desire for her daring adventure. And with the sister of my would-be murderess, who she purged from the earth, so we would not be separated by her wiles, and whom we've invited to our bed. But I can't help but wonder- and then I'm determined to let it go- whether 'the big fish' that she caught, means the end of our world," always tempted to form a theory, to defend against the personal, before he turned them to numbers and tried to escape.

But it is he who is the sacrifice, thought Nora, and she wondered if she was the next.

"Christa's shadow is in the room. I can feel the constriction in my heart. How shall we deal with it, Nora?"

"I forgot to ask myself that question. I was distracted by 'the pleasure principle'."[338]

At bottom, distracted by Nola's shadow, she knew that Sergei had been fucking it, and, drowning in the transference, she wanted to possess him. "Shall we continue our experiment and face the Sphinx of our unconscious?"

"You mean, while knowing it's a warning and not heeding what we know?"

And somehow the danger made it better, as both were eroticizing death.

'It is true what they say: no man can survive her', said Terzo to Siegfried, as they were watching them play. 'Indeed, my own life was cut short by her magical manipulations'.

'Yes, I admit she is masterful', said Siegfried. 'I am beginning to envy her art, and if I could have fully incarnated, I would have chosen her body'.

'It's a fantasy, Siegfried, you could not have kept up with her. Though you have been named for a hero, it is time that you learned your own limits'.

'I cannot help but notice you have been named for 'the third', and that you are not conscious of yours and believed you were a nymph with a penis'.

'It is what binds us together- why we are fused with our mothers. I am still trying to be the hero, and to bring her down from the father god- from the lonely rock on God's mountain, [339] where she is unable to love. It seems we have the same destiny, and the same weakness as Siegfried's. It's in the back- in the shadow,* where we are victim to their martyr complex."

Siegfried is appalled, the way he has stolen his myth, and without any conscience, as if it were perfectly natural. 'Though I admit my heroic manoeuvrings were not as grand as your own, I died to protect my own mother from the abuses of our father, and by becoming a woman, I took her lover to redeem her. You seem to have forgotten my name, you are so enamored of your own... As I became more and more like her, I became the object of her fascist lover. And when I hung myself above her, he fled from her love. It was only by taking my life that I saved her from death. But the greatest sacrifice of all was that it was never understood. We are nothing but their offerings, and were sacrificed to a vision of perfection'.

'Strange, that although we are opposites, we have the same problem', said Terzo. 'For myself, I am tired of eating boar in Valhalla with the other fallen heroes: tired of drinking the blood of immortality from the spirit of the beast. It is time to descend into a permanent body, more suited to my temperament. I am not a hermaphrodite by nature, but a boy with a dangerous curiosity, with a mother just as curious and oblivious to consequences, who under the threat of Thanatos and Eros has initiated her son into the mysteries of the feminine'.

'How many fallen heroes have been seduced by the shadow of the mother, believing they would learn all her secrets, and who found themselves between the worlds? How many are feasting with the dead'? and feeling the weight of his tragedy, Siegfried pondered the problem. 'In our identification with their hero complex, we have given our lives to their myth, and our sacrifice will not be conscious, and there *is* no glory in 'the lower trinity'.

'I will continue my non-existence in complete anonymity, and my marvelous acts will be misnamed as the defense of reversal- either in some text book by my mother, or a brilliant treatise on my suicide- exploring her complex, as if analyzing mine, and which she'll be tempted to call, *The Suicidal Impulse Of The Child*; while yours is immortalized in her novels, which are all autobiographical, as if you are her problem, for we are nothing more than their material: an anti-hero to be dissected by the critical *animus* that we are victim to. At least, *your* mother knew that you died a mythical death, like the wounded god that they adore and recreate in all their sessions, while my more personal sacrifice was compared to the death of a drag queen'.

'Don't be so modest," said Terzo. Try to remember your myth. Look at the death of the castrated Attis, who was unable to endure being possessed by his mother, and who hung himself from a tree as a sacrificial offering'.

'Thank you for recognizing what my mother has ignored. I sometimes wake up from her dream with the fear that I was only trying to escape'.

Terzo realized through Siegfried that he had the same fear. And what of Sergei, he wondered, 'was it a sacrifice of love'?

But the Sphinx didn't answer, and the three

dreamed of his death...

In Sergei's dream, he was drawn on a curved path of light, till it turned on itself into a black hole in space- a distortion of space/time, from which no light could escape: in *psychic* reality, a black hole in the mind, in which the inverted force field of gravity was the Mother of Shadow. In the throes of his dream, Sergei died in his sleep, while the shadow of Christa was gripping his heart, and as she severed the thread between the mind and the body, in her deathless delusion, believed that 'Nola is mine'...

In Nora's, she was waiting with Nola at the door of his tomb, and, somehow, his death made her conscious of how she sacrificed her son... and that 'the gift had been given as if it were being destroyed'.

In Nola's, she was drawn by love's gravity down to the mine of the Mother, where the black substance of shadow formed the stone of the *Self*. Her hand was extended, as if for an offering, and a child sat on his palm, watching the light as it curved... And then he was gone, and all that remained was the child.

CHAPTER 47
'EVERY ANGEL IS TERRIBLE'

'*Every angel is terrible. Still... I invoke you, deadly birds of the soul... knowing what you are*'[342] Nola repeated at his grave in Pere Lachaise. The stone was surrounded by physicists and philosophers, and hundreds of white calla lilies around the inscription by Leibnitz, who spent his last days confronting the problem of evil: she stared at the words she had chosen, confronting her shadow, and the deadly force it attracted that turned her lovers to dust...

EVERY SPECK OF THIS COSMIC DUST IS BOTH AN ATOM AND AN ANGEL

Inscribed on the stone... in the heart... in the mind.

Terzo was hunched on the grave and knew it was true, while Nola wept to unknowing, beneath her black veil of mourning. How she longed for the man who had taught her to transit the lights, but in the end, the dead stars had won, and had taken his body. It was nothing but a cauldron of ashes that were hidden in the stone, as if the body of shadow was fed to the Devourer: the *Mother* of *Shadow* always claiming the gift, that was tainted again by the spell of the Trickster- that by turning the trick, she was unable to renounce. As she sank to the earth, Nora was holding her up, the two alone, like her dream, with the souls of the dead.

The scientists from the Congress now knew what they lost; that what they disdained was their fear, and they threw their hats on the stone. Now they envied his courage, and knew they had not understood, as they

349

questioned their theories and reflected on his.

But Nola and Nora, who knew the gravity of love, knew it was not just a theory, but a psychic reality. And she vowed to give Terzo a home in the heart of her son- the son she saw in her dream, so he could learn to be human, and he could teach it to her, for 'her heart was as cold as the stone' (Leo's words as a warning that she would suffer her tale). And she vowed to be 'the bridge across the gulf' for the unborn child she would bear, as she passed into darkness, and Nora carried her to Snow House.

PART THREE

CHAPTER 48
SPELLBREAKER

She began the experiment on the bed that her mother was murdered on, the bed her son died on, and that she mourned for his life on, and imagined what kind of vessel could contain such a soul. When she conceived of a soul-image, she began to invoke it, and was calling it down, to give it substance and form. In the imaginal mirror that reflected his spirit, he began the descent, moving her hand on the page, to bring her son back to life, and to sustain who she loved. She tried to make out his form in the dust of the dead, and to translate the glyphs that appeared just beneath it:

Papilio onus, in Latin, for the soul of a dead person, the wings associated with a butterfly, dusting the point of my pen. The dust forms the letters as it writes the invisible... The meaning is doubled- like the creature I bear... I see the symbol inside me- the double axe of the labyrinth, the beast in its center, and the thread leading out... 'Leading to what'? I am asking: 'To a new inner order', it answers: 'a new beast being born, who will harbor 'the third'.

"Mother of Fusion," she murmured, "give form to 'the third', so I can hold him on earth, and time and space can be one."

Sergei's spirit appears and talks to Nola a while; tries to free her from guilt, so she can mother the boy. The months of labor passed quickly and still she was mourning his death, while Nora was staying in Snow House, guarding Nola from 'Lupa'.

'You see, Nola, my soul, your shadow has limits. Love and death are beyond us, and belong to the Mother. You don't really believe that you are the shadow of gravity, do you? I had a black hole in my heart that took the form of a complex, that kept it from beating in rhythm, until it finally stopped': taking the thorn from her flesh, that he knew she had borne.

But Nola wanted to feel it: her shadow had killed him: her perversion of will that made the invisible manifest, and using Sergei's experiment, it had taken his life. She prayed that the son she was bearing would not be prey to her darkness, but, as Sergei was saying, death was beyond 'her'- or was it? She would learn how to channel death's urge: she would spend her life learning how.

When the nine months were complete and the child had emerged, Nora was cutting the cord to free its soul from the past. With her beastly intuition, Nola held a mirror to the child, and saw the shadow of Christa licking its blood on its flesh. In the spirit of Atropos, Nola cut off her tongue, and, like the Medusa, who saw her reflection in the shield, the spirit of evil was petrified and its heart turned to stone.

She left a drop of her poison that Nola turned to a healing draft, drawing the cross on its lids: 'Be open', she said. The boy was immune to all illness, and the more obvious demons, and learned to recognize the lower spirits and to dispel them with a thought. All her lovers were in him and the son that she cursed, and when he was restless, she would chant him to sleep...

Spellbreaker! You struck the healing chord,
the clearest note, held the mirror up to God
and shattered the old reflection of the past.
You broke its spell, grinding the fragments
into sand that shifted with the wind of spirit.
You are the voice that moved me through
the wilderness,
that parted the scarlet sea of blood
and formed a path within the heart,
crossed me over
to the Station of the Moment
and set me down on solid ground;
How you 'gripped my straying thoughts
'like the broken pieces of a sword',
tempered them to serve the whole
and forged them in the fire of *gnosis*.
In the sheathe of will you held them fast
and when I prayed for heaven
you gave me earth,
redeemed me with the sacred Word
and made them 'home
and holy dwelling place'.[346]

She baptized the boy with the Living Water of the
heart and called him Quint, the fifth essence: the boy
that linked the five elements: Leo, Sergei, Ambrose,
Philos, and Terzo, his brother, a quintessence to guard
him.

All seemed to be well in the forest of Snow House,
as the wolf of a huntress trotted from instinct to spirit,
with the boy as the vessel of the son she destroyed.

CHAPTER 49
THE SPIRIT IN TOTO

The spirit of Terzo in Toto, on the day of Quint's baptism, sat on a rock in a glade in the forest of Snow House. Toto had named it the rock of Saint Paul, who was a mystic devoted to the spiritual body. Later, Quint asked Toto what it meant that the flesh was corruptible, and he said that when the spirit chose a body that matter was spiritualized, but if it fled from the body, the soul would be weak, for the flesh without spirit is a life without God.

'Lupa' believed- in contrast to Paul, that the animal soul was essential for the sanctifying of the body, and that when it combined with the souls of the dead, though the flesh was corruptible, the spirit was strengthened. But, like Toto, matter and spirit were at war in her breast: she had two warring souls and passed the torch to her priest. Toto would pass it to Quint, and the boy would war with the flesh, and, like the wolf girl in Nola, he was torn between instinct and spirit.

Terzo had been living in Toto, as he prepared for his vows, and it was time for a change, when Terzo left him for Quint. Terzo, not being religious, during Toto's Christian revelations, had been feeling like a hypocrite, and a stranger to God. But he made Toto conscious of his calling, though his own was in Quint, and so he prepared for the sacrifice on the day of the birth.

'I haven't abandoned you, Toto. Please try to understand. More by fate than by character, I am a thief and a trickster, and am closer to the devil than I am to Mother Church. Besides, my 'son' needs me more, and I will be closer to my mother, and he is a more fitting instrument for my spirit to dwell in. But I will always be with you, for you will be mentoring the boy, and it will not be so different, for we will have our talks through the transference. Please don't take it personally. I am not rejecting your body'.

"It feels like a death, and I will be lonely without you. You gave me a vision of the divine, when I had nothing to believe in. But I will find you in Quint, who will be needing my counsel, for the spirits take their toll, each with a will of its own."

'I will not leave you, my saint- and you will be, you know. We must avoid an exorcism of the Fathers, who would think you were possessed. You are more like Ambrose than myself, who had the gift of God's grace, and I'm more like Leo... my father... who belonged on the street... It was Leo who freed me from Snow's obsession with God, who she suffered and died for, and I no longer believe'.

"It's still hard for you, isn't it, to say the word 'father'?... as it was for myself... until there was you. When you found me in the gutter, I found the father of my fate. I have never known my father, but its mother was 'Lupa', who brought me back from the dead, when I died like the god."

'I had to father myself, and only in death did it work. As the 'father' of my 'son', I must protect him from his mother. She would devour the boy, if I let her possess him, for the love she denied me will be given to him. The guilt will make love excessive and will bind him to earth. He's confused, like myself, who his real father is. He was born of the living and dead, and soon he will grasp the inconceivable: the alchemical marriage of the Mother and Son'.

"You are speaking of the marriage of spirit and matter that you are trying to find in the body of the child. Teach me the secret of that union, for dreams are easy to forget, so I can teach it to you, and the body won't seem like a prison."

'I don't know if I can… I am still struggling with fate… Just when I think I accept it, what I learned from my death, I remember the reason I died, and why I did not want to live: how love turned to hate, and I forgot what I know'.

"But you gave it to me, and I remember it all. Why was it me that you chose?"

'We both suffered the shadow and died the dreams of the mother. When I found you and you were dying the death of the god, I wanted to give you my life, and the longing to live. I didn't know at the time that I would die the same death'.

CHAPTER 50
SHE-WOLF

Since the death of his father, who resided in the stars, Quint was re-animating his mother, who lived for the boy, and was bringing her down to the mysteries of earth. It is said that Eros was hatched from the great orphic egg, and was the first of the gods, for without him nothing would be: that new life cannot grow without the passion of love, and that the god had been mothered by the Lady of the Beasts. Others say, he was the son of Aphrodite and Hermes- a phallic god who regenerates the hearts of the dead: but the urge to *become* is born from the Mother of Earth, while Eros sparks the unconscious, and the desire to be.

It is a fact that the incestuous urge, in which the opposites are fused, was a necessary element in the lives of the gods, and no love is as strong as the love of the mother for her son. Nola, Quint's mother, was also mothering Toto, and being held in her arms was like being held by the moon, who knew the secret of change, and turned the darkness to light. But as the Lupa in Nola, she was the essence of earth, the huntress of spirit, and their lady of the beasts.

Quint, a prodigy of nine, was probing this love, that like a mystical force worked its spell on the boy. Like Toto, he was roused by his mother and her wild wolfish shadow, that had the rawness of nature, a force hidden in Terzo; the impulsive boy of the streets, who was haunting her dreams, and invested his brother, to be near her on earth. The five spirits communed in the heart of her son, and knew her core through young Quint, who had her stars in his blood; but while Sergei

357

came down, he always returned to the stars.

On the darling boy's birthday, who was as fearless as Nola, she gave him a bow and a quiver, and a she-wolf to protect him; and he would wander through the forest, hunting quail for their dinner, a bird of the senses, and a messenger of Eros.

One night, Quint sat on the rock in the sacred enclosure and talked to Lupa, the she-wolf, of his longing for his mother. "The mystery of love is as old as the earth, but why am I drawn to her body and the sins of the flesh? Am I in love with my mother, and what does love really mean?"

An inner voice seemed to answer... or was it the voice of the wolf girl? 'What you love in your mother is the freedom to wander the dark places. Now hold me close in your arms and stroke my body of fur'. Quint held the wolf in his arms and talked to the dead, who confounded his heart, for each had his thoughts on her nature, each contradictory, and at odds with his own: each obsessed with the 'Lupa', like they were on the earth. This confounded the boy, who wanted her all to himself.

In the day, he spoke to Toto, as they sat on the rock, and told him their secrets and what he learned in the night. Today, Toto illumined the meaning through the healing words of Saint Paul, and the words of the mystic were mixed with his own, who, at times, changed the meaning, to calm the boy from his dreams, that awakened his nerves for his adventures on earth...

"As the body is one and has many members, all the members of that body, being many are one: there are two selves in that body, and more in the mind: one self that is hungry, and a second self that is drunken:

meaning, do not get drunk on the spirit, *though we suffer the* selves, for the hunger will guide us to a whole mother image. The saint asks the question: "*Is Christ divided?*" And he speaks to us 'babes', who are a part of the whole. *I fed you with milk,* says the saint, *the spiritual drink,* for we long to be one with the Mother, as we were as a child. We struggle with oneness, but we are many in one, for all the gods are alive in us, as they are in the Son. Like the Son of the Mother, we suffer the shadow of self, till we transform our own *devil into the angel of light*:[352] meaning: our shadow is made conscious when we go down to the depths, and *then shall I know** through the child in the man, for, through the mind of the child, I can imagine the whole, and can be what I must in the mind of the man."

"I see what you mean, Toto, and I see something else: though I am only a child, I have the mind of a man, and the child wants to be whole and know the darkness of love."

Toto knew Nola's lovers were alive in Quint's blood- that he was learning their secrets and knew more than he should. Like the son of the mother, thought Toto, I have the heart of a child, but I am drunk on her spirit, and am in love with the wolf. Quint understood in the heart, for he was drunk on it, too, and longed for a whole mother image, while he was holding the wolf.

"You are in love with her, Toto," as if he had said it aloud. "I have always known that you loved her, who runs with the beasts, but it is only the longing of the part for the whole."

And Quint knew the man in the boy through her dead lovers' spirits, and Terzo wrestled inside him and longed for her touch, that he could only know through the boy, who she stroked like a beast; while Quint knew the Lupa in Nola through the soul of the wolf.

"Come, Toto, lets bathe in the stream, where my mother bathed with her nymph, when I watched through the trees and hid my face in my hands."

CHAPTER 51
WOUNDED EROS

Nola and Quint, the she-wolf beside them, sit on the rock and consider the mystery of Eros. It is confusing for Quint having her lovers inside him, and he studies love's patterns as he lives in love's grip...

"I've been reading your essay," says Quint, "On *Symbolic Incest and the Wounded Eros*, and how sexuality and the erotic are not always related. At first, I was confused, but now I think I understand."

"Tell me what you see, Quint, and how they are sometimes unrelated."

"I see when you are speaking of Eros and the confusion of love, when the lover is under the spell of the beloved, it can seem like an erotic obsession, and at times it is hard to tell the difference. And though it can happen that Eros is related to the senses, love and desire can be like two separate worlds."

"Can you give me an image of Eros that describes the difference between them?"

"It's like when I watched you bathing with your nymph and you were naked in the stream. The moon was reflected on your breasts and I was excited like a child, and though I was lost in your image, I did not need to touch you... It was enough just to gaze at you, and to know you existed."

"Tell me more."

"When I'm with you I want you, but it's like I'm inside you... and I know it's the memory of a man, and not a boy, like myself."

"Yes, you seem to understand it- more like a man than a boy."

"But it feels like a sin, like I was spying on your soul: that I am looking too deeply into a dark secret place, and though I love what I know, I'm not sure how you feel: if you want to be known, for I know more than I should."

"What do you know about your mother that she may not want you to know?"

"Well... I know you love Nora, the way other women love a man. I don't know how I know but, somehow, I do. I know you have the spirit of the wolf and will hunt what you want. I know you know how, because I know it, too. I know you know how to love me like the Lady of the Beasts, and I know that *I* am your beast, and I know I belong to you. Like the Lupa, I want to protect you from harm, though I am only your creature, a wild boy of the forest... I know that I love you, like a lover... and yet, you are also my mother... Can you explain it to me, mother, why I feel the way I do? Do all boys feel that way... or is it the spirit of the beast?"

"Yes, Quint, I can, but we know what we know: that Eros and instinct are not *always* opposed, though it is true we must learn to tell them apart. You have seen the way I love, and you want to love that way too: to be free in your love, and to heal the wound in the heart. You know that I want to protect you, and that we were born of the hunt: that we hunt like 'The Wild One', with the spirit of the beast; that *we* are her beasts and must learn to know her completely."

"We know what we know...said the wild boy, reflectively.... "I knew you would tell me and that you would free me from sin. Today, in the fields, when I was running with Lupa, I could feel my brother inside me, and he asked me the question. He has asked me three times now if I knew who my real father was. I thought he was being perverse and I said it was Sergei, but he smiled to himself, as if he knew something else. He said, he took you like a lover in the form of a nymph, and that I am a child of incest, of a mother and a son... Who *is* my real father? And do we know what we know?"

"It depends. You have a father of spirit and a father of matter."

"Can the two not be one?"

"They can, but not always... They are sometimes divided... and it takes time to unite them."

"I know what you mean... but what of Eros, the love god? Is it true that my spirit father is also my brother, who lives in my body to be close to his mother?"

"The spirit has a way of taking magical forms, and it changes at will, to keep the mystery alive. We don't always know how the forces of love would combine, but when I gaze at your form, I am sure that the gods became one."

"And who is my father of matter, is it Sergei or Nora?"

"I think we can say that you have the influence of both, for you are a child of science and the mystery of art... and then, there's 'the third'... and it is living inside you, so that you know what you are, and how to embrace what you're not. That is the essence of love, when you can love your own shadow."

"Tell me about Terzo, my brother: I know he's a stranger like me, but I would like to have known him as *another* person than myself, to know the difference between us, that I keep trying to find."

"Well, he had the same wildness of spirit, and was not at home on the earth, but the real difference between you is the way you work with the will, for you have the discipline of Sergei, so you can bridge the three worlds. Terzo got caught in the past and turned his will on himself. Learn from your brother not to linger in time, and to fight for your love, though your Eros is wounded by love."

Terzo was listening, and never felt more alone. He felt the wound of her love that had never been lived- the wound in the heart, scarred over by death. Now the heart was ripped open, and she knew what she'd done.

He was transported to the past, to the year he was nine, when he witnessed Snow's death and he lay on her grave; it was then he remembered dashing his head on her stone, and the words echoed through space that carved a wound in his heart: 'Forgive me for not fighting for it', and the words burned in the brain; he could feel them through Quint, who made the heart feel alive...

She saw him mourning his life, as he once mourned for Snow, when he believed he betrayed her... and was not the hero she loved.

"You see, Quint," reversing the thrust of her words, "there is no wound like the mother's, when she knows she has wounded her son." And she talks to the Terzo in Quint, who was listening in his soul: "He never knew how I loved him, and how I fight for his love."

"But his love is in *me*," Quint replied, wanting her for himself.

"Are you jealous? He is part of you. It is like being jealous of yourself."

"So it is *me* that you love?"

"Yes, Quint, every part of you."

"Even the dead part?"

"Of course, for it is part of the whole."

"Toto's saint says the part can be *changed* by the whole... and I will find what is whole in me, so I can change my dead brother- so when you love him through me, I can be more than myself."

She gazed at his beauty, the arrow aimed at her heart, and like Eros, the child god, he gave life to the dead. As he leapt through the fields with his wolf, as if moved by the wind, she felt the force of his love, and Terzo knew how he needed him: that it was only through Quint that he could change 'Lupa's' curse, and he would learn to be human, while he was near her on earth.

CHAPTER 52
SECRET SPELLS

Nola and Nora were having an imaginary session, while dining in Snow House on the quail that Quint hunted. It is a fact too much quail can make one insatiable and that the pleasure of eating it can turn into lust. Though Nola's lust was for spirit and at odds with the senses, 'Lupa' came out in the transference to the other extreme, and often played with the heart of her sons and her lovers, and with the shadow of love that confounded them all.

"He's like a miniature son/lover, who has the qualities of all of them: a crucible of souls- there's something incestuous about it," Nola was saying to Nora, who knew all her secrets (but whose analyst was who's was an enigma to both).

"Eating quail can be dangerous. You can't get enough of him, and have projected your lovers inside him, whose lives you have ended. Remember Medea and the mother complex that was named for her, who as the priestess of the Devourer, knew the art of devouring, and yet, falls under its spell and destroys her own children. Let me quote her invocation to the underworld goddess: *O Hecate, who knows untold desires that work our will, and art the mistress of our secret spells, still the smoking breath of* the fiery boar, *and tame the wild beasts, who never ploughed a field.*"[359]

"Thank you, dearest, I'll have some more quail now."

"If I were not possessed by your shadow, I would run for my life."

"We knew what we were in for in this conflagration of opposites. Love is too much, and yet it isn't enough," said Nola to Nora (something the two had in common). "It needs to be tempered this passion, for Hermes is arguing with Aphrodite. *He* wants more spirit, and she wants more love, like yourself, and are projecting it on me. Basically, the two are incompatible, the power of magic and love, and the reconciling of the two requires continuous work. How do you see it, I mean the essence of the problem?"

"What I see in the magnetic mirror is that we are all aspects of yourself. The problem, as always, is who can the other be? What are we to you? Are we reflections of *you,* or do we exist on our own? The essence of the problem? I am in love with an archetype."

"As I am, my dear, but that is inevitable."

They gather the white calla lilies for the Black Virgin in 'the round room'- that room in the psyche that rounds on itself. Nola now on her knees, in the midst of hundreds of calla lilies, prays to the Mother that she will not devour her son, and asks that she free him from wanting to be devoured; while Nora is asking her sha-dow if she is enough for the wolf one... this sword in my heart... for whom I would lay down my life.

'Tell her that the wolf is not hungry,' Nola says to her shadow, 'that it is only the quail that makes me think I want more.'

CHAPTER 53
STAR GAZER

A new 'lower trinity' was formed, bringing change and transformation, as the boy was compelled towards the rising sun of his myth, and as he struggled with the spirits he was far beyond his years. Quint, haunted by 'the third', with Nola and Nora, returned to the penthouse on Abingdon Square, and on the day he turned ten, they gave him a telescope. The teachings of Sergei developed his talent for star gazing, and he was prepared in his young mind to become an astronomer.

On most days, he was gazing at the giant Orion, the blind lustful hunting hero, an earthborn lover of Artemis, who she blinded with a scorpion for the slaying of her beasts. He recovered his sight by his longing for the sun, after being stung by the goddess and banished to the underworld. When the pain of the beast was made conscious, as he suffered her will, she resurrected the sun-hero, who became a constellation, and was the guide for dead stars that were lost in the firmament. What this meant to the boy is when the light is eclipsed by the shadow, if we bring the shadow to consciousness, like the shamanic Orion, we can illumine the darkness by the longing for light.

It was in this way that he walked into the crux of his myth, that was beginning to form in the dark of the mind. And so, the blind hunter, who died of the poison of love, and who rose from the depths and was healed by love's wound, became a life-giving symbol that would quell all his doubts...

For a boy on the earth, whose fate was to struggle with shadow, it was the myth that prepared him for the life of the hero, for whom 'there can be no resurrection without a betrayal'. He would keep this in mind, so he could bear all his wounds, as he ran with the beasts and his brother inside him, and while protecting his mother he would complete Terzo's destiny.

He began with the study of the planets as his mother's astrologer, so he could avoid all the dangers that he saw in her chart. It was hard to counsel a seer, who was identified with the Huntress, and was bearing Nola's reversals and the assaults of the self.

"You see, mother, how Venus and Mercury, the thief of her love, are in conflict and squared in the darkness of Pluto. It is clear that you will suffer love's wounds in the nether world of the dead, as it tests your love for the Mother and your faith in her Son. The negative influence can be traced to your father, who is imprisoned in Tartarus, in the twelfth house where he lives- the house of death and transformation, meaning that what has died is reborn. It will come about in the fourth month, on the day of Good Friday, when the son is 'split into atoms and eclipsed by the moon'.[362] Quint sees his own death in her solar return, and makes the decision to tell her, instead of protecting her.

"Tell me more, what do you see, Quint? How does this death come about?" asks his mother, the huntress, veiling the dread, and was dying to herself as she masked the effect.

"I see the death of the son for the transformation of the beast."

And she is drained of the life force, gazing through the lens of the past.

"We must not submit to the danger of being fatalistic," said Nora.

"That's easy to say, Nora, but look at your own fate," said Quint. "Do you not see how your Venus is squared with your Saturn, and how the shadow of the father is threatening Eros? how it's attacking its young, a recurring pattern in your chart. Again, there is the danger of death, and the slaying of love."

"How can I change it," she asked, already under its spell.

"By protecting the cub of the huntress, or she will take her own life."

"Then we have a chance," Nora said, "for I will protect it with my own."

"Look inward for a moment, Quint, and ask yourself the question: do you have the desire for death that you pursue in the hunt?" asked Nola, who would analyze the end of the world.

"From time to time, but I am working on it."

"We will work on it together and turn fate into destiny."

"I knew I could count on you, mother, to not submit to the martyr complex. You will be the first of the saints to not submit to her fate."

"And I'll be the second," said Nora. 'We saints must work harder,' repeating 'Lupa's' words to the sainted Leonardo.

"I will consult with my brother, who will not want to die a third death, and with Sergei, who is teaching me to read 'the stars in the blood'. By knowing the myths and their endings, we will learn to survive... What was *your* mother like? You never told me about her. It's as if you never had one- like you created your own."

Nola slips into reverie... to the place that never

was... rides the beast of the soul... Did I create you in my image?... the made-up face... the mask of death, as I hauled your bones from grave to grave... till I numbered and named them, and covered them with skin.

"I never knew her"... Snow was mortified... "until I knew her in myself, while she drove me on to give her meaning... and to outlive my own death."

'I have that need all the time', said the boy, but it was Terzo who said it.

"It's different for you, Quint," said Nora, "whose beast of a mother is teaching you the mysteries, while she plays out their themes and makes your fantasies real."

Snow was offended, and was feeling like *the shadow of the trinity.*

"I must have suffered in my last life with a cold reductive mother, so I would be given a passionate shapeshifter, who was able to guide me through this one: a mother who I don't have to make, and who is creating *herself.*"

"You can't rely on *Mercurius* to do the work of transformation," said Nola. "Making a mother is an art, and you must continue to make her."

Snow agreed, though reluctantly, for it was Terzo's need coming through her.

"Don't let me distract you from making a mother, for once you can do it, you can do the impossible. Make me what you will, Quint, and let me know myself in you, for you are destined to create me, and to recreate yourself through me. I want to know my creator, as I want to be known by him- even when I don't... and when I deny my desire."

"I must say I am jealous," said Nora. "I would like to be born in you."

"That's really perverse, Nora" said Quint. She is either your lover or mother. She can't be both... can she, mother?" smiling at her like a lover.

"No, Quint, she can't. Only in the mythic imagination can we be what we're not."

But Terzo had been born of such a trick- the splitting trick that *she* was born of, and knew there was no trick she hadn't turned... and that somewhere they were one...

This was his cue, and Terzo and Siegfried appeared...

'Can you believe her audacity'? asked Siegfried.

'I believe she is capable of anything. As the 'father' of Quint, seduced by a dream, I would not be surprised if she seduced him as well'.

Why do they think I can't hear them, thought Quint... but I will pretend that I can't, so I can learn what she's not as the wolf of my soul: the *shadow* of my mother that I dream in the night; but, as if she could hear him, she retreats from his eyes.

"Come back, mother, where are you? I need you on earth. 'The door is bolted, and we can't get in'."

The words from the opera, as Philos arose from within, and, in his mind, Quint was playing the song of the Hawk. He took her hand and led her down from the mountain of the moon, so he could know Nola's shadow and could separate it from his own.

CHAPTER 54
BETWEEN TIME

Terzo and Siegfried were conversing in space...

'This little reversal they're practicing, as they obsess on their sons, while making us suffer their interminable analysis, is only a hint of the problem of their compulsion for wholeness', said Siegfried, exasperated, but compelled to be known. 'If the only way to integrate them is to help them to work on their shadow, and how they unconsciously killed us, I would rather be dis-sociated; it is really more than I can bear. To think hanging myself was the only escape, so that I would not be tormented by her Oedipus complex- that her son seduced her lover to lie with his mother; that her son took on her guilt for bearing the son of her father, that he tried to avenge it by suicide, and stole her identity. The truth is, I chose to die by my own hand, rather than let her control me.... or was I trying to save her- like the hero I was named for? Why did I bother to die? Was it a sacrifice in vain'?

'You are becoming your mother in an endless self-analysis', said Terzo, who realized he was doing the same. I understand your dilemma, but it's too reductive, too Freudian. In the Jungian view, which is much more profound, you were trying to 'sacrifice the incestuous libido', but as you were identified with her shadow, you *became* the sacrifice itself. *My* martyr of a mother tried to hang herself on a cross, and on the day I was born- the day of the death the Christ. She arranged it that way, in order to glorify her myth. Is there no end to her ingenuity in turning fact into fiction? I am nothing more than a minor character, the tragic hero of a dream, though the plot turns on my demise and is the high point of her book. Am I nothing but a symbol in her drama, in order to make her more conscious? Am I never to rest as my reward for having an unbearable life'?

'My own problem, precisely,' said Siegfried. 'From now on my mother can interpret her own dreams. For my own part, I just might refuse to emerge'.

'I hope you don't mind, but you would simply be repeating your suicide. Can you honestly say that it worked when you died'?

'No, I cannot. If I had a few incarnations, like you, I'd be more conscious of my death'.

'We might as well reconcile ourselves to the tragedy of being human, and suffer our limits in a finite universe', said Terzo.

Meanwhile, the mothers continued to exorcise the past, and were confronting their ghosts as projections of their complexes.

CHAPTER 55
REUNION

The living and dead were gathered at Snow House, discussing the transference and the projections of the past, for the spirits were impeded from completing their arc, trapped in a web of preconceptions that they were trying to live. Sergei was conspicuously missing and was merged with Leonardo, and Terzo was trapped in his brother, along with her lovers, while Nola was mourning their deaths and trying to find them in Quint.

Snow began the discussion by questioning Nola, disturbed by her image of her, as a shadow with no substance: 'How would you free me from your shadow, so I was more than a complex'?

"By freeing you from yours, so the nun and the whore could be one."

'I tried that myself. It was what killed me in the end'.

"You tried it with a psychopath and death was not a gamble but a certainty."

'You have a better take on the odds. That's why you're alive and I am dead'.

"Death is not the end, for I intend to reconstruct you. Instead of mourning for the past, I have brought you into time."

'And your beast of a saint'? Leo asked. 'How will you free me? You have tried to reconcile the opposites by merging me with Sergei. But do you really think it worked? Can't you see the madness in this art? Can you imagine Sergei on the streets, shooting dice with life and death'?

"Of course. He was shooting dice with the stars.

You had something in common, though I admit your styles were incongruous, and that you studied it from different angles. Yet, you reached similar conclusions: that love bends the light. You were an expert in the art of bending, and I am your living example of that art. If you could separate the opposites, you would still have a body- if you hadn't fused with your brother."

'Or you, I would add'.

It made Terzo think and re-evaluate the situation. 'Yet, you fused me with Quint. What of separating love and death'?

And she had no answer for once, and she knew she would not.

'Do I get to live past his prime'? he continued, 'or will it be another disastrous experiment, while you shoot dice with the gods, and are playing the Self? You are still changing fate, so we can be what you want'.

"This time you will live out your destiny, and will complete it in Quint."

'How do you expect me to come to terms with being part of a whole? And what will we do with my ego, when it rises up from the grave? Will it be serving your own, or have an independent existence'?

"The whole will transmute the parts, till the parts are related to the whole, but it seems that it has already risen, and that it is poisoned by envy. Stop trying to get out, before the incarnation is complete. The tree that you sprang from depends on the earth; your spirit depends on the ether; and your soul needs 'the spirit of gravity', so that it stays in its orbit, and doesn't collide with the moon."

'It already has and it has taken your form. I am part of your dream, with no dream of my own, and while you spin out your tale, I play it out on your stage. I now believe I'm your huntress and an Arcadian wood nymph, 'the sun/moon hermaphrodite',[370] and the father of your son. Can't you see how confused I am, because of your powers of imagination? It's like I was born in a crucible and you were the alchemist; like I'm some marvelous metal you cast in the statue of a god: your magic panacea for the problems of the universe. But where am I in all this, and what do I mean to you'?

"You are the hero of my art, the spark of my creations. But if independence is what you want, I will give you back your sins, and allow you to be responsible for your ambivalent existence."

'That's very generous of you, but what about the sin of being born? Am I responsible for that'?

'That is the question I would ask', said Siegfried, brooding in a corner. 'They both think they're beyond us, our mothers, in their mutual analysis. It's the power of interpretation that makes a fantasy real. It can turn a dark dream into fate, and make the dark seem like light, and can be seen from any angle, depending on the complex of the analyst. There is no way to fight them. They are shooting dice with reality. All one can do is surrender, at the risk of submission to the martyr complex. The problem is expressed in the mythic nature of my name: a name I can't live up to, and that tormented me on earth'.

"I gave you the name of a hero," said Nora, "so you could free yourself from fate, but you identified with your shadow and the problem of the feminine. It was clear you were trying to escape me when you dressed in my clothes, and when you were penetrated by my lover you got trapped in my body. It's hard to look at a

377

problem, when it is situated in the back, and what is before you is a void that is filled by the mother."

'I'm not sure I understand'.

"You became what you feared."

'Are you saying that my becoming a hermaphrodite was a fear of the feminine'?

"You believed by *becoming* your fear that it couldn't destroy you," Nora said to her son.

"Don't worry, Siegfried," said Quint, for the sake of his brother; "I will help you find other ways to ward off the fear, without having to resort to such a primitive defense. One does not have to become a hermaphrodite to engage in the hermaphroditic process. It isn't easy, this work. I want to become her, myself, and, to be honest, I've wondered if I'll ever outgrow it."

'We are not responsible for our unconscious', said Terzo, again, "and there is nothing more unconscious than turning spirit into flesh'.

Toto was trying to come to terms with his repressed sexuality, and after taking his vows was still eroticizing 'Lupa', while Nola was more like a mother, who gave him a self.

'But you were born to be a saint', said his mother, 'and join the old religion and the new, and to redeem me from the sin of becoming the Mother of God'.

"It is time to let go of me, mother. I cannot be what you need. The last time I tried, you died on the street. I'm still repenting for your death by being a virgin."

Terzo remembered her words, when the gypsy predicted his death, and how fate became destiny and ended his life. And now? He would have to complete himself through Quint, and would only know her through the boy. His life would never be his own, and he would never be a man. He was the eternal child of a dream... that had become a reality...

Now Toto realized his problem as he saw it in Terzo. He was identified with his mother, and her Catholic/pagan split. Becoming the Christ to her Virgin was only part of the problem. He would always be a virgin and would never be a man.

"And I?" Quint was asking. "Will I ever love a woman?... an ordinary woman, who is unlike my mythic mother?"

"You're spending too much time at the seminary," said Nola to Toto, ignoring Quint's question that she would rather forget.

"A perfect place to observe it," said Nora to Nola. "When we leave out the feminine, we identify with the feminine. Christ had a similar problem and took on the properties of his Mother, and died as a virgin- like Terzo... and Siegfried- for having my lover was like being his mother... and still, he resents it, not having his own."

'I only became you', said Siegfried, 'because you were incapable of intimacy'.

"One cannot be intimate with a drag queen," said Nora, regretting that she said it, as he disappeared in the ether, to deprive her of his presence.

"What we have learned in this meeting" said Nola to the dead, is that there are just so many patterns, and they are meant to be broken."

'We created those patterns and set our 'sons' up as heroes. They are enraged with our unconscious, because it drove them to suicide, while we were defending our egos against our psychopathic *animus*', Snow confided in Nora, who she would talk to from time to time.

"It seems we have something in common, and should see more of each other," said Nora to Snow, wanting to analyze the dead.

This put Nola on the defensive. If her mother was consorting with her lover, and her lover was her analyst, was there any hope of separation and the aloneness she was searching for? Where was Sergei when she needed him... but he was fused with Leonardo. She had created an impossible dilemma and it was obvious that the trickster was at work.

CHAPTER 56
LOVE COMES IN DISGUISE

To understand the inner workings of Terzo's incarnation in his brother, we can look at the twinship of Castor and Pollux, the sky and earth brother, who are the brightest stars of Gemini. Though only one was immortal, both brought down divinity, so it could be experienced on earth, by confronting 'the conflict of opposites'. While the mythic *dioscuri* are archetypal twins, Castor, the mortal brother, once was fallen and is dead, but, as his brother's immortality, he is given a glimpse of the eternal. The two alternate in being human, and in knowing their *limits*, which can be known through the shadow in the battle with love.

In *our* story, the earth brother is elevated when the dead brother descends, each made conscious of their shadow through the shadow of their mother, and are given the taste of immortality through her projection of the hero. As they struggle for love and the heroic ideal, with the fear of being mortal and not attaining to her vision, they are *confronting* their limits in the battle with death.

As Terzo was coming and going through Quint's mortal body, he resented the vessel that his mother immortalized, and as he wrestled with his envy a conflicted love grew between them, as Toto tempered the two through the Great Mother goddess. While Quint studied the heavens, they studied each other, and Terzo vied for the love that their mother lavished on Quint, as she mourned for his soul in his tomb made of flesh.

Nola confirmed his existence by confronting her

dark side, which when he was more or less human was expressed in their dreams: in her triple identity, she was his goddess of the crossroads, and as he traveled the *trivia*, it was through the image of his mother. In his sacrificial death, he believed he'd been exalted in her eyes, the hero raging within him by avenging Snow's soul; but with the birth of the boy he began to doubt 'Lupa's' love, and to long for the earth that he denied when he lived.

Like the Mother, the hero can personify the *Self*, and, by transcending his fear, he would learn to be deathless, to redeem the shadow of love and become what he must. When 'Lupa' was moving his hand to blind Lupo the wolf man, it was the moment of glory that he had lived in his dreams, in which he was able to destroy what had held him in fear, but glory lasts only a moment in the life of a mortal, while granting the illusion of immortality by overcoming one's limits.

In these times, Nola was careful to not let him enter her body, for he wanted to possess her and to have her for his own, and like an animal she was alerted to Quint's prediction of his death. As she dissolved the delusion that Terzo had fathered his brother, she realized he would always be a boy who was searching for his mother... and looking deeper at the problem, it was not so different from her own: for as 'Lupa the wolf girl', she found the mother she was searching for, in the shadow of the archetype, from the time she was a child. It was as if the Terzo in Quint was instructed by an older spirit, and was informed by the triple goddess of earth, heaven, and hell, and was in conflict with his reason that defied the wisdom he received.

Terzo's father was observing the conflict from

within, and knew his son's nature was distorted by his incapacity to be a father: his passive role in his development that was arrested by his shadow, and was more committed in death than he was when he lived.

According to Terzo- as death made him more cynical, and the dead cease to dream, for they *become* the unconscious- like a queen on the board she kept taking his knight, and giving the glory to Quint, who she endowed with his gifts; while Leonardo and Sergei, now fused into one, were constantly splitting, each protecting their sons; both residing in Quint, while attempting to escape- each merged in the other by the shadow of Nola.

On a day when the envious spirit and his brother were sitting on the rock, with Lupa the she-wolf lying between them, they talked of their mother, who they did not want to share...

'As the whore she rejects me, but as the virgin devours me. It seems she delights in confounding me, and will not let me rest', said Terzo to Quint, probing the heart of the boy.

"I find just the opposite (not realizing the whore was so literal): as the virgin she adores me, as if I were a miniature god. Her idealism and spirit inspire all my endeavors, and without her, I'd be nothing... nothing more than a boy... She has taught me to gaze at the stars through the boundless reaches of space, to know the gods as they were, who still inhabit the spheres. She lets me course through The Hunter, who I follow when I'm lost, but as the whore she devours me and is demanding and unpredictable- more like a lover than a mother... who would possess what she loves. Yet, always the virgin wins out, and is willing to sacrifice her desire, always striving for transcendence and the purity of love," Quint says in his innocence, stroking Lupa the wolf, as if he were stroking his mother, while Terzo is seething with envy.

'As I become you, I feel what it is to be human-which I never learned in my life as a boy on the earth, and which was 'the gift' of our mother, with the heart of a beast. As I learn how to love her, I know the tragedy of love: of not possessing the beloved and anticipating loss. I don't envy you, boy for having to live in her world'.

Toto has joined them and sees that Terzo's possessed, and no longer recognizes the heroic figure he idealized. "Reverse what he says. He is saying he envies you, for you are surviving the love that denied him his own, and unless you're aware of his envy, your brother will betray you," Toto is saying in Latin, which he was teaching the boy (forgetting that Latin was 'the language of the dead').

The Leonardo in Quint remembers Lupo's betrayal: how he had stolen his life and feels the pain of separation, and Quint's senses are sharpened, as he is aware of love's shadow.

'No, I don't envy you, Quint', said Terzo to his brother. 'In fact, it's almost a spiritual relief to have left my body behind, and to be able to live through your own and not suffer the consequences'.

"He is saying, he is jealous of your body and the way 'Lupa' worships it- like the body of a god, that he wants to possess."

Quint responds to his rival with the wisdom of a child, yet with the mind of a man, taming the wiley spirit that he's hosting...

"I can understand it must be freeing to be dead and disembodied, and to not have the burden of being 'nothing but human'. Let me live for you, Terzo, and be responsible for *all* your lives, to ensure your immor--tality, so you are not trapped on the earth- like you were when you lived as a thief on the streets. You can come and go like a pharoah through the door of the tomb, while I am fixed in a self, and must bear what I am. You are made of her heaven and the dust of the stars, that I must observe from a distance, while I am bound to her earth: stars with the power of change that can alter our fate. Let me love her for both of us and bear the betrayal of love; to feel the pain of being human, as you flit through the planes."

And so, through the god's double nature, he learned the law of reversal, and believed, for a moment, that he remained who he was, while allowing the alien spirit to live in his skin; and whether a trick of the devil, or his generous nature, the twinning allowed him to know what he knew. For a moment, he banished the spirit, to be alone with himself, put his arms round his wolf, and held her close to his breast...

"I will protect you from danger, which surrounds us on every side. Now let us hunt for our dinner, for we will be hungry tonight. These spirits are devouring the food of the mother, and we need to nourish the soul, so we are strong for the fight."

And as he was tracking a boar, the spirit of Philos was guiding him, and by protecting the boy he was reversing his fate. Playing the song of the Hawk, he distracted the spirit of Lupo, for he was tracking young Quint and was plotting his death.

Though the boar signifies lust- like the pheasant he

hunted- it is sacred to Artemis, the virgin Mother of earth, and, like the chaste goddess of the moon, its tusks are shaped like a crescent. The boar avenges its wounds, with horns made for the kill – horns like the devil's that are able to tear up the earth. Quint knew that the boar attacked before dying- that it never gave up, and he vowed to outlive it.

That night at Snow House- that followed an afternoon sleep, when Nola dreamed of his death, and saw the shadow of Lupo- as a sign of his manhood and courage, Quint served up a boar. Nola kept her thought to herself, until they finished the feast, which he prepared by himself, and with invisible hands...

"It was really marvelous, Quint, and I admire your bravery, but you must learn to fear death. I had to learn it myself."

"But it was you who taught me the secret that there is no life without death, and I'm more alive when I'm hunting and confronting the beast."

"I must ask you to sacrifice such pleasures out of devotion to love. Remember your reading of my stars, in which you saw your own death. What do you think, Nora, am I being a devouring mother?"

"I don't think so. The art of hunting the shadow is knowing the odds, and it takes many deaths to believe that the hero is mortal."

They can see he is feeling a defeat of the ego, which has taken heroic proportions and is being tested in the hunt.

"You see, Quint, you are driven by spirits who have not lived out their lives."

"Please, mother, Terzo is listening."

"He needs to hear it, just as you do. Love comes in

disguise when it is confounded by death. It is not easy to die when you live for *The Thought*. It requires a sacrifice that is beyond what is human, for bringing the stars down to earth is a task for a god. Terzo knows that I need him and that I need him in you. He knows that the heart is a riddle that can change the shadow to light."

"But he wants to destroy what you need in the need of your love, and the forces are raging in the heart of the beast. He still says he's my father, and that he wants to protect me, but he is trying to confuse me, and I think he has won."

Quint leaves confounded as Sergei appears, and feeling separate from Leo is feeling a sense of authority. 'I am claiming my son. He is splitting again. I've had enough of this doubling. When will you ever get enough'? He sits between Nola and Nora, scolding Nola like a child.

Like Terzo and myself, he is competing for her love, Nora was thinking, as she devoured the boar, and, like Nola and myself, he will never get enough. He is even jealous of his analyst, though I was part of the deal.

"At bottom, you're a monotheist, beneath your pagan veneer. You believe in the one Father of unity, one love, and one science. It finally killed you and I won't let it happen to him. He needs a sense of multiplicity, with the *illusion* of unity. Have some dessert, darling," pouring him a glass of wine.

'Don't try to seduce me, like you used to', trying not to weaken out of love.

"He may have a point, Nola. Perhaps, you should listen. This split could be deadly- this doubling of the father: like Terzo's conflict with Lupo, and his real father, Leonardo: like you and Snow as his mother, repeating the doubling motif, in which the shadow of spirit was attacking the flesh."

'Thank you, Nora', said Sergei; you are as sensible as always. I am the only father of my son and am made of both matter and spirit. You are still turning your projections into reality. I watched you dreaming of Terzo in the guise of a hermaphrodite, who took you in the lilies and fathered our son. What is obvious is what you're unable to see: the 'fabulous son'[381] of your alchemy, is only the illusion of a solution.

"You seem to have forgotten in your death how you justified it in your theories. The double god is confounding you, along with my son, though it inspired all your work and the conclusions you drew."

Nora is smiling to herself, knowing she is triggering a complex: the complex of a man, who in his heart was homophobic.

'As usual, Nola, you are tempting the trickster', said Sergei. His only chance to be a man is not to merge with his mother- to not lose himself in you, and the lost souls of your lovers'.

"Have you forgotten you are one of them?" asked Nora. "I'm still alive and I forget."

"Please, Nora, try not to collude with your patient." "I thought I had won it, this battle, but it is emerging with more ferocity. Still, I am dealing with it, Sergei. Go back to the stars. And don't tell me what you think, Nora, or you can join him on Orion."

"I am biting my tongue, and I can't distinguish it from the boar."

'We all have an unconscious', said Sergei, and disappeared with the wine.

"His glass is empty," said Nora. He has proved his impossible theory: that matter can be turned into spirit, and he is the father of your son. But it seems it's not over and there will be another round of death."

CHAPTER 57
A SPIRIT POSSESSED

Toto sits on the rock with the spirit of Terzo, and is performing a psychic exorcism to purge the spirit of Lupo. To give a dead star new life in the dark of the *Self*, a tomb of pearl must be built for the transformation of the worm.

"You're degenerating, Terzo. I feel like I've lost you. If you weren't a spirit, I would say you're possessed. I understand that you're trying to know your own shadow, but identifying with it is not the way of the hero."

'I don't want to disappoint you, but I have disappointed myself. From a pure-blooded hermaphrodite, I have become an evil queen. Indeed, I'm a spirit possessed by the shadow of the father, who is poisoned by envy and is avenging his blindness. His spirit is living inside me and is tearing me apart. I am questioning everything, just as I did when I lived, and I've been asking myself if I need a priest or an analyst'.

"If you want my advice, you do not need either, but both. As your priest, I would refer you to Saint Paul, the mystic, as we are sitting on the rock that is a symbol of his presence. In Paul's words: *And we with unveiled face are being changed to God's likeness. We have renounced underhanded ways and refuse to practice cunning, or to tamper with the Word'*, which he veils to those who are lost.

'It's a bit too Godly for me. What does Ambrose say'?

'Lift the veil,' he is saying. 'Go down to the mine. Bring down the god. Come down, Terzo. Come down'.

CHAPTER 58
GHOSTS ON THE COUCH

Nola lies on the murder bed in an intensive self-analysis, reflecting on the patterns of the killings and the workings of the past. Leonardo replaces her and submits to being analyzed.

"Yes, Leonardo, how can I help you?" she asks her dead lover, with the dry wit of a seer, on the 'analyst's chair' of the mind, that has become almost visible.

'Please don't embarrass my spirit, it took a lot to appear. I have been trying to pass through the negative veils, that *I* call my death and *you* call resistance. I know that I've broken your boundaries, but I've broken my own, and I am trying to form them from negative space. I'm a man with no body, a ghost of the past, that is not able to satisfy the needs of a beast'.

"If you're speaking of 'Lupa', having a body would-n't change it."

'There was a moment in time when I thought that it could. I've been comparing myself to your other dead lovers, all trapped in your son, in the body of a boy. If you could help me get out, so I could become what I'm not'.

"Pretend I know nothing. What would that be?"

'A saint, a flutist, a priest, or a scientist'.

"What would you *not* say?"

'I was unable to act, a problem I passed to our son, and by breaking the pattern, it led to our death'.

"Try to imagine your self as part of my psyche, a dead part that I'm trying to bring back to life. Ask yourself what it is that I am unable to transform."

'That you are trapped in Snow's shadow. I have the

same problem. It keeps us from fighting for love. How many deaths will it take'?

"We will do it in this one. What have you tried?"

'I tried re-enacting Snow's murder through the eyes of my son- a suggestion of 'Lupa's'… 'She' says it's my shadow that killed her… the shadow he thought was his father... He didn't know... I never told him... he thought... he believed'... He gives up in despair… 'What do I know that I don't'?

" 'She' is saying you can't tell the difference between your shadow and Lupo's- your projection and 'hers'. Do you have a projection of your own?"

'Not yet. I'm suspended in time. I am asking you to form a boundary between matter and spirit- an impossible task, as the boundaries keep shifting. Nothing has changed. It is just as it was when I lived. My eyes were wide open, but I was unable to see… When I look through my son's eyes, the image is frozen... The knife is suspended... I'm unable to act... It's like my shadow is praying... my hands clasping the knife... like I'm praying to Nothing... a shadow prayer to the void... What I mean is... I can't feel the wound... but it was me that he killed... What I mean is...'

"What you mean is, you are identified with your shadow, that you project on your brother, and are feeling the guilt, he is unable to feel."

'Yes, that's what I mean... the guilt of killing my mother... I mean, my lover... your mother'.

"We will work on it, Leo, the killing off of the feminine."

'You mean, the act of separating 'Lupa' from her woman-hating *animus*'?

She is silent a moment... and tries to confront it.

"I'm afraid you have hit on it... the Lupo in Leo... the Lupo in me... the killer *I* who destroyed the saint in the thief, that I needed to transform, instead of living 'her' myth- in which the knife is the means to *penetrate* the feminine."

'Let's not go too deep. I might not be able to return'.

"The real fear is not being able to escape. Take back your shadow that has the shape of your brother. Your shadow is sleeping. It escapes into sleep. It sleeps with its eyes open, but is unable to see."

And he weeps like a child... like a nine-year-old boy... and remembers his brother smashing the face of the Mother...

Leo is replaced by Terzo 'on the couch'...

'I know what you want- why you're bringing me back. You want me to relive all my traumas to relieve you of yours, and free Quint from my influence so you can kill off the past'.

"I would spare you both, if I could, but it is no longer possible. Tell me, why are you trying to kill off the opposite, instead of trying to integrate the living and the dead?"

'It's Quint that you're thinking of. It's '*too late*' for me'...

Leonardo's ill-fated words... when I prayed for his death... when I was trying to kill off the opposite... instead of trying to integrate it...

"Don't you see what is happening, that the blind beast has returned? Are you going to let him possess you, or will you fight for your freedom? I know what it's like to be possessed by his shadow. It was his curse coming through me, when I robbed you of the need to be human."

'But you are still here. Are the dead able to change? Do you know what it's like to be stranded in the coldness of the stars, while Quint studies them on earth and is protected by your love; to be the shadow of my brother, the one who is feared and rejected, split off in your darkness and exiled to hell'?

"Are you going to submit to your fate, when you have a chance to reverse it? 'The devil wants to be redeemed'."

'I will try to redeem you'.

Terzo is replaced by Leonardo on 'the couch'...

'I was conversing with Sergei on his theories and finding him unbearable. He's trying to teach me to father my son, who is possessed by my brother, and tormenting his own. I finally lost him in some ethereal realm. I'm tired of hearing about the magnetic field of the dead. It's your fault we are fused. You will not let us go. How many years in his body and entombed in his son's? How many light years of lecturing me in the dark of the mind? You've gotten me back for my sins. Is there no limit to your folly? Don't you think it's enough'?

"I do. I wanted to talk to you about it, but I need your help on the matter. I've gone too far again, darling."

'When have you not? I'm beginning to feel like your creation'.

"You *are* my creation, as I am yours, Leonardo. But you are right, it's not working. It's time you were analyzed: time to endure the separation from your psychopathic brother."

'I've been enduring it for years'.

"You have endured the *illusion* of separation."

'So you are saying that death hasn't turned the illusion to reality'?

"I am saying, we have destroyed the illusion *and* the reality."

'It is you who have fused them. There's no boundary between them'.

"You are making my point. It's time to reverse it; but let's trace it back to the beginning, to how it began. The first time was *your* doing, when you fucked me to replace him- your devil of a shadow that was splitting you in two. The second, not letting me *know* that you fucked me, while I spun my dark fantasy, and became what I'm not- a psychic whore on the street. Third, when you *allowed* me to spin it, till I repeated the tragedy, and was playing the whore to deal with your shadow... while escaping my own, and slipping into the part."

'How can we *separate* the parts, without self-destructing'?

"By shifting the center of gravity."

'Can you be more specific'?

"By not sleeping with your eyes open, so you know if you're awake or unconscious. I'm not asking you to watch, while Lupo is killing my mother, but to know it through Terzo, who looked through his eyes, and thought he was holding the knife... remembering... forgetting... that he did *not* kill his mother... repeating... destroying... killing the thing that he loves... like his 'mother'... the whore... You must free him from prison- like I once freed your brother, but which led to your death, and the death of our son, and by reversing my curse he can learn to be human: not an imposter, but a boy, in a human body on earth.

'You are asking a lot. Do you really think I have the power'?

"It is time that you claimed it and stopped calling it Lupo. I am not asking for blood- a symbolic murder will do. This time, Leonardo, you will be awake with your eyes open, and will not unconsciously collude in the killing off of the feminine. He is still trying to drive me to suicide by attacking my son, and is avenging his blindness- the blindness of the beast. It will require another murder, a *psychic* dismemberment, which we will accomplish after death, by reversing the past. This time we'll remember what we tried to forget. It will be performed in separate stages, like we would work on a recurring dream, by exploring dark matter, as we work with the compulsion."

'Only you could devise such a complicated scenario'.

"The unconscious devised it."

'I'm afraid the unconscious is beyond me. But you will have what you ask: I will surrender my ego- a reflection of the past, and subject it to 'the couch', to the painful process of analysis... take the risk that I'll exist in a form that you will recognize... a thief who has run out of pearls, and the chance that I'll lose you. There is only one condition I insist on: that you don't confound me with a quark: I am asking for a separation from the inflated physicist you're merged with: the atomic madman you replaced me with, and his pretentious theories of inverted space/time. The worst part of this fusion is that I am beginning to believe him: that gravity is life, and draws us to the heart of the unconscious'...

"To the magnet of the *Self* that you are trying to

deny. You have attracted what you need, but are unable to admit it. It's hard to find an expert on the force of attraction. If you could stop being envious, you might learn what you know, but you will need some distance from your shadow, so you can know yourself in him."

'Sounds like a paradox'.

"So is the psyche. I'm sure it is just as unbearable for him. Why don't you talk to him about the problem, that is, if you can find him in yourself. I'm sure he has a scientific theory on the pangs of *separatio*."

'You're impossible'.

"How else would you find me? We will *use* the Law of Attraction to analyze the transference: the incestuous spell that your son is imprisoned in."

'And *your* son, my wolf one'?

"I must refer you to Nora. My feelings would get in the way."

'That would be a novelty. I didn't realize you had them'.

Leonardo is replaced by Sergei 'on the couch'.

'He thought that he lost me. He may as well lose yourself'.

"Still making the invisible visible?"

'While I'm immersed in your darkness, as if I were one of your experiments'?

"Try subsisting in my light."

'I am not the genius you think I am'.

"That *you* think you are, darling. Now let's get down to business. Why are you here?"

'I couldn't bear being without you: that is, without myself, doctor'.

"I know what you mean. We will continue to work on it by stripping the veils, while learning to bear being human, to be together in time, instead of trying to outwit it, and to live in inner space, in a world that we create... and compulsively destroy... Then, as a spiritual exercise in bearing the impossible, we will try to bear being separate, while being joined in the soul."

'Will I be able to touch you? Why can't I touch you'?

And then he was gone, and she was reaching through space.

CHAPTER 59
COME DOWN FATHER:
I NEED YOU

Quint questioned his relationship to the world of the spirit, and whether the beings inside him were a projection of his mother, or did they move of themselves with a life of their own, and compel him to live and explore the life of the mind? The gist of the problem was in having two fathers, a father of matter and a father of spirit; for just as he thought he was coming to terms with it, his brother intruded, confounding his thoughts.

Now that his mother was trying to temper her shadow, it was time to stop splitting and bring them into relation: clearly, matter and spirit were simply interpenetrating principles, and the mother and father world personified these opposites: a split in the psyche between conscious and unconscious. Though his father of matter was rarified and unworldly, he contributed to the study of interior space/time, and devoted his life to the theory that dead matter lives. In his theory, its psychic equivalent was in the realm of non-being, and the spark in the darkness as the foundation of life: the spirit of the feminine as the life in dark matter, the shadow of life, from which the living are born.

But it was Terzo who confirmed that the dead stars were alive, and who imparted the mystery of bringing the soul back to life. Quint, who was twelve, in his struggle for freedom, questioned himself if his thoughts were his own, or the urgings of his brother and the spirits of her lovers.

He would be beginning his studies in religion and

physics, which Nola had arranged through 'Lupa's Jesuit trick- who switched the Eucharist for his penis in the rite of Communion- the erratic head master at *Dieu et ses Anges*: the same priest she blackmailed for Toto and now for her son. He was ready to enter the preparatory school, in the elitist school for 'the chosen' as a prodigy of physics, with students four to six years his senior, who would go on to seminary; while he was preparing for Trinity College in Cambridge, for a masters in astronomy, psychology, and the philosophy of religion.

She knew that the pedophile priest would idealize Quint, who was accepted as having a remarkable intellect, but his older colleagues would be unable to keep up with the boy and would treat him as an outcast, and with the envy of his brother. More, he was a boy of the wild, who could run with the beasts, and though Nola had tamed him, Quint would be jousting with his masters.

He would have to learn to be civilized and talk the language of men, an impossible task for a boy who communed with the stars; Toto, adept in such matters, had taught him to 'pass'; but what was required in the world was to be an ordinary boy. He would have to learn the very basics of being 'nothing but human', and so he called on his father, who was more practical than his mother. Perhaps, he could give him some simple advice on how to appear to be fixed, while the spirits were raging inside him.

"Come down, father, I need you," he called through the ether, for his father was unable to stay in Quint's body, and had returned to the stars, where he felt more at home. "I need to know how to be when I enter the world. How did *you* learn to do it when you were here on the earth? Tell me the secret of the Mother of gravity, that allows the transition from the stars and the life of the spirit, to begin the journey to the ordinary and to the lower world of men."

But it was the *problem* of gravity that had stopped Sergei's heart...

'Frankly, making the transition to earth was never my strong point, but I can give you some simple advice, in order to make the descent. When I wanted to adapt and was out of sorts with the world, I observed the four rivers that run through the mind, and followed the four cardinal directions to the center of earth. By using the 'excep-tional points' of the luminaries in the heavens and the number six as the Word in the timeless region of the psyche, link the upper and lower Trinity through 'the third as the fourth'. It can also be learned by *gazing* into the heavens and studying how the inner constellations are projected in the sky'.

"It's much too simple for me, father, but I will try to follow your instructions."

CHAPTER 60
PASSING IS AN ART

At the Jesuit school in Paris, at *Dieu et ses Anges*, Quint was sublimating the senses to transform the inner man. There was a concentration on theology, with an accent on the spiritual values, but here 'a man was trained to think, and rounded out in the humanities'. Quint's prodigious talents were both envied and feared, and he was promoted at twelve to the advanced upper levels, for those who are 'called' (by the workings of 'Lupa').

Called for what was the question, but no answer was offered, and so he created his own, which was prompted by Terzo. When Quint was asked to explain it by one of his peers, which happened quite often at *Dieu et ses Anges*, he said he was called by the stars, who had asked him to free them. This left them nonplussed and they never asked him again; but they never ceased to be curious about his mastery of astronomy. It was mixed with psychology and religion, a fusion of Ambrose and his mother, while Leonardo was teaching him the game of chance with the dice, Philos transposing the numbers into Dionysian notes, moved by the god of the spirit and the mind of Apollo, as Sergei trained him in physics and the music of the spheres.

He studied T*he Old Testament* in Aramaic; *The New Testament* in ancient Greek; Constructing Christian Theology and Deconstructing World Religions; Medieval Philosophy; Freudian Psychology; Sacred Geography; Cultural Anthropology; Advanced Creative Writing; Biblical Literature; Ancient Tragedy;

Music; The History of Art; Western and Non-Western History in the Age of Anxiety; Critical Thinking and Logic; Geometry and Calculus; The Chemistry of Five Ele-ments; Astronomy and Physics; the Heresy of Alchemy to the Atomic Structure of the God-man; Analytic Chemistry; and The Metaphysics of Biology. This was accomplished in the space of three diabolical years, and would not have been possible without the help of the spirits. At fifteen, Quantum Physics, Cosmology, and The Theory of Relativity; the Symposium of Dialectic with more challenging dialogues, based on the phenomenology of Religion and The Exegesis of the Holy Books; St. Thomas Aquinas- analyzing *Summa Theologica*; and with his Latin from Toto, he would graduate in a year.

He was given special permission to take the Science of Religion class, for the brightest of students, who were going on to seminary. It was taught by the old Jesuit priest ('Lupa's' trick when she was twelve), who had a penchant for Quint and for Toto, as Nola predicted.

"To quote Maeterlinck, said the Father, *In order to commit themselves as little as possible, some scientists see in ether the element of spirit, a fictitious but indispensable basis for the phenomena of light. Others despairing of their cause, revert to the hypothesis of a universal substratum- which exacts nothing, and is no more than a nickname for the profound and primordial mystery, and which has been vainly plied with thousands of equations.* According to Maeterlinck, *the word ether is as the word God: it masks and disguises magniloquently* that *which we do not know.*[395] Let's discuss."

Quint raises his hand.

"Yes, Quint."

"The renowned relativist astronomer and physicist, Jeans, is cited by Maeterlinck 'to reconcile ether's opponents'. He said: *What we have here is a mental creation and not a solid substance, which is just as real or unreal as the existence of the poles… or the mind of the supreme law of space and the body of time*[396] (fusing Jeans with Alexander and wondering why).

"The commitment to ether is the greatest commitment of all, for how can we question that it is a psychic reality- a *transcendent* reality that exists in the space/time continuum: the fourth dimension in the unconscious, linking inner and outer space: a linking through the ether or spirit, as the universal substratum. *There is no time external to the events of the universe, says Maeterlinck, just as space exists only through the displacement or passage of matter.*[396a]

"*But* Jeans asks: *What would happen if time stopped? Nothing,'* he says. *We should have no suspicion that* it *stopped. There is no time: there are only imaginary measurements existing in the mind.*[396b]

"And *I* ask, what of sidereal time and 'the stars in the blood'? The psyche has its timing and links the mind with the stars. Linking conscious and unconscious with interior time is a psychic commitment, like the commitment to ether: a spiritual commitment, the greatest commitment of all, for how can we question that spirit is a psychic reality? In essence, if ether is God, so is gravity for Maeterlinck, and both exist in the psyche, in what Jeans calls *The Thought.*"[396c]

"Maeterlinck asks, he continues, (wishing he could

stop): *If one could suppress gravitation, which is like the power of God, interrupt it or cut it short like an electric current, would it mean the end of life, of which it is the unique source, as it acts in proportion to matter, and the force that surrounds it?*[397] My own thought is that this suppression of gravity, as a force in the psyche, would be a refusal to admit that the unconscious exists, and, in time, would result in an interior death. The real question is, are we unconsciously identified with the 'shadow of God', and what we fear will destroy us, and, by suppressing its reality, believe it ceases to exist? In essence, can we create our own death through a psychic projection? *The Thought* that spirit does not exist, and that, in the end, we're dead matter, may mean that *The Thought* of God's shadow has become a reality."

But now his devilish shadow made itself known to him: it was living inside him, and was tricking *The Thought*: 'Or is *reality* fictitious, like the spirit- or ether'? (asked Terzo, the spirit, using Quint's voice and his shape) 'Does it have any meaning, or is it the work of the trickster, a whim of God's shadow, a *deformation* of ether (our mother disguised) that we think of as spirit? (Was it ether that killed me and interrupted my current'? whispered the rogue of a spirit, transmitting the shadow of *Thought*, ('or is it our mother, who *commits as little as possible*, and who *despairs of our* cause of freeing ourselves from her will')?

Quint's *Thought* suddenly shatters like invisible glass, for now he *knows* he's possessed by his envious brother- who is falling again after a brief resurrection- as if 'colliding with a passing star'* that feels cheated

406

by fate; as if his brother was his shadow, obscuring his light.

Quint tries to subdue him, in a voice not his own, mixed with Terzo's ghost wanderings, like the fragments of dreams: the dead brother inside him, who envies the fifth, and is merged with his mother, his 'universal substratum', who 'masks and disguises' the spirit inside him.

Quint seeks his refuge in his father, the philosopher of physics, and asks *The Thought* how to free him from the rebel spirit that torments him, but he is unable to find him in the wilderness of space.

"If 'The universe begins to look more like *The Thought*'," Quint continues, under the spell of 'the third', "and we deprive it of light and of spirit, it is nothing less than the devil, or *The Thought* in reverse, in which we believe 'God is dead'. In Jean's words, Mind no longer *appears as an accidental intruder into the realm of matter. We ought rather to hail it as its governor and creator.*[398] How can we doubt, Father, that with every thought we are moved into being by ether, and that the quality of spirit, whether denser or lighter, is changed by hatred or love, and is the beginning or end of a world?"

Would his brother's hatred, Quint wondered, be the end of *his* world, whose shadow was killing his spirit and *The Thought* that is God?...

"And if *gravity is life*, Quint continues, "is the shadow of gravity death?"

Was the death of his father, the fate of his son? Quint is asking *The Thought*, as his young mind is drifting into Jeans *'reverse time travel'*.[398a] He is warned by his father to 'stand stiller than still',* but the spirit is raving inside him and he is unable to stop...

"Has *The Thought* of 'the end of the continuous creation of matter,'* Quint continues, "become a physical reality that we are unable to control? This may be the essence of the phenomenology of spirit. It is in this context that I must contradict Jeans on one point, for clearly, more than one object can occupy the same space at the same time, which, like ether or spirit, can be invisible to the eye." Where did that come from? He is trying to destroy me.

Again, he is calling on Sergei, who again is reduced to a thought in cold space, and he was unable to hold him, for his image kept doubling. Was he spirit or matter? his shadow kept asking, and so, Quint was caught in his brother's continuous reversals, and no sooner did he trust him than he changed his character and temperament; and whether father or brother, darkness or light, the two fathers inside him were at war in his soul.

"What I am saying, Father, is that *The Thought* is continually dying and being reborn, and that ether, the Mother, is the force of gravity itself, pulling us down to the source, to what we call the unconscious: to *what is unknowable and plied with thousands of equations*, that cannot be limited to logic or reason: that four dimensions are not enough, and that the fifth element of ether, *masks and disguises magniloquently the primordial mystery*, who can never be known in all her dangerous forms."

Why did he say it? Why was he telling his secrets? But *The Thought* did not answer that had turned to the trickster, as Terzo put words in his mouth that had a will of their own...

"To the mind of a superman or angel,[399] he continues in dismay, *who can grasp the unknowable,* wishing he could stop, the ether, as the fifth, can change its form and its sex, by shifting *The Thought-* that *those who can't commit* have assumed is fictitious, and yet, it is the *nature* of ether and the *mystery* of spirit to change from the masculine to the feminine, like the androgynous Christ."

His classmates looked on astonished, hating this grandiose boy, who was feminizing the theories of the master they idealized.

The priest has been mesmerized, unable to speak, but suddenly comes to his senses, for he has lost all control. "Enough! You are killing the thought of the class!" outraged by his own silence, while eroticizing the boy, drunk on a boy of fifteen, who could confound his own thoughts, like 'Lupa' once did, and make him doubt what he was.

"But this class would not exist, Father, without the problem of opposites, and though at the moment they are trying to destroy one another, they can only be reconciled by the mystery of ether, which includes the shadow of spirit, or matter, which we think of as feminine, and, yet, we know that without it, there would be no 'rebirth of the infant church'."

There is a moment of wordlessness, as the boys are stunned by the blasphemy, and their passivity in not confronting it. And yet, they were beginning to conceive of another dimension that seemed strangely feminine, and that the feminine soul and the spirit were not easily separated, for they too were under its spell, and were unable to respond.

"Where have you gone, Quint, and where can we go

from here?" asks the mortified priest, who has lost their respect.

"It is not intentional, Father. I am trying to relativize 'the poles of the compulsion, which are personified by God and the devil,'[400] and it will take some time to accomplish it."

"Where are you, Quint, and where have you come from?"

"From the door of the tomb in the fourteenth station of the cross...'opening and closing'... closing and opening... and I am only exploring what exists on the other side."

He wondered if losing his ground with the collective he might soon be an outcast, like his father before him, in the reductive structure he defied. But Terzo was shifting his effect on the minds of his colleagues, who now, in the transference, were intrigued by the impossible: by such sacrilegious meanderings disturbing the usual boundaries, and what was emanating from the ether- now known as *The Thought*. And now, they had to admit that Quint's passion was the *essence* of religion and felt almost like atheists in the midst of such fervour- for the 'called' had now realized that they knew nothing of God, or 'the spirit of gravity' as the Mother, who was disguised as the devil.

"Let me put it another way," said the priest, red with rage, "where are you *trying* to go?"

'Anywhere, so long as it's out of this world', Quint responded, from Baudelaire's *Flowers of Evil* (a favorite of Terzo's), going on like an opium addict, and in Terzo's *puer* tones that he had come to despise, but that were plucking his strings, like an out of tune instrument.

'Is anyone with me'? asks Terzo, through the body of Quint, like some maddened revolutionary storming the fortress of Catholicism, so out of Quint's character, whose eyes were lifted to heaven, and with a grandiose flourish that was more like his mother's.

A few raised their hands with the usual trepidation, feeling spiritually threatened by their daring, in the face of such perversity. Somehow, they had never realized that Quint was such a wit, and the Jesuit threw up his hands in a fit of despair… "We will *explore* it after class, Quint, and we will be looking at its dark side." (The boys knew what he meant, and sneered to each other).

'What is repressed in the shadow returns with a vengeance', his mother was whispering to the soul of her son, from the fifth essence of ether that was attuned to *The Thought*.

"I would be happy to, father. Isn't that why we're here?"

The boys were suppressing their laughter, and Quint smiles like an angel.

"All I am saying is that gravity is the Mother, whose breath is the ether, and which I think I just grasped in the gravitational field."

"Class dismissed," said the father. But the class sat transfixed.

"And I am more certain than ever," Quint continued, unabashed, "that it is ether that causes the force of attraction."

"I said, enough, Quint! Enough!"

But we have fifteen more minutes, and it is just getting interesting," said Quint, who was shaking his Jesuit shadow, looking him dead in the eye… a look reminiscent of 'Lupa's', the priest thought to himself, as he opened the door for the boys, and tried to confirm his authority, that he knew he had lost to the spirit of ether; knew they would challenge his limits and break from 'God's prison', 'Lupa's thought now intruding and merging with Terzo's.

Quint and the priest were alone in the room now. What was he afraid of, the priest was asking the ether? He thought he disguised it, but Quint and 'Lupa' were on to him, as he looked him over *discreetly* (he tried to believe), roused by the boy and the canny glint in his eye.

"That was quite a diversion from the text, Quint."

"Isn't that what discussion is about?"

"Not exactly. You will have to learn discipline and to stay within the bounds, if you want to be tops in your field. It is astrophysics, isn't it?"

"Yes, Father, it is."

"I can see that you get your theoretical bent from Gobosky, your father, the renowned astrophysicist on the electromagnetic field."

Silence.

"Your father was Gobo, wasn't he?"

"Yes, Father, he is."

"But he's deceased, is he not?"

"In a way. My father is in the ether, where such genius belongs."

The priest is amused, but his smile changes to lust. The boy is not fooled, but he plays for a while. "How quickly spirit can change, when it descends to the earth: interesting, isn't it, Father, how it hides in the senses?"

The Father knows he's been read, and by something he couldn't quite fathom… the boy was like 'Lupa', when she was whoring at twelve, and again she was using his senses to get what she wanted… He tried to cover himself, for he was aware she wanted blood, and he tried 'to commit himself as little as possible'…

"I'm going to pass you with honors… but only for your brilliance…"

Where did that come from? He was getting deeper in the mire, as if the boy was 'a mental creation and not a solid substance'…

"You can go now Quint," before he *completely* exposed himself. Again, the compulsion was building and Quint knew what he wanted.

"But what about the exploration?" asked Quint. "There is so much to know, and we have only pierced the surface." He left, as if reluctantly, teasing him to death. He had learned from his mother and her son how to work the trappings of the mind. And he would continue to learn it in ways he couldn't conceive.

'Passing is an art', Sergei said to his son, thrusting through the fifth to commune with his heir, before laying down 'on the couch' in Nola's consulting room...

'I need a session. I'm tired of passing. I want to be with you- in the body'.

"You are, darling- mine," repeating her words to Leonardo.

'Death has not dulled your wit'.

"On the contrary, it has sharpened it. But I admit that I want you, the whole self incarnate. I've been working on a formula on bringing you down, and to still be in love with you when the spirit turns to flesh. Meanwhile, I'm *perfecting* the art of passing as I'm moving through the planes."

413

'That isn't your problem'.

"What *is* my problem?"

'Staying on this one. It's what drew us together. Remember'?

"I am trying to forget. But it's clear, you wouldn't be here if your formula wasn't working. Let's begin the impossible- to integrate spirit and matter, which is always a sacrifice and requires *staying* in the body. In short, you have discovered an equation to manifest the spirit, but being visible always leads to a crucifixion of the flesh. Are you willing to endure it? The last time was insufferable."

'But only for a moment. You did it, you know. I *belong* in *The Thought*'.

"Then as a spiritual exercise, in bearing the impossible, let's return to the source, to the cross of our being, until we can bear being separate, while being joined in the soul."

She wanted to hold him on earth, to hold him back from the stars, as her hair swept through his fingers, like it did when he lived, and he kissed what it seemed was the mouth of the earth.

'I couldn't resist'.

"Neither could I. I need your dead matter to keep me alive. Why not stay for a while, so we can pretend we're in love?"

'I would not believe I existed unless I existed in you. But this time, we will measure the odds. I will come down from time to time, to not get trapped on the earth'.

"I understand, my own spirit, and if you don't mind, I will wait." She was entranced for a moment by his effusions of light, as she gazed at his beauty, passing through her entirely. He was stunning, she thought, his etheric body against her. He could not have been more... and then he was gone...

But she spoke to his soul through *The Thought*, the only way she knew how...

> You were there, as always,
> too fixed and too firm,
> chipping smaller stones of wisdom
> from the giant macrocosm
> and the great rock that you are.
> Undisclosed were the worlds within,
> veiled by detachment and forethought,
> the blue measured glance assessing
> the odds,
> weighing the unknown chance
> and quickly fending it off to be safe
> from the steady onslaught of chthonic
> feelings,
> an incalculable force, too heavy for
> shoulders
> that prefer heady ether to earth,
> already descending to the nether extreme.
> But you took me home to the mythic clouds
> beyond Olympus,
> opened the heart of God
> and bowed me down before him.
> There on a desert in space
> with no water or camel,
> we began the distant journey
> to an elusive point we called reality,
> a distant destination,
> but always closer than before.

Quint went to his mother in Snow House to prepare for his finals, to make certain the spirits were working, to ensure that he passed.

"I need to know they are with me and not off on a tangent. I want to go further. I need more of a challenge. The collective level is low, and I'm working too hard for the possible. I am not feeling expansive in such a limited atmosphere, and I'm compensating with states of possession and boundlessness. Tell me, am I being arrogant again? Do I need to work on humility?"

"Yes, Quint, you do. But I have the same problem. I long for the impossible- like your father of matter, who returned to the spirit, and who is pressing you on to find a way to combine them. It's a strange kind of discipline to mediate the collective, and to not be tainted by its lack of values, which are created by the unreflective. You will have to learn to contain, so that you can pass in this world, for breaking out prematurely would lead to a tragedy. We will challenge it together, or their envy will destroy you. In essence, do not lift the veil to the uninitiated, or you will be crucified by the mob."

"Something greater than my pride tells me that it's true. With my brother inside me, it's like I'm struggling with death: it's like he wants to destroy me, and yet he needs me to live. He keeps asking the question that I am trying to answer, but when I try he distracts me and interferes with *The Thought*. Tell me, how can I free him, so he can rest in the ether?"

"Perhaps, he is trying to pass and is the question, itself. 'Live the question,'[407] he's posing, and we will make a pearl of his death."

And she strokes his wild head and winds the curls

round her fingers, like strands of light that are mixed with the dark strands of her own.

CHAPTER 61
A PLACE TO PRAY

1990: The year devoted to Snow: 'Do this in memory of me',[408] on the site of my grave, above the place I conceived you, the day I designed my own death. Build a temple for Artemis, and with my bones build an altar. Make a shrine of her image and raise me up for the hunt'.

The temple was built, surrounding the stone on Snow's grave, and Quint made a statue of the Huntress on her altar of bones. Terzo brought it to life by inspiriting the stone, as an offering to Snow, who was slain by the beast. She was aiming her arrow at the Hunter through the opening in the dome, her she-wolf beside her, avenging her death.

Nola was trying to reverse her dark prayer ('Let it not be human... let it not be human': the prayer that was answered, though she had changed her dark mind: her spells were easy to cast but were harder to break) and was invoking The Wolf One for the blood-letting sacrifice. She built a circular amphitheatre in the forest of Snow House, a glass domed roof high above for viewing the planets and stars, where their choreographed changes were part of the performance.

Nola played the protagonist in all of the tragedies-Medea, Jocasta, Electra, Clytemnestra, all the myths she had lived, to fit the parts to the whole- but tonight was the sacrifice for the mother of tragedies. Tonight, her Medea was devoted to Snow.

Nola redeemed Snow House from the dread of the wolf man, and practiced healing with Ambrose and the nuns from 'The Mother'. She turned the forest that surrounds it to a retreat for the arts, and gave a class on the tragedies, as a sacred offering to the gods; Nora the meaning of the dramas and the art of psychology; Toto the spirit of theology; and Quint the science of the stars, which was guided by Sergei, his father of spirit and matter, and he came to terms with the split and vowed to make them combine.

Toto's first mass took place in the temple and was devoted to Artemis, the Lady of the Beasts...

"This mass for the Huntress is a warning for the hunter, who Artemis turned from a man to a beast," and he read from *Metamorphoses*,[409] changing the words when he would...

" 'It happened that Actaeon, the hunter, through unknown ways, stumbled upon the goddess on a hillside, in a place of desolation, where weary of her chase, she dropped her javelin and bow', and stripping her veil was bathing naked with her nymphs. When he saw her unveiled and her nature revealed, 'she pressed her horn mark on his forehead, and marked him for death.'*

"Now *Actaeon's forehead wore a most peculiar dress, his head branched in antlers, his* neck *grew long, ears were pointed, hands were hooves, arms stag's legs, his body a short-furred creature with spotted skin. Tears ran down his face, when he saw his reflection in the stream, and he had no words* for his grief *and made beastly cries,* for he had seen her mystery unveiled, who was 'virgin unto herself:* he wanted the body of earth, and to claim what he saw, but unwilling to make the sacrifice, he was turned to a beast. Now the hunter was prey and his hounds chased him down, and was himself the blood sacrifice to the goddess of the hunt: *If*

419

only he could speak: Look at your master', he would say. 'I am Actaeon', the hunter, *but words were lost to him, and he was torn to pieces.*[410]

"Like Actaeon, we all bear the beast in us. *Its fur, though invisible, grows on our shoulders, our fingers are claws, arms like legs, our tails sweep the earth, and when we're talking we growl, till the goddess puts bits between our teeth, driving us on**. Tame the beast in the man, so that it doesn't destroy you, as it tears up the earth in the war of the flesh and the spirit. Now let's pray to Our Lady that we may know our own beast, and know what it is to be human and make the sacrifice to earth, without losing our soul to possess what we love."

In the silence that followed, the will was aimed at the heart and all felt the grief for the blood that was spilled in her name.

Terzo, sitting in the pew next to Quint, felt a rush of remorse, and remembered the words of his father: "But the beast in the man still longs to be human. We are not born human. It is an act of will to be human," and he held his hand to his heart, that beat in the heart of his brother...

'Forgive me, if you can. I sometimes forget who I was. I am jealous of your genius, and the way she loves you when you speak'.

"She needs yours as well. We can have her together," Quint said to his brother, who was prey to his shadow.

Then he looked up at Lupo, who was slouched in the corner, his hands in his pockets, whistling *The Messiah*, and was staring at Quint with his unseeing eyes... but Quint knew he could see him and that he wanted his life...

"If I die in the hunt," he prayed to 'The Wolf One', "rip his heart from his breast, and protect the soul of my mother."

Was he identifying with Actaeon, and did they share the same fate? Only the Sphinx knew the answer and what he would meet at the crossroads. But in every beast that he hunted, he would find a piece of the riddle, and by fighting his fate, he would bear his own destiny.

CHAPTER 62
THE DEVOURING MOTHER

Nola's performance of Medea began with a ritual sacrifice, when she called on her dark side and became what she played. The soul of the sorceress, fired by the rage of betrayal, slit the throat of a boar with the knife that killed Snow. She offered it up to the goddess of hell, as its blood poured through the stone, filling the vessel beneath it, its screech in the night as she ripped off the mask, kneeled to the goddess and prayed for revenge. Hecate sanctioned the offering, for she had longed for such passion, and since the days of the matriarchy had never seen such devotion, but *becoming* Medea was the grounds for a tragedy, as she revealed to the audience that the gods were not dead.

"We must separate the opposites, before they are joined, an arduous task, like parting Venus and Mars, for love and death can be closer than identical twins," Toto was saying, as he was merging with 'Lupa', knowing the dangers of merging in his own mother's death. But he was one with the myth and his lady of the beasts, who had brought him back from the dead to become what he was.

"She knew the wild pig in its more human form, that she'd slain with a thought when she hunted for men," Toto mixing his thoughts with Ovid, his poet, as if he were praying to the Wolf One and the 'Lupa' in Nola…

This shows how Circe's magic works, the sorceress who turns men into pigs. That woman can get away with anything she chooses, which proves that all things change, yet never die. Or here or there, the spirit takes its way to different kinds of being as it chooses, from beast to man, from man to beast: however far or near or strange, it travels on, so does the soul pass through its transformations, nor does Artemis ever look the same, gazing at Nola, who shifted her form... as he merged with the 'Lupa', under the spell of her art. *She lives in the shadow of the goddess, and will rise or fall with her*,[413] as she slays the great beast in the dark of the mind.

'We slide into the forms we create', said her poet, and the Wolf One in Nola turns men into beasts: *a mixture of father/form and mother/matter**, as she tempts men to linger on '*The Blessed Isle of Forgetfulness*'... "I must be careful of loving her and being turned to a pig"...

But now the Devourer demanded a more interior sacrifice, and, as if the Mother of Shadow appeared in the play, she awakened the spirit in the souls of the dead. Athena, the protector of mysteries from the eyes of the profane, would be reminding our heroine why they were hidden, as the Wolf One in Nola was saying the words of Medea...

'*Some gods bewitched my senses, chained my will. Is this called love?... Yet each love went to death, however death had caught him,*'* her face like a death mask, as she called up the shadow.

Lupo, a beast of the Huntress (who fathered her rage, whose animal seductions were passed on to 'Lupa'), had been watching the sacrifice, waiting for his moment to appear. Leo, watching the performance, was keenly aware of his presence, till his eyes were diverted through the glass dome of the theater, where Terzo, in the ether, was standing on the shoulders of

Orion.

Both Sergei and Leo were distracted by the stunt, while Nola did her monologue of the slaying of her children...

'*They must die*,' she was saying, standing by the altar with the knife- the same knife with the cross, with which Lupo killed Snow, that had blinded his eyes through the strength of her will... '*And since this must be so, then I, their mother, shall kill them. Arm yourself in steel, my heart! Do not hang back from doing this fearful and necessary wrong. Come, my poor hand, poor wretched hand, and take the sword. Take it, step forward to the starting point, and do not be a coward.*'[414]

It was as if she were plunging the knife in her heart, and the terror of the words she gave voice to was transferred to Quint, who in the thrall of the Mother seemed to suffer their death, when a blind boar hurtled towards her that was driven by hate, possessed by the shadow of her father in the body of the beast. It had been fuming through the forest, sniffing the earth for its young, and it charged across the stage, sniffing the blood on her hands, lapping the blood of its son from the sacrificial bowl. The boar stared at her blindly with its unseeing eyes, and sensing the shade of her father as its hatred shot through her, she stabbed at its eyes with the knife that killed Snow. Lupo, merging with Leo, thought his son was his own, confounding the son of his brother with the son of the boar, and began charging Quint, who sat at the edge of the stage, who was staring at Terzo in the ether, standing on the shoulders of the Hunter.

She charged the beast with the knife, and

summoned her will, as it was poised for the kill, wanting blood for its life; then it kneeled as if praying, as if waiting to be slain- its deadly tusks shaped like Luna, the triple goddess of the hunt, that contained the makings of the *Medicine* and 'the poison that heals'.

As if submitting to the sacrifice and the need to transform, the spirit of Trickster pretended to be tamed, and seemed to reveal that all things can be changed: a moment, until it believed what it feigned, and she turned its evil against it, as she did with the pimp. Under the spell of the sorceress, it prayed to the triple-faced goddess, as if the beast was repenting the murder of Snow. Snow's shadow loomed on the stage as she was watching the rite, a dark smile on her face, as on the day of her death, as if seeing the Mother of Shadow, her hands clasped in prayer, the wolf man clasping the knife that was plunged in her heart.

Quint was cringing in terror, as Terzo watched from above, as 'Lupa' was plunging the knife into the blind raging beast. Then she chased it offstage and it escaped to the forest, mourning its 'son', who belonged to his brother, the child he abused and drove to his death.

"She reversed the outcome of the play and reconstructed the tragedy. Instead of killing her children, she had protected her son from pure evil. She has rewritten Medea," the critics reported, and the audience, spellbound, gave her a standing ovation. But the play wasn't over, for she'd be rewriting the end. Knowing her lust for adventure, Lupo lured her to the hunt, still avenging his blindness and the loss of his brother.

Sergei bowed to her brilliance, but he feared for the boy: 'My muse of astronomy',[415] under her spell, 'bring down the stars and accept my love as a sacrifice: my need to search for a body, to be near her on earth. I will give up my longing for love, if my son can outlive his death'.

'How I wish I had the courage to sacrifice my love, but it is greater than my will, which in the end is only human', Terzo said to the Hunter, as he descended from Orion.

The next day, on Good Friday, avenging Snow's death, they set out on the hunt, to kill the blind boar. Again, Nola believed she averted the danger, as she had with Sergei and Leo, in the same reckless spirit, ignoring Quint's prophecy and her own intuition. She carried her bow and a javelin, the she-wolf beside her, in identity with the Huntress, the triple-faced goddess, and all three faces were warning her, as she defied what she knew: Hecate, Artemis, and Luna, the moon, all portending the death, yet she continued the hunt.

Quint had his bow, Nola her will and a lance; Nora a pistol; and Toto his prayers. They were accompanied by the spirits, who were armed by the Huntress: Terzo. Leo, Sergei, and Snow, who appeared on Pale Lady, and wanted blood for her death; Esperanza, still shielding her son from the devil, believed she had died to prepare him for sainthood; Ambrose, who guided him, so he could live for the call; and Fatima, the Berber, as fate serving destiny; while Philos was playing the Hawk on his flute. It was a party of twelve (squaring 'the third'), while Siegfried hid in the forest, till he could call up his courage.

The living covered themselves with the blood of the boar, and waited for the ravening beast, who was possessed by the shadow, that in a fit of delusion was seeking revenge for his 'son': the son of Leo, who blinded him, and who he drove to his death. Now the blind raging boar was charging towards Quint, who was shielding his mother as it leapt on the boy. Nora aimed at its brain, but only wounded the beast, while the Lupa in Nola plunged the lance in its heart.

Quint's was pierced by its tusk; his eyes were blinded by Lupo, whose poison was mixed with the blood of the boar. Nora knew if Quint died, Nola would not want to live, and was asking Athena to take her own life. "The virgin goddess is listening," said Toto through Ovid, "for only a virgin goddess can hear a virgin prayer."[417]

'Give me the courage to protect him, whose flesh is my sanctuary, and I will accept my own limits, and give him my life', said Terzo who swung from the ash tree of fate and hung his legs round its neck, beneath its 'foam-covered jaws'.* He slit its neck with the knife- the same knife that killed Snow- the death of his 'mother' that foreshadowed his own.

Its neck is like iron, its bristles like spears, and when it howls milk-white foam boils up from its throat, Toto thought to himself, caught in the spell.

Nora was shooting it in the heart, but still the beast would not die, and as it lunged at her throat, Siegfried lived out his myth. Holding its horns, as he was crouched on its back, he drove the furious beast into the ash tree of fate, redeeming Siegfried the hero in the eyes of his mother. Leo aimed his gun at its temple, as he once aimed at Lupo,'s, and Sergei echoed the numbers to turn matter to spirit, the Berber humming them backwards from the right to the left, reversing the odds and turning death into life. Toto was kneeling by

Quint and prayed for his life, placing the palm of his hand on the boy's bleeding heart: " 'Apollo, 'slayer of darkness', brother of Artemis, *two lives are now the gift I ask you,* my wolfish mother and her son, *or he is one more life within his brother's tomb.'*[*]

Toto's mother was listening, and she prayed to the Virgin: 'Let him remember his real mother, who died to protect him', while Nola prayed for her death for the life of her son.

Ambrose knelt beside Toto, placing his hand on the priest's, that covered the hand of Quint's brother, shielding the heart of the boy: *'If there is a physical body, there is also a spiritual body. So it is with the resurrection of the dead, who inspirit the flesh'*,[418] said the healer in Toto, in the words of the mystic St. Paul; while Philos was playing the song of the Hawk on his flute, that Athena invented for the ritual sacrifice. A Hawk made five circles around the disc of the sun, and circled the head of young Quint, whose blood was drunk by the earth, as Artemis restrung her bow and fired her arrow…

'If I am slighted, no one can say that I've gone unrevenged',[418a] transferring her will to the she-wolf of Quint.

"Kill it with love," Nola said, to Lupa the wolf: "*Dismember* the beast, *scatter the bones and the blood of the wild pig that was my father. Tear the arms and legs, all hanging parts from that rough body.*"[*] And the wolf did as she said, the totem spirit of her soul, *and with wild fearful groans it fell to the earth. "Unnatural flesh that fed on flesh, on blood for its own blood, body on body,*"[*] "feel the sting of betrayal," she said to the spirit of her father. And so Lupo was slain by the animal soul of Quint's mother, *unspinning the thread and reversing the pattern of fate.*[*]

Snow was trapping its blood in the blade of the knife, and drew a cross with its fluid on the lids of young Quint, but he was seeing his mother from another world than our own, as its evil was dying in 'the blind wilderness'[*] of hate, its howl of death now replaced by the call of the Hawk, as it circled above it, to the sound of the flute, while Toto was 'invoking the power of change'.[419]

Nola held Quint's dying body, like Esperanza held Toto, like the dying god in the Pietá in the arms of his mother, and she whispered her grief to the Mother of Shadow...

'Love is as fierce as death, its jealousy bitter as the grave. Even its sparks are a raging fire, a devouring flame.'[419a]

'Listen, 'Lupa', the wind. She is coming right through you. She says she is needing your help. *Love is stronger than death'*, Esperanza was saying, repeating her words.

But Nola was saying the words of Medea...

'What use have I now for life? I would find my release in death and leave hateful existence behind me...[419b]

"Take me, Mother, I am ready now."

CHAPTER 63
'THE THIRD DAY'

Toto and Nora carried him to her bed: the bed Terzo died on, that her mother was murdered on, and Nola lay on the murder bed with her son in her arms. Terzo stood on the threshold, as she was mourning Quint's life, and he was willing to live in Quint's body, so he could restore him to life. As he gazed at his mother, who was praying for death, he knew how he loved her in the boundless universe of non-being, and that his spirit existed, so he could keep her on earth; so that Quint would return and give her a reason to be.

"If you take him," she prayed, 'bury my body beside him',[420] or let him rise on 'the third day' from the tomb of his brother." And again, in her grief, she could not bring him back, until she accepted her shadow and could surrender her will.

Toto performed the life-giving ritual, for she was lost in her darkness and wanted to die, as Nora wept for her soul and the life of her son. Siegfried knew in his heart that she was weeping for him, and for the first time, since she named him, he knew he had lived out his myth: that love curved like a bridge and returned to its source.

Quint's wound bled like the god's, till Toto's prayers made it stop, but when the pagan priest ceased to pray, the blood would flow from his heart. He read from the *Old and New Testament*, from the Kabbalah and alchemy, as Quint lay with his mother, the she-wolf beside him. The spirit of Sergei reined in *The Thought* , but no one could reach her that guarded the chamber of death. Like a martyr she suffered the death of her son, and like the Magdalen she waited by the door of the tomb.

Toto read Ovid and knew the mystery of love, that he continued to veil for Terzo and Quint... his first love as a boy, who had given him life... and, with burning tears in his eyes, he gazed at her face, and reflected in anguish on the words of his poet...

She lay silent, all her words past speech, drowned in the desert of her grief; but like a rock stands above me, gazing at earth, or lifting her eyes up to heaven, as if outstaring the gods.[421]

With the eyes of a Sphinx, she gazed at her son, but was not able to heal him, for she was dying of love... Gazed at the death that her vengeance had wrought, like a lioness mourning, whose cub has been slayed.

Snow came to her side and lifted the veil: 'Bring him back', she said. 'Rise from this bed of death and bring him back. Take Terzo's knife with the cross on it that was plunged in my heart, and cut the sign of the cross on the heart of your son- like Terzo, his brother, when he dreamed of your shadow'. And Snow put the knife in her hand, stained with the blood of the beast, the life-giving *Medicine* trapped in the blade.

Nola rose from the bed, where Snow's heart was torn open, and cut the sign of the cross on the heart of her son, and, under the spell of the Mother, reversed Terzo's ritual of death. Again, Terzo entered Quint's body and accepted his limits, whose desire to be near her gave Quint the strength for the fight. Quint's vision returned as Sergei transferred his formula, to make the invisible visible, to make the descent back to earth, proving that 'gravity is life', and that matter and spirit are one. And through Sergei, Leonardo was able to father his son: an imperfect pearl that was made from the tomb of the worm. 'The invisible thief',[422] was dissolving the ghost of 'a chain, that melted like wax before fire' and was trying to free what he loved...

'Out of *'the third' comes the one'*, said Leo to Terzo....

And Terzo received it: 'As the fifth', he replied.

The dead stars were alive and surrounded the bed, and Quint knew he was blessed when he looked in the eyes of his sphinx. "I have found 'the missing fourth'; through the life of my brother, who has passed it to me by the art of my mother."

'The god called Love has greater strength than I,'[*] said Nola to Quint. "You are born of that god and he spoke through my sons."

And so, the flesh was transformed by 'the stars in the blood', and on the sixth hour of 'the third day the lion cub returned to life';[422a] but the greatest miracle of all is that Nola came down, and accepted her shadow as a hunting companion. She had eaten its body and drunk of its blood, and 'the gift had been given, as if it were being destroyed', for she 'gave up her claim to it'[422b] and descended to earth, and she prayed for its life, for it was dying of unconsciousness.

CHAPTER 64
AFFLICTION

"What does it mean, to be born out of death?" Quint asked his dead brother, who was using his body.

Was Quint identifying with him, with his terrors and complexes? For he was restless, unquiet, his nature tinged by death's shadow. Quint understood that his brother had died before he lived, and again was infecting Quint's soul with the jealous ravings he was prey to, from being poisoned by love in his exile on earth. The thieving angel who was cursed by his whore of a mother was now stealing Quint's Eros, and diverting him with endless dialogues, and since accepting his rival and being willing to die for him, Terzo was tempted by envy and was haunting the boy.

'It's a good question, Quint, and we must explore it if we want to live. If only you could ask our dear mother for the secret of immortality: for bringing the dead back to life by turning the shadow to light. Once we knew what we were searching for, but we have forgotten what we know, and mother is an expert in these matters, which she has excavated from my tomb. She can turn a black depression to desire, and fall in love with her projection, and the greatest talent of them all, can believe what she created. In her penchant for analysis, she has sanctified her own unconscious, and finds the meaning of her dreams in the sons that she has borne. If we could only ask our mother, why I am living in your skin'.

In fact, he had tempted Quint away from her, this peevish spirit of perversity, and deprived him of her presence, jealous of her passion for the youth. As always, he was watching from within, without the capacity to act, though he was serving as 'the third' that could reconcile the opposites... "But why was he thrown by my question? Quint inquired of the depths. The answer came through his mother, who reflected it back to him...

What we are seeking is the Medicine for the affliction of the soul. The alchemists, in order to obtain it, had to loosen the age-old attachment of the soul to the body, to make conscious of the conflict between the natural and spiritual man, and rediscovered the old truth: that every operation of this kind is experienced as a figurative death. This explains the violent aversion one feels when he has to see through his projections and recognize the nature of the anima. It requires an unusual sacrifice to question the fictitious picture of one's personality.[424]

It is not as transparent as it seems... and I questioned the spirit, who was trying to confound me...

"Why after slaying the beast is your soul still attached to my body, and why am I bearing the projection of your 'fictitious personality'? Why, after my unusual sacrifice, in which I survived my own death, am I still being blinded by the primal nature of my *anima*, the Lupa in Nola, who is avenging the past? But I will not ask her these questions, or why I was kidnapped by your shadow, and will use mother's pen as a sword, while I find her inside me. Meanwhile, I will be seeking the *Medicine* for the affliction of my soul- that after dying to be free is still fused with your own."

Quint had graduated from seminary with the highest honors in the school, and at the age of sixteen, with the help of the renegade spirits, who, investing the prodigy, confronted their conflicts within him. They were kept, somewhat, contained by his heretical father, who had a genius for restraint, considering 'the nature of his *anima*'- though he had died while possessed in a paroxysm of jealousy, which not only led to his demise, but to a fission of his soul. So that his son would not suffer a similar fate, he had realigned the eternal order of his boy's inner stars, and would teach him to bear what he knew, and to survive his mother's whims.

Terzo remained twenty-one, the year that he died, whose longing for life was renewed by young Quint, who though a youth of sixteen had returned from death's threshold, and had, somehow, survived through the invocations of the mothers. Despite Sergei's knowledge of physics and 'Lupa's' other nature, Terzo's humiliating dependency on his brother's earthly body set off a chain of events that challenged the flesh and the spirit.

He seduced Quint away from his mother for two overriding reasons- for the doubling pattern of *Mercurius* was still repeating itself: his own need for her love, which could never be sated, for he was unable to feel it from his twilight position, and he needed Quint's body to know the human heart: the second was expressed in a sacrificial manner- to break Quint's projections, which affected his own, so he could recognize 'the nature of his *anima*', which, was as ghostly as Snow, but like his visionary brother's was inseparable from his mother. It was the usual alchemy of contradictions that could not be brought to a solution: a paradox of twinning natures that were forced to co-exist. But the roundness of the psyche can find a snake-like path to re-emerge, to bridge the split between the opposites, and rise beyond them through 'the third'.

They would reach to their depths, to the deeper layers of the feminine, and would recognize its triple nature, and suffer the antagonism of the elements. But the dead and living would be reconciled through the union of her sons, as they struggled within her, each the shadow of the other.

"He still doesn't realize that I am devoting my life to him, by recreating his *anima* in the twinning with his brother, while I am living his death and repenting my curse," said Nola to Nora, as they lay on the murder bed. "Has he forgotten again? Do you think he knows how I love him?"

"Not yet, but soon, I imagine, if you continue to relentlessly work on him. It will either kill him again, or bring him to birth. How many times did he die in you, and how many times will you repeat it? I'm not as strong as you, you know, and it may kill me, as well, and you would have to suffer alone, and pretend you arranged it."

"Balls! Another dinner in hell, and *you* will be writing it. What would you call it?"

"*The Balls of my Lady*- that is, if I survive them."

"If you don't, I will live for you."

"Is that a challenge or a threat? Four balls, my punishment, are tougher than two, but again, I will gamble my life, and I'm taking you on."

"Please, it will be more amusing than to threaten myself, but it is what lies in-between that sticks in my throat."

"I understand. You are not a cocksucker by nature.

But say more."

"I must. This game of survival is more than an addiction. It was always a compulsion and my fear is not for myself, but that I've contagioned you with it, and Quint who is hooked. I have mothered a shadow with the nature of a beast, who pretends he is protecting his brother from being tortured by mine."

"We will need to watch every move and reverse it at once."

"My thought precisely. I admire your thinking. Clearly, my dream, it is why I fell in love with you."

"And I who have let you, knowing the stakes. What myth will we be subjected to in the next round of love and death?"

"The myth of reality and its shadow that gets caught in the collective. Quint will enter that myth through Terzo's projection, and will learn how to break it by suffering the shadow. It is one thing fighting a wild boar in the forest and being sacrificed to it in the archetypal world, and quite another to confront it in the human aspect of the psyche, where its *boarishness* is disguised by a seductive persona, that must be pierced by the hardened tusk of experience."

It was the year 1990 when the god of change rended space, as time completed its cycle in the fourth dimension of psyche. Nola was sixty and had led a transformative life, which resembled the Count St. Germaine's who had found the elixir of immortality, and who continued through endless incarnations, as though unscathed by his deaths. And like Wilde's *Dorian Gray*, it was as if there was a hidden painted portrait, which recorded her sins of unconsciousness and the consequence of the years, so that her physical body, as lithe as an animal's, still remained as it was in the fateful year of thirty-three.

As the spirit of change in a twinned living body, Terzo kept posing the questions, the ones that turned in the tomb: the boy who was fated to outlive his own death, and to transfigure his shadow by making it conscious through Quint.

CHAPTER 65
DOUBLE CROSS

Now that Quint left his mother, it was time for him to fall in love. But who would he love but she who conceived him, and to reflect on it puzzled him and left him bereft. Not one of God's creatures could compare to his image of her, who was fused with the Huntress in the heart of the boy. He would have to blind himself to her nature to find an exogamous love, and, as if he had swallowed a love philtre, allow his senses to delude him. And what could he find in a stranger that he could not find in Nola?

The next cycle began in the ninth circle of Woodstock, where its regressive inhabitants were caught in the '60's, unearthed by a motherbound Terzo, in a cosmic disaster of time. It was there he would find a kind of surrogate mother figure, to compete in Quint's soul with the incest taboo. It would not be easy for the trickster to find an imitation of their mother, in the incestuous town, sunk in the pall of unconsciousness. Meanwhile, in the penthouse on Abingdon Square, Nola and Nora perched like two birds in a tree- where Nola had fantasized her suicide after the death of her son, but decided to write about it, instead, when she had thought her 'last thought'. And so, it continued, the analysis of their sons and the descent of the soul through their fantasies and dreams.

Terzo, playing 'the third', was leading his charmed younger brother, to the house on the mountain in the upper reaches of Byrdcliffe, where the Arts & Crafts movement produced such marvelous vessels, and the study of sculpting, metal work, wood work, and weaving were taught with a mastery that inspired Quint in his art. There he could gaze at the high places and into the valley, hidden by the vines of Dionysus and the white lilies of the moon garden, as if transported from Snow House by the spell of their mother.

It was when facing Mt. Guardian that Quint was shaping his vision, to capture the myth of reality, while being prey to its taunts. Terzo had tempted him to buy the house with Nola's trick money- that she made in the '60's and hid in an Arts & Crafts vessel. Now it was meant to be used for Quint's graduate studies, which he would begin in the fall at Trinity College in Cambridge, as the youngest person to be accepted into 'the aristocracy of the mind', and would study philosophy, theology, and astrophysics with the masters. But first, a calm summer to experiment with his separation from Nola, so that the mind and emotions could be joined by the spirit.

Where was Toto, his mentor and priestly companion, who would ask the right question and test his heart in the fire? But when he looked at himself, and asked the heart what it needed, the heart replied it was something that the priest could not give him... something of the fire of the earth... that kept shifting its form. What it was was unnamed... something of Eros and the senses: something that would awaken him to life, while Toto was celibate to the core.

It was Toto who taught him the dogma of the Fathers, and found a way to combine it with the psychology of the unconscious, to link the human and divine with the archetypal mind: but though linked in the mind, the body was missing. Like Toto, Quint never learned how to mediate the senses, and was an acolyte of the unseen and a vessel of the spirit. He could hear the voice of the Mother in the wind from the mountain, that 'Lupa' heard as a child on the peaks of the Pyrenees, where she communed in her darkness with the Lady of the Beasts, and it helped him to continue when he was sunk in despair

His spiritual gifts had kept him apart from his peers, who resented his talent to see the invisible, his profound knowledge of the worlds, and the subtle art of the paradox, that he learned from his mother, who was in touch with the goddess. It was clear he was linked to the source and it roused their fear of the unknown. His rarefied nature brought enmity upon him, and brought out the shadow in those who hadn't the courage to explore it. When they encountered in him what they had glimpsed in their dreams, they avoided the attraction to the mythic drama he personified, the fateful dangers that he reckoned with, for they sensed the hero in the boy.

But how would he bear his brother's grief, the wound of a disappointed spirit, as he confronted the dark side, which resembled an alien being: a second self he was unable to claim as his own? He had studied his mystery in the depths of his mother, who had been roaming the alleyways of psyche and searching for love, but when she had found it she would kill off a lover. Was she searching in Quint for the quintessence of Terzo, the boy she returned for on the verge of her death, to embody his spirit that she projected in Quint?

And where were the spirits of her lovers when Quint needed their guidance? Did they want him to suffer his drama by letting him stray from his course? He knew he was a magnet for the trickster, the god of reversal, and as he was laying a stone for the foundation of *Self*, no sooner did he lay it, then it would slip from his feet. Yet, the spirit of change was alive in his blood, and he felt the need for adventure, since he survived his own death. What form would it come in, in what aspect appear, with Terzo's spirit as its instrument that was working 'the third'? asked Quint of his shadow that did not yet belong to him.

A mere woman, Terzo thought- tinged with the spirit of Lupo, who again was rushing in and out of him, and plotting to destroy him: for 'what separates comes together',[432] and his evil nature was remembered.

It will be the defeat of your ego to compare her to Nola, and to never be satisfied with what will always seem less, but it is my job to convince you that you are suffering in bliss. Your struggle with evil will be my overcoming, for though 'body and tomb are the same', you are my means of incarnation, Terzo said to his soul, which he was trying to find, and which resided in Quint, who was learning his shadow.

Quint, as a recluse of *The Thought* had been studying the patterns of the psyche, and the subtle weavings of his mother who was directing his libido, and who he was trying to be free of to be his own man. Indeed, she was linking all the opposites, but first the conflict would be sharpened: what of his problem with women, and the fear they inspired? Women felt shunned by him and seemed to make no impression on him, while he was looking right through them to a burning star in the ether. If they were young, they were too young, like the quarter moon to the whole, which would never expand to the fullness of Nola; and if

442

mature on the surface, they knew nothing of her mysteries.

How would he free himself from her- from her power, her influence, so he could mark his own boundaries, whether near her or far? She was everything he was not, and he longed to be more, and to satisfy her needs, so that she needed no other. But Terzo wanted it, too, and they were under the same lunar spell: one that couldn't be broken by mere physical distance, for both were a part of her in their struggle for perfection. She was the ineluctable soul substance that held them together, and leaving her meant they were torn from their root, and at the mercy of forces that only Nola understood: forces she infused in her son who burned with her blood, the rebel angel Quint struggled with, as he swung from exile to grace.

The house was empty without her and yet alive with her presence. It appeared through the masks Quint collected, which evoked the essence of 'Lupa'; and the votive offerings to the Mother that helped him wander through time, like when he clung to her breast and felt the warmth of her flesh, and through the skin of the earth felt the fire of the sun; he remembered living in her body with its penetrating rays, which pierced her warrior armor and made her unattainable to men; when only as a child, he could gaze in her depths, and not be turned from the hunter to the beast of the hunt. She was in every stone, the wild garden, the ancient statue he sculpted: his Lady of the Beasts with her she-wolf and her taut bow and arrow; the Pan in the garden with the spirit of Philos, playing the song of the Hawk on his mythical flute.

And then what he feared really happened, when

Terzo procured 'a mere woman'. She appeared as a whore that was a parody of 'Lupa', playing her sins of the past, mixed with a '60's pagan mother figure- a 'woman without a shadow', who was merged with her darkness, but who kept it repressed to confirm her own virtue- unlike 'Lupa' who used it, and *played* with her devil. What Terzo did *not* know was by the *appearance* of 'goodness,' what occurred was pure evil; for the shadow is projected, and spared Quint nothing for his gifts.

Terzo was compelled to come down in his arrested development, and he could only do it through Quint by a crime of pure passion, and if they could turn the projection of the idealized mother, Quint would be turned from a boy to a man.

Lara personified the victim, with the kind of martyr complex that destroys one, but she would rip the veil from Quint's eyes, replacing Nola with a rival mother figure. He would learn to accept his own shadow, as his thoughts were turned into acts, and fate would spin its own patterns in unimaginable ways.

Only a trickster could find her: a forged image of their mother- who had written an infamous book on the freeing of the feminine: a woman who masqueraded as the '60's contrivance of 'Lupa': a joke of 'the fourth' that Terzo extracted from the transference, and yet her history reflected the spirit of the goddess. It was her myth that engulfed Quint in a *folie a' deux*, a delusional tryst that would change the course of his stars; while Quint's sky brother was trying to make the descent, and how would he do this but through his earth brother's fall?

When Terzo's wandering spirit seduced the shadow

of Lara- drunk on the moon in the full phase of its madness- Quint lay on his bed and was lost in his mother, and was hypnotized by a poem, like an opium dream. Lara was veiled through the eyes of two blindfolded angels, the two made of pure silver on the headboard of the bed ('Lupa's bed at 'The Mother' when renouncing the senses, reversing her will and how Terzo was born). *Was* it his mother inducing the fantasy of Lara, or was she part of the poem, for Quint was unable to tell?

In keeping with the New Age fantasies that permeated the town, and with 'the big book' of AA, which she carried with her like a bible, Lara was sure her 'higher power' had arranged the secret tryst, and believed that he was summoned from above and that things would never be the same. (This proved immeasurably true, more than a saner person would have wished).

And so, having entered Quint's bedroom as a typical *anima* woman, who was ready to give herself up to the masculine spirit, Quint carried the projection of the archetypal hero, again a parody of the myth that his mother embraced. Lost in his beautiful persona, and in Terzo's *puer* fantasy, at first she wondered at the doubling, which she projected on the planet Mercury, and, ignoring what was obvious, she was hoodwinked by the double god. We will not dwell on other fragments that tried to form themselves in thoughts, to protect the reader from contagion, but it was clear she misinterpreted the signs.

In the manner of the cult that she belonged to, she believed that she was 'powerless', and as the belief made it so, she was addicted to the thought. As 'thinking' and the 'will' were said to be part of 'the disease', she passively submitted to prevent the threat of a recurring relapse, and Quint was now the substitute of the addictions she was prey to: namely alcohol and eating, with a chaser of cocaine.

Again, Terzo was confounded by his trickery and was spellbound by his mother, and was unable to distinguish his father from the wolf man, what was Quint or himself, what was Lara or 'Lupa'. Strangely, Lara was told by a psychic that when she turned thirty-three- when the Mother mourned for her Son- her own myth would come true. It was the crux of Terzo's joke, and the year 'Lupa's' myth became a fact. Quint was unconscious of the joke, and was afraid to read his mother's book (and the part that he read was repressed in the shadow). Terzo rejoiced in this madness, and would not let him in (but the time would be coming when he wished that he had).

When Quint looked up at Lara, before she joined him in bed, she seemed like an image in one of his dreams: perhaps, a vision of Nola's that would dissolve in the moment, as she was stranded on the threshold, while he mused on the poem...

> In Zanadu did Kubla Khan a stately pleasure
> dome decree...[436]

Again, he was distracted by her presence that was so foreign to his senses. He might have thought that she was dead, more like the *aspect* of a woman. And he wrestled with the image, thinking it was conjured by his mother, and read the poem like an oracle that was revealing his fate...

> *a savage place! as holy and enchanted*
> *as e'er beneath a wandering moon*
> *was haunted by a woman wailing for her*
> *demon lover...*
>   *the shadow of the dome of pleasure...*
>   *a miracle of rare device,*
> *a sunny pleasure dome with caves of ice!*[437]

He looked up from the poem to see what form she would take, and still she stood on the threshold like a drug induced image. Was *he* the demon lover in 'the shadow of the dome of pleasure'?

Lara was startled by her revelation that by simply following her 'higher power', while practicing 'the steps', blinded to the thought and the will, what she had wished had come to pass, as if she were rewarded for her abstinence, which only lasted a day, and was replaced by the boy. Like Terzo, who found her, Quint believed that he created her, and Lara believed it as well in her magical thinking, for 'the extremes meet in the unconscious', and the cave of ice was heating up.

But let's go back for a moment, to understand how she got there (something that Lara, herself, would never know for a fact), so as not to rob her of the sympathy that a victim deserves. It must have been her double nature that magnetized Terzo, who attracted a woman that was playing his mother- his mother who needed him to inhabit his brother, as Quint needed Terzo, to trace the need to its root. Lara was drawn by the split she unconsciously mocked, that Nola transferred to her sons, who were caught in her myth.

In the day, Lara was a social worker (another parody of Nola, now a recognized analyst, a gift from the unconscious). Indeed, Lara's therapy consisted of caring for the dead: the victims of acid trips, which they never returned from, while burning their short-term memory from an excess of alcohol, mixed with barbiturates and opiates that deadened the libido: sex addicts, psychopaths, thieves, and psychotics, living in the delirium of the past and trying to repeat it. The thieving patients she attended only typified her problem, for finding goodness where there was none, she repressed the danger of the shadow. Her wicked sister, who was selling her was 'saving' her from poverty, but she believed she was a healer, and so no one ever paid her; she was grateful to her father for she realized as he raped her, and her martyr complex had convinced her that she was born to be a whore.

The goddess Lara that she worshipped, who held dominion over death, was the wolf one whose hunger kept her whoring on the street. Unable to receive, she was giving it away, and her sister Cora, her madam, taught her to profit from her guilt; rather than repenting for pennies as the altruistic social worker, she taught her to steal and use the trickster as a guide. And so, when her second self emerged in the dark of the night, the social worker would dissolve, with her superficial sense of conscience.

Donning the shadow of her sister, the thieving whore would take the lead, and, after robbing a trick, Terzo found her in an alley. The trick that Terzo arranged, by a stroke of ingenuity, was that Lara and her sister were identical twins, and had been bought by 'Lupa's' trick money, and given more than they were worth. The sisters met on the threshold of the bedroom of Quint, and were looking in the mirror, where Terzo scrawled the address: it was written in lipstick, his mother's, in his back-slanted hand, and Lara painted her lips with the letters like blood. The sisters had been guided by the spirit through the darkness of the forest, and arrived in the garden on the mountain and escorted to his brother.

Quint had been trying to focus on Lara, who seemed as transparent as a ghost, till her twin had arrived. Cora, a common hooker, *illumined* Lara's altruistic nature, and, used to this doubling, for Quint she was real. The fact they were hired by a spirit, who was playing a pimp, took a less literal form than it did on the streets, and the events would unfold in incongruous ways.

Although the twins left their bodies by habit when a bargain was made, tonight they surrendered to the senses and a Dionysian madness- the spirit of 'free love' that had hypnotized the town. Cora, Lara's double, was taken with Terzo, and, acting out the 'demon lover', he was perverse to an extreme, playing the sadist to her masochist, while escaping from the past.

There was even a moment in the transference when Cora thought she was in love, though with what she couldn't tell, as it was shifting like *Mercurius*, with one shifting form and two minds, and with a will split in half. Whether an angel or demon, or some duplex being without a name, the reflection of the spirit seemed as real as it were flesh. They tried to distinguish one another in this double pair of opposites, the spirit and the earth brother, and the simulated virgin and her shadow: the traits in the darker sister's personality and the 'nothing but' light side of Lara, twisted together with the brothers in a cross of double fate, as the nun's narrow bed seemed to expand for the tryst.

In short, something was emanating from below, from the dark of the mind, as fate seemed to turn for the sisters from the bondage they had sought; while Terzo bathed in the delusion that he was transforming the feminine. With an inflated sense of power, he felt at one with his mother, while the brothers and sisters were romping in an orgiastic frenzy, the four possessed by the beast through the rest of the night.

"How could you, Nola?" asked Nora as she lay in Nola's bed, as they watched from the maze of the unconscious, from where the two did their work.

"It seems you are transferring the qualities of Our Lady from your mythic imagination, and mythologizing my powers (pretending she had none), while I am feeling the terror of knowing that Quint must learn to be a man. After bringing him back from the last bloody round, do I still have the hubris to challenge the beast?"

"Such humility will certainly be rewarded in hell. But I can only thank the gods that my own son is not there."

When, as if conjured, Siegfried appeared, and was perched on the headboard and watching the orgy; he imagined his mother was trying to make him a man, and was trapped in the senses that foreshadowed his death.

I have not been named Siegfried for nothing, he thought, and I will not submit to her sorcery- her Medea transference with Nola, whom I am sure is behind it. Good thing I sat in on their sessions, or I'd be possessed by my shadow. Instead, I will watch, and I will learn from their trickery. This way, I will not repeat my tragic end, at least, it will not be inevitable. How is it possible that Terzo is under his own mother's spell, who has broken the boundary of death and returned as a hero? he was asking himself, forgetting Terzo could hear him, who still thought him a light-weight and took pleasure in tricking him; and, as if drawn by a magnet, he was dropped in the orgy, trapped in its lust in the midst of four tangled limbs.

Again, the bed seemed to expand to accommodate the spirit, as it had for Terzo before him, who had slipped between the sisters (on Snow's narrow bed of a nun, that was used for prayer and meditation, and that Nola had dreamed in when she returned to the nunnery).

"What have you done, Nora?" asked Nola.

"What have *I* done? It is you that is writing it and gambling our lives, sweeping us into the whirlwind of negative matter, the same negative force field that killed off our lover."

"*Our* lover?" asked Nola, amazed at the audacity of love.

The spirit of Sergei was filled with remorse, for being swept into space in the dark heart of matter, and having slipped out of time could only observe what he missed, as he listened to the two women arguing, with whom he shared all his theories. Strange to be wanting to return to what he had tried to escape, missing his body of flesh and the soul of the earth. He reflected a moment on the thrust of the transference, on his fusion with Nola and the gravity of death... Had he sacrificed science for love, or was even love just a theory, a mix of gravity and madness that he fit to his formula?... But how he longed to be with them in the illusory sphere of dense matter... that his theories could return him to Nola and a session with Nora... If he could have his own body... if he could love on the earth... and gaze at the stars with his son, not looking on from above.

Nora was asking the question that she asked every night: would I be willing to sacrifice love, to be able to survive it? She was now sixty-nine and was still trying to be rational... twenty-seven years I have known her, and though we are no longer lovers, the effect is the same, for we are companions in the hunt. And what are we hunting for, but the missing pieces of the self? It transcends the urge for survival and fires the blood- a challenge that only the sturdiest heart can endure. It has kept us together as we search in the darkness, and I would give my life to be with her, for only in Nola I live.

Take me to the limit, Nola prayed from within.

And Nora responded, as if she had spoken aloud. "What limit is that, when you have already defied it?"

"You are afraid I will join him in the timelessness of space- or is it you that is tempted, for I'm beginning to like it on earth."

Let her not disappear, for she is the face of the invisible, Nora prayed in her silence, and she is all that is real...

"Not till our immaculate conception is conceived through *The Thought*, not till then will I leave you. I promise you that."

But Nora should have known better than to believe in the impossible, for there *is* no impossible in the life of the transference.

CHAPTER 66
THE GIFT

It was Terzo's belief from inside his brother that his mother was playing the biblical Rebekah, 'the free woman' and mother of Jacob and Esau, who tricked God's blessing from the father, defying fate for free will; who turned the patriarchal order from the older to the younger- from Esau to Jacob- who was favored by his mother. Reversing the gift of the covenant, and the bond between God and his sons, she reversed the heirarchical pattern and changed the destiny of both.

In our tale of the brothers, which has the same archetypal root- though the plot and the details are at odds with the Bible- there is the same peculiar relationship between the sons and their mother, so that the gift of her love that Terzo had longed for, and considered his birthright, was given to Quint. Terzo, like Esau, resented that Quint was her heir, stealing the gift of her love, like the biblical brothers. And, as if Esau had transferred the timeless rage of his loss, he vowed to destroy him through the wiles of the wolf man; now one of Nola's beasts who she'd slain in the hunt- who returned for revenge and was residing in Terzo.

'And then there was the struggle of the son for the *separation* from his mother', said Terzo to Quint, who he depended on for life, for splitting is not separating, but a defense against union, and whether it was she that had willed it, or Terzo, himself, was a question the Sphinx might have asked, for the brothers would never be certain.

Terzo dwelled on his struggle with the Lupa in

Nola, and the anxiety of separation that he still was feeling in death, for he had died of his love, a curse she invoked from his birth (and though no longer confounded by 'Lupa' and Snow, the split in his soul still existed in the the shadow of the fathers). Quint, like young Jacob, who was favored by Nola, not unlike his brother, was craving both shares of her riches, knowing the need had its price that both were reluctant to pay.

Though the brothers were born at different times, and in a sense of different mothers- for once 'Lupa' and Nola were like two different creatures- the two sons 'clashed within her'[444] as they did in Rebekah. Clearly, her pen was performing an exorcism of the past, as she trans-ferred her will and tried to attain it in Quint.

Nola remembered the day when Quint was questioning his fate, while studying his story in the Bible in *Dieu et ses Anges*, and seeing Delacroix's painting in the church of St. Sulpice: Jacob wrestling with his angel, 'who would not let him go'.*

"Tell me, mother, I'm confused," he questioned Nola from 'Le Dieu', "who did the gift of the covenant belong to by destiny? And who did Jacob wrestle with, who took the form of his angel, 'cause I dream of that angel, but my dream's like a vision, and I can't see his face for he is hiding his nature, and that seems to be masked by a part of myself. Tell me, was it his envious brother... or was it 'the shadow of God'?

"It seems the inheritance was split and that he was wrestling with both, and that by finding 'the third' he transcended the conflict"... the split in his mother... his whore of a mother, Nola was thinking, and hoped he didn't hear. She remembered her dream after the death of her son, the first dream Nora analyzed when she saw

454

him in his tomb: replacing the image in St. Sulpice of *Jacob Wrestling With His Angel*: the painting by Delacroix that captured the split. The trick took place in the church, where she was tricking the priest. She realized the painting had inspired a religious bent in Quint, a sense of predestination, and his struggle with fate.

Nora was wrestling with the problem of what she learned in the struggle, which had almost been fatal and that they somehow survived, but they were about to repeat it in their battle with death. The question? How to turn the compulsion for wholeness into a less dangerous quest, so that confronting one's death was an occasion, not a ritual. At least, she hoped she had learned it, but only 'Our Lady' would know, who was teaching the Lupa in Nola to tame her own beast.

Nola buried her head in her analyst's breast, who held her shadow woman close to her and stroked her wolfish head. "What suffers?" Nola asked- Sergei's question long ago, as she was bearing his spirit and the soul of his son.

Nora sensed Siegfried was listening, and she asked the same question. "What suffers, my son?" as if she were asking herself.

'I was wondering when you'd ask me. You didn't ask when I lived. What suffers is the self that suffered my mother, who was unable to realize I was not an archetype but a boy'.

And she asked how to change it, and if he could help her to see.

'But I am already dead, and I am not a believer, like Quint. I have no dark angel to struggle with, to be conscious of my shadow- only you, who has mirrored it, and who is obsessed with her own'. And he escaped to the ether, where he felt more at home, leaving his mother to wrestle with the riddle of fate...

"So again, I am left with my conscience, but the drama is moving, and we have to act quickly, if we would change the old ending."

Nola agreed, for death was hungry again, and they knew it was coming, but what form would it take? Nola was writing their story in blood, and would sacrifice them all to understand their inner workings, but by writing the future, she was making their shadow more conscious, and forging a path through the heart to the depths of the earth. And this spell that she conjured, to kill the projection? would it *free* Quint from his fate and   from   the   curse   of   his   brother?

CHAPTER 67
OFFERING

How would Quint find his way, who lived in the core of his mother, while being moved on the path through the veils of her shadow? How would he free himself of her influence and her mantle of myth, when as the sphinx of his soul she wove his riddle of fate? He obsessed on this question and it would move him toward Lara: a female form he could shape, to *fathom* his fate. Could he love an *ordinary* woman, while he was caught in her tale, and was every son of the mother prey to her center of gravity?

Nola dwelled on the conflict and fashioned the cure. If she could sacrifice Sergei to Nora, she could offer her son to the goddess... but through a woman who was mortal... and who would try to replace her? Nola mused on these questions, while she was cutting the cord, as she unraveled his tale that she had spun from her core... She would overcome her obsession and set him free from her love, and if a woman worthy of his talents did not exist in the world, a dupe of herself would break the inces-tuous spell.

Only Terzo had 'realized' that she had written her in- or did he conjure her up by using her wit? A woman at odds with her ideal would help her to sacrifice perfection, and allow Quint to come down, for she held his image to God's mirror. It was time to reconcile the inner opposites, which were expressed by her sons, and to realize that if she failed to recreate them, they would not cease to exist: that her 'creations' did not depend on her power to transform them. This Lara of the Death Mother was a common copy of herself that was forged from her book, which the woman was reading: the book resurrected the myth of Lara's youth, and she used her mythic fantasy to exploit the sons of *The Lares*: the house gods of Lara the goddess (the myth she was named for), to escape her pedophile father, who was exploiting her body.

And so it began, the game of reconstruction, that was bought with 'Nola's' trick money, in what seemed another life. Once again, it attracted the three preying females, and attracted the spirit of Lupo, who would find a fitting instrument, while the third sister called Fate would be closing the deal. How it would happen, not even the author would know, but was invoked by the spirit that had risen from the dead.

Nola reflected, her pen poised above the page...Something was at work that was projected through the feminine... and Lara and her sisters would personify its madness. She traced the reason for Lara to the root of her name- to the Protectress of the Dead and the Mother of the *Lares*... the brothers fathered by Hermes- who was also her son- the protectors of the house... that was also a tomb. She would bring down the myth, so Quint could be rooted in earth, while Lara would carry her shadow, and separate him from his mother: a solution she dreaded, but a necessary sacrifice.

Soon, Moira (the third sister), who was working for her father- a redneck psycho and con man- would have their eyes on young Quint, the eccentric boy on the hill, as the myth of the outsider: Quint a mark for the locals, produced a feeding frenzy for addicts, and his peculiar demeanor was drawing attention to the house. In the small drugged-out town the shadow was 'nothing but' literal, and was exposed in each transaction, through a thief of a contractor. These 'builders' were catalysts for change by stealing the cash, and could turn a house to a tomb by the work of the trickster.

The belief Nola harbored, that she changed every man she destroyed, always complicated matters and turned her lovers to slaves: a fact she was still making conscious through her analyst and 'patient': her companion of the hunt, in the wilderness of inner space. But now she was changing an army of women, who were trying to be like her, and to free themselves from the patriarchy, and further complications would arise, while they were enslaving their men. Quint would be no exception, for she had put it in motion, and it was beyond her control now, while Terzo was driven by Lupo.

What are we in space/time but dying stars that are reborn? Nola is asking as she is writing the book. The dead lovers I live with that I invoke through my son; the soul-sparks in space that are warring in time, are now trying to be silent, so that his destiny will be his own- all but Terzo who is shifting his shape with *The Thought*. It's an exhausting experiment and there is no rest for the dead, who are compelled to transform him as relent-lessly as me.

Meanwhile, the sisters and brothers and their tangle of bodies had formed a double cross made of the shadow of the moon, and in the morning they began the arduous process of separation. It was hard in the light as reality dawned. The three tried to recall what they had done in the night, when they were moved by the god of double nature and unable to resist; or Quint would have been daunted by his mother's idealism, and, under her all-watching eye, been repelled by the act; while the mercenary whores would have asked for more money, the mercurial spell being broken, and would have found another mark. Looking at Lara that morning, it was hard to imagine that he wanted her; how gripped by the poem with its opiate images, he had tried to live through the senses in the face of mundane reality; but he was still unknowing of the joke that Terzo thought was his own: that he had finally had a woman, but one who mimicked his mother, and as far from his imaginings as the Lupa in Nola.

"Your name?" Quint was asking her.

"Lara and yours? But Quint didn't answer, and was not even sure that he knew. "This is Cora, we're inseparable," stating the obvious, a problem that mirrored his own and that he was trying to forget... Would he ever be able to live his own life?

'Don't be silly, your own life? As if there was such a thing', Terzo replied, mocking Quint's thought, but he was caught like his brother, unable to live for himself.

Cora was looking for Terzo, her own 'demon lover', trying to wrench him from Lara's- who at least could be seen, for something not visible seemed to be physically missing, and she tried to recall what she loved, when submitting to the spirit.

How could Terzo be seduced by such an inferior type? Quint was asking himself, in an obvious lapse, unwilling to realize he was seduced by her twin... but I'm forgetting he's dead, and that forms can shift through dead eyes... 'She's like a woman who is haunted, wailing for her demon lover'... It must have been 'the waning moon'... What else could it be?... But

I am also forgetting that I am fucking her twin... another doubling of the plot, in which I am caught in a web... It's not easy to look at the face of the unconscious... or is my brother the minion of my terrible mother, whose values are reversed... like the mother of Jacob? Is he acting as her psychopomp, in order to guide me to her depths? Will I return with more substance if I survive the promptings of her will... and is Terzo her instrument, so I can be what I must?

He appeared now, the spirit, and began to play with Lara's nipples and to suck them like a child, as if nursing on the she-wolf... like his drawing in his first life, after seeing the image of his mother: the unknown woman of his dreams, who turned his visions to reality. Lara was playing with herself and Quint left the three to their devices, and took a walk in the garden to be alone- with one self. Cora jealously watched as the spirit entered her sister, and Terzo felt more in control, though being written by his mother; and, as they wrestled with her wildness and her mutable nature, and he was trying to take more control of his fate, he was misleading his brother to feel his own sense of power- like the spirit that possessed him and was attacking young Quint.

Quint was amazed to find a statue in the center of the fountain, surrounded by the whiteness of the lilies that were transplanted for his mother: an obscure goddess he didn't recognize, a form of Aphrodite, a young girl with no eyes, as if she could only look inward. She was holding a dove in her hands, with its wings outspread, freeing the spirit of life, by giving it back to itself. Lara came from behind and he turned to face what he feared, but what he thought he would see

461

is not at all what he saw: a mask of goodness on her face, which before seemed distorted; something maternal about her that obscured Nola's absence.

She named the ancient stone image, diffusing his senses: "Her name is Turan, the Etruscan Aphrodite. I had a statue like this one- exactly like this one. *Turza* means offering and *turan* what is given. She's the guardian of my soul, like the statue I worshipped as a child. A miniature was placed in the graves with an image of her mother, as an offering to the dead in the ancient graveyard of Vulci, the village I was born in, and that I thought I would die in."

Again, her image was changing in the waxing of the light. She looks almost beautiful, he thought... like a stranger from another time. What was I seeing... Was I seeing her shadow?

"I would sit on a tomb with her statue that was meant for the burials, while I played all the heroines in the novels I stole. It was like I was dead and she gave me a soul. Her mother is Lara, the Protectress of the Dead, adored by the ancients, when the dead were still holy. She appears as a prostitute. The crones called her 'bitch'; her pagan name from long ago, when the dead gave life to the living. Hermes, her son/lover, and the father of her sons, told the ancients her secrets and led them down to the graves. They called him 'the son of a bitch', who takes different forms, like herself."

He is interested now, for the myth was more like his mother... or is she purging the past, by torturing her sons? Still, it seemed like the past was becoming the future, and he directed his thoughts to her relation to the dead.

"An offering to the dead... who gave life to the

living," he reflects.

"And to love" she responded, "the kind that could kill you," in her throaty Etruscan tones that seemed to emerge from the earth, to awaken the senses, at odds with his will. "She is, also, called 'Lupa, the Wolf One', who walked the streets of the town."

So, it *was* his wolf of a mother, behind Terzo's meanders in the night. But he was still not aware of the joke and his mother's past as a prostitute, the book still repressed in the shadow and protecting her myth.

"I was *named* after Lara, the mother of Turan, to bring my mother back to life, who was a manic depressive. She died when I was born, and promised to return. If it wasn't for Lara, my namesake, I would not have survived. She made me what I am. It was Lara who freed me. When I was a child, I would dream I was buried alive. I was afraid of the dark and that I would die in my sleep- that like the ritual for the dead I would be buried with her statue. I was afraid to leave the house and pass the cemetery by the church, where she'd be making love on the graves with the men of the town, taking their soul and their money, as she turned them to beasts... until she gave me a dream that I was a woman of the night... a woman free to walk the night... pretending death was an adventure."

"Are you saying death was an escape from your fear of the dark?"

"Yes, I am saying it, and I learned it from her."

"Tell me more of your death goddess," testing his own.

"She is the mother of the *Lares,* the twin protectors of the house. A house is a tomb, and the dead are the stones of the foundation. Her daughter, Turan, works

463

with the ghosts of the dead. She comes when there's danger. It is good that she's here."

Quint was beginning to question 'the nature of his *anima*', as the roots of his nerves were contracting at the base of his spine... Perhaps, it was Terzo on a tangent and not his mother who attracted her... Or was Terzo pimping for his mother, so he could have her to himself?... He was relieved, for a moment, for the trick had backfired on his brother, for though she was common, compared to his jewel of a mother, she was more like an antidote to the wiley shadow that possessed him... Or was he trying to convince himself that what was lowly was appealing?... But now the thought had assailed him that he was trying to suppress. She seemed attuned to the goddess, but she used the words of his mother, and either Nola was writing her, or she'd been reading her book. He was baffled when he remembered the extremes of his pleasure, when he had finally penetrated 'the ordinary' and it made him feel almost human.

"Lara, the mother of the dead, is a goddess of fate, an aspect of Cybele, the mother of Attis, who hung himself from a tree, after castrating himself: sacrificing his manhood to Cybele's incestuous love, who was possessive and jealous when he fell in love with a mortal. Lara has similar castrating qualities that have affected the *Lares*, her sons, who are under her spell."

Yes, his mother was in on it. He knew the Attis myth well. He remembered, he had read it in her book, when he used it as an oracle. His eyes fixed on Turan, as he tried to fathom what it meant...

"She wasn't here yesterday. How did she get here? Did you bring her?" he asked.

464

"I'm beginning to feel she brought me. How did I get here? Fate is a mystery. We don't always know how she happens, for she comes in the dark."

I am missing a piece of this whore of a goddess, who turns to a wolf, Quint thought to himself.

"Listen, I've made a decision. Let me give you your money back." Her eyes drew him in like empty graves, as she handed him a wad of bills. "You don't have to pay me. I liked it. The pleasure was almost all mine," she confessed. That never happens, she said to herself, when she practiced 'the fourth step' with her 'list of resentments'- on which men were at the top as a kind of general category, while she was doing her inventory, which had become an obsession.

Was Terzo buying sex with the money of his mother? Was he using her money to make him a slave of the senses? Quint was mortified at the thought, and asked the spirits inside him, but not one of them answered. Were they testing his wits?

"Are you saying that sex is your profession?" he asked.

"Only one of them. I'm, also, a social worker. I work with sex addicts and other dependency problems: love, alcohol, perversions, and drugs, but mostly the mother."

"The mother?" trying to hide his trembling hands.

"Heroin. Death is the greatest addiction of all. And yet, it keeps life in balance, and keeps us from wasting it. It's a constant reminder that there *is* no 'bottoming out', 'cause there's always another bottom, and it's so easy to fall."

"I was never big on balance. It is clear from my studies in physics that it is only the lack of it that

465

ensures our continuance on earth. There *is* no balance we know of between matter and non-matter… 'and the illusory heaven and hell that is disguised as the sex act'… Where did that come from, he wondered… and he realized that Terzo had added it, and was trying to confuse him with these impossible opposites… His mind wandered… to the opposite. He might as well learn about sex from an expert in the field. She was not unbeautiful, he thought, reappraising her soul (as the light was playing tricks and confounding the senses), and, most important of all, she was not ignorant of the gods. That was something in these godless times, trying to be rational. I am no fool, he was thinking… with the exception of love, but I am already working on it, and this whore will be helping me…

Of course, I will have to teach her to think, while trying to not mask her virtues, or compare her to my mythical mother, who she could not measure up to; still not fully realizing she had written her in, conceiving the transference with Lara's specific dimensions and defects, so there was no question that the girl could compare to herself. She did not *consciously* conceive that this minor character would out-mother her, but it seemed it was necessary for the withdrawal symptoms to be tolerable.

"Well, at least, he is not addicted to heroin," Nola said to Nora, "though I am being used as a substance, more dangerous than an opiate, and even harder to survive… Terzo's taste is so off… so… on his own self-absorbed track… so invested in betraying me… But what is the real question?… What am I avoiding?… Why the addiction to illusion when it comes to Terzo, the lost one, who I can only know in my dreams, and only talk to in death?" The question answered itself, inducing her own mother complex, obscuring her sense of reality that always opposed her intuition; joining his shadow with hers, like some mythical *monstruum*... Was she betraying herself in the guise of her son, by wanting to keep him inside her as her motherbound *animus*, who was stripping the questions and answers to pierce her layers of defense?

"This may seem strange to you, Quint, as we have only just met, and under extraordinary circumstances, but I have a desire to mother you... It isn't quite clear to me, but I also want your body... It's beyond me... a force of nature... or something I don't understand. Will you let me take care of you and give you what you need?"

"I have a mother already. It's... kind of you... Lara... but I won't be needing another," trying to sound like himself; hiding his *need* for a mother, evoked by her words, that enveloped his senses but not as entirely as Nola's, and it would give him a chance to free himself from her depths... "Where is Vulci? He asked, trying to split off the thought.

"It once was Tyrrhenia, and is now part of Tuscany, where the living made offerings to the goddess of earth and the dead, whose spirits were guided by Hermes in their journey to the underworld. Naturally, there were grave robbers for the treasures buried in the earth. I come from a long line of grave robbers. The Etruscans were sometimes called pirates. That's how I learned to be a thief. It's in my blood. Do you mind?"

"It's also in mine. My brother is a thief."

'Your mother was a whore', said Terzo in his ear, unable to contain it and to keep the joke to himself.

467

Quint pretended not to hear it, then split it off, like before.

Why am I drawn to this whore? he was asking the spirits; was he only drawn to her history and her relation to the dead?... more like his mother's than his own... like her lovers in his skin... and the senses that they sparked that were foreign to the boy.

"I was looking for spirit" she added, "but all I found was more matter."

How amusing, Quint thought, the opposing joke to my own. I am going to outwit my brother the pimp, and fall in love with this whore, who is not as common as she seems. He can turn a joke to a tragedy, and I will return it to its source, as my mother taught me to do, and I will practice on her. If this whore could help me to limit the dead brother inside me, so I could become the whole man that the alchemists dreamed of; only then would the joke be given meaning and purpose, so the split between matter and spirit could be finally healed.

He refused to examine the deeper motives of his mother, for she was shielding his heart from the defenses he unearthed. But if he did, he would realize that she needed Terzo inside him. And why did she need it? To complete her son's destiny- or was it her own, for clearly, the two were inseparable.

And then came the signs of his compulsive gambling with love: like Terzo... his mother... his uncles, the twins: Leo, Terzo's father... and Lupo... a psychopath. And he wondered again, if he would be able survive it, for the trickster appeared in a more volatile form: its pieces re-membered, its parts reassembled, and again had invested his brother, and was living inside him. He tried to make sense of it, but the parts kept reversing. Still, he drew his conclusions, as he tried to remain what he was.

He would mine the rich offerings in the tombs of Etruria, and, by accepting love's shadow, he would turn death into life; learn the secrets of 'Lupa' and come to terms with the feminine, and through the mystery of Turan, he would learn how to live.

Terzo recited the words of his poet, the words on the grave of Quint's 'father of matter'- the one's Nola murmured that were written in blood: *Every angel is ter-rible, but still I invoke you*, as he was thrusting through gravity, winging his way through the spheres. Tossing 'the love-dice'[459] he watched them falling through space/time, till he could gather his strength and return to his host.

With all of his will and his mother's, he made the descent, and again he committed to being embodied on earth, with nothing to gain but the nearness of Nola, and to learn to be human with his god-given limits, that now held him captive in Quint, in which 'body and tomb were the same'.

CHAPTER 68
CONFABULATION

Quint was teaching himself to keep his ego intact and not drown in her love, while Lara was drowning in Quint. In short, she illumined the problem that he was trying to confront that kept him bound to his mother, while he escaped her embrace. Still, he found his way into her, as into the rich ancient tombs, and her offerings to the dead were rousing the spirit of Terzo, who was tested beyond his ghostly endurance, as Nola was spinning, and weaving and cutting the thread.

Despite the workings of fate and the fusion of complexes, the ruse would succeed in making the shadow more conscious, than when Terzo lived in her shadow, bearing 'Lupa's' rejection. For in his nearness to Nola, in the depths of young Quint, he would learn to commune with the feminine, without being trapped in his fear: a fear he transferred to Quint, as he lived in his body- of being *bound* to the earth and held hostage to matter. The sublimation of the senses seemed to have failed, for though Quint was a sensitive, he had a tendency to merge, and while trying to free himself from the thrall of the mother, there was the need to escape from getting lost in her depths.

He knew in his young years what Nola's projections attracted, but not even Nola could imagine the madness that followed, and that Lara's grave robber father, the essence of evil, would be a psychic parallel of Lupo, who had found the right vessel- whose degenerate nature was most akin to his own, and that a Faustian contract was being forged by the fathers.

When Lara and Cora moved into the house, they

hustled Quint to hire Seth to strip the house to its essence. He would be working with Moira, the third crazy sister- and though diagnosed as bi-polar, like her delirious sisters- she was psychotic like her father, who would be making the mosaics. Soon a kiln was installed in the basement of the house and Moira lived by its side, breathing the intoxicating fumes, and, like the oracle of Delphi, she hallucinated the future, lost in the labyrinth of psyche, with the beast in its center.

Terzo had realized he was shooting dice in the dark, and that not even Nola could imagine the ending, and all were moved by compulsion and the force of love's gravity. The projections were mounting in rhythm with the reparations in the house, and one haunted year would be concentrated in a black hole of time.

When Moira first came to tea and discussed the terms of the contract, the devil's own bargain was signed in Quint's blood. The father, a 'builder', a paranoid schizophrenic, concluded that the bats had invaded the cedar shingles on the roof (an analogy to the daughters, who were invading the house). He would replace it with a copper one, with a one-way door for their escape. It would be thirty grand for the roof, fifteen for their removal, ten for the crack in the foundation, five for the mosaics: a third down, twenty thousand- and thirty for 'time and materials'. It was clear the sisters found the cash (the trick money of Nola's) that was returned to the trickster from where it was made, so that the past and the future were confounded again.

Three days from the talk in front of the statue, the child Turan was conceived by Lara and Quint, and was named for the miniature image that was placed in the

471

graves. Nine months had now passed when the girl child was born, and Lupo entered Seth's body and had his eyes on the child. His spirit was a constant distraction to the work on the house, but there were also the usual excuses contrived by a contractor, who only shows for installments to cover 'time and materials'.

On one of Seth's visits, the child was buried in a pile of earth- the topsoil he had bought to work on the garden by the fountain, and was saved by an hysterical Lara, who attacked him with a pitchfork, that she lodged in his back at the base of his spine, while the spirit of Lupo was moving his hand and blinding Turan with a big rusty nail.

Moira, who was meant to be watching the child, was hallucinating in the ferns, while Cora and Quint were fucking in the woods, for Cora thought he was Terzo, and Quint thought she was Lara. While Lara was running from Lupo and hiding from her father, clasping the child, its eyes streaming with blood, clutching a knife to protect it, she stumbled on the pair. In a borderline rage, she slit Cora's throat and sank to her knees, holding the child up to heaven: "Give it the gift of second sight," she prayed to the goddess Turan, "and I will sacrifice my body to 'The Wolf One', your mother." Moira was listening and heard a voice from below, and would follow its command and would answer Lara's prayer.

CHAPTER 69
ADDICTION TO PROJECTION

In that year of confusion, Quint had taken up statue making, and Terzo infused Quint's creations with the spirit of life. He had often resided in the Tuscan Turan, to re-animate the heart in the core of the stone. Again, he seemed to be purged of the spirit of Lupo and would appear as a house god, a son of Mercury and Lara, and would take on the qualities of a fugitive father, so that 'father' and son were completely confounded, as he protected his brother from his lover's projections. In accord with his nature, Terzo changed bodies at will: from Quint's to Turan's as the mood overtook him, and would act as her genius and psychopomp, while being healed of love's wound.

Since the death of her twin, Lara had turned on herself. Quint had begun to ignore her, and she came to hate what she'd borne, as he grew bored with her sex and was obsessed with the child. His mother worked through the ether to care for its soul, and attracted the spirit of Lupa, the blind child of *Perdue*, who died in the shadow of 'The Mother' and was searching for a body.

At times, Quint believed he imagined the child into being, a little beast of 'Our Lady' and a mystic by nature, and as they played by the fountain, he was renewed by Turan, reviving his faith that had been tainted by Lara. The more Lara hated her, the more he adored her, and he began to believe that she mediated the goddess. Soon Lara stopped eating and had given up sex and made offerings at the graveyard as she prayed to 'The Wolf One'; while Moira projected the oracle into the child, who she would sit on a tripod to interpret the tiles.

Her delirious symptoms were becoming more dominant, and she stopped taking her meds and was high on her madness. Obsessed with the Terzo in Quint, she searched for 'the third', and was trying to find it in the blind eyes of the child. The infant screamed at her touch, as if she could see in her heart, and as Moira groped at its body it recoiled like a snake. Terzo repelled her advances and found new ways of escape, to fend off the evil of her paranoid ravings.

When Lupo wheeled Seth through the garden (when Lara severed his spinal cord), he seethed at the statue that he placed in the fountain: a grave offering on the night of the Dionysian orgy, and a warning to Lara, who he molested as a child. On that night that he followed her, he watched through the window, as she was 'ravaged' by Quint and the spirit of Terzo.

Seth had abused all his daughters, but he was jealous of Lara, and no man could have her, unless they were paying. Lupo, his familiar, defiled Terzo at nine, and claimed the boy as his own, avenging 'Lupa', his mother. Again, Terzo would turn it, re-versing the spell, and when the spirit pushed Seth in the kiln, the wolf man went with him, both consumed in the flames, and were reduced to dark matter.

Meanwhile, Moira, Seth's apprentice, a pawn of the trickster, was making the 'ancient' mosaics, and inscribed them with 'glyphs', that she interpreted through the child and her 'oracular powers', and was projecting her unconscious contents in the flames of the kiln, trying to call up her father, whose spirit 'appeared' in the fire. Almost nine months had passed since the blinding of Turan, while Moira deciphered the tiles and the sibylline runes. When she was able to stop, she would await her commands, and somersault backwards through the corridors, repeating like a mantra: "Yes, father, I hear you. 'she' will obey your command," and with no transition would revert to her commonsense style- a means of simulating sanity as she listened to his voice. Quint, naïve by his nature, thought she was maddened by death, but Terzo diagnosed it as paranoid schizophrenia, and had her committed to Kingston in lock-down psychiatric.

There her bed became the kiln and she saw the future in the flames, and, bound to its bars, Moira waited for her trial. She believed in her Joan of Arc complex she'd be burned at the stake, as the willing sacrifice to her Lord for the glory of France, and that her voices were proof that she was called as a saint. But the voices from the grave were confusing her commands, though she depended on the dead to know the secret of her fate. The day finally came for her psych evaluation, and she was diagnosed with necrophilia by a necrophiliac psychi-atrist, who was aroused by the case as he interviewed his patient.

"The problem?" she asked, "I wasn't aware that I had one, but I confess I am attracted to the dead and the brother of my client. The problem, as you put it, is the spirit of the wolf man, who is keeping the job from getting done and possessing the spirit of his son, who he molested as a child and that drove him to his death. The mosaics I am forging revealed the secret of his fate."

"And what *is* the secret?"

"That he married his mother and murdered his

father."

Clearly, Moira was identifying with Terzo's Oedipal myth.

"Though I have killed my father, who molested me, I am trying to bring him back to life. I understand that he is feeling sexually deprived; he has always been jealous, and he preferred me to my sister (an obvious lie or a wish, for he rejected her for Lara)- but I cannot understand how it justified blinding the oracle, who is disguised as a child, and is interpreting the tiles."

The psychiatrist, a sex addict, was excited by the molestations of the dead, and prescribed the wrong medication that enhanced her delusions, arousing the transference and his latent psychosis.

In the next session, she disclosed she was the *tool* of her father, and as an infant was nursed by his penis and fed on his blood; that her sister Cora's demon lover abandoned the body of her client and was inhabiting his daughter, who knew the riddle of the Sphinx.

She confessed she was guilt-ridden for wanting the subtle body of a spirit, and was torn between the dead boy and the earthly body of his brother, which was complicated by the problem that he hired her to exorcise the house...

"In my dream, I am the mother of the child, who was fated to be mine, and it is not impossible that the Lord has placed me in your care, for though the child is decoding the riddle, a certain Word remains inscrutable and reveals the climax of the tragedy that I am trying to decipher. Clearly, you are fated to help me to interpret the end of the myth."

"And what is *your* interpretation?"

"That the mother of the child, will be replaced by

myself. She will be needing a mother, or the mother of the book will kill her off."

"Tell me more about the mothers."

"There are three mothers in the myth: my sister, myself, and the mother of my client- whose shadow kills off her lovers and is confusing her sons. The dead one died in the gutter, when she changed the symbols in his dreams, and now she is changing his nature and it's creating a problem in the house."

"Say more about the problem."

"I'm a Catholic and incest is considered a sin, and so I converted to a Jew, but my voices are pagan- like the shadow mother of the brothers, who is driving them mad. My sister, who I'm replacing, and is the mother of the oracle, is under the spell of the shadow, the mother of her lover. She will join our father in the underworld, and the father of the brother. As a Jew I have broken the Ten Commandments, but as a Catholic I confessed, and I have been promised absolution by a sex addict priest."

She listened for a moment, cocking her head from east to west, where the sun was setting in the mind and was indicating death....

"Excuse the interruption, but the goddess is mediating, and is giving me instructions on how to follow the command."

"What is it?"

'Find the missing penis, or it will fall into the hands of the Destroyer'.

"And who is giving the command?"

"The Great Contractor God, who is controlling the job. There must be another solution than castration or death."

She was tethered in the violent ward and considered highly dangerous, and when her emaciated body resembled a corpse it was clear her diagnosis of necrophilia was a projection of the doctor. She performed the sex acts he commanded, and he tried to fuck her into sanity, but when she brought him to a climax, she fantasized his death. As it happens in the transference, her fantasy stopped his evil heart, and, by avoiding a scandal, she was placed in her sister's recognizance. This gave Moira more time to finish the book, while she was learning the secret of making a fantasy real. By interpreting her dreams through the son of the Wolf One, she would learn to interpret the Word that was revealed in the book.

CHAPTER 70
DECONSTRUCTING THE MOTHER

It was her repression of the shadow that attracted Lara to the trickster- that revealed its double nature by leading Lara to the brothers. Now the spirit of Luce had entered the body of Moira and was colluding with her voices to take possession of Turan. Terzo was seeing Quint's death in the dreams of the sisters and he projected it back to his brother from the delirious dreamers. But how to free him from the mother, while he tried to free his brother?

Lara's 'goodness' soon bored Quint, a mix of ignorance and blind denial, with flashes of insight that were more like Nola's than her own. He realized, she was unable to experience more than one dimension at a time, and though she had several selves in one body they were unconscious and dissociated. At bottom, she could not measure up to his mother's projection of his *anima*, and could not tell the difference between inspiration and insanity.

"It is you, not Turan, who is the blind one," said Quint. "Your sister is crazy and you must keep her away from the child."

"You've become jaded and cynical, like your disillusioned brother. You are not seeing the whole person that is hiding in every fragment of her being. Imagine, if you will, that you saw in your brother only evil, and not the noble part that made the sacrifice of his mortal body to the Mother."

"How is it possible that you can be so naive? Where is the whore in you, when you are denying the shadow?"

"Your brother has changed you, and the boy I loved once has abandoned me. It was the boy that I loved, not the world-weary man. You are losing your magic, since the birth of Turan. If she can survive the evil of my father, she can survive my sister's madness."

"What do you know about madness? Madness is the gift of Dionysus that you can't distinguish from insanity."

This was wounding and she recoiled to instinctively strike, getting back through her dream, which put the fear of the God in him. "I didn't want to tell you, but I dreamed of your mother. I was telling her your secret and she cut off my tongue. In my dream, I knew what it meant: that she was castrating her son."

Was Lara confounding her fate with Lara the nymph- The Mute One, or Muta, when Jupiter cut off her tongue, before she descended to the underworld in her status as goddess? Or had Christa returned through the pen of his mother?

Quint swallowed hard. "And what *is* my secret, dear Lara?"

"In my dream...

"She was holding you back from the man you aspire to, and you were complicit in the plot- a *self-castration*, if you will. The fated boy and destined man were like one monstrous creature: one mother, two souls, and only one human body- like you and your brother- like one monstrous fusion," and he realized the sisters shared the same double fate.

"In another part of the dream- the part I didn't want to tell you...

"Before she killed me to have you completely to herself, I had two sons, like the *Lares*- a boy and his shadow: twin spirits that were struggling to separate from one another, but they were unable to do it, except through my death. Clearly, the cutting off of my tongue was a symbol of separation: like Attis, to escape from his devouring mother, so he would not be consumed by her incestuous love."

What could he say? She had done it like Nola: the castration was complete, and he had never loved her more. And why? because she'd been infused with Nola's thoughts and had destroyed him with her love. How would he ever deconstruct her, who had attracted his lover- the mother of his child, the three interwoven in his psyche?

In the next days, before Moira began acting out Lara's dream, Quint struggled with the darkest premonitions and in despair called his father. "I need you. Come down. How can I change the dream, father?"

'Can we change 'the stars in the blood'? he replied, influenced by the spirit of Leonardo.

Quint was recalling the book that he had used as an oracle, before, unable to bear it, he burned it in the forest, knowing the pattern was repeating and would end in more death... How many pages had he read before he purged it from his mind, for it was like the words were alive in in 'the stars in his blood'. Quint asked the *Lares* for help and that they take him instead, but his mother's pen would not have it, nor would she forgive the other woman- that is, on the devouring side of the uncon-scious, where the darker compulsions are at work.

In essence, the mistake Lara made was to tell Moira her dream, which her sister interpreted through the blindness of shadow: if Lara was sacrificed and made into Muta (The Mute One), Quint would be hers and would be freed from his mother, and the child would belong to her and protect her with its oracles. Clearly, the trickster was at work when Moira severed Lara's tongue- the woman named for a nymph, who could not keep a secret, and who was changed to a goddess and protected the dead.

It was Christa prodding Lara to tell Moira the dream: for Christa's was severed by Nola, during the birth of her son...

"Luce made Lara swallow it, and she was asphyxiated by the word, while Christa incanted Nola's poem for the blind child of *Perdue*- the spirit that invested Turan, and the words resounded through space"...

> *You threw a ball into Nothing that never returned...*

As Christa mimicked Nola's voice at the grave of Lupa, her namesake, mourning a self from the past that was dying its death.

Nola watched from within as Moira kidnapped Turan, hiding the child in a cave in a hidden glade of the forest. Then she offered its mother to the Lady of the Beasts, threw her body in the stream, and had a vision of the goddess: the Huntress was bathing her limbs with her nymphs, as Moira cocked her head to the west as she listened for the voice: it commanded her to drown herself, and the sisters were caught in an embrace, and like one single creature they were bound by the reeds.

When Quint, led by Terzo, rescued Turan from the cave, a stag drank from the stream as if turning death into life, for when 'the third' rises up it takes many forms.

PART FOUR
CHAPTER 71
TRINITY

1990: That day made its mark as the beginning of change: the kind that was conscious and not contrived by The Fates. Quint made the commitment to Trinity College in Cambridge, where he would work for the gift that he was destined to live. It was transferred through Nola and Sergei- an outlaw of physics, connecting the pathways in space for the dead to come down. To the British eccentrics, Quint was an oddity, and as a wild spirit was unacceptable to the 'intellectual elite'.

The year took its toll and he was feeling foreign and alone, at 'the most holy and undivided Trinity College', where he continued his studies and learned the mystery of love. His mind had been steeped in the fantasies he was prone to, as an ingenious defense against the problem of reality- a depressive reality that opposed his inner vision, for Quint was not made for a scholar of the sciences, and yet was the youngest accepted for a masters at Trinity.

But another trinity was in the making that would compensate its cold austerity, and his unusual imagination was the only way that he could bear it- while the endless resource he was born with, and that was mothered by his history, felt more like a defect than a gift of the gods. He was sure that Nola had abandoned him, unable to find the middle ground, who, in her profusion of love, never spared him from love's fall. But her immersion in the boy was abstracted by her analytic writings, and was a love that was sublimated by the mystery of transformation; while the revelations of his father blurred the limits of reality, as he led him through the heavens in his journey to the stars.

Quint's astronomy professor took every chance to reprimand him: "Quint dear boy, you are beyond yourself. Why do you insist on taking off like that? Come home, Quint, come home." But 'home' for Quint was a thing that was alien to his soul and he would long for the forest and the dark mother world; or he would leap through the ether and was lost to the depths, and the world of men and its logic would slip from his feet. Yet, he was closer to *The Thought* than he ever was before, and took his respite in the fifth, in the element of ether, where it sanctified his destiny and the *anima* realm that he was prey to. Like Jacob, the chosen one, inspired by the trickster, he received the gift from his mother, who was his corner of the earth, and he would find the means to make it real, so he would not be living Terzo's fantasy.

Lara seemed like a chimera, for he had escaped from love's spell; and Turan, who was spawned by it, was mothered by Nola, who turned the house on Mt. Guardian into an analytic center. It was a magnet for neurotics, who lived in the realm of the unconscious, and Nora and Nola, and the prophetic child she was mothering, attracted those who were curious to explore the mysteries that plagued them.

The blind child of *Perdue*, lived in the soul of Turan, who was being prepared for her destiny as 'The Seer of the Guardian', and was becoming a legend, like Nola, who was rewriting her fate. Quint communed with Turan through his visions and dreams, as 'Lupa' once did with Terzo, when she couldn't find him on earth, as he mourned the mother of his *Lares*, the nymph of his myth: her image carved in his heart, like the statue he made out of stone, and that he placed in her grave, to guard her soul after death.

Quint found Jonah and Issa in the Trinity College library, while they were searching through rare editions of *Genesis* in Aramaic. As he was looking at an image of Jacob wrestling with his angel, the brother and sister fell in love with him, and the three became a lower trinity...

"Why what have we here?" said Jonah to Issa, smiling at Quint, who was charmed by the rogue.

"Why don't we find out?" said Issa to Quint.

"Why don't we?" said Quint, "I'm up for the challenge."

Quint could feel their desire for him, and the three began their dark journey. The incestuous pair played like lovers, repeating the games of their childhood, and would quickly discover they knew nothing like Quint, who was a *new* kind of game and was defying the old one. He changed their pattern of relationship, playing 'the third,' as he challenged the fear of losing himself in the beloved, or in the call of the solitary, which he'd relinquished for Lara, who was wooing him back to the silence in the image of Muta.

And so, the three biblical 'scholars', bent on the challenge to tradition, had found one another in the constraints of academia, and realized that Trinity College in Cambridge was the perfect setting for their experiment, and yet, it could not be more in conflict with their inner atmosphere and temperament.

The two, who tended to polarize to prevent the

inevitable merging, had been needing a third and Quint appeared just in time. It all began with an argument of a philosophical nature: was Jacob wrestling with his angel, or the envy of his brother?

For Quint it seemed basic, for why not both, he was thinking, until he remembered he had asked it himself, and the shadow had answered the question when it almost drove him to death: it was both always both, in the bridging of opposites, and he would make the concept a reality, rather than *thinking* the problem. Jonah and Issa were up for it and the kind of companions he wanted, but there was the usual splitting, which they were playing to win: what was an angel for Issa was a dark spirit for Jonah, and both were wrestling with projections they were imposing on Quint.

"What are *you* wrestling with, Quint?" she asked him audaciously.

"It's not so simple for me. What of the *shadow* of Jacob and of the mother who arranged it, who is identifying with the trickster and its reversal of values?"

"What do you mean by the shadow?" asked Jonah, half-hearted, but superstitious by nature he resisted the answer. There was the fear he'd attract it and bring it up from the depths: that simply by talking this shadow talk, it would have a life of its own. Perhaps, he thought by not listening he could keep it hidden in the dark, but there are no bounds to the shadow and Jonah was used to its sting.

"The dark side of the *Self*, or the God that's reflected in *us*, and has a personal dimension that can't be measured by the ego."

"Do you mean the great whale of despair that is trying to swallow us whole? I would hardly call it personal, unless the devil is your mother."

Issa smiled at his wit, but was plunged deep in thought. She looked at her darkness through Quint and she knew what she wanted. She would have to know her own shadow to love such a creature... Was she ready to dare it, she wondered- ready to love so completely?

"I am looking at my own," Issa said, and was already daring it.

"And *your* shadow?" she asked, looking him straight in the eye.

And he knew that he still hadn't claimed it, the thieving trickster inside him, as her look pierced the wound and was rending his heart. He saw the projection on Terzo and began taking it back: how the trickster within him had desired Lara's death; how the blindness of Turan reflected his own; how he had split it off from the ego to escape his own darkness; and, under the influence of Toto, how he renounced it for spirit.

Issa challenged his manhood as she looked in his soul, and, with the same senses that duped him, he knew he had found what he sought. Her eyes had a coolness, a candour, yet with a heat that disarmed him, and compelled him to seek out its source that he was unable to trace. There was nothing about her of Nola, he was trying to tell himself, for he did not want to see it, though she was lifting the veil. As they observed one another, Jonah seemed quite controlled, but behind his civilized countenance he feared what he knew. His obsessions and compulsions were bound up with his sister's, and if this envy was shadow, he was fated to wrestle with it.

But what made Jonah so appealing? Quint finally asked himself. He had a subtle intellect that mocked him; a sinuous body that tricked him; and a heart fully bent on a sinuous path. He was a tangled mass of contradictions- a dangerous character, but it only made him more attractive, as Quint sparred with the rogue: he even thought he could tame him, instead of taming himself, but when he realized the theme, it repeated itself; he tried to be more objective as the facts merged and dissembled, and left him adrift in the swarm of the mind.

Meanwhile, Jonah's angular face hid the weak-ness that seduced him, and the fire in his eyes was the kind that consumes; while Issa's were cool and relentless, without any artifice, and seemed mild but demanding, the mind combining both sexes, not submitting to either- no matter how tempted; and regardless of which one Quint wanted, she searched for 'the third', while the stubborn lips held their view and refused to concede. No weakness there, he conjectured, but was she playing his own? The hard body like stone, the kind he wanted to touch, was in the shape of a woman that would yield to a thought, but what was beneath it made the boy in him tremble, while the man was composed and was willing to wait.

One night in a Dionysian revel, the three found themselves in bed, and Jonah fastened on Quint, who was fucking his sister. Was it Quint that he wanted, or would it always be Issa, and he watched for a while, enraged by his envy. When he took her from behind, his eyes were on Quint, who was stealing her away, who had kept him on earth. It was Issa- only Issa, who made him want to live, and without her, he was doomed to the demon of his nature.

'What have you done, Terzo? What have you done?' Quint asked his brother, who he blamed out of habit. But no sooner did he ask him, then he knew his shadow as his own… it wasn't Terzo at all… not Terzo… not his mother… but his own trickster shadow, and he took it back, the projection; tried to claim his own darkness… It would be harder to bear… but he was willing to bear it, not knowing its depths.

"What happened, do you think?" Issa asked, when they finally separated. And he was jolted back to the conflict that he would rather not face…

"Love," answered Quint. It has always been the problem." And he spared them his thoughts and resorted to an inner dialogue.

This was the beginning of confusion and Quint called on his mother…

And was writing the letter he would rather not write…

My Sphinx,
I have found myself in a dilemma, a problem of love, and with a brother and sister, who are obsessed with one another. Only you know the riddle, as you have probably written it yourself. What am I to do, mother?
Your beloved son, Quint

But he ripped up the letter, knowing he wanted her near him, and reflected on the riddle, confronting his sphinx… If I *play* out the riddle, like the unwitting

Oedipus, I will be destroyed by my devourer, the man-killer I belong to. There *is* no escape, for she is writing my life, and again has bewitched all my senses and intrigued me with incest." Where is Terzo, the tempter, so I can blame his wild spirit? (unconscious of the fact that he was blaming his mother).

And as he fought with his angel and the incest taboo, while Jonah was fucking his sister, as he tried to break from his mother, he knew from her wisdom that his real lover was change, and even Terzo had realized and kept his distance a while.

CHAPTER 72
A PHYSICS PROBLEM

The other challenge was astrophysics, despite the coachings of his father. He was up against it and he knew it, for his imaginal gifts were on the line. What was a black hole for Quint in the core of his psyche was the same complex that led to the death of his father, whose obsession with Nola shook the foundation of self. While for the man of science the fixation seemed only a star in its death throes that ceased to exist in our universe and disappeared in another, the mystic at one with her was *anima* possessed, and, at the root of his wanderings, he abandoned himself.

To divide science and mysticism, not in his work but in love, was an old way of seeing that the knowing mind could not bear. It was as if the sun and its shadow were unrelated phenomena, and, when they met at the crossroads, they attacked the root of his reason. It seems he reverted to a state that preceded analysis, when the unconscious was opposing the conscious ego in a single being- when they were trying to destroy one another, in order to survive.

For Quint, like his father, the dead stars were reborn, and it was never more pellucid than when love gripped his soul: life was born from destruction, and love was created from shadow: from the 'ghost particles' of spirit that haunted the soul in its wanderings, as the dead came to terms with the dissolution of form.

The three were presenting a paper on *The Death of a Star*, which they would discuss with great passion far into the night, and make love in between, when Jonah would be swallowed by the whale; spewed out in the void, feeling betrayed and alone, as he swung from manic to depressed at the mercy of his moods.

"*If you're traveling at the speed of light, time stands still, so nothing can change*, said Einstein," Quint was saying to Issa, as it occurred night after night. "And that's what Jonah must suffer on the manic side of his nature, when he knows he is caught on the dark side of love; devoured by depression in the black hole of psyche, when time is as still as a corpse, and it seems that nothing can change. I have become his imaginary rival, who was meant to help him escape, as he defies the dead star of love in his immersion in you, who he'll always lose to some lover, or the need to escape."

Or is his agony for Issa, a need for greater intimacy with me, as he falls more in love with me and is trying to steal my libido? In short, what is an adventure for me is an addiction for Jonah, for he depends on Issa for reason, and myself for the loss of it, and on both of us now for a sense of meaning in his chaos. He is using me to justify his masochism, when Issa feels free, and when she submits to her pleasure from being loved more than he, who was doted on by a mother that out of envy ignored her.

I will not be the Hunter, as a lover of Artemis, who, like a beast of the Huntress, is slain by her love. Teach me, you who were blind and who restored your own sight: what can't I see? Why am I sightless from love? Quint was asking Orion, the blind Hunter of love.

But it was his mother who responded, and who was secretly peeved, though she conceived it herself that he'd be weaned from her love. And she answered the letter that Quint had not sent...

My Darling Boy,

Stop splitting! 'The answer to the Sphinx's riddle can only be herself'.[484] Reverse what you think and you will know what you feel.

In All Ways,
Mother

As always, Nola's teachings were comprehensive, despite the turmoil within- for her sons represented the split in her soul. Meanwhile, Jonah was using Quint's shadow to torture himself, while Issa was using Quint's ego to break free of his love. Quint was using the dead stars to hold both sides of the riddle, holding the tension of opposites and bearing the heat. But what would he do when he couldn't? What would he do with this love?

The three, who liked getting lost- for it was not only Jonah, though Quint prided himself on his unusual discipline, got lost in each other and played 'the death game' with sex- meaning one of them would be rejected, and it was bound to end badly.

"Now I would like you to blindfold me and tie me to the bed, and I want only one of you to fuck me, and I will guess who it is", said Issa reflecting, as on a physics problem she devised.

"I have a better idea," offered Jonah, "Why not take turns being blind. It will make the distinction much clearer, between who one wants and one doesn't, or it might go to your senses instead of your head, and in your confusion not know what you love:" knowing what she was getting at and urging her towards it, though it stung to the core, before he cut off all feeling. "But if one is right," he continued, "one will demand other acts, and will *choose* who one wants and who will have the release, while the other renounces it- in a Tantric kind of way."

And so, in the end, a *psychic* death would ensue, for the one who would lose, and the mystery of love would be ended... at least for the moment, for one could not kill it forever, no matter how one had tried, thought Jonah to himself. It was absolutely diabolical, how he used his fear for self- defeat, and how each would be pitting themselves against the talents of the other.

"Sounds like you're stirring it up to create an ancient tragedy, and disguising it in Eastern mysticism," said Quint, who knew the game well, and who was also aware of its probable ending. He began to imagine he was writing the book, and Nola transmitting it, to set him free from her love, so he could master his fate and be freed of her will. "How interesting how you arranged it, so that *no one* can win: so we are all in bondage to love, and yet will *hate* what you love." Quint was saying to Jonah, hiding his passion from himself, and feigning an air of detachment that was more like his mother's.

"Have you always controlled your anxiety by *interpreting* the tragedy?" Issa asked Quint, getting down to the wound.

"Do you mean like yourself? I believe we have the same bent," Quint responded.

"That we are both more interested in the analysis than we are in the experience?" Issa replied. "I have been trying to change it. Where did *you* get it from?"

"My mother. She's a mythic mystery writer, who is analyzing God, and rewriting his will, as if it were hers."

"So Quint, it's the mystery mother disguised as a domineering lover?" asked Jonah. "I thought that might be the case. But let's return to the game. Why don't *I* tie Issa up? Your style is too loose, and she can't be trusted, you know- or don't you?" he asked.

"I know what you're thinking," said Quint. "Can she escape what she created? But there *is* no escape," he repeated, using the words of his mother. And you, you are bound much too tightly, and are projecting your fear onto Issa. But you will have to suffer the ending, while you are eroticizing death."

"You are good at this game," Jonah responds, "but though you are thinking that I robbed it of mystery, it will be harder to guess who is binding her shadow, than who is taking her body and binding her will."

"I will know," Issa said, "the heart is a huntress- though you want to create your own punishment, rather than suffering mine."

This tore Jonah up, knowing the shadow had won... that the heart wanted Quint: that love was a two-headed monster, each destroying the other- each watching its death. "Let's get on with it," said Jonah losing his patience, lost in a suicidal gesture, that was becoming compulsive.

And they played and they played, and yet none knew the other. All three were confounded by the mystery of the heart: that the real monster was love, and death its trickster companion: the two heads of the beast, and the third always changing.

The next day in physics class, Quint began an interesting dialogue. The master asked: "What did Einstein mean when he said: *A gravitational field tells matter how to move, as it acts on its substance?*"[486]

Quint raises his hand.

"Yes, Quint."

"I think what he meant, on an inner level, is that gravity is the force behind life- the unconscious will that moves us into being, and keeps us bound to the *Self*, as our own is escaping: more, that the magnetic field it produces comprises the substance of 'Thought' that allows us to know what we are, and what we will dare to become," Quint replied matter-of-factly.

"The substance of thought?" asked the master.

"Yes, the substance of mind- 'the *spirit* of gravity'- the force that allows the unconscious to rise up to consciousness."

"This thought you are speaking of is, perhaps, a class in psychology," interjected the master.

"Can physics and psychology be so clearly divided? And can we separate the two from the religious experience? If 'gravity is the force that tells matter how to move,' the first time it happened was the beginning of the world, and is the unconscious itself, the *Mother* of matter. We might say, spirit and matter are reciprocal states, and that 'the spirit of gravity' in matter is the Holy Ghost of our science that brings down the Word, or the undivided Trinity- in this case, science, religion, and the art of psychology- that is, if we dare bend the light," he expounded in a dialogue with himself.

This time, he knew his own shadow, but like a rebel of science was defying its boundaries- like Issa and Jonah defying the boundaries of love. Issa was amused, as Jonah jealously watched. She had never seen him that way... as the rebel of her thoughts.

"What I am saying is that if 'matter can generate a

gravitational field, and gravity can tell matter how to move,' then gravity and matter are reciprocal states; and it follows that if gravity is life, it is also the mystery of death."

"You seem to be having a dialogue with yourself, Quint," and though the master was agitated, and tried reigning him in, he was mystified by the boy and what was driving his thoughts.

"It certainly seems so. It's rather unfortunate. It would be an interesting discussion- the one I am having with myself, if I could have it with you, and we could go deeper than the surface."

The master reddened with rage and again Quint smiled like an angel, always the innocent, always tempting the tempter. And even the master was attracted to the boy.

Later in the sex game, Issa teased him on his theories. "Show my matter how to move, while you are acting on my substance, and move me into being as you fuck me into space/time; as you curve me like a bridge that spans the mystery of death, and bend me like the light, while you teach me how to love. As you drive me into hell by the force of gravity, itself, suck the spirit from my matter, so that it travels at the speed of light. And, please, don't let me change, Quint, unless I do it with you, 'cause I am completely in love with you, and I want you all to myself."

Jonah was seething with jealousy and unable to enter the game, and when Issa lured Quint away to the endless moors that she loved- to Bronte's mythical world, where death is the wind of the spirit- Jonah took his own life and left his remains to his sister. When they returned from the wild, they found Jonah's body on her bed, which was bathed in his blood and the force of love's gravity.

The incestuous monster, the Sphinx, was always in on the deal. If you didn't know the answer to the riddle, she would kill what you love. After a time of great mourning, Quint changed his major from physics, and was steeped in the psychology of the tragedy of being human. He would begin the experiment of writing the fourth book of the trinity, and learn to know his own shadow through the transference with Nola, while the reflection of spirit took many forms in one body.

CHAPTER 73
WHAT IS ISSA?

She was both wicked and good, both foolish and wise. She was all that existed not written by Nola. She was mine in a world where only I had awakened her. But what is Issa, I asked? Would I ever know what she is? I know that her strong legs encircle me, like a serpent an egg, and I am born in that circle to a life that is whole.

Did she believe that she killed him? No, not at all... or was it yes all at once, in the dual nature of Issa, for she lives in the heart of ambiguity, where light embraces the shadow- where nothing can stop her in the reckless abandon in love. It seems that Issa goes anywhere: highborn, it is true: but she can go to the low places, and always knows where she is. Though her mistakes can be deadly, she can bear the result, always confronting the shadow, when she thinks she cannot.

She knew Jonah was using her as a means to self-destruct, and to martyr himself in the god of the moment; knew he wanted to destroy her, while destroying himself; but though they shared the same root, they devised unique ways to express it, for as Jonah suffered the play, she played with the suffering. And I? If I was playing the hero, I wanted to emerge from the drama, and not submit to the madness, and be its victim like Jonah, who was caught between love and despair in a bi-polar vision.

The brother and sister had grown up in privilege, and thrived on their fantasies in an idealized world. Like the Brontes, they created a mythical kingdom, which they could build and destroy in their tales of love and love's death. Love had its laws for all others but they could live without consequence, protected by wealth and by the blood of the gentry. No matter what they conceived of, it would appear in the garden, whether a toy or a friend that would vanish as quickly. All the world was a mirror and confirmed their perfection, each compelling the other through their mythic imaginings.

Their father, a criminal barrister, in an inflated House of Lords, had reversed all decisions in the case of his daughter, but punished Jonah for his guilt, while betraying his mother. Clara was possessive of Jonah and envious of Issa, who her father lavished his love on, which she was unable to hold.

They learned fencing, dressage, and read German philosophy, and their lesbian governess taught Issa sex magic, that in turn she taught to her brother, who was a willing initiate. Analiesa, a lesbian and metaphysical genius, had a calling for teaching, and while Clara mourned in her bed, she read them Novalis, and taught them to romanticize death- the lure of the shadow, and the hidden world of the unconscious that compelled love and death.

> All that is visible rests
> upon the invisible,
> the audible
> upon the inaudible,
> the felt
> upon the unfelt.
> Perhaps thinking rests
> upon unthinking.
> What then should we do

in this world
with our love and faith?
Down, down,
to that sweet bride,
to Jesus, to the Beloved.
A dream breaks
our bonds apart.
We sink
into the Father's heart.[492]

This was their bedtime story, repeated endlessly before they slept, never sure they would awaken from their dark dream of love. As a creative defense, to keep death away, Issa wrote death poems and explored the teachings of the mystics, to whom light was a lover who was hung on the cross, while brother and sister wandered down the dark paths of fantasy.

No matter what revelations that Issa imparted to Clara, she projected their brilliance on Jonah, as if Issa had stolen it: he was 'the bright one', the cure for her depression, and Issa's uniqueness was merely remarked on with humor, while her brother's sharpness and wit would overshadow her own. His mother's self-absorbed narcissism had always amused him, and it worked hand-in-hand with the idealizing of himself; and like a maenad possessed, she devoured her son like the god, who she imagined would save her from the coils of dementia. Clara suffered the slights of her sex addict husband by devaluing Issa (who hid her wounds in her poems), while he spent her money on prostitutes, and then disappeared with her fortune.

Whatever way Issa played it, she was testing her courage... reminding Quint of his mother... though he

tried not to see it. Strange, how he found her in everything... but why not say I?... as she moved my hand on
the page in the reversals of love... Yes, she would love
hating Issa... I would say to myself, for the threat of our
love would be almost too much to bear. Though both
were adept at holding the opposites, in the end they
would swing to the extremes with a passionate
intensity.

I had to believe I could keep them apart: that she'd
detest the hot intellectual, who had stolen her son: the
woman who tried to replace her, after she killed Lara
off. Would she edit her out, to possess me completely...
or was Issa the antidote, the separation she devised?... a
question that plagued me as I became my own man- for
she had killed off the boy, who she drowned with my
lover.

Meanwhile, Lara was mythologized, her grave the
place of high healing, and news of Seth's retribution
spread through the town. And while the junkies and
contractors were driven to analysis, Turan's sibylline
visions- the blind prophetess of three, was revealing
The Thought, as she sat on the tripod, inspired by the
oracle of Delphi, who was a reader of souls, and, in
time, would be the vessel for the resurgence of the
Hawk boy- the mythic son of the Mother and the 'Lord
of Two Worlds'- a healer of twoness and the wounds
of the past- a balm for the wounds of the motherbound
heart... but for now death would sting, and he would
search for his own,

Terzo had fled from my flesh but I was absorbing
his gifts, and I was beginning to integrate what he knew
of the shadow. Even Issa was astounded at the
conclusions he inspired, that I was using in my studies

through the medium of spirit.

I was no longer arrogant when my peers were impressed by my talents, for I accepted it now- that my gifts were not mine. How to give up my claim to them was an ancient problem I was solving, so I would not be blinded by the blessing and accused of hubris by the gods. I was aware of the pitfalls, which I was still falling into, and was learning the paradox of not possessing what I owned. And I tried to remember that love and freedom are not opposites, for if we escape prematurely, Eros takes back the gift.

Being Issa wasn't easy as she lived for the Word, and was a poet possessed and true to mastering the art. Her devotion to her writing nearly drained her of libido, and only then was she my lover and not the ghost of her craft. If I was not as hungry as my mother, who required the blood of the sacrifice, loving Issa was Promethean, like stealing fire from the gods. Daring to love her had left me exposed and I suffered the pangs of love's binding as I was chained to her rock. I could only pretend she was mine and that I belonged to myself, and was devoured by my longing and the fear my love was not enough.

CHAPTER 74
ALASTOR

1993: Issa was honored as England's youngest poet laureate, and I had been carving her image in the rarest obsidian, a volcanic stone made from fire, with the double meaning it evoked: the stone of the philosophers and the prophetic stone of John Dee: the diviner and astrologer to Queen Elizabeth I, who communed with angels and divinities and was a student of Ficino's: the Hermetic scholar of the early Renaissance, who revealed the secret wisdom, and who my mother lectured on in Padua, and was the beginning of another tragedy (if she'd kept the secret, as intended, perhaps, Philos would have lived, the vessel of her son, who died a second death). The statue of Issa was shrouded in thought, the open book on her lap- as if it were all that exists: *STONE* was the title carved on the page: her head bowed to the book and the enigma of the word.

The spirit of my brother had invested the stone, and merged in its depth with its extraordinary properties. The dark angel I wrestled with divined the essence of 'the third' and transferred it to me as I was shaping her soul; an essence that moved me on my journey to join the shadow to the conscious mind.

The obsidian Issa was bought by Cambridge University and was veiled in the garden of Trinity College. It would be lauded by critics as a great work of art that expressed the soul of the poet and awakened the gods. Nola and Nora had come for the unveiling, and Issa would be analyzed by both, who were reading her poems. Nora had already concluded she was as elusive as Nola, but seemed just as direct, which made her more enigmatic.

When the statue was finished, Issa had a child: a boy named Jonah for her brother, and the hero who was swallowed by the whale. The mythical Jonah of the *Bible* was sacrificed to the Mother, and after three days and three nights he was spewed from her mouth, a resurrection that prefigured the birth of the Christ; but the Jonah of Issa, who had sacrificed *himself*, would rise up in Issa, like 'the *shadow* of God'.

The boy had his bi-polar spirit and was claimed by her brother: but who was his father? Was it Jonah or Quint? A question Issa was obsessed with and passed it to Quint, who turned away from the boy and despaired of the birth. Love was changing to doubt, as the shadow invaded her soul, and she *dwelt* on the doubt and the fate of her son.

I faced the morning they met with a feeling of dread- an irrational feeling I was unable to control. We were in the garden of Trinity and instead of looking at my statue, my mother was looking at Issa and observed her every change: every physical motion, every shade of ex-pression, every look at her son, and the shift of her eyes, as they returned to my mother, who appraised the 'hot intellectual'. She admitted that the British mask of neutrality had a certain appeal, but wasn't fooled by her coolness and sensed the fire at her core. Issa at once had idealized her, and in a way fell in love with her, and the wild beauty she sustained from the age of thirty-three. Nola admired her restraint, and would have invited her to tea, if her son were not involved and the testing not begun; while Nora was trying for a philosophical approach and restraining her jealousy that was at odds with her heart.

Almost at once, Issa won Nola over, who invited Issa to Jonah's baptism as an act of humility, which, under ordinary circumstances, would be the other way around. The following dawn, when my mother looked at my work, the four of us met on the Bridge of Sighs on the Cam (linking the old and the new- on both the river and mind): my studio above it, a gift from the college of St. John's, with its neo-gothic windows and mythical beasts, and a door to the bridge that seemed to be linking the opposites- Issa's part of the gift was from Trinity College that immortalized her poems, an anomaly in Cambridge, for the two colleges owned it, but were constantly at war.

Nola, playing the priest, as she did in *Perdue*, dipped the child in the river for the ritual Baptism: "Receive 'the spirit in the water', Jonah," tracing the cross on its lids, with her own mystic meaning for the myth of the moment. Nora and I left the women alone, who were facing their fear... or should I say mine?

Nola got right to the point and they had the following dialogue, that I will try to reconstruct as I heard it from my window...

"Tragedy agrees with you, Issa."

"I don't have a choice. It's an inheritance from my mother. I have accepted my tragedy- as a challenge to her madness... that she bequeathed to my brother: a gift to his death."

"But you do have a choice, and I shall prove it to you, Issa."

"How will you do it? I am curious."

"By giving you the challenge, to transform what you hate. What do you hide in your coolness that veils the fire in the heart?"

"I feel almost naked, like you already know all of me. I think I resent it, and yet, I can't help but like it. I know that I need it, but I'm not ready to admit it."

Nola was moved by her candour, "That you *want* to be known?"

"What else do you know?"

"That you love the child in the man."

"What I love is the child and the man trying to find one another. I love what you dared to create. It took courage to create such a creature."

"Are you sure you are not in love with the child of the past? That it's Quint you are in love with and not with an archetype?"

Issa reflected... "The child of the past... Yes, there is something in what you say. I am in love with a myth... and though it's the child that I love, it seems that death is my lover, so that love cannot die... for I am afraid of love's darkness... afraid I'll submit... that it will swallow me up... like Jonah, my brother, who was seduced by the dark, and thought he found it in me... as I found it in him."

Nola was disarmed by her honesty, and listened in silence... and her own fear of surrender?... It was time for some 'heart-work'.[498]

"There is a part of me, Nola, that is *unable* to love. You must have a part like that... a part that wants to destroy love- that idealizes the object, and destroys what is real. I want to love what is possible, but there is a dark angel above me, and who only appears at the moment of surrender. Do you know such an angel, Nola?"

The resistance dissolved. But would it destroy Quint

as well? The way it destroyed all her lovers? The way it destroyed her first son? Now she wanted to guard her from a fate like her own, to protect Quint from her rival and what resembled herself.

"Yes, I think I have met him and we will give him a name. When we name our dark angel, we break the spell of the unknown. Let's observe him at work, and we will know what we can."

Nola discussed it with Nora, to throw some light on the matter. "It seems you share the same angel," said Nora, "that it resembles your son" (knowing it also resembled her own). "The angel of a disappointed spirit, that is unable to live the ideal, and is avenging its fate of 'the youthfully dead'[499] (I lamented her well-spoken words and my son's early death (a miscalculated vision as I summed up the odds).

"There are not enough angels to go around. It's a mathematical problem," said Nora. We need to give him a name, for once he is recognized, he will lose his power over love. But first we must free him from the Mother of compulsion."

"Why are you assuming that the angel is masculine, Nora?" with the cunning of her *animus* that stepped aside from her imaginings, feminizing the angel of the poet, and playing with Nora, who was jealous.

"I was only assuming that the will is excessive and is interfering with the heart," not submitting to her trickery.

"I think I need one more session," said Nola. How about midnight on the bridge?"

"I will try fitting you in."

They awoke in the same bed and went to the bridge for a session...

"I fell asleep before our session," said Nola … "and had a dream about the angel"… and not wanting to reveal it, she would not allow herself to keep it…

"He said his name was Alastor, Shelley's 'spirit of solitude'…an avenging *lonely* spirit… 'the wanderer of the waste',[500] who like a disappointed lover swings from ecstasy to despair. In my dream he was solving a mathematical problem, but the equation revealed that it was a problem of love. 'One needs to love more', he was saying, and I didn't want to hear it: 'When love wants to possess, one kills what one loves'."

Too much love puts the fire out. I must turn down the heat, Nora thought.

"When Shelley drowned in the sea and his body was burned… his heart remained whole… it was burning… but whole… and I saw his heart in the fire"…

"And when I awoke I was weeping."
"So Alastor won out," Nora said.
Terzo and Siegfried winced at one another, for both believed he was the angel and was sailing through eternity, both haunting their mothers, in search of the ideal: a mathematical problem? Or the longing for love?
'Death only stings for a moment', the 'angel' was saying, but Nola knew it was Terzo, with his usual sarcasm, and she longed for her son, as he slipped from her grasp.
"Only a moment... but it lasts for eternity," Nola said to his spirit, while Nora thought the same thought.

CHAPTER 75
MYSTIC LADDER

Each rung of Jacob's ladder was a phase of Quint's moon- an inner moon that reflected the lunar stages of psyche, transforming the boy to a man, as if by a spell. Each step between worlds stripped the veils of the shadow and sparked a dialogue with the *Self* that moved him towards wholeness, as he wrestled with his angel and tried to interpret the meaning. The next day, mother and son were rowing on the River Cam, and he was trying to understand the strange riddle of love...

"Take ours, for example, and the problem of measure. If love is not burning, then it seems to grow cold, and though I know it as love, I feel its loss in my bones. It's like with Issa and I, when we lose one another, and withdraw from the heat with the fear love will die. Can you explain what I'm feeling, as only you understand it? For though I am writing your book, I'm dipping my quill in your blood."

"Let me try. We've been blessed with a vision of the boundlessness of love, and the limits elude us, until we sense love will die. At times, we may feel like we're being consumed by love's fire, and this love we are bearing feels like the death of the self. We will have to work harder to bear love's extremes, for Eros is a god on the wing, who can turn the water to air. It you try to restrain him, he plays with the fire, but you can calm him with a feather and he will not turn away. How often I've thought that Love left on a whim, but he always returns with a question that keeps me searching for more; and just when he seems to grow cold, he returns with new life. The nature of love is like the rungs of Jacob's ladder, that lead to both heaven and hell, to the light and the shadow. Take the statue of Issa that is cold to the touch, but how its soul is alive in the heart of the stone; how it hides on the surface, but burns in the core."

"I knew you would tell me what I needed to know. I am trying to love her, the way I love you, as if I were the mother giving birth to myself."

"I must not love you too much, so you can mother your process."

"If you are able to do it, then you are a saint, for you are letting me die my own death, to be reborn in your love. We haven't talked of Turan... and how I couldn't bear to see her..."

"Death needs time. She is three and is already stripping the veils. When one has no eyes, one is naked in God."

They talked through the night of the things of the heart, and as they ascended the ladder, they formed a new rung.

CHAPTER 76
THOUGHT EXPERIMENT

Talking to Nola was like having a dialogue with the *Self,* and as I worked with the transference, I continued recording the book. I could hear Issa weeping in the arms of my mother, and tried an experiment in listening and receiving their thoughts.

"Let's try something daring: a thought experiment with shadow," Nola was saying, and waited till Issa stopped weeping...

'You are thinking, it is myself that killed Jonah, so I would be free to love Quint. But Jonah has found a way back, and I need your help to contain him, so I am not possessed by his spirit and controlled by his will'.

"But it's uncanny," said Issa.

"Not really, it's transference: the unconscious projected through the mind of the other- the basis of all human relationship, linking conscious and unconscious, or how would we love, if we were not linked in the mind? 'What is *she* thinking, you are asking'? Open the door of the tomb. Let time and space become one, and let *The Thought* come right through you, and you will hear what I think."

The lids of Issa's eyes seem to close of themselves, and she receives the reflection of spirit that reveals Nola's thought... 'You are thinking... Change the shape of the fear that the thought will destroy you. Use the fear to create by *using* the shadow of the thought'...

"How precise. In the shadow is hidden the elixir of life. It is hidden in the darkness, in the stone of the *Self,* where on the verge of its death, we become what we are. This shadow that haunts you will be the spirit of change. Take back the projection to know the shadow as yours."

"I no longer know what is mine. I am possessed by the fear. My shadow and Jonah's are like one single creature…. I have thought of taking my life. I am losing Quint to the fear. I am not even sure I can love… or if my love is a curse."

I knew that this inseeing was a gift I received from my mother. Why have I embarked on such a journey, I was asking my soul? but I recorded her thoughts, as if the fear was my own. The redeeming of the dead must be harder than I thought, and I must be careful of my martyr complex, for the spirit is feasting on the flesh.

CHAPTER 77
TWO JONAHS

For a time, Jonah existed as an independent spirit, but after investing his sister he settled down in her boy. He was four now and afflicted by the gambols of the wraith, and he wanted to know the rebel spirit like the spirit of a friend; as a curious child will dismember a doll, he tried mending a self that was broken by fate.

"Where do you come from" he asked it, "and is it green like the earth?"

'From a place far below, where things end and begin. It is black, like the night, a lonely place like the moon, where dead stars have stopped burning and are waiting to be born'.

Young Jonah understood a small part of these thoughts: that the lonely place the spirit spoke of was what the boy had called home. "I know a place like that, Jonah, but now you have me."

The boy tried to give the dark spirit a soul, and he promised his namesake he would not be lonely again, but how could he know what he'd done, or how to live what he said? It was only Turan who could teach him to love, as Jonah passed him his sickness with its broken delusions, while Quint was withdrawing from Issa and his alien son.

The house on the mountain was a crucible of change, as the poison of shadow was transmuted by Turan, while Nola mothered the seer and taught her the art. Though she lived in the darkness, she was the bearer of light, and honored the grave of her mother with invisible offerings. People came from all over to consult with the oracle of seven, who was seated on a tripod by the statue of Turan. There was either a pagan conversion or a collective regression that made miniature images of the girl for the graves, and believed she embodied the goddess of the dead.

Even the devilish spirit was attracted to Turan, and would transit from the girl's younger brother to the blind seer herself. At times, it rested inside her from its manic flights in young Jonah, basking in her innocence- a survivor of the babbling tongues. She could distinguish a bi-polar 'vision' from a psychic reality, and was working with amphetamine psychosis, the addict patients of her mother, so when the spirit appeared she understood its compulsions.

After three years of harboring the hunger of the spirit, Issa had changed and was losing her will, and felt like the slave of its perverted desires. It had poisoned Quint's love, who was disturbed by the trickster, that had finally succeeded in producing a rift between the pair, infecting the boy with its manic moods and black depressions. Quint returned to upper Byrdcliffe, to bring Jonah to Turan, who would be teaching the youth how to tame the strange spirit, and turn evil to Eros through the workings of Nola.

When Turan first met her brother and held him in her arms, she saw the child that was sacrificed in her own tragic existence, an absent place in her being she was unable to fathom, that had suffered the evils of existence before she could speak. Her mother's death and her blind eyes had revealed her inner darkness and a deeper understanding of the tragedy of others. It had led her on her way to the destiny of healer- for only the wounded can heal us, who have suffered the *Self*.

On a day when boy Jonah and Turan were exploring

the wild, a viper appeared on their path and she gripped it in her fist. She called it by name, for she knew it as Jonah, and summoned *The Thought* from within as Nola taught her to do. Mesmerizing the spirit, she let it slither away, and the boy watched it turn blue and begin shedding its skin, rubbing itself on a rock, loosing the skin on its mouth, and the spirit rose from inside it, till it was free of the ghost.

"Something is dying inside me and it wants to be born," said the boy to his sister, the vessel of *The Thought*.

"Death hurts" said Turan, "but you we will make death your friend, and when it is time for the birth, it will make itself known. Like the viper renewed after shedding its skin, the poison of death is the elixir of life. Soon, Jonah, soon: I can promise you that: soon the dead will be freed and the living transformed."

CHAPTER 78
MOON EYE

As an analyst, Nola was changing the art, as she extracted the elixir from the depths of the shadow. The day of Issa's consultation, the dead were observing the session, and it was like breaking wild horses as they coursed through the mind.

"But why, Nola, why? You are the only one that I can work with."

"You're too close to me to be my patient. It's against the analytic rule."

"But what of you and Nora?"

"It was a natural progression. It would have been a blasphemy to stop."

"But that is exactly what I mean. Think of Jung and Sabina Spielrein, not to speak of Toni Wolff, both his patients and his lovers, and the inspiration for his work; both the hook for his projections, who transformed their madness through the art."

"We are not obliged to repeat the mistakes of the masters."

"At least, we are not lovers."

"Thank God, for the little things. Did you have a dream last night, Issa, so we can know if it's right?"

"Yes, we were in our first session, and you asked me why are you here?"

Nora's question to Nola, who gave her the art: finding the meaning of the complex and where it was trying to go.

"How was my question explored in your dream, and what was your own and the image it evoked?"

"Why is the death instinct stronger than the desire to

love? I'm still possessed by my brother. He keeps dying inside me. I'm losing Quint to a ghost. Why is it stronger?"

"What do you think has to die?"

"The delusion that death is my lover, and that love and death are like twins: they are trying to destroy one another, and both are claiming my soul. In my dream"...

"I was nursing a creature with the face of a dwarf... the face of Jonah, my brother, sinking his teeth in my breast: sucking the poison from my heart, but it was giving him life. I wanted it to kill him, but it kept him alive. His eyes were closed to the world, as if he hadn't been born, as if he were sleeping inside me, and I brought him to life. When he opened one eye, it expanded like the moon, but it was the color of shadow: it was blacker than black. I was in the dark with the dead, and they whispered the meaning: *'There is no resurrection without a betrayal'*."

" *'I am still trying to accept it, that I was baptized by Death'*, Terzo said as 'the third'- *'and that Death is the Mother'*. The others agreed. *'We all tried'*, they were saying, like a fugue from within. *'I will not be analyzing you alone. It has always been so'*, you confirmed. *'We need the shadow to interpret, and the dead are experts on the matter'*."

"So. Let's look at the meaning," said Nola. "It's a simple dream, really, for it reveals itself completely. The dwarf-god[509] is the symbol for the mining of the lower earth. It is working for the Mother, and is a god of invention. He's *a grotesque or misshapen god, small* *and apparently insignificant, like the impulses of the unconscious, but endowed with its power** It seems you are ready to begin. Your instincts were right. It is telling you to see through the eye of the analytic process- the moon eye, or unconscious, to know the workings of the conscious ego. The creature is shaped by the shadow, and is feeding on your soul. But to know the depths of your darkness, you must separate it from your brother's."

"I am no longer trying. He is draining my will. I can feel him inside me, struggling for light, as if he wants me to free him. But what of *my* freedom?"

"There is only one way to free him: by freeing yourself. He is binding you to him, in the compulsion to escape."

"Escape from what?" Issa asks.

"Why ask what you know? From love and love's binding, so it has a devouring quality. You must need to be bound."

'It seems you share the same myth', Ambrose was saying, still taunting her for her faithlessness. 'It wasn't long that you mourned me, replacing the saint for the scientist'.

'And Mother Church for the Law of Gravity', said Leo. 'It's a habit, you know'.

'She replaces us all', Sergei said. 'She replaced a thief for a flutist, a priest for a physicist, and a physicist for our analyst', finding his voice in the infinite.

"One exorcism at a time. Your own life depends on me, so I wouldn't be so eager to cure me," said Nola to Sergei.

"Whose analysis is this?" asked Issa.

"Both- always both (a sudden sadness inside her in

the image of Nora... and with a dread premonition she is seeing her death)... Jonah personifies the *shadow* of love. You are identified with his hunger, and you cannot get enough."

"I am drunk on him, Nola. I am drunk on his spirit. He is pulling me down to his darkness, so he won't be alone."

"Down to the Mother, to the root of the complex. Too much love can be deadly, and he is asking for more. Love is a devouring hunger that must not be sated."

Ambrose confirmed it, adding the words of Saint Paul: '*To keep one from being too elated by the abundance of revelations, a thorn was given me in the flesh to harrass me.*[511] And so, it begins, this analysis, which always brings up one's devil. I'm available for consultations if the thorn should penetrate too deeply'.

" '*It's too late... it's too late*'," Issa was saying. "I have joined him in death... the death of the spirit of love."

"You are aware that you are helping him to kill the desire and the will?"

"The compulsion takes over... as if I wanted to die. I am submitting to the death urge and renouncing the will."

"You are *identifying* with his spirit and the killing of desire."

The spirits were quiet, for they knew they were being analyzed, and the more they resisted, the longer they'd be 'on the couch'.

CHAPTER 79
THOUGHT TRANSFERENCE

The Georgian manor house of Issa's, in the kingdom of Sussex, was a gift of atonement from Clara, her envious mother. She had strangled herself with a weed in the garden, where her earthbound spirit was colluding with her son. The sojourns in the house were unbearable for Issa, who was avoiding her ghost and her mother's meetings with her brother.

But this weekend was devoted to an experiment on transference, without the ego intervening to edit the shadow. The four defied reason and forethought for the rules of the game and Nola, Nora, Quint and Issa were congregated in the drawing room for the daring affair. They would give their thoughts a free rein, while tapping the shadow, but in a more personal way, despite their secretive natures, and so were fixed on the theme, before letting it go.

Quint sat in between the three unbearable mystics, and was recording the session, as an 'objective observer', an experiment to see if their psyches were linked. It was natural that things would go strangely awry, and the unexpected would happen, as they were weaving their thoughts.

Quint was in awe of the talents of his unpredictable muse, who had learned to read the continuum that he played the deaths to understand. He was also aware of escaping the personal, as he dealt with the dark side of Issa, who was obsessed with his mother.

The three women were concentrating on not editing their thoughts, and he began the transmission by disclosing his own, as he screwed up his courage and confessed to the dread...

The desire to possess me linked my mother and lover, and I felt like a third, though they were linking through me- as I listened with 'the third ear'[513] to track the fears this inspired...

Nola responded, and kept Nora's illness to her-self, who was using her jealousy of Issa to distract from her death: (she will pretend that it's hers, and try to veil what she knows).

I was no longer possessive of Terzo and Quint, but it was transferred to Nora, who was obsessing on Issa, who was obsessing on me, as I obsessed on 'my death'. Nora feared 'the new element', and was unable to integrate it, and feared being replaced by someone young and unpredictable- who had been fantasizing an affair with the mother of her lover.

Nora was more possessive of Nola, than the life she was losing that was ebbing away, and Issa was trying to be detached as she 'listened': she could never be sure what was happening with the analysts, who were able to hide their emotions with their meanders through psyche: their interpretations obscuring what was tracking the heart. And she listened intently to Nora's response...

It's the relationship between the elements that I think is the question, and what you have projected into the crucible of youth. It seems that Quint is in love with the Nola in Issa, and, perhaps, you are a little in love with her, too.

*In love with your projection? (*thought Nola, who answered her thought). *Don't be silly, my dearest, I am as old as the Sphinx: perhaps, in another incarnation, when I've forgotten what I know. But I think you are jealous, again, and it doesn't become you.*

Nora threw caution to the Mother, and revealed a more human side...

Please don't pretend to have humility. It is completely out of character. Sphinxes take what they want in the name of the riddle, and kill off their lovers, who do not know the answer. It feels as if I were the portrait of Dorian Gray that is aging, while you have remained as you were the day that we met- the day I was crucified. I am still removing the nails.

Nola was merciless, notwithstanding her death...

You mean the death of your old self that you killed with my craft? Yes, that was a marvelous year. We must never forget. Now please don't go daft on me with this falling in love business, as if you were human and were living a melodrama. Let's keep the aging portrait in the closet, while you add another sin.

Issa listened amused, knowing it was she who was jealous; that such a love was beyond her and that she would never be enough... *Was* she in love with my mother, who was as old as the Sphinx, who looked more like thirty-three, like when Nora put her 'on the couch'? Of course, the transference was timeless, and Issa was capable of anything. But my mother? How perverse, and I hoped she could not hear my thoughts. As the inscrutable scribe, I was meant to be discreet, a rule I was dying to defy thinking my shadow was veiled, and I contained my emotions and recorded Issa's instead, as Nora was listening for her response and pretending to be objective.

The unconscious is a beast, and there are things that can't be tamed. Of course, I'm in love with my analyst and am caught in their incestuous obfuscations.

I watched Nora contract. How much could they bear? But faithful to the task, I continued to record…

It is not jealousy we are dealing with, but something more deadly (Nora continued in a complex trying to suppress the thought of death). *What I am saying, is you withdraw the projection too quickly, before you can feel it, and create another to transcend it, to not suffer love's sacrifice… and, in this case, the sacrifice is me.*

It was obvious the distraction from death wasn't working on the heart.

What you don't know either one of you (Issa continued), *is that it is I who am in love- not Nola but me, and I have taken pleasure in deceiving you: the joy of duping two mystics… and am duped by the fear- the fear of love's death… that Quint is in love not with me but his mother* (hoping Quint couldn't hear her, but she was new to the game, and he heard what he feared and their fears were confounded- Issa's with Quint's, and with Nola's and Nora's).

I was surprised that the spirit could take such a turn, as I continued to track it, as if her thoughts were my own. What makes you think I don't know, you're in love with my mother, with the shadow of love, and that you fear love will die?

Of course, you are right, Nora (Nola continued). *You have sacrificed yourself, when it was completely unnecessary* (directly to Nora, hoping the others couldn't hear). *It is my problem to transcend what is commonplace in love. But you know less about my suffering than you imagine you do, for I am even better at hiding it- this gift I was born with. I am sure that the gods have been laughing at us, while I suffer for love, which you are completely unaware of, you are so obsessed with your death.*

Both their faces turned pale. Now Nora knew that she knew. Issa knew it, as well, and I felt caught in their midst. After recording their dialogue, leaving out Nora's death, I returned to myself and let the three women read it, who confirmed it was accurate, while Nora, was steeped in a complex: the thought of losing Nola to Issa, when she was no longer here, when it would no longer matter (that is, under ordinary circumstances), but what had been keeping her alive by driving her mad.

"I think I'll have lunch alone" said Nora, with-drawn. "and continue searching for the pearl in the flaw in the heart."

She left feeling estranged and took a walk in the garden, and what they had forgotten now happened, when Nora met Issa's dead mother, who took her life in the arbor and was unable to leave it. Jonah, still bound to his mother, was talking to Clara of Issa, and discussing the problem of love after death.

"That's quite a work you created," said Nora to Clara.

'Yes, I didn't appreciate her- until I was dead. But she is rather brilliant and surpassed Jonah, my son, who was a reflection of myself, with all the limits that killed me- the limits that Issa transcended and that led to his death'. Jonah shuddered in his spirit, and tried to recover from the wound. 'She was always more gifted, but I did not want to see it. He just didn't have the courage that Issa is blessed with'.

Clara was feeling betrayed by his love, and avenged it with praise, for she had learned in her death, and was reflecting his weakness by the strength of his rival. Quint was recording it, aware that the weakness was his, for her love was a mirror, reflecting his problem with love. Was Issa using his mother through the art of projection (like her mother used Issa, to awaken the love of her son? the love he gave to her image that he carved in the stone?)

'I will be stealing the gift by living inside her', said Jonah. 'But what you don't understand is that I always knew I had fooled you; that I took advantage of your foolishness and the excess of your love. It made me a fop but I will take on substance from Issa, who was nursed on the poison of envy and transformed it to art'.

Nora understood what she had already gathered and

began thinking of Siegfried, who she robbed of his strength, and through her own preconceptions had turned to a fop. It had almost happened to me, Quint couldn't help thinking, if it wasn't for Terzo, who challenged my will.

"It's the usual conflict", said Nora to Clara. "Too much love or too little; it is always shaped by the complex, and where there is one, there's the other- on the shadow side of the equation.

And in that moment, she knew what she'd been trying to repress; not just the terror of losing her... not just jealousy... not all of it... but the inner *certainty* of death... the end of life... the end of love...

Back in the manor house, the three were reading the text, on the shadow of love and the fear love would die.

"Let me take you both to lunch," I said to Issa and Nola. "I know a place you will love that has the best oysters in the world."

Nora, somehow, knew the restaurant and was waiting for us at our table, where two dozen oysters arrived and a bottle of Cristal. Nola pulled up a chair and we left them alone, and sat at another with two dozen more. I ordered another bottle of Cristal, for the experiment had worked.

"So, you feel you've been had," said Nola to Nora.

"Of course. After escorting me to the underworld, did you really think you could fool me, by stealing the pearl in the oyster and have me agree to the theft? You are passing the gift prematurely by using the art of projection. I would have waited, myself, but we are different that way. You take what you want, while I am renouncing my claim to it."

"You are not renouncing it now," Nola said, "but I

accept what you say. I am passing the gift of the transference, the gift that you gave me. You are jealous of the transference. Don't you see your own madness?"

"I do. And I see yours as well. What have I done? you are thinking. I will never be alone again."

The refrain of the past that haunted Nola in love, for in her animal soul, in the heart of the wolf, she thought she could live without starving, if she were free of her beasts. I will only be one of them, Nora was thinking, a revelation of 'the fourth', her immortalized analyst, who is destined to be integrated, when the projection is withdrawn. I will be nothing but ether, and 'the spirit of gravity', but that's what happens to analysts in a successful analysis, convincing herself it was her only purpose on earth.

And they swallowed an oyster and sipped the Cristal, and Nola knew she would suffer the words she once said... that Nora had got it all wrong... that it was she who was jealous... jealous of death... her only rival in love.

"You are jealous of Death, your old lover, who killed off my rivals," said Nora; the dismembered stars that you loved, who were too near the black hole- yours I would add, if I were not trying to be civilized. What you fear, my black heart, is not the death of our love, but your *desire* for death, and you will survive both, as always."

Issa sat at their table, and confronted their shadow: "I want to love the way you do, down in the heart of the solitary, for you *are* 'the great lovers', the way Rilke conceived it, who are able to transcend the possession of love," (transmitting what was needed to help them remember): "while *we* try to kill off love's shadow,

530

before love can die, and pretend to not suffer the unbearable loss" (as *you* are doing right now, using me as a pawn, to escape what you fear, to forget what you know… like I am doing with Quint- I wonder if Quint can survive it?)

"I'm not really sure, but soon I will know," I replied, as I sat at their table, and endured the death of our love, that was trying to learn Issa's shadow… by knowing my own…

"How many times have I asked that question myself?" Nora said, "and I will continue to ask it, till I give up the ghost. By the way, I took the liberty of packing for 'the unborn children'." And she took in the flesh of the oyster, and saw its mystery unfold, playing the game to protect her, who she would give up her life for, as she gave up protecting herself, which she was trying to find.

"I, too, am asking that question," said Nola to Nora.

"When has death ever stopped you?"

But it was stopping her now… and she knew she couldn't change it… knew she would never love again… that desire was dead- that the experiment had worked, and she was dying love's death… that she was finally alone… like a curse that came true… like the curse was her fate…

I am willing to die, but how will I bear it without her?

CHAPTER 80
MY DEATH

1997: It was the year of my death. I am dying today. Will she find me in Hades and bring me back from the dead? Again, the death of my father creeps into my blood, and Nola is breathing her spirit into my lungs. I am trying to write it, but the pen falls from my hand, and I am losing my will and my longing for life.

How will I leave her? I am asking the *Self*, and I knew I could not and that I would have to return. To live in her head would be hell: to be her thought would be death... but I could no longer laugh. She would have to laugh for me.

"Breathe, Nora, breathe!" I could hear Nola saying...

But how would she find me in a psyche so alive with other beings?

"Please, Nora, breathe for me! Please don't give up!"

I can hear her weeping for me, praying for me... but my body is dead...

"I break," she is saying. "I break like the bread... my body is broken... and you have taken my soul... I can no longer live... but I must... for Quint... for Turan... I must live for the dead... I must live for Nora, my soul"...

Quint carries me to my bed, and he gives me the book... I must record it... her death... so she can continue *The Thought*... so she can live through the Word, so she won't forget who we are...

He puts the pen in my hand and curls my fingers around it. "You must write," he is saying. And he weeps for me, prays for me... as if it were me who were dying... and I start to write in a trance...

And then I waited... for what?

And Terzo laid down beside me...

'It is hard on the earth, but I will stay with you always'.

"Can I bear it," she asked, "this always on earth?"

CHAPTER 81
AWAKENER

Nola is kneeling on Nora's stone in the chapel, beside the grave of her mother, a simple stone from the forest, her head bowed to the earth, to the Mother of Death. She was finally alone... and she mourned for her love. 'How it rounds on itself, the infinite stream of the stars',[523] said the mystic inscription, written in blood. Her sons stand beside her and are lifting her up, as she weeps scalding tears, pounding the earth with her fists. Nora has joined her dead lovers; her spirit illumines the stone; and she waits for the words that Nora rips from her heart...

"*You* are the wind of the Mother now: you and Snow are as one. and I will stay on the earth, until you are ready. I will wait till you're ready," and she lies on the stone. Her body is prostrate in the sign of the cross: listens to the voice of the wind as 'the hearer of the Word'...

"It is said that 'the wind is the enemy of the wire walker'[523a], that it sways the air-born body from its pinnacle of balance and hurls it down to the cold hard earth. But I cannot fight you, for I am swept through your forbidden space to the primal urge of my beginnings, blasted as I'm ground against you, flinging wide the gates of hell.

"I was the stranger, who drank your will that held me captive, a wanton playing with the snake and basilisk, until memory anointed me and the starving wolf had fed the lamb. You were the elixir of love's bitterness that compelled me to complete myself, the blessed

534

weapon of my punishments, that made me dance as if possessed, like a maddened nymph around your flame. And though I fasted for the forty days and nights, denying the temptations of the flesh, like a drunken dervish I was reeling through the lonely desert of the *Self*, whirling like a slave of love in a black annihilating sun, and only paused to worship you, to kneel before the muse and lay my broken words upon your altar.

"No... not a god or angel... but a glowing point along the path... that seemed to vanish in the dark. Like an orphan child I longed for you, hunted for you in the psychic wilderness, so I could lay my wildness on your lap and let you stroke my stubborn head. Though there were certain things you would not say, as you hid behind the mask of paradox, I said them all, incanted them in mythic tongues and in a hell of wolfish feelings that dashed themselves to pieces, mingling with the marrow of the heart.

You are my great awakener, the mother of my inner son, that drove me to the cross's center, where we wrestled in the holy crucible, dissolved and reassembled, and waited for the god to set us free; and while the struggling ego fought for life, the spirit burned away the dross, reducing us to essence, as love turned away a thousand times.

How our metals mixed remains a mystery, for in such whiteheatedness we could not touch. And while on earth, I give my body to the god, down there, in the primal night, I belong to you completely, and they are one, the god and you."

And she kisses the stone and waits for the god... and on 'the third day' she rose from the tomb of the self.

CHAPTER 82
WHY MOTHER? WHY?

Nola and Turan were strolling through the lilies, while the girl was absorbing the thoughts of her 'mother'; they triggered her questions and sparked her own complexes.

"In my vision, young Jonah is the father of my son, but Jonah is my brother, and can your brother be your lover? Does love *always* end in death, the way it was for brother Jonah? Why does the world think it's wrong to be in love with your brother? And what of Isis and Osiris, who were brother and sister?"

"Osiris was dismembered, in order to separate the opposites, that in incest are fused in the desire for wholeness. The *Self* is like a magnet searching for its image in the moon, but we must not drown in our reflection, in the likeness of the self."

"Then is my vision a lie? Am I seduced by the darkness?"

"It will have a double meaning, like all the mysteries of the soul. It does not mean it's false, but it requires a rending of the veil. Tell me, what do *you* think it means?"

"I don't think I know yet, but Terzo told me his secret- the one he died to make conscious. What he said was quite simple. I would have thought there was more. He said it is the Law of Attraction that is the key to life and death, and that the mystery is the conjunction of the sun and the moon."

"An often deadly conjunction that creates an eclipse of the ego, but Terzo is a romantic, who is meandering amongst the stars, and we must be wary of acting out the eternal drama of the gods."

"When you are teaching me, 'mother', it is like I am teaching myself- like you are teaching inside me, like a fountain in the heart."

"We are really that for another, my absolute darling. It seems you are the source of what I teach you, and I am reading its essence in your eyes."

"You are seeing your wisdom in my blindness. It is your essence you are seeing."

"What I see in your blindness can only be seen in the invisible, and we will continue to interpret it, so we can be conscious of the moon. You can tell me its dark side and I can relate its outer image, and together we can see the whole, in the completion of the *Self*."

"Let's look at it, 'mother', including its dark side, like when you loved Leonardo, who loved the image of your father, who you hated in your love, and who you avenged through your sons. When you had Terzo, did you know that it was the problem of the likeness? Is that why you sent him away, to not drown in your reflection?"

"I believe you are seeing it, but I was blinded by my vision. I could not see what was before me, only the darkness in the mind."

"Is that what I am doing? Am I attracted to the darkness? Am I drowning in the fountain... or am I only searching for my birth mother? Do you think she remembers me, Nola? Did death make her forget? She never talks to me like you do, and she will never know as much as you... Do you think she knows that's the reason- that she will never know enough? Or, perhaps, like Issa, she believes that love is a prison... like Terzo in Quint, with no heart of his own... It must be hard for a spirit coming down to the earth… It's not so simple as it seems… the love of the son for the moon…It's the fear of love, isn't it, of losing yourself in your love?"

"You know it better than I do, Turan, like my story is yours, and since you can read all my secrets, you do not need to repeat them."

"But why, mother, why? It's the best story I know. It's like the Passion. Do you mind?"

"No, but he would… You are like the water of the moon, and I won't protect you from the heart. You must suffer your destiny... as I suffer mine."

Would we be able to break it, the pattern, and 'the compulsion to repeat'?[527] Nola asked Nora in the silence of the soul. She had tried to shield the blind seer from the terrors of love, but 'the stars in the blood' would attract what they would.

CHAPTER 83
MASK OF THE HAWK

When Toto came to Quint's studio and was crossing the bridge, Quint was waiting for him at the window, as if the years hadn't passed. He had sensed Toto's presence, as he worked on Turan, and it was as he imagined, for Toto was struck to the core. The marble depressions for eyes seemed to see the invisible, as she lifted the mask of the Hawk, perched on the sensuous shoulder, and, as if revealing the secret of the sun and the moon, the myth came alive, as it was for the ancients. A serpent was entering into her womb, in the *virginal* phase, to awaken the moon.

Toto was hypnotized by the image and it awakened his senses; and what was sacrificed to Mother Church, and had caused such a split, seemed to rise from the dead, as he returned to the earth. The virgin priest had a kind of conversion experience, and it changed his old way of seeing, as body and mind came together, and the desire to realize the mystery seemed to move through his matter.

"How do I know her?" he asked, "she is the eyes of your soul, for the 'light in the darkness' are seen in her form."

"I knew you would see it, Toto. It was you who gave me my faith; not the dogma of the church Fathers, but the spirit behind it: here 'the third' is inside it, and *enlivens* the stone."

Turan entered the studio, holding the hand of young Jonah, and sat before it, as if seeing the completed image of herself. After a moment of immersion in the heart of the statue, she looked into Toto, as if seeing his thoughts. "This is Jonah, my brother, my son and my lover."

Toto was enchanted by the girl and looked from her to the statue….

"Again, your father makes me conscious of what I know from his mother."

"I know what you mean, Toto. He is also doing it to me. I have always known Nola through Quint, and Quint through his mother. It is like my mother never left me, and, though I never knew my mother, I have found all of her in Nola, who is teaching me myself, as you can see in the statue."

"I see we have her in common and the gift that she gave us, and I have a feeling you will be giving the same gift to Jonah."

"Yes, I will give it to him, Toto. He is why I am here. I knew when I held him, before he was born, that we belong to one another- that he is the brother inside me. We were *born* mythic lovers, but it is only a vision, and I will protect him with my life to not make the myth become real."

"How old are you, I'm wondering, if you don't mind me asking?"

"I am seven, but I'm a woman- like I am in the statue."

"You might be the first... unless it was Nola".

"But Nola was twelve," as if seeing her, looking through the eyes of the past.

The Lupa in Nola was his first erotic experience, but it only existed inside him and he had kept it a secret. And though he still was a virgin and had taken his vows, always the Lupa in Nola would intrude on his prayers.

When Issa entered the room, she knew him at once. "Toto?" she asked.

"How did you know? I'm hiding my collar to be an ordinary man- not that I know what that is, and I don't think I want to."

"It won't be easy to be ordinary- it may be impossible. I know you through Quint. You must stay here, he needs you, but he would never admit it- his needs are a secret. I'll arrange a meeting tomorrow with the Dean of Trinity Chapel. I'm a fellow at Trinity, and the Dean's my first cousin; my uncle, the prime minister, has some influence with the college, and you will be our new priest. You *belong* in the chapel."

"But though I'm a priest and a Catholic, I am also a pagan. I believe in the old gods, 'and we need every one of them'."[530]

"I need them, too. And though the chapel is Anglican, it is more philosophical and universal. Let's think of it as a challenge to embrace the ambivalence- of the old and the new, and the shadow of both."

It was then Toto saw Terzo in the heart of the statue, and as he looked through the window, 'Lupa' was crossing the bridge. It was Nola who entered and gazed at the work, and he emerged from the stone with his devilish smile.

Toto was the first pagan priest in Trinity chapel, who embraced all the gods in his pure pagan heart, and was honored by the Church of England, and soon was known as a healer. In time, Toto was canonized and became a new kind of saint, but it was important that he 'sin', and would know what he renounced.

CHAPTER 84
TEMPTATION

It's a queer thing when the dead are compelled to enter the living, so it has what it needs to make its darkness more conscious. On a day when Terzo was driven to change bodies at will- for the work must continue, and he was changing more often- he entered the body of Toto to move the ascetic, to awaken his senses (or was it his own?), but it was also a devilish trick for unnerving his brother, ('who is the genius of my work, and is getting all the glory'), bored with the sacrificial role of playing the invisible creator. Was he claiming the gift, or testing his own virgin spirit, for not having a body, his sensations were Quint's. And by testing Quint's endurance was he testing his own, when he tempted Toto with Issa, for the boundary kept shifting.

That Toto was a virgin played a part in the decision, and that Issa needed an adventure brought the metals into play; and with Terzo's ingenuity, who moved the heart of her statue, it was not a great accomplishment to move the makings of the living Issa. She could not be more ready, and Toto's senses were fired, which had been stirred by the statue of the child in the goddess, and was quickened by the boyish memory of the Lupa in Nola. Terzo knowing Toto's passion, for he sparked the spirit in the boy, and his eventual vocation of 'turning water into wine', was privy to his weakness, and worked the shadow of the priest.

He had devoted his priesthood to redeeming his mother, for in the Catholic aspect of his nature- though the pagan virgin railed against it- as they used the *Pietá* for their survival, he was certain it had killed her, and was still doing penance by 'renouncing the devil'. As we know, the urge for redemption is the greatest temptation for the fall, which tends to work through the senses, followed by the need to be absolved- to heal the split of good and evil, and the pain of separation from the God.

Looking at it from another angle (a perversion of 'the third'), whatever vows Terzo made, he wanted the spoils of Quint's experience, and, in this case, it was Issa, and he would have her through Toto. He would be the mediator of the senses: a role he perfected as a spirit, for when he was living in his body, he was a virgin, like the priest. While baiting Toto through the senses, he used the martyr in the saint, for, without the self-denial, the priest would not be tempted by the trickster. It was Terzo's joke on God's disciple, as a rebel of the church, and whether he was destined for a change was a question even Nola couldn't answer.

Was it 'the Lupa' in Issa that attracted him to Issa's body? It had always been 'Lupa', through whom he was transiting the worlds. From the time she was twelve and his mother found her in the gutter, she told the tales of 'the Lupa,' who turned men into beasts, but who could see in their souls and had the power to heal, while tempting men into madness through the wiles of the whore. When Toto was born, he was nursed on these tales, that had the shape of a myth when she gave him new life. 'Lupa's' power of inseeing was behind his vocation as priest, while she developed his calling for sainthood through Nola's power and will.

Now he saw her in Issa in a less idealized form, and the unattainable object seemed to be within his grasp.

Until the fortuitous meeting, he had sublimated the urge, and devoted to Nola as a mother was unwilling to replace her, but what he was unable to possess he was finding in Issa, who had similar interests and strivings and who saw the god in the priest.

Issa was an expert in botany and the wonders of flora, and as they walked through the woods, she revealed all its secrets- the hidden ways of the Mother, revealed in the spirit of nature. On that day she was telling him the Roman myth of the spring: of the fertility goddess, Flora, who was resurrected in the Renaissance, and how neo-pagan revivalism had inspirited Christianity. And she whispered to Toto- as she was urged on by Terzo- that the Greek Chloris, a nymph, that dwelled in the under-world (and was an aspect of Flora), was married to the wind god, while the voice of the Mother was blowing in his ear, and, as if he were drugged, he took her in the flora.

Was it really the goddess of spring, he inquired of his conscience, or his shadow that led to the betrayal of a brother? For his faith in Quint had been equal to the boy's devotion to the stars. It was at the moment of completion that Terzo made himself known to him, and Toto realized he'd been had and it was the trickster who had Issa. Only Terzo was aware of the meaning of *Floralia*: a celebration to honor prostitutes as Terzo honored his mother. Issa was mystified by Toto's prowess and thought him an exceptional lover, not being conscious of the fact that she had been fucked by 'the third'.

As the Ambrose in Toto was watching the act, he marveled that the trickster could seduce the ascetic, until he remembered how Nola worked her spell on his flesh: how the soul can be tempted, for the devil has two faces, and one is the whore in the heart of the saint.

CHAPTER 85
CONFESSION

How could Toto tell his 'brother' that he was in love with his mother, and had taken the Lupa in Nola and not the mother of Jonah? Which would be worse? Which was Quint more possessive of? But even before he had asked himself, he had answered the question. Quint would forgive him for Issa, but Nola was taboo. How could he tell him he betrayed him... and for what? he was asking; how could he reconcile his calling with the spirit of the trickster?

It was Issa who revealed it in her off-handed way, as Quint was working on a statue, immersed in his work: "I hope you don't mind, Quint, but I had an adventure with your priest. I had the feeling that he needed it. He was a virgin, you know."

"How presumptuous of you, as if you could give him what he needs: what *she* gave to me... as if you could give it to him. It was not you who he had, but the image of my mother, but you must know that- or don't you? And who did you think *you* were fucking?"

"Why are you trying to hurt me, when you are obsessed with her, too? You were fucking the image of your mother before I existed. But the problem is twice as complex and I did not want to tell you. I was possessed by your brother, but it is not an excuse. I was not able to resist, because I wanted it, too. I knew exactly what was happening. It was your shadow that was fucking me."

Quint knew what she meant, but for a moment he hated her. "I'm disappointed in you, Issa. I thought you were beyond it." But he never revealed his real feelings, and continued working on the statue. "What do I know of human love? I am only an image-maker. I know nothing of the human heart and being caught in love's coils. You are nothing to me... nothing! And I will not die for you, like Jonah."

My foolish boy, she was thinking, don't you know how I love you? I cannot find you out there... and I don't want to need you. And she tried to embrace him, but he continued working on the statue.

He confronted Toto on the problem, unable to restrain his curiosity. Why wasn't it Toto who told him what he wished he didn't know? "What *is* unacceptable, Toto, is that you have forgotten what I know. It could only be Issa, who is merging with Nola. It wasn't Issa you fucked... And yet, how can I blame you for wanting it? To pierce the unknown... and what I imagined myself?"

"Forgive me for not knowing you."

"Somehow, I do. 'Even God's saints are tempted,' repeating the words of his mother, quoting from the book he never read... that was emerging from the shadow... and now he knew what he repressed... remembered reading like a thief... of how she worked her spell on men... how he purged it from his mind... to keep the pearl from the worm... how burning the book in the forest he had turned it to ashes... and kept the vision of his mother pure and intact...

"But why would you think you could ever know all of me? Do I know all of myself?" but he was torn to his roots, as Toto was mourning his shadow.

CHAPTER 86
WEAVER

Toto was not simple, though he appeared in simple guise. His complexity was hidden beneath his primitive beginnings. His influence on Quint was greater than it seemed, a more essential contribution to his rapid development. From the first, Quint was moved by the life of the spirit, and like a diver plunged inward was looking for pearls. Toto had also been looking by playing the crucified god, when Terzo found him in the gutter, and turned the worm to a pearl: how the Mother built a tomb from the flaw in the self and was transformed to the stone that was the symbol of Christ.

Toto was a brother to Terzo and Quint, as he searched for 'the philosophic wine', and worshipped the virgin in 'Lupa', 'the wild one' who hunted men's souls that she turned to a beast. Nola was more like his mother, but what he wanted was 'Lupa', a conflict that deepened his friendship with Terzo and Quint, who struggled like Toto with their incestuous yearnings: the need to penetrate the mysteries of the Mother of Earth. The Lupa in Nola was the lover he longed for, who had lifted him up from his ghetto in hell, and, without her image to guide him, he would have died on the street.

As his protector and mentor, Quint knew how he needed him, and now estranged from his lover, he needed his wisdom (though Toto had done what he secretly feared). As they sat on the rock in the forest of Snow House, they talked of the things of the soul and communed with earth's spirit- that took the shape of 'the Lupa', their lady of the beasts. In the Nola aspect of her being, she was a stranger on the earth, for she lived in the mind, and only *imagined* 'coming down', but both had been freed by her spirit that could either heal or destroy.

"I guess you could call it a spiritual awakening, a change of nature through my brother and a revelation of the shadow side. I had been wrestling with my angel, and I didn't call yet you came. I continued our talks every night, while I was making the statue, and saw my self face to face through the eyes of Turan: the unseeing eyes that could see in the dark. Terzo was moving my hand to give the invisible form, until the stone came alive, and then you were here."

"And the other members in your body?"

"Nola keeps them alive."

"How lucky they are, who were changed from a beast to a man: how she reversed it at will, until we knew who we were. She's done it to all of us, and only we have survived. The others, inside us, are making us conscious, as she moves them to change us, while we are changing the dead. When as a priest at St. Sulpice, I was moved to Trinity chapel, and the Parisian archdiocese conceded to the Church of England, it was one of her miracles that only she could perform... her transference with Issa is a tale in itself, and it didn't take long till I realized she'd written it in... So here we are on our rock and it is as it was... and yet nothing's the same, now that the boy is a man."

Nola is climbing the rock with Turan, finding her way through the dark, as if she had eyes in her palms. Turan sat beside Toto and she told him her thoughts...

"I knew you would come, Toto, when I saw you in my dream. You were blessing my eyes and I knew who you were."

"Can you describe myself to me?"

"Well, you were a boy with a fever, and 'Lupa' was giving you life," recounting the moment when she brought him back from the dead.

"I keep reliving that moment when I returned to myself. It is why I am here- to try to find it again."

"Yes, I knew if I didn't have my dream, you would have to wait five more years, but when my statue was finished, I knew I was complete."

"A complete woman at seven?"

"How long does it take?"

"It depends" Quint replied.

"On the phases of the moon?"

"On the whim of the goddess," said Nola.

"Yes, she has many whims and I don't want to be one of them."

"But we all are," said Nola. Why should you be an exception?"

"Because I am made out of stone, and I will live forever, like Issa. Quint has given us life and we are immortal, like Terzo. I will not die like my mother, but I will live as long as yourself, Nola."

"You don't know what you're asking. That's a very long time, and you might get bored with the rest of us, who must go on for eternity."

"I will never get bored with you. I can promise you that."

"Has it ever happened to you, Nola, that someone got bored with you?" Toto asked his obsession, trying to find her in Nola.

"Only once in this life, Toto."

"And may I ask who it was?"

"Myself, and it hurt."

"Tell me about it," asked Toto.

"And me, Nola. Tell me. I want to learn not to do it. It must be like dying and still having a body... but not able to leave it... like being bound to a rock."

"Exactly like that. You have seen the invisible. It is said that Athena, the war goddess, mastered the art of weaving, and that Arachne believed she was the weaver of destiny: that on one fateful day she competed with the goddess, and for her hubris was turned from a woman to a spider. Like Arachne, when Athena challenged me to a dual, I believed I could win when I tried to trick fate, but Athena was playing me and I was reminded I was human, and I was trapped in my web and suspended in space."

"How did you escape?"

"I wove the rope on which I hung myself, until my analyst reminded me. She said I turned love to a game and that the game turned to death."

"I see it now, why you almost stopped trying. But no one on earth can do it better than you. Can you tell me exactly how she said it? What words did she use?"

She said: "Like Athena, you are sprung from the head of a power-driven father, and you have to learn your own shadow, and the shadow of love."

"And *how* did you learn it?"

"I broke the pattern of the web and began some serious work. You see, when I tried it the first time, I was terribly young. That's when Terzo was born and I felt trapped by my fate. It became a pattern to escape and I learned all the tricks, and with every trick that I turned, she taught me the *limits* of love... more, how I threw it away, just when I knew I had found it."

"*How* did you do it?"

552

"By exaggerating the plot."

Toto is laughing, like he did as a boy.

"Are you laughing 'cause you know that no one knows all of her? I will ask for a dream- a dream from the goddess. The goddess will tell me what a man cannot know."

"You will see, child, there are things she keeps to herself. Knowing, Turan, is like three swords in the heart."

"Is it like seeing our myth without the eyes of the Hawk? Terzo once told me that feeling the swords in the heart, hurts less than the wound of feeling nothing at all. He said he's felt both, and that Nothing is worse."

Terzo, invisibly perched on the rock, is feeling the wound in the heart, when you have lost what you love. How he wished he could weep. But then spirits don't cry.

CHAPTER 87
HAWK BOY

The next day on the rock as Turan wept tears of blood- for being blind to the world, though she could see in its heart- Nola conjured the Hawk boy in the vessel of Turan. She took the girl's blindness into the hell of her heart and was asking the Mother and Son to blind her own eyes, to give her sight to Turan, who suffered more than herself...

And so, the myth of the Hawk god was born in Turan, who saw the face of her 'mother' that her fingers had searched: the face she conceived of 'on the scale of the stars'.[542]

"You have blessed me with eyes that can see like the Hawk. Though I knew the shape of your soul, when I could see in the dark, seeing the face of the earth is the gift of a sphinx." Turan touches her face, as her eyes catch the light, and like the young Magdalena, the tears pour through the veils.

'The mystery of everything is Water,'[542a] said Nola, who had taken her blindness and could no longer see. Her offering was accepted by the Mother and Son, and all that there was were the shadows, that she had known from within.

CHAPTER 88
BORN OUT OF DEATH

Nola is blind now and is dying her death. "I am coming down, Nora. Is that what it takes? Do you have to die to be conscious? as she was mourning her sight. I see you've entered my body... I thought it was Snow... that she returned to her bed, to take me with her to Lethe. But it was you, wasn't it Nora? You could never get enough."

'The inner analyst has been reflected on since the beginning of the art, but the Nora in Nola bears new reflection', said Nora. 'And so, we are finally one, said the spirit to the body'.

"You needn't have gone to such extremes to get a rise out of matter."

'It was time to get inside you for the final stage of the analysis'.

"Sounds like incest. I didn't want to tell you, but I was your mother in the last life."

'I deserved you in this one, for being fooled by your disguise. I knew something was up when you arrived as a masochistic patient'.

"Always the martyr dying my death, for the virgin is buried in the heart of the whore."

'Let's not eroticize it', said Nora.

"Once you've been fucked by the god, nothing else will quite do, but the penetration of the dead, who quicken the living."

'I only came up so you would not have to go down', Nora said.

"I'm beginning to realize I'm addicted to 'the spirit of gravity'."

'It's only the cure for lingering on the heights. A few sessions in hell has made you a better analyst'.

"*What is the meaning of the sacrifice*? Terzo's question to my mother... I think I'll write about it instead," and she rose from her deathbed.

'Call it *Turning'*, said Nora, 'for it turns on itself, when the fascist shadow is trying to control the unconscious'.

"It will kill me to write it."

'When did that ever stop you'?

"Is there no end to this experiment?" already conceiving the plot: "A study of fascism on the shadow of the father: the evil from the past, from the poison in your blood- from the beast that destroyed you that I will kill for your death. But first, I will drive it insane by turning its venom on itself, and though I'll be dying of love, I'll be avenging your life."

THE END

Notes

BOOK I

CHAPTER 1

1   Oswald Spengler, *The Decline of the West,* vol. 2, tr. Charles F. Atkinson (New York: Alfred A. Knopf, 1926

5   C.G. Jung- Transference: This bond is often of such intensity that we can almost speak of the [change] when two chemical substances combine and both are altered. *CW16, Psychology of the Transference,* tr./ed. R.F.C. Hull (London: Routledge & Keegan Paul, Ltd.) para. 358

7   C.G. Jung- Synchronicity: A meaningful connecting principle of an inner and outer event. *CW8, The Structure and Dynamics of the Psyche,* tr. R.F.C. Hull (London: Routledge & Keegan Paul, Ltd., 1960) 41

8   C.G. Jung- Space/time Continuum

CHAPTER 2

14   C.G. Jung- The Self: A psychological God that comprises the collective unconscious, the personal unconscious, and creates the conscious ego.

CHAPTER 3

17   C.G. Jung, citing medieval alchemy   **Ibid*

20   Jacobus D. Voragine, *The Golden Legend,* vol. 2, tr. Ryan & Rapperger, (London: Longmans, Green & Co. Ltd., 1941) 355

22   *Ibid* 657

23   Rainer Maria Rilke

23a   Jacobus D. Voragine, *The Golden Legend,* vol. 2, tr. Ryan & Rapperger, (London: Longmans, Green & Co. Ltd., 1941) 355   **Ibid* 355

CHAPTER 30

CHAPTER 31

CHAPTER 32

CHAPTER 33

CHAPTER 34

CHAPTER 35

CHAPTER 37

CHAPTER 38

CHAPTER 39

CHAPTER 61

CHAPTER 62

CHAPTER 63

Printed in Great Britain
by Amazon

31311587R00322